# Vallyn in Chains

## Vallyn Duet | Book One
### Maelana Nightingale

# CONTENTS

# Author's Note

Dear Reader,

Before you dive into the wild and twisting journey of *The Vallyn Duet*, I want to take a moment to acknowledge the darker waters we're about to tread together. This duet explores themes that may not be for everyone, and your comfort and mental well-being are incredibly important to me.

Inside these pages, you'll encounter on-page smoking, drinking, motor vehicle accidents, abduction, captivity, Stockholm Syndrome, gun and knife violence, hand-to-hand combat, death, murder, torture, blood, PTSD, exposure therapy, stalking—including hidden cameras and cyberstalking, and attempted sexual assault. You will also encounter graphic non-consensual sexual acts, bondage, and drugging.

If any of these topics feel heavy for you right now, please take care of yourself first. For a detailed list of content warnings, visit my website. I promise no major spoilers there—just the clarity you need to decide if this story is right for you.

Remember, this is your journey as much as it is mine. Your mental health matters, always.

Stay Naughty ♥ Mae

*For the readers who crave fictional men with fire in their eyes, respect in their hearts, and chaos in their souls—those that are badasses in the streets and the sheets—this duet is for you.*

# Vallyn's Apartment Layout

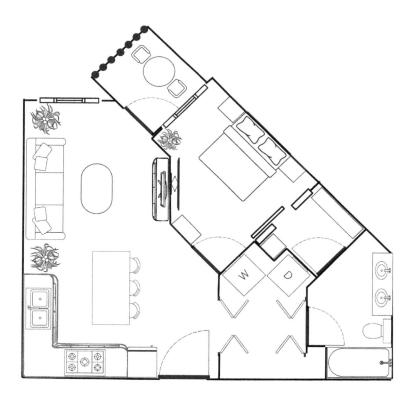

*When I wake up, everything is wrong. My head pounds, my vision is blurry, but it's the cold bite of metal beneath me that jolts me back to reality. I'm slumped in a chair—hard, cold, unyielding. I try to speak, but my lips don't part. Instantly I realize my mouth is taped shut.*

*"What if I want him to kill me? What if I just want this to be over?"*

# PART ONE

# CHAPTER ONE

# BROAD SHOULDERS

**VALLYN**

Thumping bass reverberates through my chest, blending seamlessly with the cacophony of laughter and voices. The smell of bar food mingles with the sharp tang of alcohol, an intoxicating mix that's both overstimulating and exactly what I crave tonight.

Navigating back to our table from the dancefloor is a monumental task. I weave through a sea of sweaty bodies, dodging couples practically dry-humping to the beat. Drinks slosh over the rims of plastic cups, splattering my feet and sandals as I squeeze past. Thankfully, no one's puking—yet.

With a sigh of relief, I slide into the booth next to Corey. Sasha, Tori, Carly, and Brooke trail behind me, giggling and breathless from our impromptu dance session. Sasha takes her place by my side, while the others pile in opposite us.

"Thanks for guarding the table so we could dance," Brooke beams at Corey, her smile radiant.

Corey is like a brother to me, but Brooke and Carly have both nursed crushes on him over the years. He's tall and undeniably attractive with his sandy blonde hair, caramel-colored eyes, a smattering of freckles, and stylish glasses. He catches the eye of more than a few girls whenever we're out.

But tonight, he's our table bitch, our designated purse guardian. Corey thrives in this role, securing us a spot no matter how packed the club gets and he keeps our belongings safe. He's indispensable in his role as table bitch.

Finals for the spring semester wrapped up today. As a post-grad working on my sociology doctorate dissertation, tonight's celebration is a welcome reprieve. Sasha, deep into her biochemistry dissertation, is also a TA, just like me. We have mountains of grading to tackle in the coming days, but tonight, we let loose.

Corey, who took a few years off after high school, is still chipping away at his undergrad degree. Brooke and Tori? They need no excuse to party; they're always ready to let their hair down—Carly just needs out of her fucking house anytime she can get out.

Sasha and I are physically like night and day. Her straight, medium-length, bleach-blonde hair is a stark contrast to my dark, long, naturally wavy locks. Her bright blue eyes and olive skin are the polar opposites of my dark brown eyes and fair complexion. We've been best friends since kindergarten, practically sisters. Our parents treat us like their own, and I couldn't ask for a better confidante.

Corey joined our tight-knit group in middle school, and Tori, Carly, and Brooke became part of our crew freshman year of college. Nearly eight years of friendship have solidified our bond.

"Hey, Val, it's your turn to hit the bar," Tori announces, her tone playful but insistent.

"Fiiine," I drawl, rolling my eyes for effect. "Hurricanes again?"

"Maybe mai tais?" Brooke suggests, and everyone chimes in with agreement.

The bar at this club is all about efficiency, serving drinks by the bucket or pitcher. I nudge Sasha to let me out, then plunge back into the crowd, determined to return with our liquid treasures.

As I stand in line at the bar, watching the bartenders hustle, I feel a hand slide onto my back, fingers tracing the skin just below my crop top. I turn, expecting one of my friends, but it's a stranger.

"Can you not?" I snap, my voice dripping with irritation.

"Oh, come on, you didn't dress like that not to be touched," he says, eyeing me up and down with a smirk.

"Yeah, you can just fuck off now," I retort, stepping closer to the bar and turning my back on him.

But then, his fingers wrap around my upper arm. I whirl around, done with his nonsense.

"Listen, fucker, get your hand off me!" I practically yell, loud enough for heads to turn and even the bartender to glance over. Perfect. They can summon a bouncer faster than I can.

The creep reaches for my arm again, and as I yank it away, my hand bumps into someone, sending my phone and attached wallet flying. As I look around frantically, I see a guy about my age picking up my scattered belongings. He smiles reassuringly, but I have to deal with the idiot first.

Turning back to "grabby hands," I'm surprised to find I'm staring at the back and broad shoulders of another man who's stepped between me and the jerk. He has a death grip on the creep's forearm, saying, "Didn't anyone ever tell you that no means no?"

When he releases the sleazeball, the guy shakes his arm, clearly feeling the impact of the grip, and scurries off. "Broad shoulders" turns to me. "You okay?" he asks, his green eyes locking onto mine as I look up at him.

"Yeah," I manage, swallowing hard.

Nodding to someone behind me first, he retrieves my phone and cards from the other helpful guy. I turn to thank him, and he nods with a smile.

Turning back to broad shoulders, he hands me my things. "Thank you," I say, inspecting my phone for any cracks and making sure all my cards are there. When I look up to thank him again, he's gone.

I scan the crowd. A guy like him—sexy, tall, built, and covered in tattoos—shouldn't disappear so easily, but he has. With a shrug, I return to the bar, grab our pitcher of mai tais, and head back to my friends.

Settling into the booth, I share the entire encounter, embellishing just enough to make them gasp and laugh. Their reactions remind me why I love our nights out, even when they come with unexpected drama.

"Well, at least 'broad shoulders' didn't hit on you after that," Tori quips, her eyes twinkling with mischief.

"True, although I might not have minded if he was nice about it," I reply, laughing.

Corey nudges me with his elbow. "How long has it been since you actually dated someone?"

Snorting, I answer, "I don't know, like four fucking years."

"I'm pretty sure those years were sans fucking," Sasha deadpans.

I burst out laughing, mai tai shooting out my nose and burning like hell. "That's what vibrators are for," I quip back, wiping my nose.

"Who the fuck has time to date when you're a TA working on your thesis?" Sasha asks, rolling her eyes.

"Fucking right?" I respond, raising my glass.

We polish off another round of drinks and head back to the dance floor. Sasha and I dance together, moving closer whenever a guy gets too handsy, pretending we're together to ward off unwanted attention. It works most of the time.

But there's one guy who seems different—sweet, respectful. Instead of grinding up against me, he asks to dance with me. When I say yes, he asks my name. His bright blue eyes and reddish-blonde hair are hard to miss, and his physique is definitely enticing. By the end of the night, he asks for my number, and I happily give it to him. Unfortunately, as the night wears on, his name slips from my memory.

When the lights come on, signaling closing time, the harsh reality of the bright lights makes me blink. We all order our rideshares, shuffling outside to wait.

"You sure you don't want me to make sure you get home okay?" Corey asks as we wait on the sidewalk.

"I'm good. I'll send you my rideshare tracker, though. Thanks," I respond.

My ride is the first to arrive. Hugging everyone goodbye, I promise to check in when I get home. The ride from downtown Phoenix to my apartment on the Mesa end of Tempe takes about twenty minutes.

Stumbling slightly as I get out of the rideshare, I'm grateful the driver drops me right by the elevator entrance. My apartment is conveniently close to the elevator. I fumble with my keys for a moment, thinking I haven't been this wasted in a long time, before finally unlocking the door to my one-bedroom apartment.

I drop my keys on the kitchen island to my left and kick off my shoes. Turning right, I head through the small hallway, past the laundry room, and into the bathroom. Multi-tasking as always, I strip off my pants and socks while peeing, then walk through my walk-in closet, which doubles as a hallway to my bedroom—the kitchen, laundry room, bathroom, closet, bedroom, and living room, all connect in a circle. Grabbing leggings and a tank top, I toss aside my shirt and bra, quickly changing into more comfortable attire.

I'm relieved to find my water bottle full from earlier in the day. Opening the nightstand drawer, I take a couple of ibuprofen and crawl under the blankets. Just as I plug my phone into the charger, I remember to text my friends, letting them know I made it home safely.

Me

Hey all I'm home - safe and sound

Sasha

Me too, call me tomorrow

Tori

Less than a block away

Corey

Just walked in my front door

Brooke

I'm home - was peeing lol

Me

Carly?!?!?

Carly

Just walked in my front door - patience is a virtue, you know?

Me

You know I have no patience

Sasha

Except when it comes to waiting for the perfect man lol

Me

Maybe

Tori

You've turned down so many lol – and home

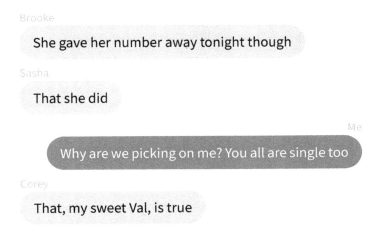

Brooke

She gave her number away tonight though

Sasha

That she did

Me

Why are we picking on me? You all are single too

Corey

That, my sweet Val, is true

After a few goodbye texts, I turn on my white noise app and drift quickly off to sleep.

# CHAPTER TWO

# FIRST SIGHT

## PHANTOM

This night takes an unexpected turn. Casen and I are in a bar that's practically a nightclub, not exactly our usual Thursday night haunt, but our mark is here. Some douchebag is cheating on his wife, and we've been hired to find out with whom and how often. Gage is out in the van, ready to handle anything tech-related.

The three of us have been a team since our discharges from the Army two years ago. Gage still does—I don't even know how much—espionage under contract, while Casen and I still do private security and mercenary work for the government now and then. Apparently, when you're skilled enough at Special Ops, they want to keep you around in whatever capacity they can.

Carrying firearms into the bar means we enter through the back, security wanting to see our credentials without causing a stir. We may not always seem like the most morally upright people, but we follow the law when we're working.

Usually, I'm laser-focused while on surveillance, especially when we're after a fugitive or someone with a warrant. Tonight, though, we're just tailing an adulterer. As we make our way from the back door to a spot near the bar, where we can see this guy in a corner booth with his mistress, a woman catches my eye.

She's laughing with her friends—her beauty striking me like a lightning bolt. Her skin is snow-white, almost like the fairy tale, and her hair is nearly black in stark contrast. That kind of complexion is rare in Phoenix, especially as summer approaches. Her cheeks are flushed pink, probably from the alcohol, and her lips are pouty, painted the color of a good merlot. As she looks at her friends, the darkness of her eyes captivates me; they're such a deep shade of brown, almost as dark as her hair.

I've been around plenty of women, usually in short spurts. My most serious relationship was back in high school, but it didn't survive my first deployment—fuck, we barely survived boot camp. Otherwise, it has been hookups, mostly one-night stands. But looking at this girl, I know my life is about to change.

Fucking hell, if this is what people mean by love at first sight, I might actually get it now. I feel like I'd do almost anything to make her mine and keep her, and I don't even know her name.

"You coming?" Casen snickers, walking ahead of me. I realize I'm rooted to the spot, my boots feeling glued to the floor.

Lifting my chin in acknowledgment, I will myself to move forward, following Casen to the front of the bar, closer to our mark. My attention is divided between our mark and the back of the pretty girl's head for a few minutes, but then, as if willed by me, she starts walking toward me. She's clearly making her way to the bar for a drink run, but I don't mind the view at all.

Leaning against a column, I watch as she steps in front of me, and I take all of her in from behind. She's about five foot eight, taller than average for a woman, but still a good six inches shorter than me. She has curves—an hourglass figure, a perfectly full ass, and thick thighs. Her wavy dark hair falls almost to her waistband. The black crop top she's wearing reveals a few inches of skin above her jeans, just enough to make my imagination run wild.

It's evident I'm not the only one who's noticed her. Some fucker decides he can just put his hands on her. My initial reaction is a gut punch of possessiveness—*mine*. She is mine, and this asshole needs to get his dirty paws off her. I've never felt this way about a woman, and the fact that I haven't even spoken to her yet tells me there's something seriously wrong with me right now.

I'm impressed when she handles him herself, turning him down so vehemently that I chuckle a little. But he's persistent, and when he touches her again, I've had enough. As soon as I have an opening, I step in.

The guy is lucky we're in a public bar and I'm technically working, or I might not have let go of his arm so quickly. Turning back to her, I ask if she's okay. When her eyes meet mine, the full force of her beauty overpowers me. My heart thunders in my chest, echoing in my ears.

This is beyond anything I've ever felt, and it emphasizes that I'll do *whatever* it takes to make her mine. It's an intensity that says I would climb mountains, swim through alligator-infested channels, kill for her, die for her, and burn the fucking world to the ground to make her mine.

A guy behind her is trying to get her attention to give her back her phone and wallet that she dropped. I lift my chin at him and hold out my hand. Right on top of the items is her Arizona driver's license. It's exactly what I need.

Standing in front of me is one Vallyn Spencer. I have her date of birth and address—she's twenty-six and lives in Tempe. In that quick second of scanning her license, I know I can find out everything I need to know about her—that's what I do every day. And Vallyn? What a unique and gorgeous name for a unique and gorgeous woman.

As I hand her back her things, she looks up at me once more, then checks her phone and takes inventory of all of her items. Before I do something really stupid, I nod to Casen and disappear out the side door of the bar.

Finding Gage in the van, I open my laptop, fingers dancing over the keys as I plunge into the digital depths of Vallyn Spencer's life. In mere minutes, her address, her school, and her world unfolds before me like a dark tapestry. Her cell phone number, carrier, social media handles—all mine now.

Her public social media profiles give me a voyeuristic glimpse into her reality, but that is a doorway I'll need to make her close behind her soon enough—she has way too much information that is publicly accessible. Tonight, she's tagged in a picture, a fleeting moment captured with her friends. I note the one male in the group—too close for my liking—but nothing more than a platonic shield, at least in the eyes of the social media world. Vallyn works with high-risk youth. The highlights on the youth center's website paint her as a saint.

I step out of the van, the night air cool against my skin as I light a cigarette. The smoke curls around me as I contemplate my next move, replaying the bar scene in my mind. I didn't approach her then—too soon, too much of a dick-move after the other asshole's display.

"Hey," Casen's voice pulls me back to reality, "the douche canoe is leaving. We need to follow him."

"Fuck," I mutter, crushing the cigarette underfoot and climbing into the van.

We trail the cheating bastard to a hotel, snapping pictures as he and his mistress disappear inside. His wife, our client, wasn't expecting him home tonight and this isn't the kind of place you pay by the hour. We decide our work is done for the night.

Gage drops me at my downtown building. I ascend to my condo, stashing my laptop before grabbing my bike keys and helmet. Moments later, I'm roaring down the freeway toward Vallyn's address. I need to see her again, to make sure she's safe—and alone.

My timing is impeccable. I cut the engine just as her rideshare pulls up. Even from fifty yards away, I recognize her silhouette, her outfit. She steps out alone, and a dark satisfaction blooms within me.

An hour passes as I chain-smoke—which is also unusual for me and hints at the anxiety brewing within me—in her parking lot, scrolling through my phone. Finally, I approach her building. Her door looms before me, a barrier I'm ready to breach. I knock softly, poised to vanish at any sign of life.

*Silence.*

I have my lockpick set in my pocket, but the handle turns beneath my grip—her door is unlocked. A careless drunken mistake, or her usual habit?

Inside, her apartment is modest but welcoming. A trail of discarded clothing leads from the bathroom to her bed, where she lies in serene slumber. The alcohol has her in a deep sleep, rendering her oblivious to my intrusion. Hopefully, she's not one of those people that are left restless and edgy from a heightened blood alcohol level.

Her phone rests on the nightstand, unlocked, white noise app still running.

*Convenient.*

I install a spyware app with practiced ease, then return the phone to its place. She looks angelic, hair fanned across the pillow, lips a shade of wine. One day, I'll be beside her, tasting those lips, feeling her warmth. But not tonight.

I explore further, finding her laptop in the living room. Another quick installation from the flash drive in my pocket means another layer of surveillance.

*This is wrong.*

I know it, feel it gnawing at the edges of my sanity. But I don't fucking care. I need to know everything about her—every move, every breath, every thought. Obsession isn't just a word; it's a compulsion burning inside me, a boundless hunger that drives me to breach every boundary and to defy every decent moral.

If someone did this to my sister, I'd kill them without hesitation. But for Vallyn, I'll cross any line, embrace every sin. I need to know her completely, to possess her utterly.

I know this is just the beginning.

# CHAPTER THREE

# CONTACT

## VALLYN

M oaning as my alarm blares in the morning, I curse myself for drinking so much last night.

*Fuck me.*

I stumble into the kitchen, desperate for caffeine. I make myself a strong coffee, filling up my ice water for good measure. I plop down at my computer, ready to tackle the mountain of finals waiting to be graded. Just as I open the first one, there's a knock at my door.

Grumbling, I throw on a hoodie out of modesty—no bra, too early for that—and shuffle to the door. Nobody's there, but a warm bag of food sits outside my door. Picking it up, I recognize the delicious aroma from my favorite breakfast spot. I check the receipt, thinking it must be for a neighbor, but it's addressed to me.

There's a note scribbled on the receipt

*Vallyn, I thought you might need some carbs and grease to help you recover after last night.*

Maybe it's from Sasha or Corey, I think. Whoever it is, they know me well. Inside the bag is my usual order—loaded hash browns, fried eggs, and pancakes. I'm definitely not complaining. A minute later, another knock at my door reveals a delivery of coffee—my usual nonfat mocha with an extra pump of vanilla.

As I devour the greasy goodness and sip my caffeine, I can feel the hangover lifting. Whoever sent these gifts is a lifesaver. I start grading tests, feeling more human with each bite and sip.

A few hours later, my phone buzzes with a text from a private number.

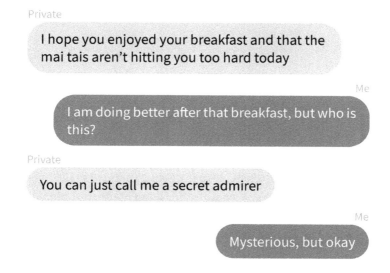

Private

**I hope you enjoyed your breakfast and that the mai tais aren't hitting you too hard today**

Me

I am doing better after that breakfast, but who is this?

Private

**You can just call me a secret admirer**

Me

Mysterious, but okay

I stare at my phone, waiting for another message, but none comes. There's a lightness to my day after that, a small mystery to ponder. It has to be someone I know, or at least someone who knows my friends. Those orders were too spot-on and thoughtful to be a random act.

I spend the rest of the day cocooned in my apartment, grading tests, curling up with a book for breaks, and napping when the grading gets too tedious. Dinner is leftover pizza from the fridge, and I get back to grading with renewed energy.

Later, as I climb into bed and pick up my book, my phone vibrates on the nightstand. Another text from the private number.

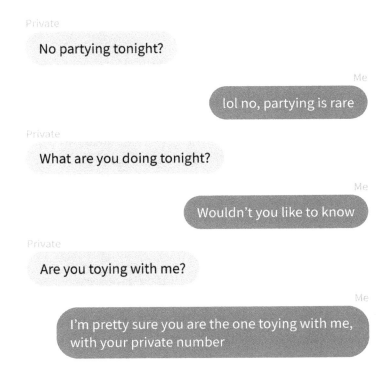

Private

No partying tonight?

Me

lol no, partying is rare

Private

What are you doing tonight?

Me

Wouldn't you like to know

Private

Are you toying with me?

Me

I'm pretty sure you are the one toying with me, with your private number

Then my phone rings, and the screen lights up with "Private Number." My heart flutters as I tentatively answer.

"Hello?"

"Hello, Vallyn," a deep baritone replies, sending a shiver down my spine.

*Fuck, his voice is sexy.*

"Are you going to tell me who this is?" I ask, almost giggling. Knowing I should be more creeped out, but I'm not.

A deep chuckle answers. "Not yet."

"Well, I can't just call you 'Private Number,'" I quip back. "So, I'll need to come up with something else to call you."

"Is that so?" he asks, his voice dripping with amusement.

"Yeah, you're so mysterious, maybe 'Phantom,'" I suggest.

Another soft chuckle on his end. "Well, if I'm 'Phantom,' then you're definitely my angel of music. But I think I'll just call you 'Little Lotte.'"

Shaking away the stunned feeling in my brain, I reply, "You mean like Phantom of the Opera? Like the Broadway show?"

"Of course," he says assuredly. "And I think 'Little Lotte' is a wonderful nickname for you."

"You know this is kind of creepy, right?" I ask, unable to wipe the smile off my face.

"I won't argue with that," he says plainly.

"Why did you call me?" I ask after a moment of silence.

"Because I wanted to hear your voice," he answers, his tone cool and deep.

"What if I hadn't answered?"

"I would have called you until you did," he says, very matter-of-factly.

"Yeah, so back to that part about being creepy," I counter.

His deep chuckle makes me smile. "Someday, Little Lotte, you won't think I'm creepy. But you'll probably think I get worse before I get better."

It takes me a moment to respond, "I don't know whether to be intrigued or terrified."

"You'd be right to be both," he replies with a sigh, adding, "but don't be too terrified. I can be scary, but I will only ever use that to protect you."

Taking a deep breath, I'm still smiling, unsure how to take that—it almost sounds like a threat.

Suddenly, he breaks the silence, "What are you doing tonight, my Little Lotte?"

I smile at the nickname and answer, "Just reading before I fall asleep. Well, I was until you called."

"What are you reading?" he asks.

"Some cheesy romance where if they just talked to each other in the beginning there wouldn't even be a story," I say with a laugh.

Snickering on the other end, he comments, "Well, that's why I'm talking to you, so our romance isn't cheesy like that."

"Oh, you think we'll have a romance, do you?"

"Vallyn, pretty girl, that is without question," he counters.

"You think I'd have a romance with someone who won't even tell me their name?" I ask with attitude.

"Oh, I like that sass—I'd also like to fuck it out of you," he states, throwing me over some edge where I can hear my blood whooshing in my ears and I feel a little short of breath.

I swallow hard. "I thought we were talking about romance," I snappily counter.

"We are," he states plainly.

"Your definition of romance and mine must be different."

"Isn't the end goal of romance, sex?" he asks, sounding like one of my professors asking a question with an obvious answer.

I don't answer him, my silence hopefully speaking volumes. Part of me wonders why I'm still on the phone with him, but I am so intrigued.

"Vallyn, sweetheart, trust me, there will be romance first," he finally says. Still quiet, I wait for him to speak, which I have learned through my education as a tactic to get people to say more. A little less cocky, he asks, "Did you enjoy your breakfast?"

"I did," I answer and then add, "although that's a little creepy too—my favorite breakfast place, and my usual order."

"That's not creepy, Little Lotte, that just shows I'm putting in effort," his voice is smooth again.

"Okay, you won't tell me your name, but what do you do?" I ask.

I hear him sigh, "That's a little complicated. But I work with both the military and law enforcement."

That hits a nerve, making me wonder what kind of guy this is who has decided to attach himself to me.

"Oh, so you really *are* a scary, creepy guy," I assert.

"Maybe," he chortles. "But my Little Lotte, you can rest assured you are the only person I have been or will ever be *this* creepy for."

A snort-laugh escapes me, "Is that supposed to be a compliment?"

"Yeah, pretty girl, it is," he says and then adds, "you are the first and only woman that I have ever completely lost my goddamn mind over."

Taken aback, I wonder if I really do know him. How could someone lose their mind over me if they haven't spoken to me? "Okay, seriously, who the fuck are you? Were we in classes together?"

"No, Vallyn, we didn't have classes together. You may not even remember me if you saw me on the street, but you are under my skin," he answers with a little growl to his baritone voice.

"You're not going to tell me anything real, are you?" I ask, hearing the anxiety and disappointment in my voice.

"I've told you a lot of real, Little Lotte, just not the things you want to know, but we'll get there, I promise," he offers, his voice deep, sending a shiver through me.

"You sound pretty confident that I'm going to let you into my life," I observe quietly.

"I *am* confident you will let me into your life, Little Lotte. It might take some time, but you will."

Sniffing through my nose, I nod and realize he can't see me nodding. Then I laugh, tears threatening to spill, and I don't know what the hell is going on with me.

"Vallyn, are you crying?" he asks, genuinely concerned, but with an edge of humor.

Laughing through a sniffle, I reply, "Yeah, but I don't know why."

"Oh, sweet, pretty girl, this is the real thing, I know it is. Maybe you can feel that intensity too, maybe not, but soon I'll be able to kiss away the tears when you cry," he says, and it's sweet. Although, I feel like I have whiplash from him going from talking about fucking the sass out of me to kissing away my tears.

Laughing again, I respond, "*Something* about this is intense, that's for sure. Still intrigued but terrified."

"That's fair, Little Lotte," he says. "I need to go, my partner needs me. But Vallyn, sweet dreams, pretty girl, I'll talk to you soon."

"Okay, bye," I say, and then the line goes dead.

I can't concentrate on reading, so I flip on the television to some romantic comedy I've seen a hundred times and drift off into a very restless sleep.

# CHAPTER FOUR

# SURVEILLANCE

## PHANTOM

I call her on a whim, a fleeting impulse I can't ignore. Her voice, when she answers, is a melody I hadn't realized I craved. She laughs when I tease her and christens me "phantom." I'd be lying if I said I didn't like it.

Morning light filters through my car window as I park outside her apartment, engine idling softly. Her text messages hint at plans, so I wait, a silent sentinel. Minutes trickle by, and then my heart quickens as two familiar faces pull up in a sleek car. Carly and Brooke, both from the night I first laid eyes on her.

Vallyn appears moments later, slipping out of the building with a grace that takes my breath away. She hurries to the car, her dark hair catching the morning sun, and slides into the back seat. The engine roars to life, and I follow, my gaze fixed on her silhouette.

They arrive at a quaint little shop. Brooke goes inside, emerging with a small purchase, while Vallyn and Carly linger in the car. I can see her laughing through the windows. My pulse thrums with every movement she makes.

Their journey continues, leading them to the parking lot of a chain restaurant. They park, and I watch as another car pulls in, the remaining three people from that fateful night spilling out. There is an air of reunion, warm embraces all around. But it is Corey's hug that catches my attention, the way he lingers, his hand slipping to the small of her back and resting there long after she has released him.

Jealousy coils in my chest, a dark serpent. I want to rip his hand off her, to pull him away, but instead, I crack my window and light a cigarette. The flame flickers as I take a long drag, the smoke curling around me as I keep watching. They vanish into the restaurant, leaving me with the heat of the day and my thoughts. I use the time to dig deeper into Corey's life. His social media paints a curious picture—no girlfriends, just endless posts of Sasha and Vallyn, especially Vallyn. After a quick text to Gage—who is the only person I've confided in with tales of my current insanity—it doesn't take long for him to confirm my suspicions, that Vallyn is his most contacted number.

A plan begins to form. I decide to test the waters, to see where I stand with her. Picking up my phone, I text her.

Me

> Little Lotte, what are you up to?

I don't expect a quick response, not with her out with friends, but my phone buzzes almost immediately.

Vallyn

> I'm having lunch with some friends, what are you doing?

Not a lie, maybe not the whole truth, but not a lie.

I know at this point she's either showing all my messages to her friends or completely ignoring them.

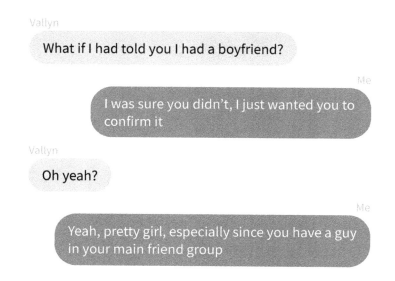

Vallyn

What if I had told you I had a boyfriend?

Me

I was sure you didn't, I just wanted you to confirm it

Vallyn

Oh yeah?

Me

Yeah, pretty girl, especially since you have a guy in your main friend group

There's a pause, a few minutes before she responds. Then, I see why, as they all exit the restaurant together. She glances down at her phone, both thumbs moving swiftly across the screen.

Vallyn

Corey? Yeah definitely not a boyfriend

Then I watch her look up, offering half-distracted hugs to her friends before following Carly back to Brooke's car.

Me

Definitely? Does he know that?

Vallyn

Definitely, and he should know that, I've turned him down enough times lol

That catches my interest—she's had to tell him no more than once—as I pull out of the parking lot behind her friend's car.

Me

That makes it sound like he doesn't know

Vallyn

Well, he should

I'm quiet while I'm driving—she's a passenger, I am not. She notices my silence.

Vallyn

You get busy surveilling?

Me

Something like that, driving

Vallyn

Okay, drive safe

As I'm following her friend's car back to her building, Casen calls.
"What's up?" I ask, after hitting the answer button on the console.

"We have an extraction mission, I said yes, so hopefully you don't have anything important this week," Casen informs me with a laugh.

I'd love to have more time to learn more about my sweet Vallyn, but I'm not going to say no to Casen.

"Where and when?" I ask, my tone slightly clipped.

Casen gives me the details, and after ensuring my Little Lotte makes it into her apartment building alone, I head back to my condo downtown. The shower I take is probably the last decent one I'll have for a while, and I savor every drop, feeling the hot water wash away the tension. I pack my bags with a methodical precision, every item a reminder of the mission ahead.

I call my parents and then my sister, sharing as much information as I'm allowed. I make sure they have all the contact information they need, my sister's voice is a comforting tether to normalcy.

Casen drives us to the airport, his eyes flicking over to me occasionally.

"Anything happen with that girl who knocked you off your game the other night?" he teases, a grin tugging at his lips.

"We've talked," I answer with a shrug, trying to sound casual. "So far, that's really it."

The question reminds me of the favor I need to ask of Gage and the small gesture I want to make for Vallyn before I leave. Feeling grateful for my sister's specific birthday request, I order a gift basket for Vallyn from a fancy bath and lotion store. I remember the coconut and vanilla-scented items in her bathroom and bedroom, so I stick with that theme.

I add some quality chocolate to the gift basket and have it delivered to her with a note. The thought of her smile when she receives it brings a small, satisfied smile to my own lips.

A little while later, while we're waiting to board a military plane to Kenya, my phone buzzes. It's Vallyn.

Vallyn

I got your little gift - thank you - it's kind of perfect

Me

I'm glad you like it Little Lotte, I may not be able to talk much the next few days, but I didn't want you to forget about me

Vallyn

You're so creepy I couldn't forget you

Me

I'll take that for now lol, hopefully you'll remember me for other reasons soon

Vallyn

I kind of hope so too

Me

Oh, pretty girl, soon you will be completely mine

Vallyn

Pretty sure autonomy is hot, but if I'm honest,
reading that was also hot

Good

# VALLYN

I'm stunned by the basket he sent me. The products inside are
luxurious, and I confirmed through a quick internet search, way
beyond anything I could ever afford. As I unwrap each item, a rich
fragrance fills the air, intoxicating and mysterious. It's as if he's
chosen them specifically for me, to make me remember him every
time I catch a whiff of their scent. The lotions are silky, the bath salts
glisten like crushed diamonds, and the candles—the candles—each
has an aroma that's both soothing and provocative. I can't help but
wonder what message he's trying to send with these lavish gifts. Why
these particular items? Why now? My curiosity is piqued, and my
heart beats a little faster as I imagine the thoughts behind his choice.

Me

I do really like this, but I have to ask where you got the idea to send this stuff to me

Private

It's some of my sister's favorite stuff, I took an educated guess

Me

Well, it's really nice, I'm almost afraid to use it lol

Private

Use it, pretty girl, I can get you more

Me

Yeah?

Private

Not even a question

Me

And what do you want in exchange

Private

Nothing - Just your conversation right now, but honestly, if you stopped talking to me, I'd still send you gifts

Me

So you're telling me I'll have to go into hiding to not get gifts from you

Private

You can't hide from me, pretty girl, I will find you
anywhere

Me

Is that so?

I stare at the three little dots for what feels like an eternity. My
breath hitches when the message finally appears.

Private

I would fight the wildest of animals and burn
the world to the ground for you. I will find
you anywhere—the darkest corners of the earth,
the deepest abyss of the ocean, or the highest,
most treacherous mountain peaks. You can't
hide from my Little Lotte, and you can't run from
me - I will find you, I will chase you, and I will
catch you.

My heart somersaults in my chest, and a deep ache forms at my
core. I should be terrified—I know I should be terrified—but instead,
I crave this phantom's touch, his presence, his understanding.

Me

Okay - back to that part about possessive or
protective lol

Private

Both, pretty girl, both - I have to go - but, Vallyn?

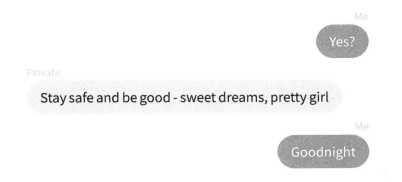

For the first time in a long while, I feel the urgent need for release. I open my nightstand drawer, my fingers brushing against my favorite battery-operated boyfriend. With a sigh, I let myself surrender to the sensations, finally drifting off to sleep, sated and at peace.

# CHAPTER FIVE

# THE YOUTH CENTER

## VALLYN

T he next few days pass quietly. I don't hear from my Phantom, and I manage to get through grading all the finals. Sam, my professor and doctoral advisor, is pleased with my progress. We have a few tasks to tackle over the summer, but I'm mostly free until the end of August, except for ongoing work on my dissertation interviews and research.

My dissertation focuses on why children in modern society are drawn into a life of crime and how early community and behavioral health interventions can prevent it. I spend a lot of time at a youth center working with at-risk kids and former gang members who became involved in crime at a young age.

The research involves numerous interviews and there are a lot of difficult histories to record. One man, about my age and reformed, so to speak, has been trying to connect me with some of his old contacts still active in gangs. I've set strict conditions if that happens—it has to be in a public place and in a gang neutral neighborhood. If I can secure those interviews by the end of summer, I should be able to submit my dissertation by winter break.

Today is a youth center day. Corey often accompanies me; his concern is sweet. We've been friends for fourteen years, and though he's wanted more at times, he understands and respects our friendship boundaries now. Still, there is a comfort level there, so he just knocks lightly on my apartment door before he lets himself in. He has a spare key, too, in case I ever need it.

"Hey, Val, you almost ready?" Corey calls as he finds me typing away on my laptop on the couch.

"Yeah, just need to finish these last few sentences," I reply with a smile.

"Wanna grab dinner after?" he asks.

"Sure, what are you thinking?"

"Just something nearby, nothing too fancy," he suggests.

"Okay, we can figure it out," I say, closing my laptop and slipping it into my backpack. "Let's go."

Corey drives us to the youth center in the heart of Phoenix. The staff, volunteers, and most of the kids know me by name. I have spent my time getting to know them, asking about their families. Many have parents or older siblings who are incarcerated, and I try to identify patterns in their stories.

One of my favorite kids, Xavier—though everyone calls him Zay—is there today. He has three older brothers, two of whom are incarcerated, while the third has recently started becoming involved in gang activities. I've only met one of his brothers; Zay just talks about the others. His dad is absent, but he has nothing but praise for his mom.

Zay believes his brothers succumbed to peer pressure and is determined not to follow their path. However, he's aware that Marcus, his youngest older brother, felt the same way but still joined the same gang. Zay's faith in his ability to stay out of trouble seems to waver as he watches Marcus's descent.

Zay is twelve, so we talk about school, shoot baskets—though I'm terrible at it—and then play some games on old consoles. He beats me at everything. Corey sits back, quietly observing.

A few hours later, Zay's mom arrives to pick him up. We exchange pleasantries, and then Corey and I head to dinner. Choosing a nearby hole-in-the-wall burger place, it's familiar and comfort food in some ways. The meal is good, and it's nice to decompress with Corey, discussing the day's interactions from an outside perspective.

"I think it's noble that you're researching this and that your work might actually help kids like Zay in the future," Corey says with a shrug.

"I hope it does," I reply. "And I hope I can continue making a difference while making a living."

"You'll figure it out," Corey reassures me.

The stuffy air hits me as I step inside my apartment, so I promptly adjust the thermostat. Seventy-five degrees inside won't cut it. The air conditioning hums to life, and I breathe a sigh of relief as the cool air begins to circulate.

Grabbing a sparkling water from the fridge, I collapse on the couch and turn on the TV. I haven't watched anything new in months, and Brooke recommended a couple of shows. I start one, ready to lose myself in it, but then there's a knock on the door.

Opening it, I find a flower delivery person holding a vase of white orchids and a teddy bear. I thank them, set the vase on the kitchen island, and open the card.

Little Lotte,<br>
I'm out of the country, but I'm thinking about you. I thought my pretty<br>
girl needed pretty flowers and something to snuggle with.<br>
♥ Your Phantom

The brown teddy bear is irresistibly soft, its plush fur inviting my fingers to sink into its comforting embrace. It's not overly large, yet not too small—just the right size, comparable to a standard pillow, making it perfect for snuggling. The orchids nearby fill the air with their exquisite fragrance, their delicate petals adding a touch of elegance to my apartment.

I pull out my phone, hesitating for a moment before attempting to text him. There's no contact number saved for him—I don't even know how he gets these messages. Uncertainty gnaws at me as I tap out a message, wondering if it will even reach him out of the country.

Me

> Out of the country, huh? That sounds prestigious. The flowers are beautiful, thank you.

I'm surprised when he answers right away.

Private

> I wish it were prestigious Little Lotte - it has been a lot of sand and heat lol. I'm glad you like the flowers.

Me

Sand and heat? Like you know Arizona? Lol

Private

lol different sand and heat, did they bring you your bear too?

Me

They did, it's very soft

Private

Snuggle with it tonight, then I can be jealous of a stuffed animal

Me

Not like you've attempted to snuggle with me in person

Private

Soon pretty girl

Me

Still not going to tell me your name?

Private

Someday

Me

how long are you out of the country?

Private

I should be back stateside tomorrow, but not
back to Arizona for another day after that - I have
to go Little Lotte - but snuggle the bear and have
sweet dreams tonight

Me

Goodnight

After I set my phone down, I realize I'm hugging the bear tightly to
my chest, and I can't wipe the smile off my face. The simple comfort
of the soft toy brings an unexpected joy. I make my way to the couch,
sitting down and putting my feet up on the coffee table. With my
knees bent, I rest the bear on my lap, positioning it so it faces me.

I gently tug at one of its ears, smoothing the plush fur away from
its beady eyes. A warm feeling spreads through me as I look into its
innocent face. Unable to contain my thoughts, I say out loud, "What
am I gonna do about this guy?"

# CHAPTER SIX

# SUDAN & THE BEAR

## PHANTOM

T he heat of Sudan wraps around us like a suffocating blanket, each moment a battle for survival in an extraction mission too financially tempting to refuse. Casen, with his effortless command of the native language, is our lifeline, guiding us through the labyrinth of danger.

The hours stretch into a relentless haze of gunfire and sweat as we huddle in the shadowed corners of an abandoned building, our only company the constant rattle of bullets and the ticking clock of our lives.

"This is why it pays so well," Casen quips, a glint of dark humor in his eyes as we share scant portions of freeze-dried food and sip from our dwindling water supply. The payout is a fleeting thought compared to the true prize—two families, now safely in Kenya, spared from the chaos we've waded through.

The return to Camp Simba in Manda Bay is a surreal transition from hell to something resembling normalcy. The relief of hot showers washes away layers of grime, almost making us feel human again.

Casen checks in with Gage, making sure everything is good at home. Then his expression shifts to one of bewilderment. "Gage says to tell you mission accomplished," he announces.

I laugh, a rare sound in our world right now, and shout, "Thanks, Gage," knowing he can hear me over Casen's satellite phone. When the call ends, Casen's curiosity gets the better of him. "What mission did you have Gage on?"

"Just something for that girl I can't get out of my head," I say, dismissive but not untruthful.

Back in the barracks, the transient sanctuary before our journey home, I open my laptop to check on Gage's progress and Vallyn. His email is thorough, detailing every step. With a new password and encryption, I ensure even Gage can't penetrate the surveillance. Three cameras now stream live feeds from her apartment, capturing the intimate spaces of her kitchen, living room, and bedroom.

The dark satisfaction coils in my chest as I watch, like a predator in the shadows.

As an afterthought I text Gage.

Me

You didn't watch her did you?

Gage

Of course not, man, you know all the ways of torture

Me

Lol, you'd be right to remember that

Her apartment is empty when I check the feed. I take a long swig of water and pull up the GPS on her phone; she's at a restaurant a few blocks away. A quick Google search later, and I've ordered her flowers—orchids, because she's far too special for basic roses. The florist's website suggests a stuffed bear, and I think, why the hell not?

Fortune seems to smile as she's home when the delivery arrives. When I get her text, I pull up the feed. Saying goodnight, I watch her hug the bear to her chest, snuggling with it on the couch. That's promising—at least she isn't too creeped out by me.

Before boarding the plane to Germany, I check the feed again. She's in bed with the bear, and I can't help but grin like an idiot. I almost want to call the flower company and thank them for the up-sell.

The plane ride is noisy, but the hum lulls Casen and me to sleep. It feels like no time before we're off the plane in Germany, then back on another headed for Annapolis. Exhausted, we sleep through most of the flight.

In Annapolis, we transfer to commercial airliners for the final leg to Phoenix. While waiting at the gate, I pull up Vallyn's apartment feed. There she is, sitting on her couch with her laptop, the bear nestled beside her. With that image locked away, I also sleep peacefully on the flight back to Phoenix.

"There's my big brother," my sister, Keri, exclaims as she bursts into my condo, her voice a force of nature. "You don't get to tell me you were locked under live fire for two days and not have me come check on you in person."

Her unannounced visit jolts me, making me rethink the wisdom of giving her the code and key. "Keri, I'm good, you could have called," I reply with a laugh, masking my surprise.

"Not good enough," she retorts, thrusting a bag of sealed food containers into my hands. "Besides, Mom wanted me to bring you food. Apparently, she thinks whatever you eat while you're getting shot at and on stakeouts isn't good enough."

Laughing, I take the bag from her and head toward the kitchen. Keri wanders into the living room, and it suddenly dawns on me that I have images of Vallyn strewn across the coffee table.

*Fuck.*

"What did this chick do? She's kind of pretty," Keri comments, her tone laced with curiosity.

*Double fuck.*

I turn the corner into the living room and meet Keri's inquisitive gaze. We look a lot alike—same hazel-green eyes, same straight nose, same dark brown hair.

"Actually, she didn't do anything. But you're right, she's pretty, and I kind of like her," I admit, deciding that honesty is my only refuge.

"Um, you know it's obvious these weren't all taken on the same day, right? Like, not even the same two days?" Keri almost interrogates, her eyebrows arching in skepticism.

I sigh, running a hand through my hair. "Yeah, I do realize that."

"And she doesn't know you're taking her picture?" she accuses, her tone sharp and unyielding.

"No, Ker, no she doesn't," I confess, feeling like my guts are spilling onto the floor.

"There's a word for this, you know? It's called stalking," she states, her voice heavy with disapproval.

"I've talked to her. We've texted, talked on the phone, but yeah, I'm a little obsessed with her," I admit with a shrug, a twisted form of pride mixed with shame.

Keri scoffs loudly. "You know if she finds out you're doing this," she gestures to the pictures on the table, "she's not going to talk to you anymore. I know the military and your job fucked you up, but come on, you have to know that you can't do this if you want to be in a relationship with her."

"Are you just here to lecture me?" I ask, shaking my head, my tone darkening with frustration.

"No, but maybe don't stalk your girlfriend," she adds. And while I know the stalking part is probably true, I can't help but savor the way "girlfriend" sounds.

A few days later, I find myself stalking Vallyn—Keri is right, that's exactly what I'm fucking doing. She and her friend Sasha are headed for brunch, followed by a shopping spree. I park my car down the block from the quaint café where they're sitting, thankfully by the window.

The telephoto lens on my camera is getting a serious workout today, capturing every laugh, every smile, every moment.

As I'm snapping pictures, a woman raps on my window, her face twisted in outrage. "What kind of asshole takes photos of women without their permission?" she demands.

Thinking fast, I hand her my private investigator business card and muster a convincing explanation. "I'm catching some douche canoe cheating on his girlfriend," I say with practiced nonchalance.

Her expression softens into approval. "Keep up the good work," she says, giving me a nod before moving on.

I return to my surveillance, the telephoto lens bringing Vallyn's world into sharp focus.

There's a ping, alerting me that Vallyn received a text message. I check the screen on the camera and notice her surprised reaction. She got a message from a guy she apparently gave her number to.

Unknown

> Hey, Vallyn (I hope I spelled that right) this is Tom from the other night, you gave me your number

I watch as she looks at her phone and then smiles, saying something to Sasha, before replying.

Vallyn

> Hey, I do remember giving you my number, what's your excuse for not reaching out to me sooner? Lol

Tom

> I don't have a good excuse, just been busy, but I would like to get to know you better.

I'm sure you would, Tom, I think sarcastically to myself, but Vallyn is mine.

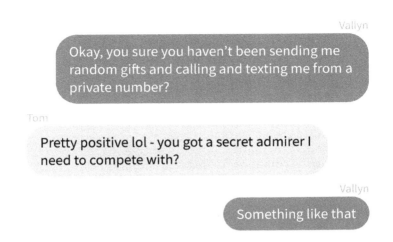

> **Vallyn**
> Okay, you sure you haven't been sending me random gifts and calling and texting me from a private number?

> **Tom**
> Pretty positive lol - you got a secret admirer I need to compete with?

> **Vallyn**
> Something like that

Oh, Vallyn, shut this guy down. He is definitely not me. Now, I decide to distract her, curious to see how she reacts. I set the camera on the dash, zooming in on her face, so I can see her clearly on the screen. Picking up my phone, I compose a text message to her, my fingers moving quickly over the screen.

> **Me**
> Hey pretty girl

> **Vallyn**
> Interesting

> **Me**
> lol, what's that?

> **Vallyn**
> You sure you're not some guy named Tom?

> **Me**
>
> Definitely not a Tom

Just then, Tom texts her back.

> **Tom**
>
> You want to meet up for coffee or drinks sometime?

She leaves him hanging for a moment and talks to me.

> **Vallyn**
>
> I haven't heard from you since the day you sent me orchids and a teddy bear. Are you back in Phoenix?

> **Me**
>
> I am Little Lotte

> **Vallyn**
>
> Apparently I'm not high on your priority list

> **Me**
>
> Vallyn, you are my priority list

> **Vallyn**
>
> Then why haven't I heard from you?

Now, this has my full attention because she *wants* my attention. She misses it, maybe craves it.

Me

Little Lotte, pretty girl, I did have some family stuff to deal with

Partial lie, but okay.

Me

I will call you tonight

Vallyn

Okay

I think the intervention is successful, she still hasn't answered Tom, but then she does.

Vallyn

Yeah, we can meet for coffee sometime, what does your schedule look like?

I roll my eyes and hit my steering wheel with the palm of my hand.

Tom

Great! I work the next two days, but then I'm off the three after that - name the time and place

Vallyn then goes on to give him a day, time, and place, and I am seething. She's *mine*, and if she doesn't realize that yet, she will soon.

CHAPTER SEVEN

# THE CONFESSIONS

## VALLYN

"Wait, you have some shadowy figure sending you gifts and texting you?" Sasha's eyes widen, caught between fascination and a flicker of irritation, miffed I'd kept this tantalizing secret.

"Yeah, he's intense, in that dark, magnetic way. Confident, maybe a bit too cocky, but not enough to push me away," I say, a shiver of excitement running through me. "I don't know, Sasha, there's something there. It's like he's hiding for a reason. Maybe I'm crazy."

We burst into laughter, the absurdity filling the space between us. Sasha, ever the pragmatic one, smirks and shakes her head. "There's definitely something flirty and sexy about it. But, considering you work with criminals and their families, it could be something dangerous."

I inhale sharply, shaking my head slowly. "I don't think it's that. Those men are a different kind of cocky. It's almost like... " I hesitate, "like he wants me to fall for him before I see him or know what he does. Does that make any sense?"

"Maybe he's disfigured or something," Sasha teases, her smile playful. "Hiding his appearance for some reason."

"Maybe, but I get the feeling his life is... interesting. The kind of interesting that nice girls should avoid," I say, trying to downplay the turmoil inside me with a casual shrug.

"What makes you think that?" Sasha's curiosity sharpens.

I take a long sip of my mimosa, savoring the bubbly sweetness, meeting her gaze. "He won't tell me his name or what he does. And then there's the fact he's been out of the country, in a desert—makes me think military or something. I don't know, Sasha. It's weird, but I kind of like it," I confess, trying to shake off the lingering doubts.

An hour after returning from brunch with Sasha, a knock at the door sends my heart racing. I open it to find a delivery person holding a vase of white orchids. The sight of the pristine blooms against the dark granite of my kitchen island is almost ethereal, their delicate petals glowing softly in the afternoon light. These are nicer than the last orchids.

With a mix of excitement and curiosity, I reach for the card nestled among the flowers, feeling a shiver of anticipation as I open it.

*Little Lotte,*

*I'm sorry I didn't reach out to you as soon as I was back in Phoenix, but you are on my mind every minute of every day. You're woven into every corner of my mind, an inseparable part of me. Even when my attention is demanded elsewhere, much like the sweet scent of orchids, the essence of you lingers, like a gentle whisper, a constant reminder of your perfect existence.*

♥ *Your Phantom*

The sweet fragrance of orchids does fill the air as I smile at the romantic words on the card. This man, whoever he is, might truly be as obsessed as he claims. A sudden knock startles me, and the door handle turns to reveal Corey. I'd completely forgotten our plans.

"Fuck, Corey," I react quickly, my heart racing. "You scared me, and I forgot we had plans. Give me a minute to get ready."

"Why are you so jumpy?" he chuckles, raising an eyebrow.

"I was just focused," I reply, forcing a smile.

I retreat to the bedroom, shutting the door behind me to change clothes. Corey's voice filters through the door. "Who are the flowers from?"

"My secret admirer," I laugh, stepping out and meeting his gaze.

Corey's expression hardens as he holds the card. I swallow hard, offering a soft smile. His eyes meet mine before he masks his reaction.

"Phantom?" he asks incredulously.

Laughing uncomfortably, I nod. "Yeah, I told him I couldn't keep calling him 'private number.'"

Corey tosses the card onto the island, his demeanor shifting to anger. "You've talked to this guy?"

"Yeah," I reply, feeling my own irritation rising. "Do you have a problem with that, *dad*?"

"Yeah, I do, and your actual dad would too," he snaps. "Val, you don't know who this guy is. He has your phone number and address, and you don't know him."

"If he has those things, I must know him in some capacity," I retort.

"Seriously, Vallyn?" Corey's frustration is palpable as he runs a hand through his hair. "Am I really that bad? That some guy you don't know, who could be a serial killer, is a better choice?"

His words sting more than they should, but maybe exactly as he expected. I steady my expression and soften my voice. "Corey, we've been through this before. I thought we were past this."

"Well, there hasn't been anyone else in years. Maybe that gave me hope," he confesses, turning away towards the windows.

I let the silence linger before speaking. "Corey, you're like a brother to me. I really thought we were past this, and I'm sorry."

"So, I don't even get friend-zoned. I get brother-zoned?" he scoffs, turning back to face me.

"Maybe we shouldn't do this today," I suggest.

"You're right. I need time to process," he admits, then adds, "And Sasha said you have a coffee date with some other guy, too."

I nod, letting out a breathy, "Yeah."

Corey exhales slowly. "Yeah, Vallyn, I'm going to need a day or two."

He approaches me, looking into my eyes before cupping the back of my neck and pressing a gentle kiss to my forehead. I remain stoic, arms crossed, but I offer him a gentle smile as he walks away.

As soon as the door to my apartment closes, I let out a breath I didn't realize I was holding and press my palms into the edge of the kitchen island, leaning against it. After a few breaths, I pick up my phone, and text Sasha.

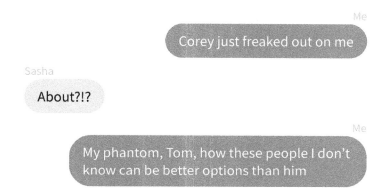

Me
Corey just freaked out on me

Sasha
About?!?

Me
My phantom, Tom, how these people I don't know can be better options than him

Sasha

I always wonder if he's just waiting around for you to change your mind

Me

It won't happen, there is zero chemistry there for me, he's a nice guy, maybe even a good partner, but there is zero chemistry

My Phantom however sent me the most amazing card with more orchids

There's a pause in our conversation while I take the picture and send it.

Sasha

Holy fuck, girl, that's straight poetry, I definitely can't say he's not putting in effort lol

Me

Right? Everything he has done has been over the top, even if it is a little creepy lol

Sasha

I think you need to push him, you need to know more, need to know he's safe

Me

Maybe, he is kind of romantic though, I feel something when he talks to me, I think it is chemistry

Sasha

Just be careful Val, also I'll give it a few hours
and then check on Corey, don't want it to be too
obvious we talked

Me

Okay, Sash, thank you

Sasha

When are you meeting Tom?

Me

Tomorrow morning for coffee

Sasha

You'll have to update me

Me

I will

Later in the evening, I'm curled up on the couch with a soft blanket
and a book, my ever-present stuffed bear nestled beside me. My
phone rings, the screen lighting up with "Private Number." A smile
tugs at my lips as I answer, "Hello?"

"Hey, pretty girl," the deep voice purrs, sending a shiver down my
spine.

"Hi," I reply, my voice soft. "The flowers are beautiful and smell amazing, and the note was sweet, too."

"Yeah?" he asks, a hint of warmth in his tone. "It's all true."

"Can I ask you something?"

"You can ask me anything," he replies, his voice cool and laced with humor. "Doesn't mean I'll answer."

I laugh softly. "Well, hopefully you'll answer this one. What does this timeline look like? When do I get to actually know who you are?"

"Oh, Little Lotte," he sighs, a touch of melancholy in his voice. "There's no definitive there—the answer is really when I feel it's time. But don't worry, I don't have infinite patience either."

"You know my friends think you're a serial killer or something," I say with a laugh.

He chuckles, the sound dark and rich. "Definitely not a serial killer. I'm not a bad guy, Vallyn, just a complicated one."

"Where were you when you were out of the country?" I ask.

"Africa, on business," he answers quickly, nonchalantly.

"What kind of business?" I probe, pushing the line of questioning.

"Government business," he replies, surprising me with his candidness. "It was a rescue mission, intense but well-paid."

"A rescue mission?" I echo, intrigued.

"Yeah, a rescue mission, Vallyn."

"Are you like a secret agent or a mercenary?" I ask, half-joking.

"Something like that," he answers. "But those are just side gigs. That's not my everyday job."

"What do you do every day?" I press, eager to keep him talking.

"Mostly follow cheating spouses to get proof for their better halves. Sometimes, life gets more interesting, and we go after fugitives and bail skippers," he explains.

"So, you're a private investigator, a bounty hunter," I clarify.

"Yeah, pretty girl, that's exactly what I am," he confirms.

"Look at you, actually talking to me," I flirt, a smile in my voice.

He chuckles again. "Little Lotte, it's not that I don't want to tell you things. I just don't want to scare you off."

"You know, you could've just asked me out for coffee," I suggest.

"Too basic. You deserve more than basic," he replies.

"Is this how you woo all the girls?" I tease.

"Vallyn, I haven't attempted to 'woo' a girl in over a decade. You are it. Like I said, I think I've lost my goddamn mind over you," he admits, his voice raw.

"Can you at least tell me where you know me from?" I ask, the silence that follows is heavy and uncomfortable.

"The only thing I'll tell you right now, Little Lotte, is that we have exchanged words in person. Not many, but we have," he answers, leaving me more puzzled.

"Why didn't you just ask me out then?" I ask.

"It wasn't the right time for either of us, pretty girl. But soon it will be. But I need you to know something," he says, his tone darkening.

"What's that?" I ask, my heart pounding.

"I consider you mine, and I protect what's mine. If any other guy lays his hands on you, they will end up dealing with me," he declares, the threat chilling me to the bone. My heart lodges in my throat, a lump of fear and thrill.

"That's the first thing you've ever said that actually scared me," I admit, my voice shaky and timid.

## CHAPTER EIGHT

# REASSURANCES

## PHANTOM

I draw a deep breath, my pulse a drumbeat in my ears. "Vallyn, don't be scared," I murmur, my voice a velvet whisper edged with steel. "I have no intentions of hurting you."

Reading those messages between Vallyn and Sasha earlier today infuriated me. To know that Corey is pressuring her was too much for me. The saving grace of that exchange was Vallyn talking about how she thinks she has chemistry with me.

Her body language shows a palpable defiance, her irritation a tangible force as I watch her on the small screen of my phone. "Maybe not, but you just threatened anyone else who touches me."

A chuckle rumbles from my chest, dark and rich. "Little Lotte, that sass of yours—that fire," I purr, "I love it. And it's not a threat. It's a promise. You are mine, and they need to understand that, too." My voice is calm, too calm, a serpent's hiss.

"You don't own me," she snaps, her voice sharp and rising in pitch. "I don't even know who the fuck you are."

"You *don't* know who I am," I reply, a smirk playing on my lips, "but you're wrong about me not owning you. I do, even if you don't recognize it yet."

She falls silent, her eyes darting to the window, tension coiling in her frame.

"Little Lotte," I say, softer now, "all I want is to protect you, keep you safe, and eventually love you the way you deserve."

"Why couldn't you just ask me out like a normal fucking human being?" she demands. "Were you worried I'd say no?"

"No," I reply, a dark laugh escaping me, "I think you would have said yes. But it would have been a dick move on my part at the time."

"So playing games with me was the answer?" she taunts.

"Generally, I don't play with my food before I eat it," I quip, my grin widening.

"Oh, now I'm food," she scoffs, throwing her arms up in frustration, pacing back towards the kitchen.

I laugh, the sound echoing through the connection. "Vallyn, baby, I would love to taste you, but no, you're not food, just an expression."

Silence descends again, heavy and charged, as she paces. I watch her, like a predator savoring the anticipation.

"Vallyn, tell me about the youth center," I urge, my tone gentle but insistent.

"So you can threaten them, too?" she retorts, venom in her voice.

"Now you might be getting a bit histrionic and theatrical," I tease. "No, Vallyn, I genuinely want to know what you do there, what you do with the kids. It's endearing."

She lets out a dramatic huff. "Did you seriously just call me histrionic? That's the most misogynistic gaslighting thing I've heard in a long time."

"Focus, Little Lotte," I command softly. "I said you *might* be getting a little histrionic, not that you are. And I genuinely want to know."

She goes silent again, but she's not hanging up. Clearing my throat I offer a consolation, "Okay, if you won't talk about you, I'll give you some bread crumbs about me."

She stops moving for a second and then sits on her couch, I watch her put the phone on speaker and set it on the coffee table. Smiling to myself, I continue, "Vallyn, just so you know I have a good family, I was brought up well. My parents are great, my sister, Keri, is great. She knows about you and even berated me a little about you."

I let that sit there, seeing if she'll bite, eventually does. "Great," she begins, "I know your sister's name, but not yours." Scrubbing her face with her hand, she sighs and then continues, "What did she berate you for?"

"Her words, not mine, but for stalking you," I admit with a smirk.

"You *are* stalking me," she replies.

"I know, pretty girl, but it's more like me doing my PI job, learning about you before I leap," I confide.

"I'm not a subject, or a mark, or whatever you call it," she says, her defiance making my eyebrows shoot up, eyes widening in surprise.

"How do you know words like mark?" I ask, genuinely curious.

"Maybe you should stalk me better and you'd know," she quips, a sly smile tugging at her lips.

"Is that a challenge, pretty girl?" I ask, incredulous at her boldness.

"I don't know anymore," she sighs, her shoulders slumping as she sinks back onto her couch, her head tilted back in apparent defeat.

"Vallyn, baby, you're not a mark. You're right," I sigh, the weight of her words settling in.

Her hands cover her face, and I let the silence hang heavy between us. Eventually, she sits up, peering at the screen, likely checking if I'm still there.

"I feel like..." she starts, rubbing her hands over her face again before hugging herself. "I feel like I shouldn't even be entertaining you, entertaining this. This should be terrifying, really."

I let her confession linger, too long perhaps. "Then, Little Lotte, why do you keep answering me?"

"I don't know, because you're intriguing, and the mystery of who you are has me questioning everything," she admits.

"Just give me a shot, pretty girl. I told you, I don't have infinite patience either," I plead.

She's quiet for a bit, then nods, her voice breathy as she says, "Okay."

"Okay?" I clarify, needing to hear it again.

"Yeah, don't make me say it again," she responds, exasperated.

"You want to tell me what you do at the youth center now?" I ask, easing the conversation forward.

"It's part of my dissertation. I interview and talk to kids and their families for research," she answers, her voice resigned, then turning sassy again, "But you know, if you stalked me better, you'd know that."

I let out a dark chuckle. "Vallyn, that mouth has to be good for more than all that sass, but thank you for answering me."

"Will you answer a question for me now?" she asks, her tone shifting to curiosity.

"Maybe," I reply honestly.

"Okay, I'll start basic, although you won't tell me your name," she begins sarcastically, "How old are you?"

"Thirty," I answer. That one is easy.

"Are you from Phoenix?" she asks.

"You said one question," I chide, then relent, "Born and raised, yeah."

"Is your sister, Keri, your only sibling?" she inquires.

"She is," I confirm.

"What do you do for fun?" she asks.

"Besides stalk you?" I reply, and she genuinely laughs.

"Yes, besides that," she finally says.

"I don't have a lot of downtime, honestly, but I spend time training in multiple ways, and every once in a while, I turn on the television," I answer honestly. "What about you, what do you do for fun?"

She clears her throat. "During the school year, I have no time. In the summer, I hang out with my friends and catch up on shows. I read a lot."

"Yeah? All cheesy romances?" I tease.

"Not all, no," she answers, laughing a little.

"Vallyn, have some faith in me, okay?" I ask, knowing I need to go shortly.

"I'll try."

"I need to go. I don't want to, but I need to," I say.

"Okay."

"Goodnight, Little Lotte. Sweet dreams," I whisper.

"Goodnight," she replies softly, and I disconnect the call.

I watch her on the screen for a few minutes longer. She finds the bear in her bed and pulls it to her chest, staring at the ceiling. She stays like that for a while, and though I really have to get moving, I hold that image in my mind, lingering on her vulnerability.

I know Vallyn is going to meet this Tom guy for coffee. The thought gnaws at me, but pushing her too hard will only make her shut down, and then I'll truly lose my goddamn mind. I'll follow her and intervene only if necessary.

She's meeting him at a coffee shop—I know the place and time, which makes my job easier. But with the temperature soaring well into the triple digits, hiding in a hoodie and hat is out of the question. My telephoto lens will have to do the work.

Gritting my teeth and clenching my jaw, I watch him hug her when they first meet. She's polite as they sip coffee and nibble on pastries, but her body language is closed off. She spends a lot of time looking around.

Is she avoiding eye contact with him, or is she worried I might be lurking, doing exactly what I'm doing? The question gnaws at me. I don't get to see the end of the date because Betty, Casen's and my secretary of sorts, calls.

"Got a bail recovery contract. We know where the subject is," Betty says quickly.

Reluctantly, I pull away, trusting Vallyn to make good decisions. I'll find out soon enough if she texts Sasha about it, and that will be revealing.

# CHAPTER NINE

# THE OTHER MAN

## PHANTOM

"Well, that was fucking easy," Casen says as we walk back to the car, having just dropped off a bail-skipper at jail.

"I'm good with easy money," I admit, shrugging.

Gage, who's in the backseat, didn't really need to be there for this one, but his presence is always a plus. As we drive, he taps me on the shoulder. "How's Vallyn?"

"Still figuring that one out," I reply.

"That the girl you've been pining over? Vallyn?" Casen asks.

"You mean the girl he's been stalking?" Gage says with a smirk, but Casen shoots me a disapproving look.

Shrugging, I respond, "It's not full-on stalking, just making sure I know what I'm getting into."

"So you're casing her out?" Casen presses.

"Something like that," I agree.

"Just don't be doing illegal shit," Casen warns, while Gage, who knows better, scoffs.

"What did you do?" Casen interrogates, his tone hard.

Shrugging again, I opt for honesty. "There might be cameras in her apartment, spyware on her phone."

"You are a stupid motherfucker, you know that?" Casen snaps, shaking his head.

"I know, I'm obsessed and doing really stupid shit. Trust me, I fucking know," I confess.

Despite Casen's disapproval, I can't help myself. Talking about her makes me pull out my phone to check for any updates with Tom. There's a text exchange with Sasha, where Vallyn mentions there's no chemistry, or maybe her Phantom is just in her head too much. I snicker at that.

Tom had sent her a follow-up text that she hasn't answered yet. For now, I decide to leave it be, content in the knowledge that probably isn't going anywhere.

Later that evening things get interesting though. Tom continues to text her, and she finally answers him, that he's a nice guy, but she's not interested. He is persistent and texts her almost begging for one more try.

So, now I'm looking up Tom, finding information on him. And within an hour, I'm knocking on his door, and I don't use my nice knock—I use my bounty hunter knock.

When he opens the door he takes a step back, I'm a few inches taller than him, and certainly more built than him. That step back wasn't a smart move. I move into his apartment with him, and shut the door behind me, then speak.

"Look, Tom, you seem like a nice guy, but you really need to learn that when a girl says 'no' she means 'no' capiche?"

"Who are you?" he asks, his voice timid.

"I'm nobody to you, and everything to Vallyn. She's mine. Don't text her, don't call her, don't even ever fucking *think* about her again or you get to deal with me. Okay?"

"Geezus dude, fine, can you leave now?"

"Absofuckinglutely, have a nice day," I say and then slam his door open before heading back down the hall.

Less than thirty seconds later there's a ping and Tom texted Vallyn.

Tom

So did you have to send this guy to come threaten me? Seriously I get the point, sorry to have bothered you

I watch the dots as Vallyn goes to reply, but then it stops and instead I get a text.

Vallyn

What did you do?

Me

Pretty girl, I'm going to need more data to go with that question

Vallyn

Did you threaten the guy I had coffee with

Me

Did he touch you?

It's a long few minutes before she responds.

Vallyn

Just a hug hello and goodbye, were you fucking watching?

Then she goes silent on me. No more texts, no more calls. Not even to Tom. Instead, she finds solace in Sasha, and together, they plan a night out with friends. I make a calculated decision to let her go. I can't shadow her every hour, every minute. There must be room to breathe, even from me.

I reach out to my parents and arrange dinner—it's been too long. I manage to drag Keri along as well.

"Still playing the stalker boyfriend?" Keri teases, her tone laced with irony.

I shrug, a nonchalant mask. "Not as much. Things are progressing."

She rolls her eyes but keeps her thoughts unspoken, and for that, I'm grateful. Dinner unfolds with stories from Sudan, carefully edited for parental ears, and then shifts to updates on their lives, a dance of normalcy.

Later, as I straddle my bike, I light a cigarette and pull up the feed from Vallyn's apartment. The moment the screen flickers to life, regret pierces me, sharp and cold. Maybe I should have kept a closer watch. Maybe giving her space was a mistake.

There's no audio on the cameras, but what I see makes my blood turn to ice. And I feel the familiar, dangerous stirrings of something dark and lethal in my gut. I'm going to fucking kill him.

# VALLYN

I am seething with anger at my Phantom, terror clawing at my insides over the things he's done. His interference with Tom crosses a line, a boundary he had no right to breach, even if I didn't want that to go further. The part that truly ignites my fury? Tom has seen the face I have yet to see. And that realization makes me despise myself even more.

Sasha proposes a night out, a distraction, so we go. It's all of us—Sasha, Brooke, Tori, Carly, Corey, and me. By the time I down my eighth shot, my secrets spill out, my Phantom's secrets. My hatred, my love, my confusion—everything. My filter has vanished.

Tori and Brooke romanticize the whole ordeal, their eyes sparkling with fantasies of bad boys and dark allure. Sasha and Carly offer support, no matter my choice. Corey, however, remains unnervingly silent.

As the night draws to a close—many more shots later, Corey insists on accompanying me home, his concern for my safety palpable. Too intoxicated to protest, I agree. But as soon as we cross my apartment's threshold, regret washes over me.

Corey traps me against the kitchen island with his arms, his eyes darkening with a dangerous intent. "If it's a bad boy you want, Vallyn, I can be a fucking bad boy," he growls.

I laugh, a nervous, uncertain sound, but his hand grips the back of my neck, attempting to pull me closer for a kiss. I twist away, slipping beneath his arm.

"Fucking A, Vallyn," Corey spits, frustration evident. "You're all turned on by this mysterious guy, but you won't let me touch you? Do I need to disappear and just start randomly texting you? Fuck?"

He lunges again and manages to cage me against the wall. When he moves in, trying to put his mouth on mine, I dodge, but stumble, the alcohol making me clumsy.

Falling hard, I end up on my back, the wind knocked out of me momentarily. Corey comes crashing down on top of me, and panic surges as he pins my wrists with his hands and he spreads my legs with his.

"Stop, Corey, please! You've been my friend for so long. This isn't you," I plead, tears brimming in my eyes.

We freeze as my phone rings, the shrill sound piercing the tension. It's after midnight. It has to be him—it has to be my phantom. Relief floods through me.

The sound of the ring loosens Corey's grip on my hand as he thinks about reaching for the sound himself. I manage to grab my phone from my pocket, see the private number, and slide it to answer before Corey can stop me.

"Corey, fucking stop," I yell as he snatches the phone and throws it to the side. "Corey, what the fuck is wrong with you? Get off of me."

My Phantom's voice comes through the speaker—his voice sounding distant with my phone across the room, calling my name, and then I swear I hear an engine revving.

"Corey, you don't want to be here when he gets here. He'll probably fucking kill you," I warn, my voice loud enough for my Phantom to hear.

Corey snaps out of whatever trance he is in, realization dawning. "Fuck you, Vallyn," he mutters, standing.

"Seriously? You're willing to end our friendship because I won't fuck you?" I ask, pushing myself up.

"I don't fucking understand you, Vallyn," he says, storming out.

I crawl to my phone, the line still open. I hit speaker, listening to an engine roar.

"Hello," I say, my voice weary.

"Vallyn, I swear to everything I'm going to kill him," my Phantom growls.

"Don't kill him. He was drunk, and he's gone," I reply, my tone too casual, my words slurred. He doesn't respond.

I laugh, a broken sound. "You know what's funny?"

"What's that?" he asks, his voice rough, heavy, and completely without humor

"It's so fucking wrong, but I was relieved when I knew you were calling. I knew you'd rescue me," I confess, giggling. "*You're* supposed to be the scary one. I'm supposed to be scared of you, and instead, I wanted you."

CHAPTER TEN

# THE THREAT & THE TUCK-IN

## PHANTOM

Her words linger in the air, wrapping around my mind like smoke. She hadn't talked to me since she texted, upset about me threatening Tom.

I take a deep breath, the tension loosening slightly in my chest. "Where is he going, Vallyn?" I ask, my voice low and dangerous.

She giggles, the sound like broken glass through the Bluetooth in my helmet.

"I'm not telling you that just so you can kill him."

"Vallyn, I'm not going to kill him. Where is he going?" My patience thins, each word edged with steel.

"Probably home," she answers, her tone casual as if discussing the weather.

"Which is where?" My fingers grip the handlebars of my bike, knuckles I'm sure white under my gloves. "Vallyn, answer me. You know I'll find out anyway."

"You're not going to kill him?" she asks, a hint of fear seeping through her drunken haze.

"No," I promise, my voice a dark vow. "But I will make sure he never touches you like that again."

She hesitates, then gives me the address. I pull over, punching it into my GPS with aggressive precision before revving the bike back to life.

"Hey, Phantom man?" Her voice is a flirtatious whisper.

"Little Lotte?" I reply, a smirk playing on my lips.

"After you don't kill Corey, you should come tuck me into bed," she giggles, the sound laced with mischief.

"We'll see, pretty girl. Lock your door, though," I instruct, my voice a rough command.

"I'm pretty sure that won't stop you," she muses, a hint of challenge in her tone.

Snickering, I respond, "No, it won't stop me. But it will stop him."

"Mmmmm," she seems to concede in a hum, her voice softening.

"Vallyn, baby, I'm ending the call now. But I'll call you back or come tuck you in, okay?"

"You better, or I'll be mad at you," she says, another giggle bubbling up.

Laughing, I respond, "I can't tell if I like you drunk or not, pretty girl."

"I have no filter, so this is honest me," she sighs, her vulnerability stark and raw.

"So honest Vallyn likes me?" I inquire, my tone teasing yet sincere.

"All Vallyns like you," she murmurs sleepily, a yawn following her words.

Sighing, realizing the entire conversation has fizzled out my anger, I reiterate, "Lock your door. I'll call you back."

"Okay," she whispers, and the line goes silent, her words lingering in my mind like a ghost.

Pulling up to Corey's address, I kill the engine and wait. I knew I'd beat him—I was closer to his place than Vallyn's, so he'll arrive soon enough. The anticipation coils in my stomach like a serpent waiting to strike, each second ticking by in a silent countdown.

A car pulls up, the glow of a rideshare light in the window. Sure enough, it's him. I pull up my hood, the motorcycle jacket shrouding me in darkness, and adjust the bandana over my face. The moment his ride pulls away, I move.

"Corey, fucker," I call out, my voice cutting through the night like a knife.

He spins around, eyes widening, but tries to stand his ground. "You her fucking stalker?" he sneers, shaking his head in disbelief.

I don't answer. In three swift strides, I have him in a headlock, dragging him to the wall of his building. The brick scrapes against my Kevlar jacket as I move and pin him across the chest with my forearm.

"Listen, fucker," I growl, my voice a deadly whisper. "You're lucky she still wants to keep you as a friend. If you ever pull that shit again, they'll find pieces of you scattered across several states. You fucking understand?"

He's rattled, his bravado crumbling. He thought he could exchange a few words and be done with it. I release him, brushing off his shirt as if to erase the touch of my violence. "I've never killed anyone for fun, and I'd hate to start with you. But seriously, what the fuck is wrong with all you guys who can't take no for an answer?"

He regains some of his swagger, a twisted smirk on his lips. "Hasn't she told *you* no? I don't think you'd take no for an answer either, fucking stalker."

Anger flares, but I keep my voice steady, icy. "She hasn't told me no, fucker. She *won't* tell me no. And *if* she did, I wouldn't force myself on her. You're supposed to be her friend. Fucking act like it."

The words hang in the air, heavy with threat and promise. He stares at me, the reality of his situation sinking in, as I turn, I make sure to adjust my jacket so he sees the gun and holster, before I disappear into the shadows, leaving him to contemplate his actions.

Starting up the bike again, I make my way back to Vallyn's apartment. The night air bites at my exposed skin, but I barely feel it. The adrenaline pumping through my veins keeps me warm, focused. I arrive and keep my hood up, the bandana still covering my face. As I check her door and find it unlocked, a fresh wave of anger surges through me, hot and violent.

Stepping inside, the dim light reveals her crumpled form on the living room floor. She's out cold, phone clutched in her hand from our last call. The sight twists me up inside, a volatile mix of protectiveness and rage.

I crouch beside her, my gloved hand gentle as I shake her. She barely stirs, a soft murmur slipping from her lips. Scooping her up, I try not to think about this being the first time I've *really* touched her before I carry her to her bed, her body feels light and fragile in my arms. Carefully, I pull off her shoes and socks, leaving her otherwise dressed. I plug in her phone on the nightstand and place her bear beside her. For a moment, I just watch her, memorizing the peaceful rise and fall of her chest.

I find a piece of paper and scrawl a note for her to find in the morning, making sure there's water and ibuprofen within reach. She needs to know I was here, that I cared enough to be here.

With a hint of hesitation, I pull down my mask, leaning in to press a kiss to her temple. Removing my glove, my fingers stroke through her dark, wavy hair, the silky strands slipping through my fingers.

As I leave her apartment, I cast one last glance toward her bedroom. Making sure her door is locked on my way out, I straddle my bike, and ride home.

# CHAPTER ELEVEN

# AS REQUESTED

## VALLYN

The sun blazes through my bedroom window, a merciless glare that tells me it's already late morning. My memories of getting into bed are as hazy as the dream I just woke from. As I push back the covers, I find myself still clad in ripped jeans and a bra under my shirt, my head not throbbing like a hangover but spinning as if I'm still drunk.

I reach for my water, and that's when I notice it—a handwritten note on my nightstand. The writing is legible but scratchy, each letter more jagged than I'm used to.

> *Little Lotte,*
> *Drink water. And for the love of everything lock your door next time before you pass out on your living room floor. You've been tucked in - as requested.*
>
> ♥ *Phantom*
> *PS I didn't kill your friend, but we did have a chat*

*Holy fuck.*

He was in my apartment. I stare at my jeans that I never would have climbed in bed in, my shoes tucked neatly next to my bed in a way I would never do. The realization crashes over me—he put me in bed. Instantly, the hair on my arms and neck stands on edge, a chill running through me.

Rubbing my eyes, I shake my head, trying to remember the events of last night. Corey—Corey fucking attacked me, and I'm pretty sure I passed out almost right after he left. What would have happened if my phantom hadn't called me?

Then, the words I said to him come back, haunting me—I told him I was relieved he called, that I knew he would rescue me, that I liked him, that I wanted him to tuck me in. I look back at the note, *"You've been tucked in - as requested."*

I hate drunk Vallyn, but I hate even more that he was here and I passed out and didn't see him. He was in my apartment. He touched me, held me, and was gentleman enough to leave my clothes on me. He could have done anything to me, but he didn't.

Picking up my phone, I plan on texting my Phantom, but instead, I'm distracted by a slew of missed calls and texts from Sasha and Corey. I am not in any mood to talk to Corey right now, even if it's to hear him grovel.

"Vallyn, are you okay?" Sasha's voice is frantic when she answers.

"I'm fine," I chuckle a little, "although I think I'm still drunk, not hungover."

"What the fuck happened last night with Corey?" Sasha asks.

"What did he tell you?" I counter, trying to buy time.

"He said that your stalker threatened him when he got back to his place," Sasha replies. "Said he was fucking psycho and we should hold some kind of intervention for you."

Now I'm pissed, and I snap, "Did Corey happen to tell you that he attacked me, that he had me on the floor of my apartment and I'm pretty sure he was at least contemplating raping me?"

There is a deafening silence, and then Sasha's voice is softer, "Wait, Corey or the stalker?"

"Corey, Sasha, fucking Corey. He went on about how if I wanted a bad boy, he could be a bad boy. Then mister private number called, and the sound of my phone ringing halted Corey long enough for me to answer it, but then he threw my phone. My phantom man heard the struggle, Sasha, he heard me yelling at Corey to stop," I elaborate, still pissed.

Sasha is very, very quiet. The silence is deafening, so I take a deep breath and ask, "What did Corey tell you?"

"He said that a big masked and hooded guy put him in a headlock and told him if he ever touched you again his body would be found in multiple states, and then flashed a gun at him," Sasha says, her voice flat.

"Of course he flashed a gun at him, he's a fucking bounty hunter, he probably has three guns on him at any given point in time," I rebut, my voice cold.

"Vallyn, what the fuck?" Sasha retorts, clearly confused. "He threatened Corey."

"I gave him Corey's address," I confess, and I'm met with silence again. "Sasha, let me spell this out for you. Corey tried to *rape* me. If my phantom hadn't called, he probably would have succeeded because I passed out shortly after. I did beg him not to kill Corey, and then in my drunken state, I asked him to come tuck me in, and he did."

"Wait, he was in your apartment last night, too?" Sasha's voice is colored with concern.

"Yep," I say matter-of-factly. "He took off my shoes and put me in bed. Left me a note, too. And I don't remember any of it."

"Val, he could have done anything to you," she states, again, concern coloring her voice.

"But *he* didn't, and Corey fucking did," I reply, I know I'm emotional and I shouldn't be having this conversation. "Sasha, I just woke up, I need to pee and process, but come over later, okay? Let's have a girls' night in, and I'll tell you everything that I know right now."

"Okay, Val, I'll be there around six. Call or text if you need anything before then," she answers.

Stumbling into the bathroom, I feel the pressing need to pee but also the urge to wash away the remnants of last night. I scrub my face, brush my teeth, and decide to strip down for a shower. The hot water cascades over me, washing away the grime and tension. Emerging, I feel almost human again, slipping into comfortable clothes and grabbing my phone as I head toward the kitchen.

But as I step out of my bedroom, I stop dead in my tracks. Corey is standing there, leaning against my kitchen counter with his arms crossed, looking at me with a mix of guilt and defiance.

"You need to leave," I say firmly, my voice cold and unwavering.

"Vallyn," he scolds softly. "I'm sorry."

"Yes, you sound very sorry," I retort, the sarcasm dripping from my words.

"I am *worried* about you," Corey insists, his voice a bit softer, almost pleading.

"Why? Because my best guy friend attacked me last night?" I counter. "And apparently used his spare key to be standing in my kitchen right now."

"I'm sorry, Vallyn," he repeats, stepping toward me. I flinch, taking a step back, and he raises his hands in surrender, stepping back himself. "I had too much alcohol last night too, and that wasn't like me. I'm struggling, I admit that, and I'm sorry."

I don't respond, my silence is a wall between us.

"Your stalker guy, though, he *is* fucking crazy and you *should* be scared of him," he proclaims, his voice rising.

"I'm pretty sure he was really restrained with his reaction to you—at my request—so maybe you should just feel lucky you're

walking today and your face is intact," I counter and watch his jaw clench in reaction to my words. "I haven't talked to him yet today, but I feel like I'll trust his version of what happened more than yours right now."

"He threatened to kill me, Vallyn," Corey says, his voice cracking, a hint of vulnerability showing through.

"*If* you touched me again?" I clarify.

"Yeah, that is accurate, but still," Corey stammers, desperation seeping into his tone.

"Corey, I could call the cops on you right now, you know that, right? Tell them what happened last night and that you are trespassing now," I say pointedly, my voice steely.

"Val," he sighs, defeated. "I'm so fucking sorry okay? I don't understand, he fucking said that you haven't told him to stop or go away. I don't understand you."

"You know, Corey, he came here last night, after he dealt with you. I was passed out and all he did was carry me to bed and leave me a note. I don't think you would have had that much self-control," I say bitterly.

"I really fucked this up, didn't I?" he mutters, looking genuinely remorseful.

"Yeah, you did, and I think you need to give me my key back now," I demand, holding out my hand.

With a show of reluctant compliance, he pulls his key ring from his pocket, unhooks my key, and leaves it on the kitchen island instead of my hand before turning to leave.

"Don't come crying to me when your stalker turns out to be a villain," he throws over his shoulder just before he walks out the door.

I follow, securing the deadbolt behind him, the click echoing in the silence. My phone rings, breaking the stillness.

# CHAPTER TWELVE

# THE ANALYZATION

## PHANTOM

T he amount of restraint it takes for me not to drive to her apartment when I know he's in there is near-infinite. And, fuck, I wish this feed had audio. I'm supposed to be on surveillance, but all I can focus on is the live feed to Vallyn's apartment.

*I am so fucked up over this woman.*

Corey keeps his distance from her. I know he means something to her, and I won't interfere unless I have to, but I need to hear her voice after whatever encounter just happened.

"Hello," she answers, a smile playing on her lips on my screen. Her voice is soft and sultry, sending electricity down my spine.

"Little Lotte," I murmur, her nickname rolling off my tongue in a low purr.

"Thank you," she says, her voice tender, almost a whisper.

"For which part?" I ask, amusement lacing my tone.

"For dealing with Corey without hurting him, for tucking me in, for calling me last night because I don't know what would have happened if you hadn't," she says with a sigh, slumping down on her couch.

"You know, pretty girl, you should be better about locking your door," I warn, a hint of dark humor in my voice.

"Well, it won't stop you, and Corey had a key, so there wasn't much point," she replies nonchalantly.

"Corey *had* a key?" I ask, feigning ignorance.

"Yeah, I asked for it back," she says.

Rolling down the window of my SUV, I light a cigarette and take a long drag, the smoke curling around me as I continue to play dumb. "You saw him after last night?"

She clears her throat. "He showed up here, yeah," she says, and then the sass shows up when she adds, "He didn't touch me, don't go murdering him."

"What did he want?" I ask, my voice low.

"To apologize, to tell me you're scary," she says with a soft chuckle.

"He probably does think I'm scary, pretty sure that was the point of our chat," I observe, my tone low and amused.

"I asked him for my key back, and he left," she finishes, not addressing my statement directly.

"Vallyn, you should have your complex change your locks. He could have made copies of your key," I suggest, watching her freeze on the feed as if the thought hadn't occurred to her.

"You're right," she finally says, her voice tinged with realization.

"Also, maybe don't drink so much," I offer with a chuckle, unable to hide my amusement.

"Yeah, that was bad. I swear I rarely drink, just two bad nights," she says, running her hand over her face in a gesture of weariness.

"Why were you drinking so much last night?" I ask, my curiosity piqued.

"Because you threatened Tom and I don't know what to do with you," she admits with a sigh, her voice filled with exasperation.

"You were drinking over me, Little Lotte?"

"Yeah, pretty sure I was," she says as she stands and makes her way to the kitchen, her movements graceful and fluid.

"I kind of liked drunk and honest Vallyn last night," I tease as she opens her fridge and pulls out a can of flavored tea.

"Oh fuck, what did I say to you?" she laughs, the sound light and musical.

"You said you liked me and asked me to tuck you in," I remind her, my voice a low, teasing rumble.

"I knew that. I was worried I said something when you were here," she scoffs.

"No, you were pretty fucking passed out. I tried to wake you, but you were out," I admit, the memory still fresh in my mind.

"I'm sad that you were here and I slept through the whole thing," she confides, opening up her tea can and leaning forward into her kitchen island. "Thank you for being a gentleman about it, though."

"I told you, pretty girl, I'm not a bad guy, just a complicated one," I offer, my voice softening. "Unlike your so-called friend, if I'm going to *really* touch you or fuck you, you're going to be willing."

"Pretty sure I'll have to see your face and know your name to be willing," she teases back, her voice playful.

"That's fair," I agree, taking another long drag of my cigarette, the smoke drifting out the open window on my exhale.

Clearing her throat, she offers another truth, "My uncle is a bounty hunter. Well, was. He's retired, so I may understand more of your complicated than you think I do."

*How the fuck did I miss that?*

"Maybe I *do* need to stalk you better, Little Lotte," I say with a chuckle, my mind racing with this new information.

I hear her snicker and see the smile on her face. "Corey told Sasha you flashed a gun at him. I remember my uncle had at least two guns and two knives on him at all times, so they both thought that was shocking. I didn't."

I pause, deciding how much information to give her. "Pretty girl, I'm always armed unless I'm somewhere I legally can't be. But with my clearances, that's not many places in Arizona."

Sighing, she says, "I figured. I'm not a fan of firearms. Like, I don't like handling them, but I figured."

"I can probably make you more comfortable around them, at some point," I offer, my voice trying to be a soothing promise.

"Maybe," she says, and I see her shrug on the screen, a casual gesture masking deeper thoughts.

"What are you doing today, Little Lotte?"

"I made plans for tonight with Sasha, but otherwise nothing. Why?" she asks, her curiosity piqued.

"Plans with Sasha, huh? More drunken debauchery?" I joke with a chuckle.

She laughs, a sweet sound that fills the silence. "No, no alcohol for a while, just a girls' night in. Probably watch some chick flicks, decompress after last night."

"You going to gossip about me, Little Lotte?" I ask, my tone flirtatious, more so than usual.

"Probably," she answers, laughing.

"Say nice things, maybe let drunk Vallyn do the talking," I tease, my voice a playful growl.

"Sober Vallyn likes you too," she says, her finger tracing patterns on the dark granite of her island.

"Yeah?"

"Yeah," she agrees, and fuck, does that make me want to drive over there, but not yet. Soon, but not yet. I let the silence hang between us for a few moments, then she adds, "I don't know why. I don't even really know you, and you *are* kind of creepy, but I like you. And for some reason, I believe you when you say you're not a bad guy."

I take a deep breath, the weight of her words sinking in. "Vallyn, I know I'm not perfect. I know that the way I'm doing this is fucked up, but it's me."

"How much do you know about my academic life?" she asks.

I clear my throat and chuckle. "You have an undergrad degree in psychology and a master's in sociology, working on your doctorate."

"So, I could analyze the fuck out of why you are the way you are and do what you do," she replies. "But what I'm going with right now though is, it's all you know. Your entire adult life, you've operated by conducting steps of surveillance, recon, and planning before the execution of almost anything you do. It's all you know."

*Fuck me.*

That hits me like a ton of bricks. I didn't even know why I was doing this—mostly just thought she was driving me insane.

Clearing my throat, I respond, "I don't know exactly how to respond to that, pretty girl. But it's probably very accurate." The silence hangs heavy between us for a few moments. "You know, Little Lotte, I'm supposed to be doing surveillance on someone else right now, but I'm talking to you instead. I've always been laser-focused at my job, but you have found a way to distract me without even trying."

Snickering under her breath, she asks, "Isn't that a bad thing? Isn't it dangerous to be distracted?"

"It can be, yeah. Maybe that's why I haven't really dated anyone in over a decade," I confide.

"This isn't dating," she informs me with a laugh. "You're still just stalking me. I just happen to be more willing than some."

"I know this isn't dating, pretty girl," I reply with a laugh. "Again, pretty sure name and face are vital parts of that."

"Glad you're catching on," she quips. "Also, this is the most normal conversation we've had, and I'm grateful for it."

"Me too, Vallyn. And to think it's all because I threatened to kill your friend last night," I quip back.

She snort-laughs. "That shouldn't be funny, but it is."

"I agree with that, too," I say. "Listen, Vallyn, I think we're at a point where I should tell you these things. I'm going to be out of the country again starting tomorrow. Hopefully, less than a week."

I watch her swallow, her shoulders sagging. "Where are you going?"

Chuckling, I answer, "That's classified, unfortunately."

"Okay," she says, her voice tinged with disappointment. "I guess that means I can't ask you to tuck me in again anytime soon."

"No, Little Lotte, but soon I hope I'm doing more than tucking you in when I put you to bed."

"God, it feels wrong to say I'll miss you, but I think I will," she admits, her voice soft and vulnerable.

"Little Lotte, I'll miss you too. I'll have my phone, though, and should mostly have service, so it really won't be that different," I reply, trying to reassure her, fuck, trying to reassure both of us.

Apparently, I have *real* feelings here, and that is not something I am used to.

# CHAPTER THIRTEEN

# THE CAMERAS

## VALLYN

J ust before six  Sasha shows up, she has food and ice cream with her, along with stuff to stay the night, if she decides not to go home. Her embrace is tight, searching, as she looks me over with piercing blue eyes.

"You sure you're alright?" she asks, her voice a soft caress yet edged with concern.

"Yeah," I nod, a bitter smile tugging at my lips. "Corey is firmly lodged on my shit list, but I'm okay."

Her eyes narrow. "Do you seriously think he was going to rape you?"

A shiver runs down my spine. "It sure fucking seemed that way," I murmur. Sasha shakes her head in disbelief, and I add, "I got my key back from him. They're changing my locks tomorrow."

She leans back, smirking. "He said your stalker is huge, like tall and built, and that he rides a motorcycle, in case you care."

"None of that surprises me—I didn't know that, but it doesn't surprise me," I respond, matching her smirk with my own.

We settle into soft, plush blankets, the chill of the air conditioning, making that necessary. Takeout containers balanced on our laps, we immerse ourselves in the flickering light of the screen.

Thirty minutes pass in a haze of movie scenes and muted conversation when a knock interrupts the peace. I approach the door, peeking through the peephole.

With a roll of my eyes, I open it to yet another delivery—white orchids and a bottle of merlot.

*Little Lotte,*
*More pretty flowers for my pretty girl and a bottle of wine for your girls*
*night. I know you said sober Vallyn would say nice things, but drunk*
*Vallyn definitely says nice things.*
*♥ Phantom*

The orchids join their ghostly companions on the island, a trio of haunting beauty. "He sent the wine for both of us," I tell Sasha, a smile playing on my lips.

"Well, yay for stalkers, I guess," Sasha retorts, a skeptical edge in her voice before she bursts into laughter.

I retrieve two glasses from the cabinet and a corkscrew from the drawer, the pop of the cork echoing through the room like a distant promise. As I pour the rich, crimson liquid, Sasha saunters over and picks up the bottle, her eyes widening.

"Wait, that's expensive wine," she remarks, inspecting the label with a practiced eye.

"Yeah?" I ask, feigning nonchalance.

"Uh, yeah, like a few hundred dollars," she responds, incredulous.

"I don't think he's hurting for money," I laugh, a bitter edge to the sound.

Her eyes bore into mine, searching. "You're really okay with this? With the way this is happening?"

"Okay with it? No," I scoff. "Accepting of it? So far."

Sasha shakes her head, her expression a mix of disbelief and concern. "I'm trying so hard not to judge you. I just don't understand it. I think I'd be scared to death."

I sigh, a weight settling on my shoulders. "I don't know, Sash. I understand him somehow, but I know it's insane. We had a very normal conversation today. There's something about him that just feels right, like gut instinct, feels right."

We retreat to the sanctuary of the couch, cocooned in blankets. The ice cream is a fleeting comfort as the movie flickers on, but my mind drifts to the orchids, the wine, and the man who sent them. My thoughts are filled with an unsettling mix of fear and intrigue, and the shadows of doubt dance at the edges of my consciousness.

A few days later, my brother, Quintin, calls, his voice is a lifeline tethering me to reality. Quin pays my rent, a safety net in my otherwise financially precarious existence as a TA. His support keeps me afloat, just above the surface, in a world where every dollar counts.

We plan dinner, a rare chance to catch up. When he arrives at my apartment, his eyes immediately lock onto the orchids. The fucking orchids are impossible to miss, their presence as glaring as neon.

I offer him a half-truth, spinning a tale of a secret admirer whose identity I only partially grasp. "Be careful, Vallyn," he warns, his tone soaked in brotherly concern.

"I know, Quin. Really, I do," I assure him, though the reality is more complicated than he can imagine.

He sighs, glancing at the sweltering view outside my window. "It's so hot out. How about we order in?"

"Oh, I love you more for that," I respond, relieved.

We order food, and while we wait, I delve into my thesis, showing him my research. My laptop becomes a bridge between our worlds, a portal into the depths of my academic endeavors.

Quin shares photos of his recent vacation with his fiancée. For a while, it's just us—sibling warmth and easy conversation, a temporary escape from all the dark edges of my life.

When it's time to wrap up for the night, Quin gives me a big bear hug, and a kiss on the cheek, before I send him back out into the universe of his job and fiance.

The next day, I make my way to the youth center alone, feeling the weight of the situation with Corey pressing down on me. Zay is there, his presence oddly comforting despite the fact that he's twelve and I barely know him.

"Where's your boyfriend?" he asks, a smirk playing on his lips.

Laughing, I respond, "First, he's not my boyfriend, and second, he doesn't have to come with me."

"He's *not* your boyfriend?" Zay's pre-teen attitude is palpable, challenging.

"No," I reply, my laugh light but masking the complexity beneath.

"He acted like your boyfriend, all protective and stuff," Zay comments as we settle on the couch, gaming console in hand.

"You thought he was protective?" I ask, recalling how Corey would lurk in the shadows while I worked, more of a silent sentinel than a guardian.

"It seemed that way," Zay shrugs, eyes focused on the screen.

We fall into a brief silence, the game's background music filling the void.

"How are things at home, Zay?" I ask, breaking the stillness.

"Marcus got arrested. They let him go, but he got arrested for illegal possession of a weapon or something," he says, disappointment lacing his tone.

"When you say they let him go, what does that mean?" I probe, needing clarity.

"I don't know, he came home, that's all I know," Zay replies, frustration evident.

"How's your mom?" I ask gently.

"She cried when he was arrested, but she's doing a'ight," he answers, his voice steady but burdened.

"And you? How do you feel about it?" I glance at him, trying to gauge his reaction.

"I'm mad at him. He said he'd never get involved in that shit—sorry, stuff—like my other brothers. I'm just mad at him," Zay admits, his anger barely contained.

"That's understandable," I assure him. "I have a brother, and I don't know what I would do if he let me down like that."

"I doubt your brother is the type to let people down. He came from the same place you did," Zay observes, and he's right. Quin and I had privileges kids like Zay could only dream of.

"There's some truth in that, Zay. You're right, and that's very insightful," I agree, feeling a pang of guilt.

As I say goodbye to Zay and his mother, he teases me, "Don't forget your boyfriend next time."

I smile and laugh, but the comment makes me think of my phantom. Sitting in my car an hour later, I pull out my phone and text him.

> Hey, haven't heard from you since you left, I just wanted you to know I was thinking about you.

There's no immediate response, so I drive home, the silence heavy. As soon as I step into my apartment, my phone rings. "Private Number" lights up the screen, and my heart flips with excitement.—my body's reaction surprises me.

"Hello," I answer, a smile tugging at my lips.

"Vallyn," he says, his tone off.

"Hey, you okay?" I ask, the concern in my voice surprising even me.

"I don't know, Vallyn, honestly," he says.

"Um, you seem all pissy, why did you call me?" I ask, trying to lighten the mood.

"What did I tell you about letting other men put their hands on you, Vallyn?" His voice is dark, dangerous, and disturbingly hot.

"Um, to not to?" I reply, my voice high-pitched with nervous humor.

"Who the fuck was at your apartment, Vallyn? Hugging you, kissing you?" His tone is furious, and I'm so fucking confused.

"What are you talking about?" I'm floored, bewildered.

"Last night, you had a guy there," he states coldly. "You had dinner, laughed over pictures or some shit, and then you hugged him, he kissed you on the cheek. Who the fuck was that, Vallyn?"

I start giggling, realizing he's talking about Quintin.

"I don't know what the fuck you're laughing about, Vallyn. I warned you," he growls.

"Calm the fuck down, that was my broth—" I begin and then freeze as it hits me.

*How the fuck does he know all those details?*

My blinds have been closed, so it didn't come from outside my apartment. Panic sets in, and I start scanning my apartment.

"Wait? How did you even know all that? Do you have fucking cameras in my apartment?" I'm half yelling, half crying. "Where the fuck are they?"

I frantically search with my eyes, but nothing seems out of place. "Answer me," I beg.

"That was your brother?" he asks quietly, sounding a bit defeated.

"Yeah, it was, and I'm calling the cops. We're done. Leave me the fuck alone," I yell, hanging up and running into my dark closet, closing the door, and collapsing on the floor.

## CHAPTER FOURTEEN

# THE PLAN

## PHANTOM

*F* *uck. My. Life.*

Squeezing my phone so hard I'm surprised it doesn't snap in two, I start laughing at my apparent inability to surveil her—stalk her—well enough. The bitter irony gnaws at me. If she *were* a mark, I would have figured out who was with her, without asking and that's what I should have done this time, as well. I really have lost my goddamn mind.

I take a few deep breaths, forcing myself to open the window of this cramped, suffocating hotel room. The night air is thick and oppressive, but I need a cigarette.

I light it, watching the smoke swirl and dissipate into the night, my mind racing with thoughts of what to do next. Calling her back now is pointless. She won't answer. She needs time to process, and if she really is going to involve the cops, it will only complicate things further.

"You okay, man?" Casen asks, stepping out of the bathroom, his concern masked by a casual demeanor.

I shake my head. "I'm a dumbass, but yeah."

Laughing, he replies, "Oh, I've known you were a dumbass for years. What time do we have to leave in the morning?"

"Flight is at noon, so probably by ten," I answer. Tomorrow I'll be back in Phoenix, where it will be much easier to handle this.

Pulling up the camera feeds from Vallyn's apartment, I see she did it—she called the cops. Four uniforms are in her apartment, searching for cameras. They won't find them. Gage is too good at his fucking job. But this gives me an idea, and another plan begins to form in my mind.

They'll try to track me through the flower deliveries, but it's all charged on prepaid credit cards that I bought with cash, they won't get anywhere.

I spend some time on my laptop, putting plans into motion. Some are easier than others, but I will get us back to where we were. The game isn't over yet.

As the building manager hands me the keys, a sinking feeling settles in my gut. Again—I've lost my goddamn mind.

Vallyn isn't home; she's at Sasha's apartment. I saw the texts come through her phone. She didn't tell Sasha anything other than she wanted girl time, and I hope it stays that way.

Opening the door to my brand new apartment, three doors down from hers, makes me question my sanity. But this way, if she flips out, I can disappear easily. By tomorrow evening, it will be furnished, and life will be good. Gage ensured the cameras in this part of the hall weren't working, so I'm home free.

Back at my condo downtown, I take care of a few more things. I need to be a better stalker to pull this off, so I dive deeper into Vallyn's life. Her uncle is a retired bounty hunter, one Casen and I know relatively well and have worked with. And, fuck, I hope Vallyn hasn't involved him yet.

That *was* her brother in her apartment—Quintin Spencer, a tech software designer and Vallyn's financial lifeline. His name is on her lease, as a cosigner.

*How the fuck did I miss this?*

I was so focused on *her*, on finding out about *her*, that I missed everything important in her periphery. I didn't pay enough attention.

Knowing she's back home, I send her flowers. I know she'll probably throw them straight in the trash, but it's something I need to do. I send them with an apology note and a promise to do better by her.

I watch as she opens the note and reads it. I can read her body language—she's torn, and that's the point. Even though the flowers and the note quickly end up in the trash, I'm playing the long game now.

Texting her may be cowardly, but I know she won't answer the phone.

Me

> Vallyn, pretty girl, I'm sorry - I'm going to make this up to you, I promise

I watch her read it on the screen. Those three dots appear and disappear repeatedly, and I can see her type and erase, type and erase, through the camera in her kitchen. My hope rises and I chuckle a little.

She fucking cares—she cares about her response, she cares how she comes across to me. I know it's going to be vicious when it comes, but she still fucking cares. Finally, she smashes her thumb on the screen and then sends her phone skidding across the kitchen island. Miraculously, it stays balanced on the edge; it would have been a money shot in some kind of shuffleboard.

Vallyn

> It's too late for apologies and making shit up to me. If you just could have asked me out like a normal fucking human being instead of being creepy, stalker, phantom man, maybe this could have gone somewhere, but you ARE scary, you fucking terrify me now - leave me alone

Interesting. She chose to tell me that this could have gone somewhere.

Me

> Little Lotte, I am scary, I'm not going to argue with that, I still promise I have no intentions of hurting you. All I want is to protect you, to keep you safe.

She picks up her phone, rolls her eyes, and goes to set it down, but she can't resist the pull, the impulse to respond.

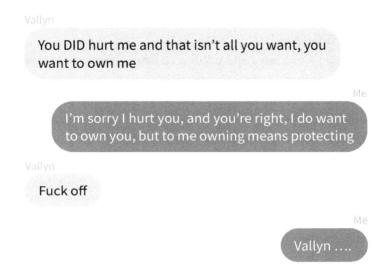

Vallyn

You DID hurt me and that isn't all you want, you want to own me

Me

I'm sorry I hurt you, and you're right, I do want to own you, but to me owning means protecting

Vallyn

Fuck off

Me

Vallyn ....

She doesn't respond again, so now it's time to put the rest of my plan into action.

"Something going on that I don't know about?" Betty's voice cuts through the hallway as Gage and I pass her by, heading to the tech room.

"Always, Betty, always," I tease, throwing a smirk over my shoulder.

Betty, in her mid-fifties, is a fixture in our office, her vibrant red hair—a bold defiance against the encroaching gray—bobbing as she moves. Though she's a bit plump, she can still tackle a police obstacle course with surprising agility, and every now and then, she vests up and hits the field with us.

Her brown eyes pierce into mine, a knowing and maternal glint suggesting she's well aware I'm up to no good.

Once we're safely ensconced in the tech room, the door clicking shut behind us, Gage turns to me, concern etched into his features. "Does Case know anything about this?"

I shake my head. "Nope."

"Is there some reason you trust me more than him with this?" His brow furrows in curiosity.

"Because," I say with a shrug, "he gives me that disapproving glare whenever I bring up Vallyn. And frankly, I'm not in the mood for an 'I told you so' from him just yet."

Gage's eyes narrow slightly. "You really think you can grovel your way out of this?"

"Not in one go, no," I admit, a bitter laugh escaping my lips. "But I can get there—unless she's talked to her uncle. And even then, part of me wonders if he'd help."

"Who's her uncle?" Gage asks, a note of apprehension in his voice.

"Jeremy Kincaid," I reply, watching as Gage's eyes widen in shock.

"How the fuck did you miss that?" he nearly shouts, incredulity painting his face.

"Mother's side, different last name. I was too obsessed with learning about her to look at the people around her," I confess.

Gage lets out a low whistle. "Well, if she told him and he finds out it's you, it was nice knowing you."

I chuckle darkly. "Jer wouldn't go that far, but his disapproving glare would be worse than Casen's."

Gage nods, then shifts gears, launching into a detailed rundown of what I need to do to disable the cameras in Vallyn's apartment. It's been years since I handled this kind of task—Gage usually handles all the tech for us now.

As he speaks, I try to focus on his instructions, but my mind keeps drifting back to Vallyn, and the tangled mess I've woven around her.

A few hours later, I find myself at my new apartment—a place I have no intention of truly living in but need to make look convincing. Furniture deliveries arrive, and I dutifully accept them, arranging the pieces to create a facade of normalcy. Despite my plans, I know—depending on how long it takes to break her—I may need to hole up here from time to time, so it should at least be comfortable.

As I wait for the darkness of night to descend, the weight of my obsession presses down on me like a ton of bricks. I occasionally check the feed from Vallyn's apartment, waiting for the moment when I know she is well and truly asleep.

It's well past midnight when I finally make my move. Breaching her door is more challenging than expected—she's added a chain lock. A part of me wants to whisper, "*Good girl*," even as I curse the added obstacle.

Inside, Vallyn sleeps on her side, her hands resting delicately next to her face. It will make this next part easier. Ensuring my mask is securely in place, I slip the pre-formed zip-tie cuffs over her wrists, careful not to wake her. She doesn't stir as I gently secure them to her bedframe.

She's a heavy sleeper, apparently. I pause to look at her, marveling at how vulnerable and beautiful she appears. The wrongness of what I'm doing twists in my gut, but I push it aside. I know she'll call the cops once she can, but I just need a few minutes. I think this is going to be a long process—a marathon, not a sprint, but I'm prepared for it.

# CHAPTER FIFTEEN

# BONDAGE

## VALLYN

I hear my name in a gravelly voice—soft yet deep and unwavering. At first, I think it's part of my dream, but as I start to wake, I try to wipe the sleep from my eyes and realize I can't—my hands are pinned above and behind my head.

Panic floods me as I blink away the fog of sleep and grasp the reality of my situation. This is a real-life nightmare, the one everyone tried to warn me about. I had some kind of faith in this man, but now, I know I was wrong.

My bedroom is shrouded in darkness, but I can make out his silhouette standing near me. I dig my heels into the bed, trying to scoot as far away as possible. My wrists sting from whatever binds them, and I know I stand no chance against this towering figure in my room.

Tears spill over, and I take a deep breath to scream, but his hand clamps over my mouth.

"Vallyn, pretty girl, shhhh," he murmurs, his voice tinged with regret and calmness. "Stop struggling. You'll hurt yourself, and I don't want to see you hurt."

I look up at him, his face obscured by a hood that nearly covers his eyes and a mask over his mouth and nose. His eyes are dark, almost black, yet there's something hauntingly familiar about them.

Through my tears, his figure blurs, but I blink and nod, trying to relax. Slowly, he removes his hand from my mouth. I open and close my mouth several times, unsure of what to say, uncertain of what he'll allow me to say without reacting. I sniffle, and he gently uses the cuff of his hoodie to wipe the tears from my cheeks.

"Little Lotte," he almost croons, his voice a low growl that sends an electric current through me, my body betraying me with its reaction. He runs the back of his knuckles over my cheek, and I want to lean into his touch and flinch away at the same time, so I remain still.

"You have no clue how much I wish you were awake the night you asked me to tuck you in, Vallyn," he confesses, his voice heavy with regret. "I hate that this is how it is right now, and I don't want it to be this way. I just need a few minutes of your time tonight."

I stay silent, trying to adjust my wrists as I lean against my pillows. Still a little panicked, I study this looming figure. Corey wasn't exaggerating when he told Sasha how huge he is. Even through his loose clothes, I can tell he is built, his head nearly grazing the ceiling fan lights.

My uncle's advice from years ago rushes back to me. I try to take in as much as I can—his skin tone, height, size, anything identifiable about his clothing. But he's covered from head to toe; no visible tattoos, no scars, no jewelry—nothing identifying I can see.

"Vallyn, I'm sorry," he says sincerely, sighing deeply. I hate what his voice does to me, the ache it stirs at the apex of my thighs isn't what I want to feel right now.

He crouches next to my bed, looking up at me. "I'm going to take the cameras down tonight. It's part of why I'm here. Also, fuck..."

He pauses, shaking his head before continuing. "There's tracking software on your phone, and I'm going to uninstall that too."

My eyes widen, and fresh tears flow as I look away from him. How can this man, someone I don't even really know, utterly break my heart? Because that's how I feel—broken-hearted, not angry, not even scared. Everything I had hoped he could be to me shatters.

Tucking my knees up to my chin, I wipe my tears on the blanket against my knees, a painful reminder of the helpless position I'm in with my hands. My uncle's words and the lessons from instructors and textbooks run through my mind. I don't think I need to humanize myself to him, but maybe it would help.

In a quiet, raspy voice, I begin, "For some reason, I trusted you, and I never should have." I sniffle. "Fuck, I don't even know your name, but I trusted you not to hurt me. I defended you to my friends. I *have* friends, parents, and a brother who love me. He's getting married in July, and I'm a bridesmaid in his wedding. I have aunts, uncles, cousins—people who care about me, people who won't just ignore the fact that this happened. Just please don't hurt me."

"Vallyn, pretty girl," he says, his voice placating. He reaches up with the cuff of his hoodie to wipe away my tears again, then moves his hand to cup the back of my neck. The sensation of his fingers threading through my hair, his gentle touch on my neck, sends unwanted shivers through my body.

When my eyes meet his—his hooded eyes, the color indiscernible—he continues, "I don't want to hurt you. I never wanted to hurt you. I know my obsession is pure insanity. I'm down this rabbit hole, and I'm trying to climb out. I think you know why we're here better than I do. Your observation about how I am used to surveilling and planning before executing is true—even tonight, there was a lot of planning that went into this."

His hand moves to the side of my face, cupping my jaw, and his thumb runs over my cheekbone. "Please don't be afraid of me. I meant what I said after I dealt with Corey that night—I'm not going to hurt you and I'm definitely not going to hurt you *that* way."

My tears betray me as I fight the urge to lean my cheek into his hand, but then the hurt comes again. "Says the only guy that has ever actually restrained me to a bed," I say, my voice dripping with attitude.

Trying to contain a short, dark chuckle, he responds, "Seriously, Vallyn, I love that sass. I never want you to lose that fire."

Standing, he drops his hand from my face, and his presence really is intimidating, looming over me. "I'm going to go pull the cameras now, and then we'll take care of your phone. Then I'll leave, but Vallyn?"

He pauses long enough that I feel compelled to look up at him.

"I'm not done with you," he says, and I suck in a sharp breath. "I don't mean that as a threat. Everything I've ever said to you is true, you're mine." He growls the end of that, sending a delicious shudder through me, even as my brain screams at my body not to react that way.

He leaves my bedroom, and I hear him moving through the kitchen and living room for a few minutes. When he returns, he shows me two very small black circles, smaller than the camera lens on a phone, resting in the palm of his hand. "They're military grade, Little Lotte, it's why the police couldn't find them."

I don't respond. He holds my phone up to my face to unlock it, letting me see the screen the whole time, perhaps to assure me he isn't doing anything but uninstalling the software. I watch as he uninstalls it, then deletes some files from my phone, followed by emptying the trash. He wipes down my phone and locks the screen before placing it back on my nightstand.

When he's done, he crouches on the floor again next to me, looking up at me. "Little Lotte, I *am* sorry. I know those words aren't enough, but I will make it up to you. I wanted you to *know* that I took the cameras down, that I can't spy on your phone anymore. Otherwise,

I could have done it all without waking you. I wasn't sure how you'd react, which is the *only* reason I restrained you at all."

Scoffing first, I swallow, unsure how to feel about all of this. Rolling my eyes, I try to think of a way to respond, but nothing comes. But then, as he stands, it does.

My voice is a whisper, "I wanted you to be the magic I thought you were. I wanted you to be the connection that I somehow instantly felt with you, even though I knew nothing about you."

He moves closer, removing his glove, his fingers threading through my hair as I continue, "I'm not scared of you." His fingers find my chin, tipping my head up slightly so he can see my eyes. "I'm hurt. I feel like you broke my heart, which is stupid because how could I feel like that when this is the first time I've even kind of seen you and I don't even know your name? But I do. I feel like you broke my heart."

The words tumble out faster than I can control, no filter in place, as I turn away. "When you called and asked about Quin, about my brother. I was so excited to answer the phone, so happy to hear from you, which seems foolish now, but I was. And then everything I hoped for was shattered in mere seconds."

My phantom is silent for a moment. *My phantom*—why does that still feel so right?

He inhales deeply and squats again. The back of his knuckles graze my cheek, causing a shudder I can't hide. I know he sees it.

"Vallyn, pretty girl, I *am* sorry, but that gives me some hope. I don't want you to be scared of me. There's no reason for you to be scared of me. I'm not going to hurt you," he says.

"But you *did* hurt me," I blurt out. "And I'm not scared of you. If you wanted to really hurt me or rape me, you could have done that already."

"I know I hurt you emotionally, I know that. I'm not going to hurt you physically," he says, and I start laughing.

"Because the cuts on my wrists right now aren't some kind of physical harm," I quip, venom lacing my voice.

"Vallyn," he sighs my name, then reaches into his back pocket and pulls out a knife. He moves toward me with it, and I don't even flinch; I fully believe he has no intent of harming me. Reaching above me, he cuts the zip tie hooking my wrists to the slat above my head, though my wrists are still bound together.

"I don't *want* to hurt you," he says, almost exasperated.

"Then stop fucking hurting me," I spit back in a retort.

"I'm fucking trying," he says, his tone severe as he shakes his head. "I'm sorry, Vallyn," he adds with a sense of calm.

Then he puts his glove back on. In a clearly pre-planned move, he grabs scissors off my dresser and places them in my lap, next to my hands. "Sweet dreams, pretty girl."

I hear the front door of my apartment close moments later. Grabbing the scissors, I maneuver them at an awkward angle but manage to cut the zip ties apart and off my wrists.

Immediately, I grab my phone and dial 911.

# CHAPTER SIXTEEN

# THE RECOVERY

## PHANTOM

I knew she'd call the police, it's the whole reason that I have this apartment three doors down and the main reason I left her bedroom camera in place. I'm not quite ready to give up all my access to her, yet. I also left the spyware on her laptop.

There's no surprise when I get a text from Gage.

Gage

Uniforms in less than three

Me

I'm clear - thanks for the heads up

Gage

What are friends for, if not for helping stalk girls?
*eye roll emoji*

I can't hear what's being said in her apartment, I hear some commotion in the hall. According to Gage there are at least eight of them—both uniforms and detectives, but they won't find anything. There is no video coverage of this small section of hall between her door and mine. I haven't been in the elevator or stairwell for hours, probably nobody has.

There's no evidence of me being in her apartment except the zip ties and the marks they left on her, and that could have been self-inflicted. They'll have nothing, nothing that says I was there, nothing that hints to who I am—no evidence at all.

I don't sleep and neither does she. I watch her in bed, picking up her phone and putting it down over and over again. Then finally she types and my phone buzzes moments later.

Vallyn

How did you disappear?

Me

I'm a phantom, remember

Vallyn

Why do I still miss you even though I hate you?

*Fuck me.*

Me

Pretty girl, but do you hate me?

Vallyn

I want to hate you

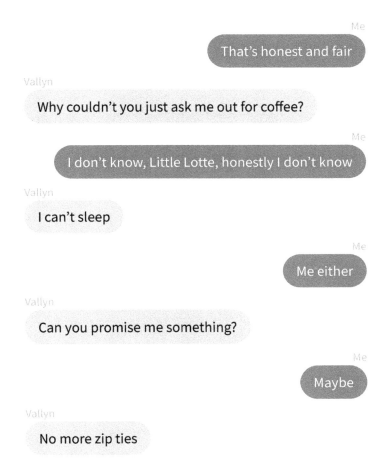

Me

That's honest and fair

Vallyn

Why couldn't you just ask me out for coffee?

Me

I don't know, Little Lotte, honestly I don't know

Vallyn

I can't sleep

Me

Me either

Vallyn

Can you promise me something?

Me

Maybe

Vallyn

No more zip ties

I chuckle a little to myself, because that's almost as good as her asking to see me again.

Me

What would you prefer?

Vallyn

Something softer

Now this doesn't feel like stalker talk, it feels like something else entirely and my cock reacts, the same way it did when I was in her bedroom a few hours ago.

Me

Little Lotte, are you volunteering for me to tie you up again?

Vallyn

No, but I know you will

Me

That depends

Vallyn

On what?

Me

On how much you fight me

Vallyn

I didn't fight you at all tonight

Me

If you weren't restrained what would you have done?

Vallyn

Honestly I don't know

Me

Pretty girl, you're giving me a lot of encouragement here, I just need you to know that

Vallyn

> Well discouragement didn't work, so maybe I'm
> trying a new tactic

I glance at the feed from her bedroom and she's smiling. And holy fuck, how did this go from her calling the cops two hours ago to this? Part of me wants to go back over there right now and sweep her up in my arms, but my entire life is now hanging by a thread with her. I have given her the power to unravel my entire existence.

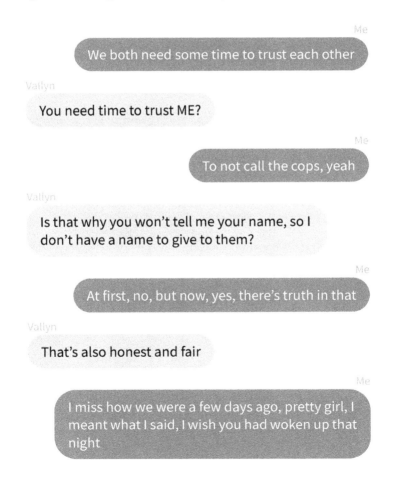

Me

We both need some time to trust each other

Vallyn

You need time to trust ME?

Me

To not call the cops, yeah

Vallyn

Is that why you won't tell me your name, so I
don't have a name to give to them?

Me

At first, no, but now, yes, there's truth in that

Vallyn

That's also honest and fair

Me

I miss how we were a few days ago, pretty girl, I
meant what I said, I wish you had woken up that
night

Vallyn

That wouldn't have changed the fact that you had cameras in my apartment, fuck, you probably still do

Me

No, it wouldn't have, but it would have made that first face to face time much better, back when drunk, honest Vallyn was telling me to tuck her in and how much she liked me

Vallyn

Drunk, honest Vallyn would probably still do that - Sober, cerebral Vallyn thinks drunk Vallyn should shut up

Me

Oh, Little Lotte, I like drunk, honest Vallyn

Vallyn

You would

I let that sit there for a minute, I watch her stare at her phone, waiting for a response, and then finally, I do respond.

Me

I like all Vallyns, I like your sass and your fire, even though the absolute gorgeousness that is you drew me in first, your fire sealed it for me, I don't want to put out that fire, pretty girl, I don't want you to ever think I want to put out that fire

Vallyn

I'm pretty sure you once said you'd like to fuck the sass out of me

Me

lol – I would - temporarily, I'd also still like to kiss away your tears

Vallyn

Maybe starting with not being the cause of my tears would be helpful

Me

I completely agree, pretty girl

Vallyn

Why can't I hate you?

*Oh, Vallyn.* I take a deep breath before responding.

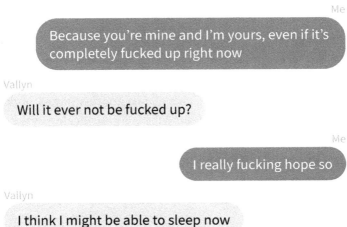

Me

Because you're mine and I'm yours, even if it's completely fucked up right now

Vallyn

Will it ever not be fucked up?

Me

I really fucking hope so

Vallyn

I think I might be able to sleep now

I glance at the feed and she's lying on her side, staring at her phone.

Me

Sweet dreams, pretty girl

She doesn't respond, I watch her put her phone down and roll over, and part of me really does want to walk back down the hall and pull her close to me.

*Soon.*

"You ready?" Casen's voice cuts through the dimly lit armory as we load up our gear.

"As ready as ever," I shoot back, strapping on my holster.

A nod from Gage as we climb into the van is all we need; we have done this so many times before, it's all just another day at work.

"Get any sleep last night?" Gage asks, his eyes flicking over to me.

I shrug, "No, but it's not the first time I've done this on no sleep."

Casen shoots me a look, the kind that says he disapproves but trusts me regardless. We've been through hell and back together, operating on adrenaline and only the ghost of rest more often than not.

"What's the intel?" Casen's gaze shifts to the rearview mirror, catching Gage's eyes.

Gage taps on his laptop, "Subject is at his mother's place. Two other potentially armed males inside—one's a brother, the other a friend. No sight of the mother or anyone else in the last twelve hours."

"Entrances?" I ask.

"Front and back doors only," Gage replies without missing a beat.

I nod, glancing at Casen. "What's the play? You want to knock or watch?"

Casen chuckles darkly, "You knock. You're on no sleep; might as well get the adrenaline going."

We roll onto the block, our eyes scanning the surroundings. The house is hemmed in by a six-foot fence, leaving little room for escape. I clamber into the back of the van with Gage, strapping on Kevlar. The AR-15s aren't fired often, but they're good for intimidation. Once we're suited up, we move out.

Casen circles the house, giving me a nod before disappearing around the back. I pound on the front door, the sound echoing like a war drum. "Bail recovery agent! Open up!"

Gunfire erupts from inside, splintering the wood around me. I duck behind the brick column, eyes locked on Casen's silhouette moving through the shadows. Gage's voice cuts through the chaos, his urgent tone buzzing in my earpiece, "Uniforms are en route." The sound of gunfire fueled Gage's instinct to call in backup. I think I can already hear sirens wail in the distance.

I skirt the house's edge, finding Casen standing over two prone figures. Another figure rounds the corner, gun in hand. I raise my AR-15, voice steady, "Down on the ground, now!"

Three men lie on the ground, weapons kicked aside by Casen. Normally, we'd be dragging them in ourselves, but the blaring sirens and flashing lights signal that won't be our job today.

As the police cuff the bail-skipper and his friends, we regroup. The house is cleared by uniforms and we head back to Betty at the office. The whole thing takes less than ten minutes, but the chaos makes it feel longer. The adrenaline rush begins to fade, and the realization of the impending paperwork sets in—the part of the job that we all hate.

Once we're in the van, I pull out my phone and reach out to Vallyn, because I know this is probably going to take some major effort.

Me

Little Lotte, I hope you were able to get some sleep

Vallyn

A little, did you?

The joy I feel at the instant response and the normalcy of it is overwhelming. It feels like comfort food for my soul right now, providing a much-needed sense of stability amidst the chaos.

Me

I didn't, but I managed to get shot at and not shot, so I guess I'm doing alright sleep deprived

Vallyn

You were shot at? Are you okay?

Me

Oh, sweet Vallyn, yes, I'm okay

Vallyn

Have you ever been shot?

Me

A few times

Vallyn

A FEW TIMES - you say that all casual?

I chuckle and Casen and Gage both look at me.

"Um, I take it that even though she called the cops on you, you're good?" Gage asks.

Laughing, I say, "Yeah, I knew she was going to call the cops, but it seems we are at least kind of good."

With the shoulder strap of the seatbelt behind me, I almost hit the windshield with how fast Casen stops the van on the side of the road.

"Fuck, Case, what was that?" I demand.

"What the fuck are you doing with this girl that she'd call the cops on you?" Casen demands in return. His anger is justified—we're business partners, and if I get myself arrested, it will impact him in big ways too.

So, there on the shoulder of the highway, I explain it all to Casen. I expect a lecture, but he bursts out laughing, calls me a dumbass a few times and then we continue our drive back to the office, and I continue my conversation with Vallyn.

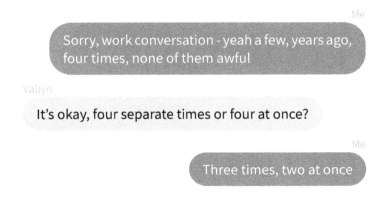

Me

Sorry, work conversation - yeah a few, years ago, four times, none of them awful

Vallyn

It's okay, four separate times or four at once?

Me

Three times, two at once

I look up from my phone, side-eyeing Casen. "There's probably something else I should tell you," I admit.

"What's that?" he asks.

"She's Jeremy Kincaid's niece," I declare with a smirk.

"Are you fucking kidding me?" Casen barks.

"I wish I were, and no, I didn't know that early on," I admit.

"Does he know?" Casen inquires.

"I don't think so, but she might have told him," I offer.

"I don't think so," Gage interjects, "there hasn't been anything in the tech world that says he's trying to figure out who you are, but anything is possible. I thought maybe Jer would put in a good word for him, but I think he's too far down that rabbit hole now."

"I am *definitely* too far down that rabbit hole now," I reply. "I need to win her over on my own now."

That question is intriguing.

I let that hang there, but then I order her more orchids and another bear, since she threw the other one away.

# Chapter Seventeen

# The Realization

## VALLYN

There's a knock on my door and I'm cautious, checking the peephole, but a smile plays on my lips when I see the orchids. This is a large, potted orchid though, not the kind in a vase, and there's another bear. It's much like the other one, but it's gray. After I set them on the island, I open the card.

*Little Lotte,*
*I figure the other bear went in the trash and you might need another one. Also, these orchids will last longer, which I'm hoping says something about us, too.*
*♥Phantom*

I hug the bear to my chest. I still don't know why this fucking man—that I should not even remotely be attracted to—seems to hold *all* the keys to my heart.

I text Sasha before I reach out to him.

Me

> Hey, I need to decompress, do you have time this afternoon or evening?

Sasha

> Yeah, I can do late afternoon, want me to come to your place?

Me

> That would be great

Then I text my phantom.

Me

> Thank you for the new bear, I kind of regretted that one

Private

> I figured you might, Little Lotte

Me

> You confuse me

Private

> I confuse me too

Me

> Sasha is coming over this afternoon, I just thought you should know, in case, you know, you decide to do something creepy

Private

When have I ever been creepy while the sun was out?

Me

That might be a fair point

Private

I have to do a shit ton of paperwork, you want me to send you and Sasha some wine again? Lol

Me

lol not this time, but thank you for making me smile

Private

That's my biggest goal in life right now - to make you smile

Me

Maybe you can call it mission accomplished for today then

Private

This thread sounds an awful lot like you forgiving me

Me

This thread sounds an awful lot like my brain not being able to overpower any other part of my body

Private

*Any* other part?

**Me**
I said what I said

**Private**
Vallyn ...

**Me**
No name ...

I giggle after I hit send on that one.

**Private**
Oh, pretty girl, you're very distracting right now

**Me**
Maybe I'm trying to be

**Private**
Maybe I should make you angry and tie you to the bed more often

**Me**
No on the first, maybe on the second - different circumstances

**Private**
Who are you and what did you do with Vallyn?

Me

It is me, I just can't hate you, I want to hate you, but I can't - like stockholm syndrome or something

Private

Vallyn ...

Me

Didn't we just do this?!?

Private

Pretty girl, I'm glad you don't hate me

Me

I'm sure you are - now go do your paperwork

Private

Yes ma'am

The entire interaction makes me smile, a warmth blossoming within me that I hadn't felt in a while. I want to be mad at him, knowing full well the gravity of his actions. But, remembering the effect he had on me when he touched me, even when I was so hurt and angry, leaves me wanting. So, instead of being mad, I clutch the bear to my chest, inhaling the sweet scent of white orchids, and I can't help but smile.

A knock on the door pulls me back to reality. Opening it, I find Sasha standing there, her expression a mix of curiosity and concern. I hadn't breathed a word to her about the whirlwind of the last few days, and now there was so much to unload.

"Listen, Sasha, I need you to not judge me," I say, my voice tinged with desperation.

"Um, did you sleep with him?" she asks, eyes wide.

"No, but it might be worse," I warn her, and then I let it all spill out. The hidden cameras, him in my apartment, the zip ties—it all comes tumbling out.

"Val, I'm trying not to judge you here," she says, her voice steady but laced with confusion. "I really don't understand this."

"It just *feels* right," I murmur, my voice cracking and then groaning. "*He* feels right. I hear his voice and I melt. And, Sasha, when he touches me, even in the most innocent ways, I feel it everywhere. I've never had this kind of chemistry with anyone."

Sasha takes a deep breath, her eyes searching mine. "Okay, I'm going to say something, and I don't mean it judgy. I just want you to think about it, alright?"

"Okay," I nod, bracing myself.

"What you're describing sounds a lot like an abuse cycle," she says softly, raising her hands in a conciliatory gesture as I start to protest. "I know he hasn't hurt you physically, but he's being psychologically manipulative. He does things he knows he shouldn't and then grovels and apologizes."

"Okay, I'm not trying to make excuses for him," I say quickly, "but I don't think he *knows* how to do this. He seems to think he couldn't have asked me out when he first met me. I don't know, Sasha, but I just... I don't think he has bad intentions. I think he has good intentions behind bad actions."

"Well, you know they say the road to hell is paved with good intentions," she points out, tilting her head slightly. "But Vallyn, I am your best friend and I will ride this out with you."

"Thank you," I respond, feeling the weight of her support. "Have you talked to Corey?"

"I have, and I think he *is* really sorry about what happened. Maybe you can extend some of this forgiveness you have to him?" she asks gently.

"Different situation—he was trying to rape me. Stalker man has had multiple opportunities to do that and hasn't come close," I say with a shrug.

"I still don't think Corey ever would have raped you," Sasha states, her tone firm.

"You weren't here that night, Sasha. He was on top of me, had my legs and arms pinned. I managed to free one arm when my phone startled him," I explain, my voice trembling slightly. "Maybe someday I can forgive him, but that is going to take time."

"I just don't understand how you can forgive the phantom guy but not Corey. It doesn't make sense to me," Sasha pushes, her brow furrowing in confusion.

"Because phantom guy rescued me from Corey and tucked me into bed without touching me. Outside of what happened with the zip ties, he has never physically harmed me. He's like a secret admirer on steroids. Corey is a guy who literally can't take no for an answer after years of hearing, 'no,'" I explain, feeling my patience fray.

"Sasha, I know you don't think Corey is capable of what happened that night, but he lost his shit. And I get that he was drunk and overwhelmed by some stuff. I *am* willing to cut him some slack, and I probably will talk to him again, but he *did* attack me—verbally, emotionally, physically, in every way he attacked me," I state with finality.

Then, for good measure, I add, "And he knows it, which is why he hasn't reached out to me. He knows what he fucking did."

"Okay," Sasha says, her voice contemplative. "And if I remember right, your 'phantom'" — she makes air quotes — "called and that ended it, right?"

"Right. If he hadn't called, I don't know that Corey would have stopped. If I hadn't been able to answer him, I don't know that Corey would have stopped," I agree with a shrug. Then it hits me like a wave crashing over me. Sasha sees the look on my face and looks at me questioningly.

I feel like I'm going to hyperventilate, panic rising in my chest and I pull my hands up to my now blood-drained face. Sasha's hands are immediately on my arms.

"Val, what's wrong?" she asks, her eyes meeting mine, wide with concern.

"The cameras," I whisper, my voice barely audible. Sasha squints at me, confusion written all over her face.

"Sasha, he saw. That's why he called," I say, my voice shaking. "He watched Corey attack me and somehow didn't hurt him when he got to him."

"Wait, do you think he has that footage?" Sasha asks, her voice tinged with shock.

"I don't know," I say, staring at my phone.

I don't know what to do, so I text him.

My phone rings moments later, the vibration slicing through the silence, and I answer after one ring. His voice, immediate and concerned, pours through the line. "Vallyn, are you okay?"

"How do you know I'm not okay?" I retort, my voice edged with a raw tension.

"I assumed. You've never asked me to call you before. What's wrong?"

"I'm putting you on speaker because Sasha needs to hear this," I inform him, my tone steady but cold.

"Vallyn," he warns, the sound of my name a low growl.

Ignoring the warning, I continue, "You're on speaker. I have a question."

Silence.

I can almost feel his displeasure about being put in this position through the phone. "Do you have footage of Corey attacking me?"

My voice wavers, betraying my calm façade. I hear him take a deep breath—but I'm unsure if it's out of relief or hesitation.

"I do," he says, the words heavy, then adds softly, "I kept it in case you ever needed it, if you ever wanted to press charges or if he did anything else to you."

The dam breaks. Tears stream down my face, my voice cracking. "So you saw that night? You called because you saw? You were *trying* to interrupt it?"

"Vallyn," his voice is almost a soft plea.

"Just answer me," I barely whisper between my quiet sobs. Sasha wraps an arm around me, pulling me closer.

He sighs deeply. "Yes." There's a long pause. "It was by happenstance. I wasn't sitting there staring at it or even checking it very often. I only opened the feed to see if you were home because I had just gotten done with something with my family. All I wanted to know was if you were safe and home. When I turned on the feed, he already had you backed into the wall. It was a coincidence that I caught that moment in time while it was happening. And I'm sorry, Vallyn. I'm sorry I didn't tell you earlier."

Sasha's eyes are rimmed with tears as she looks at me. "I'm sorry, Vallyn. I'm sorry I didn't completely believe you."

On the other end of the phone, I hear a deep breath. I pick up the phone, taking it off speakerphone. "You're not on speaker anymore," I say.

"Vallyn, I'm sorry," he rasps.

"Do you know how fucking grateful I am right now that you had those cameras in here? It's like fucking whiplash for my emotions," I admit, my voice a mix of gratitude and anger.

"Did Sasha not believe you?" he asks quietly.

"Not really, not completely," I whisper.

"Vallyn, fuck," his voice is an apology—an apology for someone else.

"Can you send us wine? Then you can talk to drunk Vallyn later," I say, a snicker breaking through my tears.

A dark laugh echoes on the other end. "Little Lotte, I will happily send you wine, and then later tonight, if you want, I'll come tuck you in."

It's the "if you want" that gets me. I nod, even though he can't see me, and say, "I'll text you."

"Okay, pretty girl, let me know if you need anything," his voice is a low purr, sending shivers down my spine.

# Chapter Eighteen

# Roses & Lingerie

## VALLYN

L ess than an hour later, there's a knock at my door. I open it
to, surprisingly, find a vase of bright red roses, not quite fully
bloomed, and two bottles of wine. For once he didn't send orchids.

"You say jump, he says how high," Sasha teases, watching as I
uncork the first bottle.

"I don't know that for sure yet, but with this, yeah, he did," I
respond, trying to suppress the flutter of excitement in my chest.

Sasha and I don't bother with a movie or any distractions. We just
talk, our conversation meandering as we share a bottle and a half of
wine. Eventually, Sasha decides it's time to leave—work calls in the
morning, and I have youth center duty tomorrow. We both know we
should get some sleep.

After closing and locking the door behind her, I lean against it,
my head spinning slightly from the wine. I find a rubber cork and
plug the remaining bottle, then take a moment to inhale the scent
of the roses on the kitchen island. Their fragrance is soothing to my
tumultuous emotions.

I head to my bedroom, feeling like I'm riding the most intense emotional rollercoaster of my life. Anger and gratitude swirl within me—like a messed up swirl cone of ice cream. The cameras he installed probably saved me from being raped. He saw what Corey did, and yet, when he caught up to him, he still didn't hurt him, he only threatened him.

I can't stop thinking about all the things my phantom has done—and hasn't done. The opportunities he has had to actually hurt me, to cross lines, and how he hasn't crossed them. It's been over four years since I've been with a man, since I've even kissed anyone. An inexplicable urge takes over me, propelling me into action.

I throw my hair up in a tight bun to keep it mostly dry and hop in the shower. I shave... well, everything, exfoliate, and scrub myself clean, then apply lotions and a touch of perfume when I'm dry. I dab a wine-colored lip stain on my lips, feeling the anticipation build.

Opening a rarely-used drawer in my closet, I dig through it until I find what I'm looking for—a red, lace babydoll and thong set that no man has ever seen me in. I pull it on and look in the mirror. The sheer fabric over my breasts provides just enough coverage to obscure my nipples, but the rest of the outfit is tantalizingly transparent, revealing the thong, the apex of my thighs, my belly button—everything except my nipples.

With a mix of nerves and excitement, I grab my phone, running a brush through my hair. I type out a message, my fingers trembling slightly as I hit send.

Me

> I'm tucking myself in, but not-completely-sober Vallyn thinks you should still come tuck me in anyway

Phantom

Is that so?

Me

She might be disappointed if you don't

Phantom

Little Lotte, I wouldn't want any version of you to be disappointed

Me

*heart emoji*

After I lay down in bed, the wine lulling me toward sleep, I purposefully kick one leg out from under the blanket. On my side, my bare, thonged ass faces the bedroom door, sheer red fabric draping seductively over my hip.

A soft touch on my wrist stirs me. As my eyes flutter open, they focus on my phantom's masked face inches from mine, his fingers deftly securing my hands above my head.

"Hi," I rasp with a sleepy smile.

His dark chuckle reverberates through the room as he finishes with my wrists and stands above me. "What are you doing, pretty girl?" he asks, his gaze scanning down my body.

"Trying to tell you that I forgive you, even though I know I'm probably crazy and stupid for it," I murmur, shrugging slightly before glancing up at the soft fabric binding my wrists.

"You said no zip ties, so no zip ties," he replies, his voice a deep baritone that resonates in my very bones. My toes curl involuntarily, and I feel a growing ache at the apex of my thighs.

I giggle softly. "When the wine came, Sasha said that I could say 'jump,' and you'd say 'how high?' I think that might be accurate."

"Only to some extent, Little Lotte," he responds, a hint of a smile in his tone. "But there is a lot of truth in that."

I watch, mesmerized, as he starts removing his gloves, one finger at a time, making sure I notice every movement. My eyes are drawn to the slow, deliberate actions.

Once his gloves are off and tucked into his pocket, he shrugs off his jacket. It's not leather, but a thick, riding jacket. Underneath, he wears a long-sleeve black t-shirt. My gaze shifts to the weapons on his body—the holster with two guns, the utility belt laden with knives, handcuffs, and other tools of his trade. Methodically, he removes these, placing them on my dresser.

The lower half of his face remains covered, but his dark hair is visible now. Not buzz-cut short, but a bit longer with a slight wave. It looks familiar, stirring a memory I can't place.

I realize I'm biting my bottom lip as I stare at him. I'm acutely aware of the contrast between us—his almost fully covered body and my nearly bare one. The vulnerability, the anticipation, it all swirls within me, a tempest of emotions and desires.

Standing on my left, his fingers lightly graze the outside of my right thigh, trailing up to my hip. The touch sends a shiver through me, and I inhale sharply. He gently tugs at the hem of my top, his eyes locking onto mine.

"I like the red," he murmurs, his voice low. "Is this for me, or is it your usual sleeping attire?"

"You're the stalker. You should know," I reply with a playful smirk.

A soft chuckle escapes him. "I'm pretty sure it's for me, but I wanted you to say it."

Looking up at him, I take a deep breath. "It's for you."

His eyes scan down my body again, but his touch has vanished. "Vallyn, pretty girl, fucking *sexy* girl," he growls, his gaze lingering on me. "I'm not going to fuck you tonight."

Hoping the disappointment doesn't show on my face, I ask, "Is there a reason for that? Since, you know, you say I belong to you."

"Oh, you do belong to me, Vallyn. You are mine, that is without question," he declares, his voice deep and commanding, sending vibrations through my nerves and bones.

He reaches into his pocket and pulls out a black bandana, moving toward my face. He demonstratively folds it into a blindfold, placing it over my eyes and tying it behind my head. The faint scent of cigarette smoke mixed with a spicy, musky cologne fragrance fills my senses, heightening my arousal. Blindfolded and bound, the anticipation makes my body tremble with desire and my cunt literally vibrate.

I feel his presence leave me momentarily before his fingers return to my ankles. I gasp as his weight shifts onto the bed. His fingers glide up my legs, and my chest heaves with each deep breath. When his lips touch the inside of my thigh, I realize why he blindfolded me—he took off his mask.

His soft lips, his tongue, and even a few playful nips travel up my thigh, the slow pace almost torturous. My hips rise involuntarily as he reaches the apex, his breath hot against my wet panties.

"Fuck, you smell good," he rasps, the warmth of his breath sending another wave of desire through me. But then he leaves me wanting more as his fingers trail up to my belly, his mouth moving to my hip and pressing kisses in a slow, deliberate trail up to my breasts. His hands graze the outside of my breasts while his mouth travels languidly up my sternum.

His weight shifts again, and hands find my upper arms above my head. One of his legs presses against my pubic bone, and I push into the pressure. Lips fall to the soft part of my neck, leaving a trail of kisses up to my ear before gentle teeth nibble on my earlobe. I gasp as I realize I'm grinding against his thigh.

As he trails soft kisses to my mouth, I part my lips, craving his kiss, but he doesn't oblige. Instead, he speaks, his voice a tantalizing whisper.

"Vallyn, you *are* mine," he murmurs, his hand slipping between my thighs, fingers brushing dangerously close to my aching cunt. "This pussy is mine. I can't wait to taste you, to feel you with my fingers and fill you with my cock, to suck your swollen clit into my mouth until you come undone."

I whimper as his fingers glide up my skin, over my hip, under my babydoll top. His thumb brushes the bottom of my breast while he presses a soft kiss to my neck again.

"These are mine," he whispers against my lips. "Handfuls of lusciousness, and I'm sure perfect, suckable nipples, for me to enjoy while you writhe under me. And this mouth is most definitely mine—sass, fire, and all," he whispers, grazing his lips and nose back and forth across mine.

"*You*, my sweet Vallyn, are mine," he rasps, a little louder. He rests his forehead on mine, our breaths mingling. My chest heaves under him, his hard cock pressed into my hip while his thigh pushes into my pubic bone.

"But you're not sober, and when I fuck you, you need to be sober," he declares gently. "And without the restraints and blindfold."

"Let me see your face," I rasp in response.

"Not yet, Little Lotte," he whispers, laughing softly, the act jostling my entire body. "Just last night you called the cops on me. And while I care *much* more about you trusting me, names and faces will come when I know I can trust you."

"Kiss me," I almost beg, feeling him freeze as he processes my plea.

"Not yet, pretty girl," he whispers, pressing a soft kiss to my cheek. "Soon, but not yet, and not because I don't want to."

Slowly, his hands trail down my arms and sides until they land on my hips. He completely removes himself from me, leaving me feeling unsatisfied and bereft, but I won't beg. He gave me a lot—edged me some—but gave me a lot. Also, I felt his erection pushed into my hip and I know he's leaving unsatisfied, too.

# Chapter Nineteen

# The Seductress

## PHANTOM

The sight of her lying there, all flushed, and visibly turned on in front of me is not an easy one to walk away from, but when I fuck her—and that *is* a when—I want to make sure she is *all* in, because as obsessed as I am with her now, as soon as I'm buried deep inside her, it's over—I will never let her go.

Not kissing her when she asked me to took a feat of strength, but I know I'm doing the right thing. I've made so many wrong moves here, I need to start making some right ones.

Pulling my mask back into place first, I pull off her blindfold, and when the lust and fire in those dark eyes hits me, it almost shatters my resolve.

"You okay, pretty girl?" I ask, looking down at her, knowing full well, she is completely unsatisfied.

"No," she says with a deep breath, "but I will be."

Laughing softly, I ask, "What are you doing tomorrow?"

"It's youth center day," she answers without hesitation.

Smiling under my mask, I say, "Then you should get some sleep, Little Lotte."

"Oh, and I have to go to my bridesmaid dress fitting or my almost sister-in-law might kill me," she adds with a sigh.

I'm not going to lie, I like having normal conversations with her, even if she is restrained to a bed while it happens. "You said the wedding is in July?" I clarify.

"Yeah, July 20th," she answers.

"Vallyn," I start and sigh, "it's very odd to be having such a normal conversation when A: you called the cops on me and hated me less than twenty-four hours ago and B: you're tied to a bed looking sexy as hell."

She laughs, and then points out, "One of those things is very easy to fix." Then her eyes cast up to her wrists.

"This is another way," I tease and grab her blanket, tossing it completely over her and then pulling it down slowly until her face is uncovered.

Then Vallyn laughs, genuinely laughs and it's music to my ears after the last few days, fuck, the last month since I first saw her in that bar.

"You should get some sleep, Little Lotte," I say, not wanting to risk this going to hell at this point. I move toward her and lean down very close to her face before asking, "Are you going to call the cops on me tonight?"

She shakes her head, and says, "No."

"Good girl," I praise in a soft growl and then drop my mask just enough to press a kiss to her forehead, not long enough for her to move enough to see me.

Then I walk back to the foot of the bed, put my belt and holster back on, then my jacket and my gloves. I feel her eyes on me the entire time.

Finally, just before I go, I reach over her head and unstrap her from the bedframe. My gloved fingers run through her hair and then I quick-release her hands from the soft cuffs and hurriedly leave her apartment.

Three doors down, in my own temporary abode, I pull out my phone and watch the live feed from the camera still hidden in her bedroom. She hasn't moved. She didn't try to follow me. Instead, she throws her blankets off and picks up her phone. I brace myself, certain she's about to call the police, but she doesn't.

She turns on the flashlight and uses it to search her nightstand drawer. This amazing fucking woman pulls out what I'm almost positive is a small vibrator.

*Fuck me.*

Then she doubles down and pulls out a glass dildo. I'm so fucking grateful for the resolution on this camera right now.

My cock has been pressing hard against the zipper of my dark jeans since I first walked into her bedroom and saw her laid out in red lingerie. Now, seeing this, I know I have to do something about it.

I quickly rid myself of everything above the waist and my belt, lying down on my leather couch and propping my phone up to watch her. Her fingers move over her tits and down into the front of her thong. I free my cock, stroking it slowly as I watch.

The fact that this woman—this woman I fucking *dream* about—is so turned on by me that she has to do something about it makes my cock even harder. As she pushes her thong down her perfect legs, over her knees, and kicks it off her ankles, I wrap my hand tighter around my shaft.

*Fuck this woman.*

She squeezes her tits one more time before pushing the dildo inside her perfect pussy. While I've seen her naked on camera before, I've never seen her spread like this.

*Fuck, she's perfect.*

Slowly, she starts moving the dildo in and out of herself, then picks up the small vibrator with her other hand, hooking it onto one of her fingers. Stroking myself, I watch her use both hands to fuck her own pussy. It's one of the most erotic things I've ever seen.

Finally, her thighs crash together, and her back arches. I watch her mouth open in a moan or a scream, and I don't care which. She pulls her hands away for a few breaths, but apparently, one orgasm isn't enough for her. She goes back in for another one, and when she comes this time, so do I.

One day, I'll have to admit that I still had a camera in her apartment to tell her about this. But I will, because this was one of the hottest experiences of my life.

I'm also grateful I can replay it.

Back at my condo the next morning, I stand under the scorching spray of the shower, scrubbing away the remnants of my own fluids on my body. Today's agenda is all about adultery surveillance with Casen. This case is lucrative, because it's a high-stakes game for our client—her prenup hinges on catching her husband cheating, and the difference in the divorce settlement is substantial.

We're camped outside the guy's office, our eyes trained on the entrance, waiting for him to emerge. Casen, ever the conversationalist, breaks the silence. "So, how are things with Vallyn? Still calling the cops on you?"

I chuckle, the memory of last night flashing in my mind. "No, I think we're past the cops phase. But I'm giving it time before I trust it completely. She *did* try to seduce me last night, though."

"Tried?" Casen's voice drips with incredulity.

"Yeah, tried," I affirm. "Don't worry, I made sure she didn't feel rejected. Might have teased her a bit, but she understood why I didn't fuck her last night."

Casen raises an eyebrow. "I'm just surprised. The way Gage describes your obsession, I'm surprised you didn't given the opportunity?"

"Casen, she's the one," I confess, my voice dropping. "I feel it deep down. I'm not rushing this."

Casen laughs, shaking his head. "I can't believe you stalked her. Hell, you're still stalking her."

I shrug. "It's what I know. Even if I would've hit on her the night we met, I'd have probably stalked her."

At that moment, our target exits his office. We slip into shadow mode, tailing him discreetly. Over the course of the day, he has rendezvous not with one, but two women at different hotels. The guy is a walking cliché of infidelity.

As we document his indiscretions, my thoughts drift back to Vallyn. She'll never have to worry about this kind of betrayal from me.

Back at the office, surrounded by the hum of computers and the click-clack of keyboards, Casen and I are deep in the rhythm of our work, compiling data for a high-profile client. The sudden simultaneous chime of our phones shatters the monotony and can only really mean one thing.

"Holy shit," Casen mutters, his eyes wide as he scans the screen. "Check that one out, five grand a day."

I glance at my phone, curiosity piqued. It's a high-risk extraction mission in a volatile warzone. My heart quickens as I read the details. "How long do you think that would take?" I ask, already calculating the logistics in my head.

"Six days minimum," Casen replies, his voice steady despite the excitement flickering in his eyes.

"Yeah, that's what I'm thinking too. Maybe ten days. But fifty grand is hard to turn down," I say, a soft chuckle escaping my lips.

Casen meets my gaze, his expression resolute. "I think that's *impossible* to turn down."

We exchange a knowing nod. The higher the pay, the greater the danger, but also the more meticulous the planning. I've taken bullets on what were supposed to be simple executive and private protection details before, but these high-stakes missions are a different beast altogether. We've faced rapid live fire, hunkered down under intense pressure, yet always emerged unscathed.

Casen's phone call confirms our commitment. Hanging up, he turns to me with a mischievous glint in his eye. "Remember how to use a parachute?"

I roll my eyes at his question, a smirk playing on my lips. "Seriously? Dropping in, huh?"

"Yep," he confirms, the anticipation palpable between us.

The exhilaration buzzes through me. This mission will be fraught with danger, but it's the kind of thrill that makes the blood in our veins sing. It's a game we know well, and one we are more than ready to play.

# Chapter Twenty

# Young Love

## **VALLYN**

Z ay is practically bouncing with excitement when I arrive at the youth center. His eyes sparkle as he grabs my hand, pulling me toward a quiet corner where a young girl stands, nervously fidgeting with her hands.

"This is Kiara," he beams. "She's my friend—my *girl*friend."

"Oh my," I murmur, taking in her shy demeanor. Kiara is around Zay's age, with a sweetness that makes me instantly protective.

Zay, never one to miss an opportunity, starts recounting my life story with a fervor. "Vallyn is getting her doctorate. She's studying why and how kids in certain areas or with certain backgrounds end up being criminals, like my brothers. Someday, she'll help kids not become criminals," he declares proudly, flashing me a wide grin that's all innocence and hope.

I chuckle, returning his grin. "That's the basic gist, yes."

Kiara's cheeks turn a faint pink. "You're really pretty," she says softly. "I can see why Zay's brother talks about you so much."

Raising an eyebrow, I glance at Zay, who is suddenly very interested in the floor. "Marcus, she's talking about Marcus," he clarifies in a rush. "He thinks you're pretty, but he's still like eight years younger than you, so even if you don't have a boyfriend, don't listen to that."

I laugh lightly, nodding. "Got it."

Kiara's voice drops to a near whisper. "My brother is in jail, too. He's supposed to be out next month though."

"What's he in for?" I ask, trying to keep my tone casual as we begin setting up a puzzle.

"Robbing a gas station," she replies with a nonchalant shrug, like it's the most normal thing in the world.

I strive to match her casual tone, but my heart aches. "Well, that doesn't sound good."

Kiara shrugs again, her expression unreadable. "We didn't have any food. He was just trying to make sure we had food."

Her words pierce my heart. This is exactly why I'm doing my research—to understand, to help, to change these heartbreaking stories.

"But," she adds, her voice softer, "he did it with a gun, so that was really bad, I guess."

"Yeah," I agree, my voice gentle. "Guns rarely make those things better. What about your parents, Kiara?"

"My mom is kind of lazy, but she's around. I've never met my dad," she confides, her eyes downcast.

"Story of our lives," Zay interjects, gesturing around the youth center with a resigned smile.

I reach out and squeeze Kiara's hand gently. "Well, Kiara, you're welcome to hang out with me and Zay whenever I'm here."

For the next two hours, we lose ourselves in the puzzle, the pieces slowly coming together to form a picture. Just as we snap the last piece into place, Marcus arrives to pick up Zay.

"Oh, it's a Ms. Vallyn day," Marcus declares with a little swagger, his tone dripping with a mix of respect and playfulness.

"It is," I reply, my smile matching his. "How are you, Marcus?"

"Been better, but I'm okay," he nods, turning his attention to Zay. "You ready?"

"Yessir," Zay chirps, his enthusiasm palpable. He glances at Kiara with a soft smile. "I'll see you soon."

Kiara nods, her shyness holding her voice captive.

Just as they're about to leave, Marcus turns back, his expression softening. "Take care, Vallyn. Thanks for being good to my brother."

I smile and nod, feeling a warmth spread through me. I turn to Kiara. "Do you know when someone is coming to get you?"

She shakes her head, so we settle down with a couple of coloring books, letting the vibrant hues fill the silence for the next two hours until her aunt arrives.

Once Kiara is safely with her aunt, I check in with the staff and other volunteers, ensuring everything is in order before heading to my car. My destination—a dress fitting.

The dress shop is nestled in the heart of downtown Phoenix, a place that always feels a bit too chaotic for my liking. I'm more of a suburb girl, and, really, even more of a rural girl at heart. The thought of parallel parking downtown is enough to make me break out in a sweat, so I find a less intimidating garage and opt to walk a few blocks.

The heat is oppressive, the kind that makes you question your life choices—like why did I not leave Phoenix for Anchorage when I had the chance? By the time I reach the dress shop, my skin is glistening, and the blast of air conditioning as I step inside is pure bliss.

"Vallyn!" Sonia, my future sister-in-law, exclaims, her face lighting up as I enter.

"Hi! I didn't think you were going to make it," I greet her, surprised and pleased to see her.

"Well, Quintin was pretty convincing," she admits with a smile. "He said you and I haven't had much time together without him."

I return her smile, and we dive into the bridesmaid dress fitting. The tailors fuss over the fabric, pinning and marking, while Sonia and I chat.

After the fitting, Sonia suggests an early dinner. "Sure," I agree, eager for more time together. We head to a nearby restaurant, conveniently closer to my car.

Dinner is delightful. Sonia's curiosity about Quintin is endearing, and she asks about his childhood quirks—his favorite stuffed animal, whether he liked the crust cut off his sandwiches, and other silly questions. Her nose wrinkles with a sweet smile at each little detail, and I'm filled with gratitude that my brother has found someone who loves him so deeply.

She drives me back to my parking garage, and I finally find my way home, the day's events swirling in my mind. The youth center, the dress fitting, dinner with Sonia—all these moments blending together, creating a tapestry of positivity for my day, but I am also exhausted.

Opening my apartment door, I'm momentarily stunned. I know he has the skills to break in, but this is something else—my entire kitchen island is a plethora of colors and fragrances, overflowing with orchids, roses, and lilies. The heady scent makes me sneeze almost instantly, I suppose a small price to pay for this lavish spectacle.

I glance around, my heart racing as I half-expect to find him lurking in the shadows, but the apartment is still and silent. There's no note, no sign of him—just this beautiful chaos he's left behind.

Unable to suppress my grin, I pull out my phone, my fingers trembling with a mixture of excitement and trepidation. I can't help but smile, a giddy thrill bubbling up inside me.

Me

You know since you're just going to come in anyway, maybe you should just have a key

Private

That wouldn't be nearly as fun

Me

lol, I'm assuming the allergy fest going on in my sinuses now is your fault

Private

Some girls would just say "thank you"

Me

I'm not some girls

Private

That's why I like you

My phone rings, and my heart skips a beat.

"Hey," I answer, my voice barely above a whisper.

"Hi, Little Lotte. How are you?" His voice is a dark melody that makes my pulse quicken.

"Tired, but okay," I reply, slipping off my shoes, savoring the coolness of the floor against my hot skin.

"How was the youth center?"

"It was good," I respond, a smile tugging at my lips. "This little boy I hang out with a lot introduced me to his girlfriend today. It was cute. How was your day?"

"Earned some money catching an adulterous fucker, but otherwise mostly boring," he answers, a hint of amusement in his tone. "But Vallyn?"

"Yeah?"

"My partner and I are leaving in a couple of hours for an extraction gig. I might be gone for a while," he informs me, regret threading through his words.

"How long is a while?"

"At least a week, maybe two. Hopefully no longer than that," he says.

"Is that why there's a flower shop in my kitchen?"

"Yeah, pretty girl, that's why there's a flower shop in your kitchen," he answers with a soft chuckle. "I don't know what our communication will be like. We're parachuting in and then we'll have to request a helicopter to get out, so I doubt we'll have cell service. We'll have a satellite phone."

I nod, inhaling deeply. "Okay. I feel like I should say things like 'be safe,' and all that, but I don't know what's appropriate for this non-relationship we have."

"Vallyn, you're mine, there is nothing 'non' about our relationship," he says with a severity that sends shivers down my spine.

"Maybe I'll agree with you when I know your name," I retort, incredulously.

"Oh, sweet Vallyn," he sighs. "I'll give your number to our partner that is staying stateside in case something bad happens, but we'll be okay. We know what we're doing."

"Can I have their number?" I ask, the silence stretching between us.

"Maybe—I'll think about it," he says, sincerity in his voice. "But we'll have to leave here shortly."

"Okay, mister phantom man, I think I'll miss you, I'll definitely worry about you," I say and then swallow hard. "Reach out when you can. I'm sure you have my email address, that works, too."

He chuckles deeply. "I do indeed have your email address. And Vallyn, don't worry too much about me—we really are good at what we do. Plus, I could buy you an actual flower shop if this ends up taking two weeks, so there's that."

"Seriously? That's a lot of money," I declare, shaking my head.

"Seriously, Vallyn, and I don't need it, but maybe it will help me spoil you more," he says, and I can hear the smile in his voice.

"You know I'm not a very high-maintenance girl, but you have taught me that apparently I do have expensive taste in wine," I tease, laughing.

"Open your fridge, pretty girl," he suggests in a seductive tone.

I move to the kitchen, pulling open the fridge door to find several bottles of wine.

"You're so creepy and so amazing at the same time," I say, marveling at the gesture.

"I try—on both," he answers. "Listen, Little Lotte, I have to go, but know I'll be thinking about you—I'll reach out when I can."

"Okay, be safe," I say softly, before the line goes silent.

# CHAPTER TWENTY-ONE

# THE SPY

## VALLYN

The next few days pass in a haze of routine and reflection. Brunch with Brooke and Carly offers a welcome reprieve from my endless dissertation work. The clinking of mimosas and soft chatter serve as a soothing backdrop, a temporary escape from the mounting pressure of my research. I also spend time at the youth center, where my heart finds a strange solace amidst the chaos.

Kiara has started to cling to me more, and I find an unexpected comfort in her small, trusting presence. Her wide eyes, filled with a mix of innocence and resilience, remind me of why I'm here. Today, her older brother came to pick her up. He's much edgier than Marcus, Zay's older brother—scarier, maybe, with a hardened exterior that speaks of a life lived on the fringes. There's a danger about him, a stereotypical criminality that sets my nerves on edge.

In the moments between, I engage with a few other kids I haven't spent much time with before, interviewing them and simply talking. Their stories are a poignant reminder of the fragile line between innocence and the harsh realities of life. Each smile, each shy glance, is a silent plea to stay untainted by the world's cruelty.

The youth center is a sanctuary of sorts, a place where I can lose myself in the effort to preserve their innocence. I find myself more and more entwined in their lives, each day drawing me deeper into their world.

At home, I spend countless hours haunted by the specter of my phantom. My mind is a constant whirlpool of questions, spinning faster and faster until I'm dizzy with longing and confusion. Is he okay? When will I hear from him again? Am I utterly insane for missing a man who has violated me in ways too many times and too dark to recount?

By the light of day, when I force myself to sit down and think logically, a harsh clarity strikes me. My own cognitive dissonance is glaring, like a cruel spotlight illuminating my own twisted reasoning. I see it, plain as day—how I've normalized his transgressions, how I've rationalized the psychological anguish he's caused me. It's a perverse dance of self-deception, my mind playing tricks to soften the brutal truth and I am smart enough and educated enough to see through it.

Yet, in the shadowed corners of my heart, a different story unfolds. There's a pull, an inexplicable draw to the man who has somehow left indelible marks on my soul. His touch, both a curse and a comfort, lingers like a ghost, a reminder of the darkness we've shared. The thrill of his presence, the danger that clings to him, has become a part of me. It's a toxic symbiosis, a relationship forged in the fire and lasting embers of his acts and whispers.

I know I should run, sever the ties that bind me to my phantom. But every attempt to escape feels like tearing away a piece of my own flesh. There's an addictive quality to the anguish, a twisted sense of belonging in the chaos he brings. He's the dark mirror to my soul, reflecting back the parts of myself I'd rather ignore.

The silence between us is a torment, a slow-burning agony that eats away at my sanity. Every day without him is a battle against the rising tide of my own obsessive thoughts. I tell myself I'm better off without him, that his absence is a blessing. But the lie crumbles under the weight of my need for him, a need that defies all logic and reason.

I'm caught in a vicious cycle, oscillating between self-awareness and blind desire. I know I'm dancing on the edge of a precipice, but the pull of the abyss is irresistible. It's a dangerous game I am playing—this tightrope walk between self-preservation and surrender.

As I sit here, unable to concentrate on anything else, lost in the labyrinth of my thoughts, I can almost feel his presence beside me. It's a chilling comfort, a reminder that even in his absence, he owns a part of me. My phantom, my tormentor, my twisted solace. The very thought of him is a double-edged sword, cutting deep yet drawing me in with a magnetic force I can't deny.

Perhaps one day I'll break free, find the strength to shatter these chains. But for now, I remain trapped in both his darkness and his light, a prisoner to my own desires and the ghost of a man who has become my obsession.

The shrill ring of my phone startles me out of my daydreams. Brooke's name flashes on the screen.

"Hey, Brooke," I answer, trying to mask the weariness in my voice.

"Val, girlfriend, we're going out tonight. You should come," she insists with her trademark enthusiasm.

I'm not really feeling it, but at the same time, I know I need to get out of my head. Maybe this is exactly what I need.

"You know what, Brooke, yeah. Is Sasha going?" I ask, curious.

"Everyone is going, Val. It'll be fun. Tori is bringing her new boyfriend," she replies.

"Everyone" probably means Corey, but I don't know if anyone besides Sasha knows what happened between us. I doubt he would have told anybody, and I don't think Sasha would have either.

After getting the details from Brooke, I get ready and call a rideshare to meet them at a bar. As soon as I walk in, I spot Corey. He's in a booth with Sasha wedged in next to him. Taking a deep breath, I approach the table. Brooke and Carly hop up to hug me right away, and Tori introduces me to her new boyfriend, Tyson, then immediately asks what I want from the bar.

"Whatever you're drinking, but a lot of it," I reply, and she laughs. My eyes meet Sasha's, and she gives me a cautious smile before I drift over to Corey. We both nod awkwardly at each other.

I find the chair at the end of the table, while they all sit on bench seats. It feels both odd and liberating to be separate, yet still a part of the group. Tori comes back and places a stoplight in front of me. It's crazy because, up until the last six weeks or so, I had only been out really drinking two or three times in the last two years. Now, it feels like a habit.

But, fuck, I need it. I need to shut my brain down. The stoplight goes down quickly, and Tori drinks shot for shot with me before heading back for more. I'm about seven shots in when I take out my phone and text my phantom.

I'm surprised when moments later I get a text back.

Private

Hey Vallyn - I'm not him, but he has me monitoring your messages while he's gone - are you okay?

Me

Wait he what?

Private

While he's behind enemy lines, he wanted to make sure that if you needed anything someone would answer, so he has me monitoring his messages

Me

This is weird

Private

I know, but do you need something, are you okay?

Me

Yes, no, I don't know

Private

Where are you?

Me

Pretty sure you already know that

Private

I don't, but you're right I could

Me

I'm just drunk dialing, ignore me

Private

Do you need someone to make sure you get home okay?

Me

lol - no, maybe to make sure my friend doesn't follow me and assault me again - no that's kind of a joke - you're not him, I'm okay

Why am I saying all this? I wait to see if he says anything else, but he doesn't. The silence feels strange, leaving me with mixed feelings. On one hand, he's ensuring someone answers me, but on the other, it's just weird.

I'm nursing a glass of ice water, chatting with Carly about our plans for the Fourth of July, when I hear my name. Turning toward the voice, I see a man standing right next to me. My eyes fall on his thighs first and then I trace my gaze up his built body to the light brown hair and blue eyes peering at me through glasses. He's in jeans and a long-sleeve t-shirt, which is odd for Phoenix in June.

When our eyes meet, he asks, "Can I talk to you?" Then he gestures with his head.

"Who are you?" I slur drunkenly and giggle.

Those blue eyes glance down at my phone on the table, and I understand. I gulp and nod, telling Sasha I'll be right back. Picking up my phone from the table, I stumble a little as I start to stand, and this stranger catches me. My eyes travel up to meet his again. I know he's not my phantom; everything is different, and there's no chemistry when our skin touches. But he carries a similar intensity.

His hand stays firmly and protectively on my upper arm as he leads me to the side of the room, away from my friends.

"Hey," he begins. "My name is Gage. I work with," he pauses and swallows, "well, I work with him. His way of texting you goes through a highly secure app, so he gave me access to it while he's out of communication because he wanted you to have a contact."

Laughing uncontrollably at first, I regain my composure and say, "So I'm allowed to know your name and see your face, but not his?"

Gage smiles. "I guess that's accurate. Are you okay?"

Suddenly serious, I ask, "Is *he* okay?"

"I would know if he wasn't, so yes," Gage answers.

I roll my eyes and shake my head. "You might think I'm crazy, but do you want to join my friends and me for a bit? Then you can escort me home, which would probably make him happy since Corey is here."

Gage's blue eyes widen slightly before he smooths his expression. "Yeah, Vallyn, I can do that. And you're right. I was just going to watch you from a distance because after those texts, he would want to kill me if I didn't. But then I saw Corey here, and that's why I decided to approach you."

Nodding in understanding, I walk back to the table and grab another chair from an empty table. All six pairs of eyes fall on me. "This is Gage. He's going to hang for a little while and then make sure I get home okay."

Sasha looks at me questioningly, and I give her a short shake of my head. I know she's wondering if this is my phantom and that is a definite no. Tyson is the one who breaks the awkward silence.

"So, Gage, what do you do?" Tyson asks.

Gage is quick to answer with a smile. "I'm a covert tech specialist."

"Like for the military?" Tyson clarifies.

Nodding, Gage replies, "In the military I was a Cyber Warfare Officer until I was discharged. I still do some work for the government, mostly foreign espionage. But now I use my skills in the private sector."

In their drunken state, my friends lose it. Brooke starts laughing. "Did you just say espionage? Like you're a real-life mother-fucking spy?"

Gage snickers and shrugs. "Pretty much."

"How do you know Vallyn?" Corey asks, wiping the smile off Gage's face. The intensity returns as he holds Corey's gaze.

"I work with someone you both know—he met you outside your building the last time you hung out with Vallyn," Gage answers, holding Corey's gaze until he looks away. Then Gage smiles, looking around the table. "And that's part of why I'm here tonight."

Gage rests his hand on the back of my chair, not touching me, but making it clear that he is in possession of me right now. Under normal circumstances, it would probably make me uncomfortable. But with Corey sitting at the table and it being the first time I've spent time with him since getting my key back, I appreciate this extension of my phantom. I'm relatively certain Gage is just as lethal, and from a quick glance at Corey, I'm sure he is aware of that as well.

All my friends, except Sasha, look utterly confused. Then Sasha clears her throat. "Work with or friends with?" she asks.

"Both," Gage admits with a shrug.

My psychology brain tries to analyze why I trust a total stranger—who is friends with my stalker—more than the guy I've been friends with for years. When it comes down to it, my trust in Corey is so far gone that these are the lengths I'm willing to go to.

When we're getting ready to leave, Sasha looks at Gage. "I'm going to steal my best friend for a minute." Gage nods, and Sasha grabs my arm.

"Are you sure about this? Do you trust him?" Sasha asks.

"Well, my phantom will murder him if he hurts me. He's my fucking bodyguard basically. I'm good, Sasha. I'm probably safer with him than in a rideshare," I say with a shrug.

"Okay, well text me when you get home," she requests.

Nodding, I hug her and then join Gage again.

# CHAPTER TWENTY-TWO

# THE PANEL VAN & THE PARENTS

## VALLYN

Gage leads me to an unmarked black panel van, and I can't help but giggle at how stereotypically suspicious it looks. "This doesn't seem like a serial killer's vehicle at all," I tease as he opens the passenger door for me. The humor fades quickly when his shirt lifts as he holds the door open, revealing a gun, knife, and some kind of chemical spray strapped to his belt. He offers me a soft smile, but the sight of his arsenal is sobering.

Once inside the van, I feel like I've stepped into a scene from a spy movie. Gadgets clutter the dash and console, and as I turn to look through the small window to the back, I see a legitimate desk with monitors and everything. My eyes widen at the locked weapon rack.

I'm still staring at the setup when Gage opens the driver's side door. His eyes meet mine through the lenses of his glasses. "I know this is probably overwhelming," he says. "I would totally understand if you'd rather take a rideshare."

"And the chances that you wouldn't just follow me anyway are exactly what?" I ask with a smile.

"Absolutely zero," Gage agrees with a smirk and a shrug.

"It's okay. Just like him, for some reason, I trust you," I admit.

"More than Corey, at least?" he asks knowingly, and I nod.

"Also, I'd tell you where to go, but I'm pretty sure you know that, too."

He chuckles. "Yeah, Vallyn, I know that, too."

Gage's confidence is both unsettling and reassuring. As he starts the van, I feel a strange sense of safety despite the arsenal and the high-tech surveillance equipment. The silence between us is heavy but not uncomfortable, filled with unspoken thoughts.

After a few minutes, Gage breaks the silence. "Look, I know he's not doing this the right way, but in some weird way, I think it's self-protection for him. I don't think he has ever felt as strongly about anyone as he felt about you instantly. He even used the words 'love at first sight,'" he confides, pausing to chuckle a little and glance at me.

I swallow hard and nod, then reply, "There's a part of me—the same part that thinks I shouldn't be in your van right now—that thinks I'm insane and completely stupid for entertaining it at all. But I feel like I understand him."

As I finish speaking, my phone vibrates. I check it and immediately laugh at my group chat.

Brooke

> Sooo, Vallyn, is your friend single? And is he seriously a spy?

Tori

> Lol, I mean I have Tyson, but Gage is hot

Sasha

> Hot but creepy

Laughing again, I look at Gage. I think about it for a second, but then say it anyway, "My friends think you're cute."

"They think I'm mysterious. That's different. We're used to it." He shrugs, and I look at him questioningly. "We basically have groupies," he explains with a laugh. I feel the tendrils of jealousy at the comment, though.

"How many of you are there?" I ask, just grateful to have someone answer questions for me and a face to put with any of this.

"Three, well, four if you count our secretary type," he answers. "They're both off on the same extraction mission." Gage's voice softens with empathy as he adds, "Vallyn, he'll be okay. He always is. They always are. I know this is weird, but he will be ecstatic to know you actually missed him and were worried."

Nodding, I take a deep breath and then ask, "Do you have any idea how much longer they will be?"

He shakes his head. "No, they're not to their target yet, or weren't as of a couple of hours ago. But once they get there, it could go really fast, or they could end up needing to take time to find or get to an extraction point."

As we pull up to my building, I look at Gage and thank him. Then I ask, "So, can I tell my friends you're single?"

Laughing, he answers, "I am, but not yet. Let's get you two settled before adding any more complexity to this for you both."

Gage walks me to my door, his presence a mix of reassurance and apprehension. Before leaving, he reminds me to lock it, and I feel an odd sense of connection to my phantom—and also I'm a little pissed that I now have a name and a face to go with Gage, but not for my phantom.

Inside my apartment, I lean against the door, my thoughts swirling. This night has been a whirlwind of emotions and revelations. My phantom's world is dark and complicated, but it's also thrilling and impossible to resist. As I lock the door and head to my bedroom, I can't help but feel the pull of this twisted romance, knowing that I'm probably in too deep to turn back now.

I collapse onto my bed, staring at the ceiling. My phone buzzes again, and I glance at the screen, seeing another message from the group chat. For a moment, I consider telling them everything, but then I decide against it.

Me

I'm home, safe and sound - Gage is gone and my door is locked lol

Brooke

But is he single?!?!?!

Me

lol, I'll find out

Lying there, hugging my bear, the weight of this new reality begins to sink in. My life is now entwined with secrets, danger, and a love that defies logic. The thought crosses my mind that this may be precisely why he started our relationship the way he did. A man like him, immersed in a world of shadows and peril, probably needs to be sure that anyone he brings into his life romantically can handle certain things.

Maybe, whether it was subconscious or intentional, it's a test.

Meeting my parents, Sonia, and Quintin at a chic, dimly lit restaurant for his birthday offers a refreshing distraction from the chaos of my thoughts. The warm ambiance, the hum of conversations, and the clinking of glasses provide a comforting backdrop as I settle into the familiar embrace of my family. Unlike so many others who find their parents a source of irritation, mine are a rare breed of wonderful.

Brian and Christine Spencer, high school sweethearts, have always seemed to share an almost picture-perfect relationship—at least as far as we kids could see. They move together with a grace and ease that speaks of years of deep, unwavering affection. I can count on one hand the number of times I've seen my mom snap at my dad. Fleeting moments of frustration that quickly melted into their usual playful banter.

"How's the dissertation coming along?" my mom inquires, just as the waiter drops off the bread basket and fills our wine glasses.

"It's going," I reply with a smile. "Loads of research. I just wish I could do more for these kids."

"I bet some of it is heartbreaking," my dad says, his brow furrowing in sympathy.

"Are you ever scared of any of the people at or around the youth center?" my mom asks, her voice tinged with concern.

I shake my head. "Not *at* the youth center. I feel pretty safe there. But there are definitely some people who set my teeth on edge. If I weren't in a place I felt safe, it might be different."

The conversation smoothly transitions to Quintin and Sonia's wedding planning. My mom is practically buzzing with excitement at the thought of wedding preparations, eager for a bigger role than just a minor player. So, she can't wait for me to get married now. Yet, she's gracious for the involvement Sonia and her family do offer her.

"It was nice meeting Vallyn for her dress fitting," Sonia says with a smile.

I nod. "Yes, dress fitting and dinner with my future sister."

Talk of the wedding dominates the conversation for a while, until Quintin turns to me with a teasing glint in his eye. "You still have a secret admirer?"

The heat in my cheeks is instantaneous, but I manage to clear my throat and nod. "Yeah, although he told me he was out of the country for a while, so I haven't heard from him lately."

I can feel my parents' eyes on me. "What's this?" my mom asks.

"Vallyn has a secret admirer who sends her orchids and wine," Quintin chimes in, grinning.

"Are we happy about this?" my dad asks, a mixture of curiosity and concern in his voice.

I chuckle softly, opting for a guarded but truthful answer. "Yeah, I think it's actually kind of special and sweet. But it is weird that I have no clue who he is."

"Do you know anything about him?" my dad presses, clearly concerned.

Nodding, I say, "Yeah, I know we've actually met, and I know he has a sister, and... " I pause, hedging, and clear my throat "...he's in the same line of work as Uncle Jer." My parents stare at me, their expressions unreadable, as I rush to continue, my pitch rising with discomfort. "Hence why he's out of the country."

My parents seem at a loss for words, their disapproval of Uncle Jeremy's career choices evident in their eyes.

"Have you talked to Uncle Jer about this?" my dad asks, regaining his composure.

I shake my head.

"I think you should, honey," my mom advises gently. "Also, I am a little worried that you know so little about him."

"That world is pretty small," my dad adds. "Your uncle probably knows the guy and can give you some feedback."

"Okay," I say, eager to change the subject.

"Orchids?" Sonia interjects, her tone impressed and excited. "That's special. Anyone can give roses, but orchids are a different story."

I elbow Quintin and tease, "You hear that? She wants orchids."

The mood lightens around the table, and I am grateful for it.

Later, as I lie in bed, I contemplate their words. I know Gage, and I know he's a covert tech specialist. Just that much information would probably give my uncle enough to identify my mysterious admirer. But it feels like I would be cheating in this game we're playing.

Maybe one day, but not now.

# CHAPTER TWENTY-THREE

# THE BROTHERS, THE UNCLE, AND THE SPY

## VALLYN

Z ay and Kiara practically jump out of their seats when I walk into the youth center. Their excitement is palpable, a contagious energy that lifts the room.

"I've been waiting for you to come back," Zay exclaims, his eyes shining with eagerness.

"Yeah? Why is that?" I ask, intrigued.

"My brother and his friends want you to interview them. I'm supposed to help set that up," Zay replies, almost bouncing on his toes.

"That would be great. I have some rules, but your help would be really useful," I say, offering him a reassuring smile.

Kiara, usually the quieter of the two, finally speaks up. "When Zay told me his brother was willing, I talked to my brother, and he is, too. Except..." Her voice trails off, and she glances nervously at Zay.

"Except what, Kiara?" I prompt gently, sensing her hesitation.

"Except Eli, Elijah, he's in a rival gang of Marcus's. They don't get along, so you couldn't do it at the same time," she explains, her voice barely above a whisper.

I nod, understanding the gravity of her words. "That's fine, Kiara. One of my rules is to meet them in a public place, neutral territory. It's probably better if I don't meet them together, for many reasons."

Her shoulders relax visibly, the tension easing. I can't help but think of the Romeo and Juliet situation they have, their brothers in rival gangs while they navigate their own budding friendship. It's a harsh reality, one that I never had to face with my childhood crushes.

We settle down to play a board game, the three of us lost in a world of colorful pieces and playful banter. They fill me in on their lives outside the youth center, their stories weaving a tapestry of youthful resilience and dreams. When the board game ends, we move on to a puzzle, piecing together fragments of a picture just as they piece together their lives.

Marcus arrives to pick up Zay, his presence commanding yet not unfriendly. We talk briefly about the interview, and I lay out my requirements. He agrees, and we exchange phone numbers, a step toward the final steps of my dissertation research.

Not long after Marcus and Zay leave, Elijah shows up for Kiara. He's still more intimidating, that hardened edge to his demeanor, but as we talk, that facade softens. He's still a teenage kid, one who's made some bad choices in a world that offered him few good ones. He was dealt a bad hand and then played a worse one. Our conversation mirrors the one I had with Marcus, and he agrees to the terms as well.

As Elijah and Kiara walk away, I can't help but feel a mix of hope and apprehension. The world these kids and their families navigate is fraught with danger and hardship, yet their willingness to trust me, to let me in, is a beacon of hope. Their stories are just beginning, and I'm here to help tell them.

I'm comfortable on my couch, the glow from my laptop casting a soft light on the room, when my phone rings. The name on the screen makes me pause. Uncle Jeremy—he never calls. My stomach tightens as I realize my parents probably roped him into their concern. With a deep breath, I answer.

"Well, hi Uncle Jer, how are you?" My voice comes out too cheerful, masking the anxiety clawing at my insides.

"I'm good, Vallyn. How are you?" His gruff tone carries the weight of his past, a testament to the rough life he happily chose to lead. It reminds me of my phantom and makes me ache for him a little.

"I'm good, but I'm guessing Mom talked to you," I say, cutting to the chase.

He chuckles, a rough, familiar sound. "She did. Want to tell me in your own words?"

I sigh, sinking deeper into the cushions. "Depends. Are you going to hunt him down and shoot him?"

"Depends on who it is," he teases, but then adds seriously, "No, if you're happy and I don't see any red flags, I'm not doing anything. I think your mom is overreacting, but maybe not."

Clearing my throat, I decide to lay it all out. I recount everything—the gifts, the visits, the cameras, Corey, and Gage. He listens quietly, his silence urging me to continue.

"The camera thing pisses me off," he admits, and I can hear the irritation in his voice. "But guys like him, guys like me, we don't function well in the real world. We're used to recon, master plans, backup plans. It's hard on relationships, even mine with your Aunt Mary."

He pauses, letting his words sink in. I stay silent, waiting for him to continue.

"There's only one Gage I know in Phoenix who's a tech specialist. I know who he works with; I've worked with them. If you want details, I can give you them, but I don't have concerns about them hurting you, no more than any guy you date, in fact I probably trust them more than someone you just met randomly."

"Part of me wants to know, but another part doesn't. I want this to play out naturally—or I guess his way, but I can't believe you're okay with me having a stalker," I say with a nervous laugh.

"It's a stalker I know," he replies, a hint of humor in his voice. "I'm pretty sure I can even guess which one it is because I think he's the only one of the two of them that would do this. Honestly, Vallyn, I'm not going to lie to you and say we're not all fucked up in the head from the shit we've been through and the shit we've done. I'm not going to tell you he'd be the perfect man, but I have no room to talk there. We're talking about someone that I would trust with my life, so, yeah, I'll trust him with yours."

I swallow hard, nodding even though he can't see me. "Okay. And what are you going to tell Mom?"

He laughs. "A very watered-down version of this conversation. One more thing—does he know you're my niece?"

"He definitely didn't at first, but I mentioned you, so I think he does now," I answer.

"Good to know," he says. We exchange a few more pleasantries before saying goodbye.

As the call ends, I stare at my phone, processing. Uncle Jeremy's support is unexpected, but reassuring. My twisted web of secrets and danger, is something that maybe, just maybe, I'm not navigating alone.

The pang of loneliness hits me hard, a fire of longing that burns deep. I can't take it anymore. I decide to reach out, knowing this time it's probably Gage on the other end.

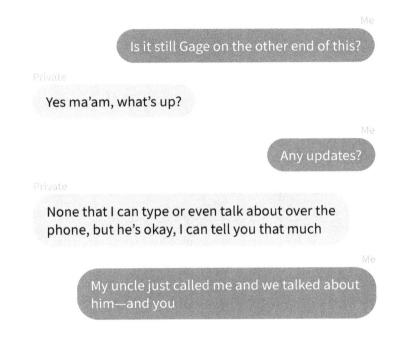

Me

Is it still Gage on the other end of this?

Private

Yes ma'am, what's up?

Me

Any updates?

Private

None that I can type or even talk about over the phone, but he's okay, I can tell you that much

Me

My uncle just called me and we talked about him—and you

A long pause. He's probably thinking I'm making a threat.

Me

Don't worry, he's surprisingly okay with everything

The silence stretches, and just when I'm about to give up, my phone vibrates again.

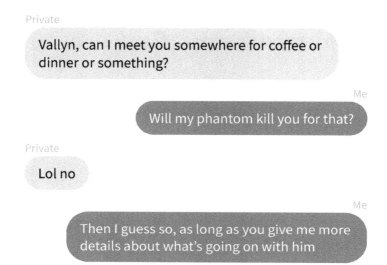

Private

Vallyn, can I meet you somewhere for coffee or dinner or something?

Me

Will my phantom kill you for that?

Private

Lol no

Me

Then I guess so, as long as you give me more details about what's going on with him

He agrees, and we quickly set up the details. An hour later, I'm slipping on my sandals, my heart pounding with a mix of excitement and anxiety. I head out the door, making my way to a small café just down the street.

The café is dimly lit, even in the middle of the day, it ironically feels like the perfect setting for a clandestine meeting. I spot him immediately. Gage sits at a corner table, his eyes scanning the room, alert and cautious. He stands as I approach, offering a tentative smile and gesturing for me to sit.

"Vallyn," he greets me, his voice a mix of relief and hesitation.

"Gage," I reply, sliding into the seat across from him. The air between us feels thick with unspoken words.

"I'm glad you came," he says, eyes locking onto mine with an intensity that makes me a little nervous.

"Me too," I admit. "Now, tell me what's going on with him."

"First," Gage says, leaning in, "tell me about the conversation with your uncle."

"I told you, he's not pissed," I say, rolling my eyes. "Maybe a little about the cameras in my apartment. But, he says he knows you and knows them, and that he would trust you all with his own life, so he trusts you all with mine."

"Did he give you names?" Gage's eyes narrow slightly.

"He offered. I turned it down," I confide, watching a mask of relief pass over his face. "Is that what you were worried about? The reason for this meeting?"

He shrugs. "Mostly, yeah, because he would want to know if everything was out in the open. I think he'll be surprised you turned it down."

I shrug back. "Gage, to be honest, I get him, and I get that he needs to do this in his own way, even if other people don't understand it. I didn't reach out to him and the whole conversation with my uncle felt like a betrayal of some kind, even though I know that's dumb. Now can you please tell me what is going on with him?"

"He's okay," Gage pauses, choosing his words carefully. "Honestly, I shouldn't tell you any of what I'm about to, but I'm going to anyway. They have their target. They're making their way through a ghost town of a city a couple of miles to an extraction point. They're not out of danger yet, but on top of the two of them, there are four more, and it's going well."

"How do you get your updates?" I ask, curiosity piqued.

"Illegally," he says, trying to leave it at that.

"You hack the military?" I whisper, eyes widening.

Smiling, he cocks his head and then shrugs. So, that's the answer.

"I also have GPS tracking on both of them, in case the decide to abandon them somewhere and pretend they didn't send them," he says nonchalantly. "And honestly, Vallyn, if that happened, Jeremy Kincaid would be one of the first people I'd call."

He looks at me, letting his words sink in, and sink in they do. Not only does my uncle trust them with his life, they trust him with theirs.

Gage and I continue with small talk, things that don't seem very important, but are in this situation.

As we part ways outside the café, I feel a strange sense of comfort. Maybe I don't have all the answers, but knowing what I do makes the uncertainty a little more bearable. There's no panel van this time. Instead, I watch Gage straddle a sleek black Yamaha sport bike. As he slips on his helmet, I can't help but think of my phantom and wonder if he rides the same kind of bike.

With one last wave, he roars off into the evening, leaving me standing there, alone but strangely reassured. The city lights blur as I make my way back to my apartment, thoughts swirling with newfound clarity.

# Chapter Twenty-Four

# The Fourth of July

## VALLYN

With the Fourth of July fast approaching, my friends and I start buzzing about our plans in our group chat. The messages come in rapid-fire.

Sasha

> We doing the normal thing?

Carly

> Tempe Beach?

Brooke

> Yeah that's the plan

Corey

> What time?

Sasha

> Maybe meet there around six? Then we can
> chill for a bit, eat some really fattening food, or
> whatever before fireworks

Tori

> Sounds good, I'll bring Tyson too

A part of me winces at Corey's participation, pretending like nothing has happened. True, we've been friends for almost fifteen years, and he's never pulled a stunt like that before. He was drunk that night, and he didn't actually get anywhere, but it still feels unforgivable.

Me

A few days later, I dress for the occasion in cute denim shorts and a red, white, and blue crop top with strategic cut-outs across the cleavage and sides. After slathering on sunscreen to protect my pasty skin, I apply minimal makeup—knowing I'll sweat it off anyway—and head down to the park to meet my friends.

I spot Carly and Brooke first. They look adorable, and Brooke hands me a hard lemonade almost as soon as she sees me.

"You bringing your cute spy friend?" Brooke asks, prompting an eye-roll and a laugh from me.

"Wasn't planning on it," I respond.

"Is he seriously a spy?" she asks.

"Well, I think he mostly spies on cheating spouses now, but yes," I answer, not entirely sure of the accuracy of that statement.

"And he's friends with that secret admirer guy of yours, right?" Carly chimes in.

"Yeah," I say with a smile.

"And you still don't know who that is?" Brooke asks, her disbelief evident.

Shaking my head, I reply, "No, but I do know he's been out of the country, or at least that's what they both tell me."

"So, you've met cute spy man, Gage, but you haven't met your secret admirer?" Brooke questions, her tone tinged with incredulity.

"Pretty much," I nod. "I know it's crazy. I don't get it either, but no, I still don't even know his name. But I know Gage's."

"Have you talked to Gage since that night?" Brooke asks.

Shaking my head, I lie, "Once, but it was quick, that's it."

The three of us quickly find Tori, Tyson, Sasha, and Corey. Corey hugs Brooke and Carly but doesn't touch me, and I'm grateful he doesn't even try. He does give me a quick nod and smile.

Why do I feel guilty for being so angry at him? He deserves all my fucking anger and more. How can I feel guilty for being angry and also feel frustrated that Sasha isn't angry? Fuck, you'd think having a degree in psychology would make this easier.

Alternating hard lemonades and waters seems to be my pattern. Carly and I find a hot dog stand and a funnel cake. It's a holiday—we can indulge a little. As the sun starts to set, we get ready to watch the fireworks. Sasha lays out some blankets on the grass for us to sit on, and as everyone settles in, it only leaves a spot for me next to Corey.

I gulp and then excuse myself to the bathroom, maybe even embarrassing myself by basically saying my stomach is upset.

"Hurry back, don't miss the fireworks," Brooke calls out as I walk away.

I do find my way to the port-a-potties, fucking lovely, and then as the fireworks begin, I stall a little more, buying a bottle of water and some glow bracelets from a vendor.

Walking back toward my friends, I can't bring myself to sit next to Corey. I just can't, so I stand about thirty yards behind them a few terraced steps up. Regret fills me for even coming, knowing Corey would be here. I can see him looking around, back up toward the bathroom area—he's looking for me.

I wrap one arm around my waist and hold my water bottle with the other, bringing it to my lips a few times, watching the display of colors and noise in front of me. Looking back down, I don't see Corey. I have no clue where he went; the rest of my friends are there, but he is gone.

Suddenly, an arm wraps around my waist from behind. I turn to yell at Corey, but the voice—right next to my ear, buried in my hair—and the grip of the arm stop me.

"Don't turn, Little Lotte," he murmurs, his voice a rich baritone that reverberates through my skin. He towers over me, more than Corey ever would. My breath catches, and my eyes fixate on the inked arm snaked around my waist, its coolness starkly noticeable in the Phoenix summer night air. Each whispered word, each brush of his breath against my neck and ear, sends shivers down my spine, igniting a fire deep within. The electricity of his proximity thrums through me, a tantalizing ache forms at my center for the man whose face remains a mystery, yet whose presence is undeniable.

Emotion surges within me as I realize he's here, he's back, and the tears prick at the corners of my eyes. My hand drifts to his arm, a tender caress rather than an attempt to break free.

Finally, I find my voice. Leaning back into him, I let my body meld with his, feeling the crook of his neck and the solid comfort of his collarbone behind my head. "You're back?" I ask, my voice a rough whisper.

"I'm back, pretty girl," he murmurs, his tone low and soothing. "And I'm not going to let that fucker touch you," he adds, a growl underlying his words. "Let me just hold you until the fireworks are over."

Swallowing hard, I nod and tighten my grip on his forearm, still securely wrapped around my waist. I focus on the rhythm of his breathing, the rise and fall of his chest against my back. Every now and then, I steal glances at his tattoos, intricate designs etched into his skin, but mostly, I watch the fireworks and let him hold me, feeling a sense of safety and belonging I don't think I've ever felt before.

When the fireworks show ends, his breath tickles my ear as he whispers, "Don't turn, pretty girl. I'll find you later."

"Wait," I plead, my fingers digging into his skin as he starts to loosen his grip. His strong arms tighten around me once more. "Come tuck me in?" I ask, my voice barely above a whisper. He chuckles softly in my ear, sending a shiver down my spine.

"Let me see your face," I add, desperate to connect with him. His thumb trails gently over the bare skin below my crop top, leaving a tingling path in its wake.

"Your friends are coming, but I'll come tuck you in," he promises. "And if you're a good girl, I'll take the mask off."

I inhale sharply and nod, my heart pounding as his hands slip away from me. Glancing up, I see Brooke and Carly approaching from about twenty feet away, their faces lit up with excitement.

"Hey, you really aren't feeling well," Brooke says. "You're so pale, you look like you've seen a ghost."

Laughing uncomfortably, I reply, "I mean, can my skin actually get more pale?"

"Apparently it can," Carly answers, and then the rest of them are right behind, walking up to me.

"I think I do need to get home," I admit.

Tori, Tyson, Sasha, and Corey quickly join us, and Corey also looks like he has seen a ghost. I make eye contact with him for a second and his jaw sets. I know instantly that he knows—he saw.

Suddenly, it hits me that's why my phantom decided to do what he did—because Corey was approaching me. He *did* say he wouldn't let him touch me. I don't think it registered before because I was too busy registering *him*.

*Fuck.*

Now my head really does start to swim. Before I was just turned on and wanting to run after my phantom, now I feel sick.

Did he save me again?

I must zone out because the next thing I register is Brooke saying, "Earth to Vallyn."

"What?" I ask, shaking my head, then adding, "Sorry."

She laughs, but then asks sympathetically, "Do you want me to drop you off at home before we head out?"

Hugging myself, I nod. Everything feels weird right now. I'm quiet in the car on the way to my apartment.

"Are you sure you're okay?" Brooke asks.

I nod and answer, "Yeah, I think I just need to cool off and lie down."

She nods and watches me walk into my building before she drives away. My mind is racing as I take the elevator to my floor.

As I put the key in my deadbolt, the door opens from the inside. A strong hand grabs my arm and pulls me inside. My face is buried in his chest with his arms around me before the door even closes behind me.

"Fuck, Vallyn, I missed you," he says, almost growling in my ear.

I laugh a little uncomfortably and point out, "I think this is the first time you've hugged me."

He chuckles softly near my ear and then almost whispers, "I needed to hold you."

My arms find their way around him and it does feel natural, it feels like home and I know how insane that sounds, given all the circumstances. Fuck, the guy just broke into my apartment to wait for me.

"Did Gage tell you about our conversations?" I ask quietly.

"He did," he says, and then his voice is coated in humor as he adds, "and I got a call from your uncle almost the second I was back on US soil."

That freezes me, but I keep my face buries in his chest—fuck, he smells good. "You what?"

"Yeah, Little Lotte, he called me. We're good, he's good, we can talk," he says. "But for right now, I just want to hold you."

# CHAPTER TWENTY-FIVE

# THE TALK & THE REVEAL

## PHANTOM

Three days ago, we finally made it back to the British military base. Casen and I connected with Gage right after. The debrief was standard, a mechanical recounting of events and updates from Gage about what happened at home in our absence. But then Gage asked to talk to me privately.

My stomach already churns with the aftermath of the last few days of the mission before I even talk to him. I force myself to stay composed as Gage reveals he met her in person. I'm momentarily relieved when he tells me about Corey, but then he drops the bombshell—she talked to Jeremy, and he knows who we are—who *I* am. Paranoia tightens its grip around my chest. Paranoia and fear—not fear of Jeremy, fear because I don't want to lose her.

Despite the reassurances that Gage provided and the fact that Jeremy offered to give her my name and she didn't want it, the fear of losing her gnaws at me. After charging it for a few minutes, I turn on my phone, see the messages between her and Gage, and then another message from Jeremy, telling me to reach out when I'm available again.

Suddenly, I feel like a fourteen-year-old boy about to talk to his first girlfriend's dad. I text Jeremy, letting him know my expected arrival time at Fort Carson in Colorado, and mention that Gage will update him if anything changes.

I want to write to Vallyn, but I decide to wait until I have all the information. If something is happening that could work against me, I don't want to make it worse. However, I do pull up her feed, it's still relatively early in the morning there and she's still in bed—snuggled up to her bear—and the beast in me starts to quiet.

As soon as Gage knows we're on the ground, my phone rings. When Jeremy's name flashes across my phone screen, I hesitate. My thumb hovers over the screen before I finally slide it. "Hey, Jeremy."

"Hey, I hear you've been stalking my niece," Jeremy's voice crackles through the phone, laced with humor.

"Something like that, yeah," I admit, trying to match his light tone.

"You didn't know she was family?"

"No, I did not," I confess. "Not until she mentioned her uncle being a bounty hunter. Then I started digging."

"Why didn't you reach out?"

I sigh, the weight of my decisions pressing down on me. "I think I was in too deep at that point."

He sighs heavily on the other end. "Listen, I knew it had to be you and not Casen, and Gage confirmed it. I need you to know that I completely trust you with her, but maybe don't have cameras in her apartment. I'm pretty sure you probably still have some up, even after taking a few down. Just don't do that, man."

"Understood," I sigh, feeling a mix of relief and guilt. I don't admit there is still a camera in her apartment, but I don't deny it either, and I'm sure he realizes that.

"For whatever it's worth, I think she really likes you, or at least the you she knows so far. She seems to understand our messed-up brains and relationships in a way that might not make sense to the rest of the world. I don't know if it's because of me or her education, but she gets you. Here's my request," he pauses, waiting for me to respond.

"What's that?" I ask, running my hand over my face.

"Don't draw it out. You're a good-looking kid, only a few years older than her, and she already feels safe with you. Just don't drag it out."

"Yeah, okay, I get it. And Gage said she didn't want to know my name?"

"Not from me she didn't. I'm pretty sure she *wants* to know it and see your face. Now that she's seen Gage's, she thought that was pretty fucked up. Give her some raw honesty, okay?"

Nodding to myself, I finally vocalize my agreement. "Okay, Jer. Give me a little while after I'm back, but okay."

"I don't have you on a time clock, man, just offering you some advice," he concedes.

I land back in Phoenix late on the night of the third. Gage works out Vallyn's Fourth of July plans for me, and my intention is to watch her from a distance, to see her, then surprise her at her apartment. But as always with best laid plans, things go awry.

She excuses herself from her friends and heads to the portable toilets, lingering on one of the terraced risers, watching the fireworks begin. That's when I see Corey, that fucking douchebag, walking toward her. I have to intervene, it's a compulsion, not a choice.

I'm in short sleeves—it's triple digits still, even after sunset, no gloves, no mask—and I know Corey will see me. She'll see my tattoos at the very least, but protecting her from him is more important. Besides, I *need* my hands on her. My addiction to her hasn't had a fix in weeks. I need to feel her, smell her, hear her voice—I need all of it.

I almost break as my arms wrap around her—I'm like a junkie taking that first hit after jonesing for days. My fingers tremble, desperate for the feel of her, but I fight to keep them still. My voice is a low, rough whisper, every word costing me a piece of my sanity. Her warmth seeps into me, grounding me, and yet, setting my nerves on fire. I can feel the slight tremor in her body, the subtle quiver that tells me she's barely holding it together, too.

I want to lose myself in her, to let go and drown in the scent of her hair, the softness of her skin. But I can't. She needs me to be strong. She needs me to be her protector, her shield. But I will take this fireworks show, and while to some it might seem long, the grand finale comes too fast for me.

After letting her go, I ride to her apartment, letting myself in. Waiting for her is torture, but when I hear her, I open the door and pull her into me. She doesn't even realize I'm not wearing a mask yet as I pull her face straight into my chest so fast.

This is the first time I've ever fully hugged her. I've held her, carried her, tasted her skin, touched her in almost intimate places, but I've never hugged her.

"I just want to hold you," I request. She acquiesces easily, and not only does she let me hold her, she holds me back.

"I missed you, too," she admits, her voice soft.

"Vallyn, look at me," I finally say, unwrapping myself from her and pushing her back a few inches.

At first, her eyes are focused down on my arms. I smile a little, using my fingers to tilt her chin up. She expects to find me masked. When her eyes meet mine, she gasps. Not only am I not masked, but

I've never been in light as bright as her kitchen lights with her. It's probably her first time really seeing my eyes.

After her jaw clamps shut, her hand runs up my chest to my face. The palm of her hand first rests on my neck, then moves to my cheek. The reactions that flood through my system are overwhelming, but I mange to hold my shit together.

"I *do* know you," she says softly. "I'd know you anywhere from just those few seconds that night."

Her words make me wonder if she felt the same things I did that night, but I pull her close to me again, her face buried in my neck and chest. Eventually, I ask, "Are you hungry?"

She sniffles before answering, and I realize she has tears. "Yeah, I could eat," she says.

"Vallyn, baby, why are you crying?" I ask, with genuine concern.

She shakes her head, wiping her eyes and stepping back from me. "I'm just overwhelmed, I think."

"You want me to put the mask back on?" I ask playfully.

She shakes her head and laughs. "No, but do you want to know something?"

I raise my eyebrows at her and she responds, "I had a dream one night that it was you."

*Fuck me.*

"I had named you 'broad shoulders,'" she pauses and snickers, rolling her eyes, "when I got back to my table that night, so I guess you have that moniker now, too."

Hiding my initial reaction to that I laugh and suggest, "Let's order some food and we'll talk. We can talk about your uncle and everything else, but Vallyn, I'm glad you missed me and you're happy to see me."

"Which way?" she asks with a laugh. "In general or your actual face?"

"Both," I say with a smile. I drag her toward me and press a gentle kiss to her forehead.

"Why now?" she asks.

"First, you asked, but honestly, with your uncle knowing who I am, if I piss you off or you want to call the cops on me, I have no anonymity anymore," I shrug. "So, I was already planning on this tonight."

"Are you mad at Gage?" she asks.

"No, pretty girl," I admit, threading my fingers through hers. "I'm glad he came to rescue you that night. I know he told you, but I would have been pissed if he hadn't gone to watch over you after the messages you sent. And I'd be even more pissed if he had let Corey fuck with you. So, no, I'm not mad at him."

I look at her and she doesn't say anything—she's studying me. "And if I had been around, you probably would have seen my face that night, too."

Crossing her arms around her waist, she asks, "Was that tonight, too? Were you not going to approach me if Corey hadn't looked like he was going to?"

"I don't know about that, Little Lotte, you were pretty irresistible standing there, but him walking toward you clinched it for me," I answer with a smile. She's quiet, so I add, "Gage also said you were worried about me—missed me."

She nods. "Uh, yeah, of course I was and I did. It was a long time and I knew it would be dangerous because, you know, you said it would be enough to buy a flower shop," she says and laughs.

"It *was* enough money to buy a flower shop, or a lot of other expensive things," I answer with a shrug. "Come on," I suggest, "let's sit and order food."

The way she stares at me, like she doesn't believe I'm real, makes me want to sweep her up in my arms, to kiss her, to touch her, to fuck her—to do whatever I need to so she knows I'm real.

"Vallyn, pretty girl, I'm here, I'm not going anywhere. I'm not going to hide my face from you again," I promise and reach up to touch her face.

I watch her shiver in response to my touch, and I fucking like it.

# CHAPTER TWENTY-SIX

# FALLING INTO NORMAL

## VALLYN

I'm stunned when my eyes meet his, and I make out his face.

*Broad shoulders.*

His chiseled face bears the evidence of a life lived hard, weathered by years of sun and stress. Yet, it doesn't make him look older than he is and he's undeniably handsome. His skin is a few shades darker than mine—my own is ghostly pale in comparison, but most people can say that. The scruff on his jawline looks like it's just a few days old, maybe a permanent shadow of stubble that he maintains deliberately. It was like that the first night I saw him, too. The first time I saw him, I thought his eyes were green, but now I see the truth in the light—they're hazel, flecked with gold and brown that draw me in deeper every time I look.

His hair, which I've only ever seen in low light, is dark brown, just a touch lighter than my almost raven-colored locks. It's longer than I'd expect for someone with his background in military operations, yet it's not really long and it suits him perfectly. The first night I saw him,

I thought he was handsome, hot, and incredibly sexy. That feeling hasn't changed—in fact, it's only intensified.

"Come on," he says, wrapping his fingers around mine. Electricity shoots up my arm at his touch, and I fight back the shudder that threatens to ripple through me.

As he pulls me toward my own couch, a mix of humor and exhilaration bubbles up. I can't help but laugh softly.

"What?" he asks, glancing back at me with curiosity.

"This whole thing is just... so not normal," I reply, as he guides me the last few steps to the couch.

He pulls me down beside him and holds me close, as if we've been in this position countless times before, though it's really the first. I turn to look at him, which separates me from his torso, but hitch one leg over his, craving the connection. His hand falls instinctively to my bare thigh, exposed by my shorts.

The natural ease between us is almost unnerving and I can't help but marvel at how effortlessly we fit together. I take a deep breath, trying to steady myself. His presence is a paradox—calming yet disconcerting. He leans in slightly, his eyes searching mine, and I feel a flutter of something unfamiliar but undeniably wonderful.

Thoughts swirl in my mind, the words caught in my throat. How can I explain the whirlwind of emotions he stirs within me? How can I convey the relief that I feel when I know he should scare me?

His touch is warm, grounding me, and the fear loosens its grip on my heart every time I look at him. I don't know what the future holds, but sitting here with him, feeling the natural ease between us, I'm willing to take the leap.

"Vallyn," he sighs my name, looking at me like he's trying to read my mind.

I run both hands over my face. "I think I'm trying to decide if I'm dreaming," I say quietly, a slight scoff at the end.

"You're not dreaming, Little Lotte," he whispers, his fingers tracing patterns on my inner thigh. The currents of fire that run through my skin straight to my center are almost overwhelming—it clenches and tingles in response to his touch. I want this man so fucking much, and I don't even really know him.

Taking a deep breath, I find the courage to meet his gaze. "Tell me about your conversation with my uncle."

He clears his throat, pulling his hand off my thigh and tangling it with my fingers instead. The sensations are still intense. Holding my gaze, he says, "Let's order food, then we'll talk."

Nodding, I reply, "Okay."

He pulls out his phone, searching for food options while my mind races with questions. I want to ask him everything, but I don't want to overwhelm him.

After giving me a few choices, I finally pick something, and he orders. Then he puts his phone down and looks at me.

"Pretty girl," he begins, brushing a few strands of hair out of my face, "Jeremy is okay. I think he's mostly okay because you're okay. He wasn't happy about the cameras, but neither were you. We've actually worked together a lot, both here in Phoenix and overseas. He only retired a year or two ago and he's not fully out. I don't know how I missed that at the beginning of this, or what it would have changed, but we're good. That being said, I'm pretty sure if I fuck this up going forward, he'll kill me—maybe literally."

Swallowing, I nod and then ask, "Okay, so do I get to know your name now? Your phone number?"

His eyes drift to the ceiling, a thoughtful nod accompanying his next words. "Little Lotte, phone number, yes, but name, I'm not sure," he says, and I start to protest. He squeezes my thigh and explains, "It's not because I don't trust you or even that I don't want you to know. I told you that I wouldn't sleep with you until you knew my name, and I want to keep that barrier for right now."

I scoff lightly, a sarcastic laugh escaping my lips. "You need to not tell me your name so that you don't sleep with me? You know that sounds crazy, right?"

"Oh, I know, pretty girl, but this whole thing has been crazy," he answers, his hand finding my chin, tilting my face toward him. "You told Jeremy you wanted to give me my own timeline on that. That's all I'm asking for."

Rolling my eyes, I shake my head but then nod. "Okay. It's weird, but okay."

A knock at my door breaks the moment. My phantom checks his phone and shakes his head. "It's not the food. It shouldn't be."

Untangling my leg from his, I get up and peek through the peephole. Taking a deep breath, I close my eyes, put on a mask of a smile, and open the door.

"Hey, Corey, what's up?" I greet him hesitantly.

"Can I come in?" he asks.

"Absolutely not," I answer, keeping my smile and pleasant tone intact.

"Are you okay?" he inquires, his Adam's apple bobbing nervously.

"I'm okay. I think I was just hot, that's all," I reply.

"I saw—" he hesitates, "I saw you with him."

"Yeah? And?"

"Vallyn, we're all just worried about you. I just want—" He stops as his eyes track behind me.

I close mine, taking a cleansing breath through my nose. Turning back, I find those hazel eyes and say, "I have this. I'm okay."

He stops a few yards behind me, his concern palpable.

Looking back at Corey, I plaster the smile back on my face and ask, "Did you tell the rest of them?"

"No," he answers, shaking his head. "I wanted to make sure you were okay with whatever happened, but it seems you are, so I'll go. Your secret, or whatever this," he gestures between me and my phantom, "is, is safe with me. At least for now."

"I'll talk to Sasha in the morning," I say matter-of-factly.

Corey nods and turns to walk away, saying, "Have a good night," as his back is already to me.

Closing the door behind Corey, I turn to find those hazel eyes fixed on me again. He approaches tentatively, his expression a blend of concern and determination. Without a word, he steps past me and opens the door of my apartment.

"Don't," I say quickly, my voice a sharp command.

"Vallyn, he has to stop," my handsome phantom says, pausing in the hallway, his frustration evident in the grinding of his molars and the strain of the muscles in his neck—it stirs something primal in me.

"I know that and he knows that. Give him this one," I plead softly.

I watch his jaw set more, the tension visible. He's not happy, but he knows he has to respect my wishes. His eyes flicker to the ceiling as he takes a deep breath before stepping back toward me and into the apartment.

"I just don't know if he would have left if I hadn't been here, pretty girl. He has no boundaries," he says softly, cupping my face with a tenderness that makes my heart ache.

Once the door is closed behind him, I can't help but laugh. "So says the guy who likes to break into my apartment."

He cocks his head, closing his eyes and taking a deep breath. We both know it's different—it's an insane kind of consensual—but he has no room to talk when it comes to boundaries.

Meeting his gaze, I ask, "Can I give you a key now so I can at least pretend I have a choice in that?"

"Do you want me to leave?" he asks playfully.

"No, I do not want you to leave," I admit a little salaciously while threading my arms under his, hugging him around his waist, he reciprocates and pulls me closer. "Speaking of which," I begin, then sigh, "how long are you staying?"

He chuckles softly, "How long do you want me to stay, pretty girl?"

*Forever.*

Shrugging, I answer, "I don't really want to let you go, so I can't answer that right now."

"Remember, you hated me a couple of weeks ago," he reminds me.

"No, I *wanted* to hate you, that's different," I confess. "I'm pretty sure I tried to seduce you right after that."

"You might have," he agrees with a soft laugh.

"Unsuccessfully," I add with a shrug.

"Little Lotte, don't think I don't want you, because I do. I didn't do all the crazy shit I've done over the last two months to not fuck you," he says, squeezing me tighter and causing blood to rush to all my most sensitive areas. "I just want it to be right in every way."

His watch vibrates, pulling us back to the present. He glances at it and then back at me. "Food is almost here," he announces.

Nodding, my heart still pounding from the intensity of our exchange, I pull away from him. "I'm covered in sunscreen and sweat. I'm going to clean up real quick," I say, and he nods at me before pulling me close and kissing my temple. His lips are warm against my skin, and I want to melt at his gentleness.

All the parts of him get to me—the soft and gentle parts, the masked and mysterious parts, the parts I'm positive are violent—they all make me want him more. There's a raw magnetism about him, a dangerous allure that pulls me in despite the alarm bells ringing in my head. I flash a quick smile at him and then step into the bathroom, closing the door behind me.

I do need to pee, so I take care of that and then throw my hair up, washing my face and arms. The cool water feels refreshing, washing away the grime of the day, and cooling me off. I add lotion—lotion he sent me—the scent of vanilla and coconut wraps around me, reminding me of him.

I hear him answer the door and make my way to the closet, getting rid of my denim Daisy Dukes and my patriotic crop top. I replace them with butter-soft, black leggings and a tank top with a built-in bra that casually shows off the girls. A clean pair of socks, and I feel much better than I did five minutes ago. I wasn't lying about feeling overheated at the park.

Quickly, I pull my hair down and brush it before putting it back up in a high ponytail—it's so long it still falls below my shoulder blades. I walk out the other side of my closet, through my bedroom, and I hesitate for a moment when I see he has left his things—his weapons—on my dresser. I swallow, but then I also realize that means he fully trusts me. I know the sight of them should also scare me. Taking a deep breath, I walk back into the living room.

He has our food set up on the island in the kitchen with the bar stools. Looking me up and down quickly when I step into the room, he smiles and says, "You look cute, more comfortable, too."

His eyes linger on me, dark and intense, and my pulse quickens. There's an electric charge in the air. His presence fills the room, and I can't help but be drawn to him, like a moth to a flame, knowing full well that flame will burn me.

Clearing his throat, he moves to the fridge and pulls out a bottle of wine, the kind he has sent me before and I really like. He moves with an unsettling familiarity, like he's done this a million times. Without even glancing around, he reaches into the cabinet and pulls out the wine glasses.

As he turns around and sets the glasses on the island in front of me, I hop onto a bar stool, narrowing my eyes at him.

"What?" he asks, his voice smooth and casual.

"Funny how you know where my wine glasses are," I tease, a hint of accusation in my tone.

He snickers, a mischievous glint in his eye, and shrugs, his silence more telling than any answer he could give.

As we eat, the conversation flows easily, a mixture of light-hearted banter and deeper confessions. The connection between us feels more tangible, more real with every passing moment. I know there are still so many secrets, so many layers to uncover, but for now, this is enough. This is more than I ever expected to become reality.

The evening stretches on, the food disappearing, the wine warming us from the inside out. Eventually, we move to the couch, the familiarity of our earlier position resuming as if we'd never left. His hand finds my thigh again.

"Stay," I whisper, my voice barely audible.

"Yeah?" he asks, pulling me closer.

"Please," I answer, nestling my head into the crook of his neck.

# CHAPTER TWENTY-SEVEN

# BEST LAID PLANS

## PHANTOM

"S tay."

The word shouldn't surprise me, not after everything else, but it does. Then she follows it with a soft, desperate, "please," and I know I'm not leaving her tonight.

Nothing since I left on this last mission has gone to plan with her. Her uncle and Gage accelerated what was supposed to be a carefully laid plan to keep her at a distance while I studied her, learned her.

Obsession claws at me, unhealthy and undeniable. That's why I cling to the last piece of this mystery—my name. Holding on to it feels like a thin barrier, a way to protect her from the unreasonable compulsion that still gnaws at my sanity—the need to know everything she does, everything she is, all the time.

The urge to protect her battles with the urge to possess her, and it's a losing fight. My self-control was strained to its limits when I resisted the temptation to chase that fucker to the parking lot and remind him she isn't his. But her request, that simple plea, won. She won, just barely.

It sounds foolish, unreasonable, but I feel like if I can hold on to this last boundary, if I can keep my name from crossing her lips, I can shield her from the rest of the madness inside me.

"I'll stay, pretty girl," the words come out quieter than usual, almost against my will. Her smile in response—genuine and real—makes my heart stumble.

*Fuck, I'm so far gone over her.*

Trying to shift the mood, a tease slips out, "But no lingerie and no cops." The blush that rises to her cheeks, creeping up her neck, is impossible to ignore. She backhands me lightly in the chest, lighthearted but with a spark that sets something off inside me.

Vallyn's eyes narrow, playful and flirty as she shoots back, "I'm pretty sure I don't care about your name anymore when it comes to crossing those lines. So, keep it to yourself."

"Oh, yeah?" My tone matches hers, the challenge unspoken but understood.

She bites her bottom lip, a move that nearly undoes me. "Yeah. I mean, I already tried to seduce you, and that was before I saw your face."

"You were pretty irresistible that night, Vallyn, not gonna lie." The honesty slips out before I can second-guess it.

"Apparently, I still wasn't *that* irresistible, though," she sighs, a hint of vulnerability in her voice. My hand finds the curve of her neck, thumb tracing along her jaw until her eyes meet mine.

"Vallyn, I've fucked this up so much, I know that. But I'm not gonna fuck *that* up. I want to make sure we're in a good place first." Her eyes lock onto mine with an intensity that no one's ever looked at me with. Then, tears well up, and she blinks, looking away.

No words feel right, so instead, I pull her closer, letting her bury her face into my chest. The intensity of this—of us—is unlike anything I've ever known, and there's no way to explain it to anyone, except to her. It's something only the two of us seem to fully understand—and I'm not sure that we understand it all.

Laughter spills out of her as she sits up, and my grip loosens, confusion etched on my face. She's still chuckling when she says, "So, I know you're crazy," another burst of laughter, "but I'm crazy too." Her eyes, still glistening with tears, meet mine as she wipes them away with her thumb. My eyebrow arches, waiting for her to continue her thoughts.

"Gage told me y'all have groupies," she says, her voice tinged with something darker. "It made me so fucking angry, thinking about little thirst traps trying to do their thing. I felt so possessive all of a sudden." She laughs again, covering her face, and I'm left stunned, processing what she just said.

"Wait, he told you what?" The words slip out, more disbelief than anything else.

She fans her face, struggling to stop laughing. After a deep breath, she explains, "My friends, especially Brooke, think Gage is hot. I told him that, and he said they don't think he's hot, just mysterious. Then he mentioned y'all having groupies because of what you do."

A smile tugs at my lips. "That made you jealous?"

"Yeah, a little. Really, more possessive," she admits with a shrug. "And for the record, Gage is wrong. He's hot *and* mysterious—they're not mutually exclusive."

Feigning offense, I raise my eyebrows. "So, should I be worried about Gage now?"

She snort-laughs, shaking her head. "No, he touched me—or, more like caught me—and there's zero chemistry there." Her voice shifts, eyes glancing up at me through her lashes. "I think my nervous system is all you—all phantom, all the time."

"I like it that way," I admit, the words carrying more weight than I expected. "But why did he have to catch you?"

"When he came to the bar that night, I was pretty drunk. I stood up to talk to him and kind of fell into him," she confesses, shrugging as if it's no big deal.

"Why were you drunk that time, Vallyn?" The question slips out, memories of her last drunken night flashing through my mind.

"You, Corey, I don't fucking know," she admits, shoulders slumping. "I'm glad Gage showed up, though. Pretty sure he scared the fuck out of Corey, even though he didn't say or do anything like you would. Just stared him down."

I sigh, the weight of what she said settling between us as her eyes well up again.

"Sorry," she murmurs, wiping her eyes. "I don't usually cry this much."

Tipping her chin up so her eyes meet mine, a playful smirk tugs at my lips. "I don't usually do the shit I've been doing with you either." Her expression sobers, the fog in her eyes clearing as she licks her lips. Every instinct screams at me to kiss her, like a siren's call.

Cupping her face, my thumb traces her bottom lip, her eyes close. *Fuck me.*

"Vallyn," her name slips from my tongue like a prayer, laced with reverence and desire. Her eyes flutter open, and she leans in, the moment electric between us. It takes everything in me, but I press a kiss to her forehead instead, extracting myself from her warmth as I stand. Her sharp inhale echoes in my mind as I walk to the kitchen, pouring another glass of wine.

"Do you want another glass?" My voice barely registers, a rasp betraying the feelings inside.

She studies me, then nods. Pouring hers, I hand it to her, the weight of what we're not saying heavy between us. "I'm sorry, pretty girl," the words come out soft, an apology for the lines we won't cross tonight.

She swallows, understanding in her eyes, knowing I'm holding back for now. It's not because I don't want to—I need to give her time to fully trust me.

"What do you have going on tomorrow?" The question is casual, a shift in conversation.

"Nothing tomorrow, but I've got some big interviews lined up for my dissertation the day after that," she says, her voice tinged with anticipation.

"But nothing tomorrow?" I confirm, watching her sip her wine.

She shakes her head, glancing down before taking another sip. All I really want right now is to hold her. "Are you tired?"

"Actually, yeah," she admits, setting her glass down.

"You want to let me hold you while we sleep?"

A smile tugs at her lips, the corners lifting as she looks away, then back at me. "That's all I get? Holding?"

A chuckle escapes me, nodding. "Yeah, pretty girl, for tonight, that's all you get."

"Then, sold," she says, finishing her wine. "I need to pee, brush my teeth, but yeah, I'd, honestly, really like that."

"Okay, Little Lotte, do what you need to," a smile creeps onto my face as I take her empty glass.

She hands it to me, placing her hand on my chest as she passes by, she lets it fall deliberately grazing the fly of my jeans. My cock responds instantly, and she lets out a playful, "Oops," as she heads to the bathroom.

All I can do is laugh and shake my head, already dreading how hard it's going to be to not cross any lines tonight.

Rinsing the wine glasses, they clink softly as I place them in the dishwasher. The wine bottle gets corked and put back in the fridge. Cleanup from dinner follows, the motions almost automatic.

Stepping out of the bathroom, Vallyn's voice pulls me from my thoughts. "You didn't have to do that."

"It's the least I can do, pretty girl," I reply, keeping my tone light. "Come out on the balcony with me for a few minutes?"

Her raised eyebrows ask the unspoken question, so I answer it. "Nicotine fix. I know it's a bad habit."

With a shrug, she says, "I knew you smoked. I can smell it. That's fine. I probably need to check my phone anyway."

Judgment or just an observation? Hard to tell, but her movements are easy to track as she grabs her phone, glancing at me before heading toward the balcony door. Midnight's come and gone, but the heat still lingers in the air.

Leaning on the railing, I make sure the smoke drifts away from her as she checks her phone. The glow from the screen lights up her face. Her scoff catches my attention, and I look over, questioning.

"Despite what he said, Corey told my whole friend group you were here, so now they have questions," she says, turning off her screen and setting her phone down with a little more force than necessary. Her hands cover her face as the weight of it all settles.

"What do they want to know?" My voice stays low, careful.

"Basically if I'm okay," she murmurs.

"Did you answer them?" The scowl she shoots my way is a little adorable. "I take that as a no? You probably should, or they'll just keep blowing up your phone."

Another drag of the cigarette, another sigh from her. "Corey is an asshole."

"Yeah, I could have told you that," I chuckle, catching the side-eye she throws my way. "You know you're kind of adorable when you're agitated and sassy."

Her giggle, bright and sudden, makes her all the more confusing. After a moment, she calms down, looking at me. "I'm sorry," she says, trying to stifle more laughter. "I just remembered what you said the first time you called me sassy."

*This fucking woman.*

"Pretty girl, you have a one-track mind," I tease, watching as her eyes narrow. "Not that I mind—but not tonight, Little Lotte."

Breathing in deep, she smiles and nods, then picks up her phone. "He told them he was worried about me. I have like a hundred texts in different groups and from all of them individually. It's just fucking annoying."

# Chapter Twenty-Eight

# Deeper Conversations

## VALLYN

"You want advice or are you venting?" His eyes bore into mine, unyielding and a little intense.

My heart skips a beat, and I feel the weight of his gaze pulling me in. "Did you seriously just ask that?" I challenge, but there's a teasing lilt to my tone, a smirk tugging at the corner of my lips. "That's like emotional intelligence 101, and I'm surprised to hear it from you."

His mouth curls into a knowing smirk, matching mine. "That's not an answer, Vallyn," he says, voice low and laced with something dark and thrilling. He holds my gaze, daring me to look away, but I won't give him the satisfaction.

"I was just venting," I admit, my voice softening as I let down my guard, "but now I'm curious, what's your advice?"

Not missing a beat, he replies, "Text the group, tell them you're fine. Send a selfie if they need proof, but let them know you're fine and going to bed. Reach back out tomorrow."

The suggestion is so practical, almost disarming. I chuckle, the sound more bitter than sweet. "That's pretty much what I was going to say—though I was planning to call them assholes first."

"They're your friends," he replies with a hint of playfulness, but there's an edge to his voice that suggests he's only half-joking.

"Corey doesn't believe you'll actually kill him because he keeps pushing his luck," I admit, the levity slipping from my voice. There's a tremor there, a vulnerability I hate showing but can't hide.

Watching him, I see his expression darken, the shift in his demeanor palpable. "If he touches you again, he'll find out how fucking serious I am," he growls, and the words hang in the air between us, thick with promise.

Silence stretches, taut and uncomfortable. His eyes never leave me, a storm brewing behind them. Then, softer, almost tender, he asks, "Can I ask you something, though, pretty girl?"

I swallow, my throat tight. I can't find the words as he stares me down, waiting, so he fills the silence. "Why do you want to keep him as a friend?"

The question hits like a punch to the gut, and I know my face betrays me. I drop my gaze to my hands, my fingers trembling slightly. He doesn't press, just turns back to the railing, taking a slow drag from his cigarette. The smoke curls around him, ghostly and fragile, as he gives me space to gather the pieces of myself and my answer.

Finally, my voice, small and fragile, breaks the silence. "Because I think he wasn't himself that night, and whether out of embarrassment or something else, I don't want my other friends to know it happened."

The confession feels like lead on my tongue, weighing me down. He turns back to me, his eyes softening. "Vallyn," he says, and there's a tenderness in his voice that almost undoes me, "that same forgiving heart is part of why I'm standing here right now. I'm not going to judge that. And, clearly, I don't know Corey, but if I hadn't seen—if I hadn't called—"

"I know," I cut him off, my voice shaky, fragile like glass. I think about that night, the tension, the confusion. "When he came here the next day, he was pissed off because he said I hadn't told you 'no.' I'm not sure what conversation you had with him, but it made me pause. At that point, I hadn't told you no, and that confused me, too."

Hesitating, words form on my lips, and I'm unsure if I should voice them. But something about his presence, the way he looks at me as if I'm the only thing that matters, gives me the courage to speak. "But this," I gesture between us, the air thick with unspoken truths, "whatever *this* is, feels real. It feels like the realest thing I've ever felt, and I don't understand it. I *get* why they don't understand it, I wouldn't understand it if I were in their shoes, but I know how I feel. I think I know you feel the same, and for me, that's enough."

His breath catches, just for a moment, and I see the raw emotion flicker in his eyes before he takes one last drag from his cigarette, stubbing it out on the concrete. In a heartbeat, he's in front of me, squatting down, looking up into my eyes as if searching for something—anything—that might contradict what I've just said. But he won't find it, because it's the truth, all of it.

His hand comes up, warm and rough, resting against my cheek, thumb brushing softly over my skin. "Vallyn, pretty girl," he whispers, voice hoarse, almost desperate, "I think I need to hold you now."

My only answer is to nod, the gesture small but loaded with everything I can't bring myself to say. He stands, his presence looming like a shadow I'm desperate to cling to. I glance down at my phone, the screen lighting up with a flurry of messages in response to my hastily sent text. With a swipe, I put it on Do Not Disturb, severing that connection to the outside world. Right now, all that matters is the man in front of me.

Clearing my throat, I stand and force a smile, trying to bridge the gap between us. "You going to sleep in your jeans?" The words come out light, almost teasing, but there's a tension beneath them, a current of something deeper that neither of us has yet dared to name.

His grin is slow, curling up one corner of his mouth before spreading into something that makes my chest tighten and my smile widen in response. "No, pretty girl. I hoped you'd ask me to stay, so I might have prepared for it." The way he says it—soft, yet full of intent—sends a thrill down my spine. Then, he leans in and presses a feather-light kiss to my forehead, the touch so tender it almost breaks me. Without another word, he turns, opening the door back into the house. His hand finds the small of my back as I step through the threshold ahead of him, his touch both grounding and electrifying.

This feels so natural, so effortless, and that's what terrifies me. How can something so intense feel so easy? My mind spins with the thought, caught between the comfort of his presence and the fear of what it means.

He moves with a quiet confidence, my phantom, heading straight to the kitchen sink. I watch as he washes his hands, the mundane action somehow intimate, like he's carved out a space in my world. My thoughts swirl, tangled and confusing. Is this real? Is he real? Can I trust this feeling, trust myself, trust him?

When he turns around, his hands still wet, he catches me staring. His eyes narrow, not in suspicion but with a knowing look. "What?" he asks, a hint of amusement coloring his voice. He grabs a paper towel while I answer.

"Still trying to figure out if I'm dreaming," I reply, the words soft and tinged with vulnerability.

He laughs, a low, throaty sound that reverberates through the room. "Vallyn, pretty girl, this isn't a dream," he says, his voice warm, soothing. "But if it were, I'd be dreaming right alongside you. And even though this is real, it feels like a dream—because you're everything I've ever wished for."

Heat rises to my cheeks, and I know I'm blushing, the warmth spreading from my face to the tips of my fingers. "You don't even know me," I whisper, the words almost lost in the space between us.

He moves toward me, closing the distance with an easy stride. His hands find my hips, the weight of them reassuring, as my hand instinctively presses against his chest. I can feel the steady thump of his heart beneath my palm, a rhythm that anchors me to this moment. "Little Lotte," he begins, his voice that deep baritone that seems to resonate through my entire being, pooling electricity at the apex of my thighs, "the first time I saw you, I knew. And just so you know, that was before you saw me. I saw you while we were walking into the bar."

My eyes snap to his, disbelief flickering across my features. "Seriously?"

"Seriously," he echoes, his tone sincere, almost reverent. "Vallyn," he pauses, his thumb brushing a loose strand of hair behind my ear with such tenderness that it makes my breath catch, "it was pure luck that you ended up right in front of me when you did, but I was very aware of you before then."

I swallow, the weight of his words sinking in. Looking down, I'm unable to hold his gaze as I admit the next part. "Gage said you talked about love at first sight."

He takes a deep breath, muttering under his breath, "Fucking Gage." But then his expression softens, his hand tilting my chin up so I have no choice but to meet his eyes. "Yeah, Vallyn, I did say something about that. At least, obsession at first sight. I felt very possessive of you from the second I saw you."

"Protective," I correct, my voice steady even as my heart races.

"Both," he corrects right back, a playful glint in his eyes that makes me smile despite the intensity of the moment.

This time, I don't try to look away. His hands tighten slightly on my hips, pulling me closer, until there's nothing between us but the promise of what could be. The air is thick with unspoken words, the kind that don't need to be said because we both already know. And in that moment, I'm not afraid. I'm not overthinking, not doubting. I'm just here, with him, and for now, that's enough.

His lips brush against my temple, the touch barely there but enough to send shivers down my spine. "If it means anything at all, I have a hard time believing this is real, too," he confesses, his breath warm against my skin. His hand cradles the back of my head, pulling me into the solid warmth of his chest. There's something so disarming about the way he kisses the top of my head, a gentleness that makes my heart ache with a mix of fear and longing.

I can't help but chuckle, a soft, tired sound that seems to come from deep within. "I really am tired," I murmur, the admission feeling like a surrender, not just to the exhaustion but to the strange, undeniable pull between us.

"Okay, pretty girl, let's go to bed," he agrees, his voice a soothing balm against the chaos in my mind. "I'm going to steal your bathroom for a minute though."

I nod, too weary to do anything but comply. "Okay."

# CHAPTER TWENTY-NINE

# PEACEFUL SLEEP

## VALLYN

As soon as he disappears into the bathroom, I move with purpose, filling up my water bottle and heading to my room. The routine of it feels grounding, a small anchor in the whirlwind of emotions that's been building between us. Once in my room, I peel off my leggings with a smirk, a mischievous little act of rebellion. If he's going to hold me, I'm giving him as little between us as possible. There's a part of me that respects his restraint, the way he's drawn clear lines around our physical relationship, but another part—perhaps the darker part—craves more. The denial only fuels my desire, making me ache for him in ways that make me feel both wild and reckless.

I settle under the blankets, the cool sheets a stark contrast to the heat coursing through me. I'm plugging in my phone when he emerges from the bathroom, dressed in gray sweatpants and a green T-shirt. I can't help but smile at that; he did come prepared after all. The sight of him like this, casual and comfortable, sends a rush of warmth through me.

Our eyes meet, and there's a question in his that makes my heart stutter and it must show on my face. "You sure you want me to stay?" he asks, his voice tinged with something that might be concern—or maybe hope.

"As ridiculous as it sounds, I'm as sure as I've ever been about anything," I reply, my voice steady but laced with an undercurrent of something deeper, something that feels like certainty.

His smile is slow, almost cautious, but it reaches his eyes as he crosses the room to the other side of the bed. I've always been a creature of habit, and even though I've rarely shared a bed with anyone, I always sleep on one side, leaving the other half untouched, waiting. As he slides under the covers, it's like some unseen force pulls us together, like magnets drawn by an invisible connection. His arm wraps around me, and my head instinctively finds its place against his chest, where I can hear the steady, reassuring beat of his heart.

Fingers, warm and gentle, begin to comb through my hair, down my back in slow, soothing strokes. His other hand finds my forearm draped across his torso, tracing lazy circles that send a shiver through me, not of cold but of comfort, of a deep-seated peace I didn't know I was searching for. I hitch a leg over his, drawing him closer, needing the contact, the reassurance that this is real. And just like that, the exhaustion that's been weighing on me all night finally catches up, pulling me under with a suddenness that surprises me.

"Thank you," I whisper, the words slipping out before I can think better of it.

His chest rumbles with a silent laugh, vibrating through me. "For what, pretty girl?" he asks, his tone playful yet laced with genuine curiosity.

"For stalking me," I reply, my voice light, teasing, but there's a kernel of truth buried in the joke. Because if he hadn't pursued me, hadn't pushed past my defenses, we wouldn't be here, wrapped up in this strange, intoxicating moment.

He pulls me even closer, his arms tightening around me as he presses another kiss to the top of my head. "You're welcome," he murmurs, and the words, simple as they are, feel like a promise. A promise that, for tonight at least, I'm safe in this cocoon of warmth and quiet, a sanctuary from the storm waiting for me on my phone.

And as sleep finally claims me, I can't help but wonder if maybe, just maybe, this isn't as insane as it feels. Maybe this is exactly where I'm supposed to be.

The room is cloaked in the heavy stillness of pre-dawn when I slowly come to, the world around me wrapped in quiet shadows. We've shifted in our sleep, our bodies finding new ways to intertwine, yet we're still bound together by an invisible thread, his warmth surrounding me like a second skin. I'm the little spoon to his big spoon, nestled into him so completely that I can feel the steady rise and fall of his chest against my back. One of his arms is tucked beneath my head, serving as my pillow, while the other is draped protectively around my waist, his hand resting in front of me.

A sense of safety wraps around me, a rare and precious thing, but the dull ache creeping into my arm tells me I need to move. The last thing I want is to disturb the delicate peace of this moment, but the discomfort in my shoulder becomes too much to ignore. Slowly, deliberately, I roll toward him, burying my face into the solid warmth of his chest. The movement stirs him, and he adjusts instinctively, his hand finding its way down my hair, smoothing it with slow, deliberate strokes that send shivers down my spine. His touch is soft, reverent almost, but then his hand drifts lower, tracing the curve of my back, finding the bare skin just above my waistband where my shirt has ridden up.

My breath hitches, the sensation electric, sparking a chain reaction inside me that I can't control. I feel it—a current, a charge that arcs between us, drawing a soft gasp from my lips. His response is immediate, a sharp inhale that I can feel as much as hear, the sudden tension in his body unmistakable. His chest rises against me, his breath warm and shallow.

My heart races, and I tilt my head up, my eyes searching for his in the dim light. His gaze is already on me, intense and unreadable, his eyes dark with something that makes my pulse quicken. "Hi," I whisper, my voice barely breaking the quiet, yet it feels like the loudest sound in the world.

His lips twitch into a smirk, the kind that sends heat flooding through me. "Hi, pretty girl," he murmurs, his voice rough with sleep, and maybe something more. His fingers brush a stray lock of hair from my face, the touch so tender it's almost painful. "You should go back to sleep."

The words are gentle, but the hand on my back, the fingers that had just traced my skin like he was mapping out something sacred, betray him. "Well, then you should stop touching me like that," I retort, my voice hushed but carrying a challenge, the kind that dares him to act on the tension thrumming between us.

He laughs softly, the sound rumbling through his chest, a quiet acknowledgment of the game we're playing. "Okay, I'll try," he promises, though there's a playful note in his tone that tells me he's not taking it too seriously. He trails his fingers through my hair one last time, a parting caress that makes my heart flutter, and then he presses a quick, soft kiss to the top of my head, the kind of kiss that feels like a secret, just for me. He settles his hand behind my back, his fingers curling possessively against my spine.

Closing my eyes, I burrow my face back into the hollow of his chest, under his chin where the scent of him is intoxicating, something distinctly him. Wrapped up in his warmth, in the comfort of his presence, the world fades away. The tension ebbs, replaced by that same bone-weary exhaustion that I no longer have the strength to fight. His breath is a steady rhythm above me, lulling me back into sleep, the kind of sleep where dreams and reality blur, where his touch lingers even in the darkness behind my eyelids.

When I stir again, the room is bathed in soft daylight, the curtains letting in just enough sun to cast a warm, golden glow over everything. We're still entwined, just as we were when we originally drifted off—his body a solid, comforting presence beneath me, my head cradled on his chest like it's the most natural place in the world. He's awake and the faint glow of his phone screen gives him away. Even before my mind fully surfaces from sleep, I can feel him, feel his awareness of me, the way he's tuned in to my every move, waiting for me to join him in the waking world.

As I blink away the last remnants of sleep, his voice greets me, a low murmur that sends a thrill through my still-sluggish body. "Good morning, pretty girl," he says quietly, his arm tightening around me, pulling me just a little closer as he sets his phone aside.

"Morning," I reply, my voice thick with sleep, as my hand instinctively glides over his chest, tracing the contours beneath the fabric of his shirt. And fuck, this man is built like a fortress. The firm planes of muscle beneath my fingertips are a reminder of the strength he carries, both physically and in the way he holds me, as if nothing in the world could break us apart. "Have you been awake long?"

"Not very long, honestly," he answers, his tone casual, almost lazy, like we have all the time in the world. "But it *is* almost noon."

I push up onto my elbow, looking at him with a mix of disbelief and surprise. "Seriously?" I ask, my voice incredulous. He picks up his phone, holding it out to show me the time. Sure enough, the numbers glare back at me, confirming the absurdity of how late it is. "Well, okay then," I mutter, more to myself than to him, trying to wrap my mind around how I slept this late.

He cups my face in his hand, that familiar gesture that makes my heart race, as if he's about to kiss me. His thumb brushes across my cheekbone, a slow, deliberate caress that sends sparks shooting through me. "I have to go do something with Gage this afternoon," he says, his voice soft, almost regretful, "but we can have brunch or whatever if you want."

Nodding, I rest my cheek back down on his chest, savoring the warmth of his skin. "When do you need to leave?" I ask, not really wanting to know the answer, already dreading the moment when he'll have to walk out the door.

"As long as I meet him by three or so, we're good," he replies then squeezes me closer, like he's trying to make the most of every last minute we have together. "You want to order food or go get something?"

A snicker escapes me, and I lift my head just enough to meet his eyes. "As much as I've given you shit about not just taking me out for coffee, I think I want to order in. Keep you to myself a little while longer."

His laugh is soft, barely more than a breath. "Okay," he agrees, his voice full of that easygoing charm that I've come to crave.

"I have to pee," I admit, my voice a little sheepish, breaking the spell of the moment with the mundane reality of life.

"Well, you should probably go do that," he teases, his lips quirking into that smirk that drives me wild. He loosens his hold on me just enough to let me go, but the warmth of his gaze stays with me, like a promise that when I return, he'll be right here, waiting.

As I slip out of bed, I can't help but glance back at him, at the way he's watching me with that lazy, contented expression, like he could stay here forever and never get bored.

# Chapter Thirty

# New Normal

## PHANTOM

As Vallyn slips out from beneath the sheets, my eyes immediately gravitate to the curve of her bare legs, the soft rise of her hips, and the glimpse of her ass as it peeks from beneath her panties. My breath hitches, and I wonder if she catches the way my gaze follows her when she looks back, but she says nothing, simply strolling towards the closet with a casual grace. Her form is like a siren call, pulling at something primal within me, and even as she steps into the bathroom and closes the door behind her, my mind stays tethered to the sway of her hips, the line of her back.

When she finally returns, slipping back into bed with a relaxed ease, I can't help the smirk that spreads across my face. There's a teasing glint in her eye, something mischievous, and it draws me in even further.

"What?" she asks, feigning innocence.

"Do you always sleep three-quarters naked?" I counter, my voice low, threading through the air between us.

She lies on her side, looking up at me with a lazy, half-hearted shrug. "When it suits the situation." The words are playful, but the twinkle in her eye tells me there's more beneath the surface—games, maybe, but ones I'm more than willing to play.

"You playing games with me, pretty girl?" My voice drops, turning dark, almost a challenge.

She scoffs, her lips curling into a smile that's both amused and defiant. "You've played more than enough games for the both of us."

A laugh rumbles in my chest. "That might be true," I concede. "What do you want for breakfast?"

"Okay, stalker, you know my favorite breakfast order. Annnnnd my coffee order for that matter, so do your stalker thing," she jokes, her tone light, but there's an edge there, a flirtation that hums with her words.

I shake my head, reaching for my phone. Her breakfast order is the last thing I placed, with the exception of dinner last night, so it's easy—too easy. "Alright, breakfast and coffee will be here in about twenty minutes—you know, in case you want to put on pants."

She raises an eyebrow, her expression challenging. "I can just let you answer the door."

The way she throws down the gauntlet, so effortlessly, ignites something in me. I fucking love this side of her—bold, teasing, just a little bit wicked. But she needs to know I can play, too. With a quick, decisive movement, I grab both of her wrists and pin them above her head—her wrists under one of my hands, my grip firm but not harsh. My other hand slides down to her bare thigh as I roll into her, pressing my body against hers, my thigh slipping between her legs. The moment our bodies connect, she grinds against me, her need evident in the way she moves, the way her breath catches.

I watch her eyes darken, the playful gleam giving way to something deeper, hungrier. Her gaze locks onto mine, and I can see the desire swimming there, thick and heady.

*Fuck, I want her.*

I want her so badly it's like a physical ache, a need that pulses through every inch of me.

I lean in, trailing kisses along the curve of her temple, down the line of her jaw, brushing over the sensitive skin of her neck before moving back up to her ear. My breath fans against her skin as I whisper, "Vallyn, pretty girl, I want you. I want you so fucking much. But I don't want you to regret this, to regret me. Just give it some time."

She's trapped beneath me, but that doesn't stop her from tilting her head, her lips finding the skin of my neck. The kiss she places there is rough, hungry—teeth and tongue and heat—and it sends a jolt of electricity straight to my cock. It's all I can do to keep control, to hold back the urge to claim her right here, right now.

"Little Lotte, you're perfect," I murmur against her skin, my voice barely more than a breath. "I promise you won't have to wait forever." With that, I press a soft kiss to her neck, lingering just a moment longer before releasing her wrists and rolling off her, the loss of contact leaving me aching for more.

Our breaths are heavy and uneven, filling the quiet room with a rhythm that feels almost too intimate. She lies next to me, her chest rising and falling in time with mine, eyes fixed on the ceiling as if searching for answers in the plaster above us. The silence stretches, thick and palpable, until finally, she breaks it, her voice softer than I've ever heard it. "I won't regret you."

The words hang in the air between us, delicate yet weighted, like they could shatter with the wrong touch. I turn my head to study her profile, the way her lips part just slightly, the vulnerability in her tone a stark contrast to the confidence she usually wears like armor.

"How do you know that, pretty girl?" My voice comes out rougher than I intend, tinged with something I can't quite place—fear, hope, maybe both.

"I just do," she murmurs, her shoulders lifting in a small shrug, as if that simple motion could dismiss the complexity of what she's saying. "It's been a long time. I don't let guys in—behind my walls—and all I've ever wanted to do is let you in."

Her words hit me like a punch to the gut, and I can't help but think back to the night she first called the cops on me, her reaction like a cold slap in the face. "I think I remember a time when you didn't," I remind her, my tone carrying the memory of that night.

She turns her head slightly, the corner of her mouth twitching in a wry smile. "Even then, I'm pretty sure just a little while later, I was texting you."

I nod, the memory as clear as day. "You did." The room falls into an uneasy quiet, the kind that presses down on your chest, making it hard to breathe. I break it this time, needing to know, needing to understand. "Vallyn, how long *has* it been?"

She scoffs, the sound tinged with self-deprecation. "A little over four years."

The revelation sinks into my bones. "Why?" I ask, the seriousness of the question evident in the way my voice drops, the vulnerability she's showing pulling something similar from me.

Her shrug is small, almost imperceptible, but I see it, feel it. "I've been really busy, but I know it's not just that. I don't know, I've had a few dates, but nobody that I really felt anything for." She turns to face me, our eyes locking, and in that gaze, I see a lifetime of guarded walls and the fear of letting them crumble. "I felt something in the bar that night. If you had hit on me, I'd probably have gone for it, but I also get why you think it would have been a dick move. But then again, the stalking thing was also a dick move." She laughs, the sound lightening the tension just enough to make it bearable.

I can't help but join her in that laughter, the absurdity of our situation hitting me all at once. "I agree, Vallyn," I admit, my voice softening. "I didn't think I'd take it as far as I did. Figured I'd look you up, learn a little about you, but I'm obsessed with you, pretty girl." I pause, swallowing hard, the dryness in my throat making the words stick. "I told you I lost my goddamn mind over you, and I wasn't lying."

She shifts closer, rolling into me, her body warm and inviting despite the cautious tone of our conversation. She's still three-quarters naked, the blanket barely covering her, but all I can focus on is the way she looks at me—like she's found something she didn't even know she was searching for.

Then she admits, "This, last night and this morning, it's been nice. It grounded me in the feelings I've been feeling, and makes me feel a lot less crazy."

Her words wrap around my heart, squeezing tight. "Well, pretty girl, I want to have a lot more time like this," I confess, my voice barely above a whisper. The tension in the room shifts, replaced by something softer, something almost tender.

I glance at my phone, a distraction from the intensity of the moment. "Food will be here in like two minutes." I start to sit up, playfully smacking her ass through the blankets, the light touch a contrast to the heaviness of our conversation. "Put on some pants."

She grins, that playful spark returning to her eyes. "Maybe," she teases, her voice laced with mischief as she shrugs.

She finally slips on a pair of pants, much to my relief, and we settle into brunch spread between us. The conversation flows easily, the kind that feels natural and unforced, filled with light banter and snippets of our lives that we've yet to fully share with each other. It's a moment of normalcy, a brief respite from the intensity that we normally share.

My phone buzzes, breaking the calm, and I glance at the screen—Betty. I shoot Vallyn an apologetic smile as I swipe to answer. "Hey Betty, what's up?"

She jumps right into business, explaining that we've got a contract from one of our regular bondsmen. They've got an informant, and things could move quickly. I nod along, mentally preparing myself for the shift back into work mode. "Thanks for the heads up," I say before hanging up, my mind already beginning to calculate the logistics.

When I turn back to Vallyn, she's watching me, that same soft smile on her lips. There's something comforting in the way she looks at me. "What do you have going on tomorrow, pretty girl? Interviews for your dissertation?"

She nods, tucking a stray piece of hair behind her ear. "Yeah, I'm meeting one of them around ten and the other around two, so I'll be busy most of the day."

"Got it," I say, already thinking about how our schedules will align—or won't. "I may have to fly on a moment's notice in the next couple of days. But after I'm done with Gage this afternoon, you want me to come back here?"

There's a pause, just long enough for me to wonder what she'll say, and then she nods, her voice softening. "If you want, it would be nice to maybe do dinner."

Her answer is simple, but it sends a sense of relief through me that I didn't quite expect. "Okay, I don't know if you want me to stay, since I could have to run in the middle of the night."

"Honestly, I *do* want you to stay," she admits, her tone shifting into something more vulnerable, more honest. "But I know I need some time to decompress with Sasha and my girlfriends, and tomorrow morning I need to be on the top of my game." She flashes me a playful grin. "Even though I clearly slept really well last night," she adds with a laugh that's light and carefree.

"I get that," I say, reaching across the table to brush my fingers against hers. "You can talk to Sasha, and when you're done with your interviews, you can check in with me. Hopefully, I'll be done with this contract, too."

She nods, her eyes meeting mine with a mix of anticipation and understanding. "Okay, so dinner tonight, though, right?"

"Absolutely, dinner tonight," I confirm, my voice firm but gentle. "I'll call you when I'm on my way back."

As the time nears for me to head out to meet with Gage, there's a shift in the air between us—a subtle tension, the kind that comes with the end of something good. But it's not a bad tension; it's more like the anticipation of the reunion.

When I stand to leave, she steps into my space, wrapping her arms around my neck and pulling me close. The hug is warm, familiar, like it's something we've done a hundred times before. She leans up and presses a soft kiss to my cheek, and the gesture feels both surreal and completely natural, all at once.

As I walk out the door, the feeling lingers—a mix of amazement and disbelief that this is happening, that she *is* mine, and it leaves me with a strange, almost ridiculously giddy feeling that I take with me.

# CHAPTER THIRTY-ONE

# GETTING TO KNOW ALL ABOUT YOU

## VALLYN

Watching him walk out of my apartment is like watching a dream slip through my fingers, and I feel a sudden, sharp ache in my chest. It's an unexpected pain and I have to blink quickly to push back the prick of tears threatening to spill over. I didn't expect to feel this way, not so intensely.

A part of me wonders if things would have been different—less complicated, less consuming—if he had just been a regular guy who casually asked me out. But then, the instant attraction was there, undeniable and electric, so maybe it was always meant to be this way, with all the tangled emotions and unspoken words.

I shake my head, trying to dispel the thoughts, and reach for my phone to call Sasha. She answers on the second ring, her voice sharp with concern, cutting through my haze.

"Vallyn, what the fuck?" she snaps, and I can practically hear the worry dripping from her words.

"Well, hi to you too," I retort, trying to inject some levity into my tone, but it comes out a little strained.

"We were so fucking worried about you," she continues, her voice softening, but the edge of worry is still there, clear as day.

"I'm fine, better than fine, really," I reply, letting out a small sigh of relief. "He is good, we're good, he stayed the night and I'm still alive."

"He stayed the night?" she repeats, her voice dropping to a whisper, as if saying it too loud might shatter something delicate.

"Yeah, and no, nothing happened. We just talked and cuddled, that's it," I explain, a small smile tugging at my lips. "He said something about not wanting me to regret it, so he won't do anything more physical yet."

"Why was Corey so freaked out if you're fine?" she asks, her voice laced with confusion.

"I don't know, probably because he wants you to be on his side of his crazy-ass delusions," I reply, a hint of the sass my phantom has come to love sneaking into my tone. "He didn't even threaten him. He stared at him, stepped up a little, but he didn't even talk to Corey. He was just... here."

"He said he was at the park, too," she adds, her voice full of curiosity.

"He was," I admit, feeling a small shiver of something—excitement, fear, I'm not sure—run down my spine. "He surprised me there."

"Is that why you looked like a ghost?" she asks, concern coloring her voice.

"Yeah, I'm sure it is. Sasha, I'm fine. I promise, we're good. You can even meet him sometime soon, I'm sure," I assure her, trying to soothe the worry I know she's still holding on to.

"What's his name?" she asks, the question hanging in the air between us, loaded with all the normalcy this situation lacks.

Laughing, I respond, "That's the only thing he hasn't told me. I have his real phone number now, though, and my uncle knows his name, so..." My voice trails off as I realize how absurd it sounds when I say it out loud.

"Vallyn, seriously?" Her tone is incredulous, almost disbelieving.

"Seriously," I confirm, though I can't help but laugh at the ridiculousness of it all. "But it's okay, it's like the last piece of him he's holding on to, besides y'know his dick," I add with a laugh, and the sound of her laughter on the other end makes something inside me unclench, the tension easing just a little.

"You're really okay?" she asks, her voice softening, the concern still there but less urgent now.

"Yeah, I'm really okay, better than okay, actually," I say, a genuine smile spreading across my face as I realize it's the truth. Despite everything, or maybe because of it, I feel more at peace than I have in a long time.

"Can we do lunch tomorrow?" Sasha asks, and there's a note of hope in her voice that makes me wish I could say yes.

"Not tomorrow," I reply, a touch of regret in my voice. "I have those interviews with Zay's and Kiara's older brothers. But maybe the day after?"

"Yeah, that works for me," she agrees. "Just me, or the girls?" she asks, her voice tinged with curiosity.

"Either, really. If they're worried about me, then sure, they can come," I reply, trying to keep things casual.

"Okay, I'm glad to hear your voice, Val. I'll talk to you soon," she says, the relief in her voice palpable.

We say our goodbyes, and as the call ends, I feel the weight of the last twenty-four hours settling over me. It's not a heavy weight, not anymore, but it's there, a reminder of everything that's happened and everything that's yet to come.

I decide to take a shower, hoping the warm water will wash away the lingering tension in my muscles, calm the overstimulation that's been buzzing through me since I walked in my door yesterday. The sound of the water is a soothing backdrop as I step into the shower, letting the steam envelop me, and I close my eyes, letting myself relax, if only for a few precious moments.

Even though I know it's probably a bit futile, I find myself slipping into nice underwear—black lace that feels indulgent against my skin—and a pair of flattering shorts that cling just right. I top it off with a soft, fitted tank, something casual but undeniably tempting. He mentioned the possibility of going out for dinner, but there's a part of me that selfishly wants to keep him all to myself tonight, to wrap us in the intimacy of my apartment where the outside world can't intrude.

The timing is perfect; as soon as I'm finished getting dressed, my phone buzzes in my hand, and his name lights up the screen. My hair is still damp from the shower, clinging in loose waves around my shoulders, but otherwise, I'm ready.

"Hey," I answer, my voice warm, a little breathless.

"Hi, pretty girl," he replies, and just hearing that familiar rasp in his voice makes my heart skip. "You still want to have dinner?"

"Of course I do," I respond, letting a hint of flirtation color my tone, imagining the way he's probably smirking on the other end of the line.

"Order in or out?" he asks.

"I want to keep you to myself," I admit, the words slipping out before I can second-guess them.

He chuckles, a low, almost dangerous sound that makes my pulse quicken. "Okay, Little Lotte, I'll see you soon."

True to his word, about thirty minutes later, there's a knock at my door, and it throws me off balance for a second. He never knocks.

"You're not supposed to knock," I say as I pull the door open, a teasing smile on my lips. My eyes drop to the bottle of wine he's holding, and I can't help the grin that spreads across my face.

"Oh, I'm not, huh?" he replies, an eyebrow rising in amusement.

"No, it's weird, and seriously, you should just have a key," I laugh, the sound light, almost carefree, as if we're already living in that fantasy he envisioned from the beginning.

He shakes his head, a smile playing on his lips, but he doesn't argue with me. Instead, he steps inside, the door clicking shut behind him, sealing us in our own little world.

Before long, we're snuggled up on the couch, just like we were last night, our bodies naturally falling into the same rhythm, the same closeness. His arm is draped around my shoulders, pulling me into him, while his other hand scrolls through food options on his phone. It doesn't take long for us to settle on something and place the order, the ease between us so natural, it's almost unsettling.

"What were you doing with Gage? Or can you not tell me?" I ask, my curiosity getting the better of me as I tilt my head up to look at him.

"He had new body cams for us, for when we're out and he's in the van, so he has better resolution or whatever. I don't know, he was excited about it," he answers with a chuckle, the sound warm and rich.

"You still might have to bounce at any second?" I ask, trying to keep the disappointment out of my voice.

"Yeah, unfortunately," he admits, his tone regretful, "but hopefully by tomorrow night we'll be good. Maybe tomorrow night I can take you out on a real date."

"Hey now, don't go saying crazy things," I tease, though there's a flicker of hope in my chest that I can't quite tamp down. "But that would be nice."

"Maybe someday this will feel normal between us," he jokes, though there's an undercurrent of sincerity in his words that makes my heart ache.

"It does feel normal in a lot of ways, but your name might help," I suggest playfully, trying to lighten the mood, though the truth of it hangs between us like a question waiting to be answered.

"Soon, pretty girl," he promises, flashing me that smile that always makes me weak in the knees.

Dinner arrives, and as we eat, the conversation flows easily, dipping into more personal territory as the night goes on. He tells me about his sister and his parents, painting a picture of his life that feels so normal. I share stories about Quintin and my parents, the warmth of those memories mixing with the new warmth I'm building with him. It feels less like a casual night in and more like a second date, the kind where you start to peel back the layers, revealing more of who you are, daring to let the other person see.

Eventually, he decides it's time to leave, insisting I need my sleep to be ready for the interviews tomorrow. With a quick, tender kiss to my forehead, he's gone, the door closing softly behind him, leaving the space feeling a little emptier, a little colder.

When I finally lie down, I think the whirlwind of the night will keep me awake, that I'll be left tossing and turning, replaying every word, every touch. But the exhaustion catches up with me, pulling me under, and before I know it, sleep takes over. The last thing I think of is the feeling of his lips on my forehead, a ghostly imprint that lingers even as the sunlight begins to flood my bedroom, waking me to a new day.

# CHAPTER THIRTY-TWO

# SUCH A PERFECT DAY

## PHANTOM

As soon as I'm awake, the first thing I do is grab my phone, my fingers tapping out a message to Vallyn before my thoughts even fully form.

> Good morning, pretty girl, I hope you have a perfect day

I hit send, and my heart does that annoying little jump it's been doing ever since last night. It doesn't take long for her reply to buzz back.

> Good morning, and thank you, go catch bad guys so I can see you tonight

Her words bring a smile to my face, the kind that lingers even as I stretch and roll out of bed.

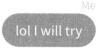

Her next message comes just as I'm stepping into the shower.

The warmth that spreads through me at her response is more than I expected, but I don't have time to dwell on it.

After a hot shower, I make my way to the office where Casen and Gage are already waiting. The air is thick with the anticipation of a hunt. Our informant had eyes on the guy earlier, but there's been no confirmation that he's still holed up in the house. Patience is a virtue—even when it's grating on every nerve.

I lean back in my chair, casting a glance at Gage, who's scrolling through his phone with that ever-present smirk of his. "Vallyn told me her girlfriends think you're cute," I tease, breaking the silence. "I bet we could have a double date or something."

He raises an eyebrow, the smirk only deepening. "You know what I'm going to say," he says knowingly, and I do. Gage is... particular when it comes to women, and while I respect it, I can't help but wonder how long it takes to find someone who meets his needs.

"Who knows, maybe one of them is what you're looking for," I counter with a grin, taking a sip of water as if this conversation isn't about to get us both ribbed by Casen.

Before he can respond, Betty's voice slices through the quiet, yelling from the front of the office. "Boys, informant is on the line!"

Casen picks up his phone, and I can practically see his brain clicking into overdrive as he scribbles down an address. Less than a minute later, we're out the door, the quiet morning replaced with the adrenaline-fueled rush of a chase.

As Casen drives, Gage fills us in on the details. But half my mind is elsewhere, stuck on Vallyn and the promise of tonight. I just want this done, the mark caught, so I can see her without this hanging over my head. The thought of leaving her in the middle of the night to chase some asshole across the state isn't exactly appealing.

Casen and I start suiting up—Kevlar, weapons, the usual drill. Our informant has the mark holed up in some dive of a restaurant. It's an enclosed, public space, so we go light—handguns only. We've done this enough times that it isn't necessary to discuss that. We move in sync, a well-oiled machine honed by years of experience.

Gage spots the two lookouts as we pull onto the block, their stance giving them away even before we see their faces. He swings the van into an alley, out of sight, and we exit quietly. Casen slips into the rear entrance, warning the staff, who start moving the front crew to the kitchen and then out the back. They also inform us that the only people left inside are a single group "of about five people," they're all together.

We don't have the luxury of interior cameras, so we're going in blind, but that's never stopped us before. Casen nods at me, and we move. Gage is positioned at the back door, ready to breach, while

Casen and I make our way to the front. The second the lookouts spot Casen's Kevlar with the bold "Bond Agent" lettering, they panic, weapons flashing in their hands.

"Drop the weapons, on the fucking ground now!" Casen's voice is a whip crack in the tense air, and they comply, their youth betraying them. They're kids, probably not even old enough to vote, but here they are, playing gangster. Casen secures them as I turn the corner into the restaurant, Gage at the back—we breach the dining room at the same time.

The mark is there, his recognizable tattooed arm and buzzed head unmistakable. I shout his name, identifying myself as a bond agent, my gun trained on him. The room is a mess of bodies—at least six men, all armed. Gage has his gun leveled at the two closest to him. My eyes sweep the room, taking in the scene, assessing the threat, when suddenly, everything freezes.

*Vallyn.*

She's here. In the restaurant. She was sitting at the same table as the mark. But now she's on her feet, caught between Gage and me as everyone else rises from their seats, too. My heart slams against my ribs, the adrenaline that's supposed to keep me sharp and focused turning into a cold, paralyzing dread. I've been through hell and back—flashbangs, live rounds, bombs too close for comfort—but nothing has ever made me freeze like this.

My gun stays locked on the mark, but my mind is clouded, foggy with fear—fear for her. Casen bursts into the restaurant, but because I'm not doing my job, he doesn't see the guy right by the door. He's disarmed before I can even react.

*Fuck. This. Shit.*

"Vallyn!" I yell, my voice sharp, desperate. "Get the fuck over here!" But I realize almost instantly it's the wrong move. The men who hadn't already drawn their guns do so now, three of them pointing their weapons directly at her.

"You a fucking narc?" The mark sneers at Vallyn, raising his hands as he backs away from the table. He nods to his men, and he and two others are flying out the front door, moving behind the guy that has a gun trained on Casen, leaving behind chaos.

My gun swings between the guy aiming at Vallyn and the one who has Casen in his sights. My ears ring with the sound of my pulse, my heart pounding in my chest like a drum of war. I don't give a fuck about losing the mark right now; the only thing that matters is the three people I care about the most in this goddamn world have fucking guns pointed at them.

I force myself to take a deep breath, trying to slow my racing thoughts. In moments like these, a calm mind can mean the difference between life and death. Even though everything around me is moving at breakneck speed, I need that second to think clearly, to act.

There's shouting all around—Vallyn's voice, trembling, denying she's told anyone anything. Gage's voice, commanding, trying to keep the situation from spiraling out of control. Casen's silence is the most unnerving—he's hurt, I don't know how badly, but he's not moving, and that terrifies me.

Tears streak down Vallyn's face as she pleads with them, her voice cracking, raw with fear. The man in front of her shifts his grip, adjusting his aim, and I see his finger twitch on the trigger. Time slows to a crawl as I realize what's about to happen.

*I don't think. I just react.*

My gun fires, the sound deafening in the enclosed space. Three more shots ring out in quick succession, blending into one another as if the whole world is collapsing in on itself. In the distance, I hear the wail of sirens, but they're just background noise to the chaos unraveling around me.

I don't know who fired. I don't know if everyone's still standing. All I know is that Vallyn is in the middle of it all, and I'm praying to whatever god is listening that she's okay.

# INTERLUDE

# GAGE

I see Vallyn before he does, and my gut twists with a sickening certainty—this is about to go downhill and sideways fast. The tension thickens like a storm rolling in, suffocating the air around us. There are too many of them, and with her in the mix, everything spirals into chaos. My eyes lock onto his face the moment he spots her, and I know he's already lost his edge, his fine-tuned game slipping through his fingers.

When he yells at her, it's like watching a slow-motion car crash. I feel it in my bones, the wrongness of it. He shouldn't have done that. If they were protective of her—and they might have been—we could've had a chance, a way out. Her presence could've been our saving grace, maybe a smoother exit, but the second they see we recognize her, it's over. They think she's a rat, an informant, and that's the kind of thinking that almost always leaves bodies in its wake.

My gun stays steady, aimed at the nearest threat, but my senses are on high alert, tracking every movement behind him. When the mark bolts, my mind spirals some—this mission is already circling the drain. But our survival trumps everything, and when he takes two of them with him, the odds shift slightly in our favor.

But Casen—Casen isn't moving. I watched them disarm him, saw it happen in real time, but nothing about it looked deadly, or even harmful. Yet there he is, slumped against the doorframe, a lifelessness clinging to him that makes my blood run cold. One of them still has a gun trained on him, ready to finish the job.

I catch sight of the guy aiming at Vallyn, his focus narrowing in as he steadies his hand. The gunshot reverberates through my skull as he crumples and falls, and before I can process it, my body reacts, instinct taking over. The man in front of me hesitates, glancing back, and I don't waste the opening—I pull the trigger. He drops, but

there's no time to breathe because another shot cracks the air, aimed
at Casen. My legs propel me forward, my left arm wrapping around
Vallyn's waist, dragging her with me as I fire at the last guy, dropping
him as he turns his gun on Vallyn and me.

Two down by my hand. They're dead, they were clean headshots
so I know it, but Casen—his chest is still rising and falling. I leave
Vallyn against the wall, her body trembling as she clutches herself,
and I clear the front of the restaurant. Blue and red lights strobe down
the street outside, the wail of sirens approaching.

I tap into the dispatch line, my voice calm, but the adrenaline
pumps hard through my veins. "We need ambulances, multiple
down. I believe the scene inside is secure." When I turn back, Vallyn
hasn't moved, tears carving rivers down her cheeks, arms hugging
herself like she might fall apart at any second.

I'm still at the door, every muscle coiled, ready for anything,
because there are still three more of them out there, plus the two
lookouts who've gone ghost. "Blake!" I shout, urgency cracking
through. "Check on Casen, fuck, man!"

He snaps out of whatever trance he's in, his eyes wide with
realization. He's at Casen's side in a heartbeat, ripping off the kevlar,
hands shaking as he assesses the damage. "Fuck," he curses, the word
heavy with fear. "He's got two wounds—fuck, I think they stabbed
him when they disarmed him."

The uniforms flood in, their expressions a mix of shock and grim
determination. Part of me detaches, thinking about the mountain of
paperwork, the hours we could be trapped at the station, reliving
this nightmare in painstaking detail. As the paramedics descend on
Casen, Blake stands and steps aside, wiping his blood smeared hands
across his jeans. He turns to Vallyn.

"Blake?" Vallyn's voice is a broken whisper, raw from crying.

"Vallyn," he breathes out.

And in those single words, just their names, I see it—this moment
will scar and bond them both in ways they may never fully recover

from. The world has changed for them, irrevocably, and nothing will
ever be the same.

# PART TWO

# CHAPTER THIRTY-THREE

# THE CHAOS

## VALLYN

T he ringing in my ears is relentless, a high-pitched scream that drowns out everything else, and yet somehow, I hear Gage yell his name—*Blake*. The sound cuts through the chaos like a knife, and for a moment, I wonder if I'm still in shock, still unable to fully comprehend what is happening. But the name registers, slicing through the fog in my brain, grounding me in the horrifying reality of the situation.

The day had started off so well, so normal. I'd met with Marcus earlier, and the interview had been more productive than I could have hoped. We talked, connected, and I felt a sense of accomplishment as I left, thinking that maybe things were falling into place to finish my dissertation. I grabbed a quick lunch in my car, enjoying the solitude before heading to meet Eli. It was supposed to be just another interview, just another step in my carefully planned day.

Eli had been polite, engaging even, and I'd spent a good forty-five minutes talking with him and his friends. They answered my questions with surprising honesty, giving me insight into a world so different from Marcus's. I was learning, piecing together the puzzle, and for a while, it felt like I was doing something meaningful.

But then everything changed.

As if them storming into the restaurant, weapons drawn wasn't enough, I saw it—the shift in Eli's expression when he heard my name. The way suspicion and accusation darkened his features, turning the atmosphere heavy and dangerous in an instant. And I froze. My body locked up, my mind going blank as fear surged through me like ice water. I couldn't move, couldn't think, couldn't even scream. I stammered out a defense, but mostly I was just... there, trapped in the moment as it all went to hell.

I didn't even know Gage was in the room until after he moved me, his hand and arm rough and urgent as he pulled me to safety. His gun had been so close to me when he fired that I not only heard the deafening crack, but felt the recoil reverberate through his body, through mine. The shock of it still vibrates through me, even as I stand here, trying to make sense of the carnage.

And now, my phantom—*Blake*—is standing in front of me, covered in blood. His bulletproof vest is still in place, but his eyes... his eyes are wild, haunted, like he's grappling with demons he can't shake off. He wants to hold me, I can see it in the way he hesitates, his hands hovering, but then he looks down at those same hands, stained with wet blood, and he pulls back. The distance between us feels like a chasm, impossible to cross.

I barely register Gage's voice as he talks on the phone, the words slipping in and out of focus. "Hey Jeremy," he says, pausing briefly. "Yeah, not so good. Listen, Vallyn was just in the middle of a bond pickup that went really fucking wrong." Another pause. "Physically, yes, Casen was hurt though." Then he rattles off the name of the restaurant, the location of the nightmare we're trapped in.

He looks at me and Blake—*Blake*, his name echoes in my mind, but it feels foreign, like it belongs to someone else, someone I can't quite reconcile with the man in front of me—and says, "Your uncle is on his way." His tone is soft, meant to comfort, but there's a gravity to it that makes my stomach twist. "We're all going to be here for a while, and you may need a support system that understands what's happening."

I can only nod, my eyes drifting from Gage to Blake, and back again. The weight of the situation presses down on me, making it hard to breathe, hard to think. Paramedics swarm around us, checking on the other men—Eli's friends—confirming what I already know deep down. They're dead. I watched them die, watched the life drain out of them as the gunshots rang out, all three of them shot in the head, a testament to both of these men's skills. Casen is being loaded into an ambulance, his fate still uncertain, but the others... they're gone. They check the three of us, make sure we're not physically injured. I'm not, but mentally... mentally I'm not okay.

The torment on Blake's face is etched deep, and I know that neither of us has the strength to help the other at this exact moment. I've never seen anyone die before today, and now I've seen too much, too quickly. The images are seared into my mind, and I can't shake the feeling of those guns pointed at me, the lethal metal, the threat of death hanging so close.

Officers move in, taking Blake's and Gage's guns, along with the weapons from the dead men. It's all so methodical, so clinical—they have clearly done this too many times before. It feels surreal, like I'm watching it happen from outside my own body.

The officers finally lead me out to the front of the restaurant, away from the scene, but I can still feel the weight of it, pressing down on me like a suffocating blanket. They question me, their voices distant, telling me I might need to go to the station later, but they'll let me know. Their words barely register—I'm too numb, too lost in the aftermath.

And then, finally, my uncle arrives. The sight of him makes my knees nearly buckle with relief. I've never been so happy to see him in my life. He had to walk in from a block away because the street is blocked, but they know him, and let him through the barricade on foot. He wraps his arms around me, pulling me into his chest, and I bury my face against him, letting out a sob I didn't even know I was holding in. His embrace is strong, protective, and I cling to him like a lifeline, the dam finally breaking as I let myself cry.

I don't know if he's ever hugged me like this before—even as a young child, with so much intensity, so much understanding, but it's exactly what I need right now. In his arms, I feel a small measure of safety, a tiny refuge in the storm of visions that are still raging in my mind. I sob against his chest, the tears hot and unrelenting, and he just holds me. For the first time since this nightmare began, I allow myself to let the fear, the grief, the shock wash over me. And in his arms, I let go.

Through my foggy, tear-filled eyes, I spot Blake, still deep in conversation with the officers and detectives, his posture tense, every line of his body radiating exhaustion. Gage, however, breaks away from the scene and makes his way toward us. I don't turn to him as he begins explaining to my uncle what happened. I catch snippets of his words, fragmented pieces of a story that's still too raw, too close. He talks about how Blake froze, how my sudden appearance threw him off in a way that has never happened before. There's something unsettling about hearing that Blake, my phantom, was shaken by my presence, that I have the power to unravel him.

Gage's voice lowers as he recounts the details—how they believe Casen was stabbed before being shot, how he was conscious when they loaded him into the ambulance. He lays out the sequence of events, the reasons behind the gunfire, the chaos that followed.

"So this has nothing to do with Vallyn and Blake together? This was all coincidental?" my uncle asks, his voice tight with concern.

"Completely," Gage confirms, his tone steady. "If we had interior cameras or even decent exterior ones, we would have known she was here, but we didn't."

"Or if he still had spyware on my phone," I rasp, my voice rough from the shock and strain, and then a dark laugh bubbles up from my throat, a little manic, a little wild. "Then he would have known where I was meeting them."

Gage and my uncle exchange a look, one that speaks volumes. I'm right—it's wrong for Blake to have that kind of oversight on me, but in this twisted scenario, it might have prevented this whole disaster. When I look back at Blake, he's still tormented, his eyes searching for mine every few seconds, longing to be close to me, to decompress with me. But the reality is that he's still embroiled in this mess, still talking to officers, still locked in a situation neither of us can escape just yet.

"You gonna have to go to the station?" my uncle asks Gage.

Shaking his head, Gage responds, "We don't know yet."

"If you need to go, I'll go with you," my uncle says, addressing me directly now that I'm a little more composed. "You've never had to do this before. Why were you even here?"

I scoff, the sound bitter in the back of my throat. "I was interviewing their mark for my dissertation."

"I think Blake assumed you were doing it at the youth center," Gage interjects gently, his voice tinged with concern.

"No, because they're active in their gangs, I wanted to be in gang-neutral territory," I explain, the words coming out more sharply than I intend. "He brought more people with him than my last one, which was just a few blocks away."

"He probably brought more people because he skipped bail," Gage points out, his tone calm, factual.

"I didn't know, obviously," I say, though there's an edge to my voice, a defensive note I can't quite shake.

"Obviously," Gage echoes, his voice softening.

As we talk, my eyes drift back to Blake, who's finally ripping at the velcro on his vest, his movements sharp and agitated. Someone with the ambulance offers him some wipes, and as he starts to clean his hands, his eyes find mine again and again, a silent plea written in them. I can see it in the way his shoulders sag, in the way he looks at me—he's just as shaken as I am, just as stunned to find himself—or me—in this situation. The weight of everything hangs heavy between us; he saved my life at the potential cost of his friend's, and I can't even begin to untangle the emotions that realization stirs in me.

But I know one thing—I need him. Right now, in this moment, I need to feel him, to know that he's real and here with me. As soon as he tosses the wipes aside, blood still staining his hands and starts walking my way, I move toward him, fast but not running. I slam into him, my arms wrapping tightly around his waist, my cheek pressing against his chest, sweat-soaked shirt and all. The second his arms close around me, I break down again, the remaining sobs I've been trying to hold back tearing free again, shaking my whole body.

I vaguely hear my uncle greet him. He releases me with one arm to shake his hand before embracing me fully again. "Thanks for coming," Blake says, his voice rough with emotion.

I have no clue what my uncle thinks about me being wrapped up in my phantom like this, and frankly, I don't care. Right now, he is all I need. We're standing outside in the blistering heat, the sun beating down relentlessly, but at least we're in the shade. Together, we're covered in sweat, tears, and blood—this tangled mess of emotion and violence—but in his arms, I feel a flurry of something solid, something that might just hold me together.

The three of them continue talking, their voices a low murmur in the background, but I tune most of it out, lost in the steady beat of Blake's heart beneath my ear. I catch bits and pieces—Blake saying, "They aren't going to make us go to the station right now. Gage and I need to go to the hospital, can you take her home?"

My uncle responds quickly, "Yeah, is she going to be safe at home?"

"Does he know where you live?" Gage asks, his voice sharp with concern.

I shake my head, not trusting my voice at first, and then manage to whisper, "No, he doesn't even know my last name, his little sister doesn't either."

Gage nods, the tension in his shoulders easing just slightly. "Good."

Blake's grip on me tightens for a moment, and I know he's trying to reassure himself as much as me. As much as I want to cling to him, I know he needs to go, to deal with everything that's happened, to check on his friend. But the thought of letting him go, even for a few hours, sends a spike of fear through me. It's irrational, I know, but after everything, the idea of being apart feels unbearable.

"Go with Gage," I murmur, lifting my head to look up at him. "I'll be okay with my uncle."

Blake looks down at me, his eyes softening for a moment before he nods. "I'll come to you as soon as I can," he promises, and I can see in his eyes that he means it, that he needs it as much as I do.

With one last squeeze, he releases me, and I force myself to step back, to let him go. As he and Gage head toward their panel van, my uncle wraps an arm around my shoulders, guiding me toward his car. I'm still shaky, still trying to process everything, but there's a strange calm settling over me now, the adrenaline finally beginning to fade.

As we drive away, I can't help but glance back, watching the scene as it disappears from view. I don't know what comes next, don't know how we move forward from here, but I know one thing for sure—even though I'll never be the same, I can't let this break me—break us.

# Chapter Thirty-Four

# The Hospital

## BLAKE

The hospital is a blur of sterile hallways and cold, clinical light as Gage and I rush in. Reality hits us a little like a sledgehammer when we find out Casen is already in surgery. The words hang in the air, heavy and suffocating, but at least they are working on him.

Gage immediately springs into business mode, his calm efficiency a stark contrast to the chaos currently spinning in my mind. He starts making the calls, his voice steady as he informs Betty, Casen's parents, his sister, and then our lawyer. Each conversation is empathetic, but short and clipped, the weight of the situation palpable through the phone, even from where I'm sitting.

As fucked up as it is, Casen getting shot we know somehow justifies everything that went down. In some twisted way, it means our actions won't be questioned as deeply, that we did what we had to do. We'll step back, let the police do their thing, put ourselves on a sort of administrative leave like any law enforcement officer would be on if they were in our position. But the thought doesn't bring any comfort. Instead, it leaves a bitter taste in my mouth, one that only deepens as I watch Gage finish his last call.

When he finally hangs up after explaining everything to our lawyer, I turn to him, my voice thick with gratitude and something else—something darker. "Thank you," I say, meaning it with every fiber of my being. But the words that follow are heavier, laced with regret. "And I'm sorry." I let out a heavy sigh, the weight of the day crashing down on me. "I know I froze. Fuck, Gage, I've taken live fire while trying to take down a terrorist holding a baby as a human shield, and I didn't freeze."

"I know," he says, his voice steady, reassuring. "I know you were thrown off your game. I know that you were shocked to see her there. The informant didn't say anything about a woman at all—neither did the staff. We had no cameras."

I shake my head, the reality of it all sinking in. "Gage, you probably saved both Casen's and her life, so thank you." The words feel like they're made of lead, heavy and unyielding, and I can barely get them out.

Trying to lighten the mood, his voice is tinged with that dry humor he always uses to defuse tension. "It's a good thing that I'm not '*just*' a tech guy," he says with a small smile. "Also, I don't know if it was just the adrenaline, but Vallyn felt tiny when I moved her."

I laugh, but it's a hollow sound, lacking any real joy. "She's not exactly tiny, but yeah. I can't believe she was fucking there. This feels like a nightmare, Gage." My voice dips back into seriousness as I scrub my face with my hands, trying to wipe away the fatigue and the guilt.

"I know," Gage murmurs, and as I rest my elbows on my knees, he pats my back, a small gesture that feels like it is meant to keep me grounded right now. "And sorry I gave her your name, too, man."

"Honestly, that's the least of my concerns," I admit, shaking my head. "I know it hit her, though. I think we're beyond games now. Frankly, we were before shit went wrong today."

"Well, the way she collapsed into you, I'm pretty sure she feels the same," Gage observes, his hand still on my back, offering silent support.

I let out a long sigh, the kind that seems to come from the very depths of my soul. "I just need Casen to be okay."

"You and me both," he agrees, and in that moment, the weight of our unspoken fears hangs between us, heavy and inescapable. We sit there in silence, the beeping of machines and the muffled sounds of people bustling around the hospital fading into the background as we wait for news—any news—that Casen is going to pull through.

Eventually, the waiting room fills with more people—Betty, Casen's parents, his sister. The unnatural, fluorescent-lit space feels like it's closing in around me. The weight of the unspoken fears of everyone hangs thick in the air. We're just holding vigil, a group bound together by anxiety and hope, waiting for any word, any sign that Casen is going to be okay.

When the news finally comes, it's like a lifeline thrown into a churning sea. The surgeon steps into the room, his face calm, professional, and my heart clenches as I wait for him to speak. "He's out of surgery," the doctor says, and I can hear the collective breath we all release, a sound of tentative relief. "He had one stab wound and one gunshot wound, but we were able to repair the damage. He's awake and in post-op." He then explains in more detail about the wounds and infection risks, focusing his words on Casen's parents.

The relief is palpable, but it doesn't erase the guilt that clings to me like a second skin. We'll let his family see him first; that's the right thing to do. Gage and I hang back, giving them their moment, but every minute feels like an eternity.

When Casen's parents return, they look reassured, and as Gage is talking to them, their tone is lighter. The tension in me starts to ease. But that anchor of guilt still weighs me down, even as I'm grateful beyond words that Casen is going to be okay.

Finally, it's our turn. I let Gage go in first, hesitating, trying to gather my thoughts. But when I finally walk in and see Casen lying there, propped up in the hospital bed, something inside me releases, and I feel like I'm exhaling for the first time in hours.

"Hey, man," I say, my voice thick with emotion I can't quite hide.

Casen gives me a half-smile, his expression tired but relieved. "I caught up to you now," he says, and there's a dark humor in his tone that almost makes me laugh.

I know exactly what he means. I've been shot four times before; this makes four for him. "I guess we both have five lives left," I respond, trying to match his levity, but the words feel heavy, like they're pulling me down.

Casen's eyes narrow slightly, and then he asks, "So, that was Vallyn?"

"Yeah," I nod, the weight of the situation settling on my shoulders once more, my tone resigned.

"Why was she there?" His question is simple, but it slices through me like a knife.

I let out a long breath. "She was interviewing him for her dissertation. She didn't know he had skipped bail. She told me the person she was interviewing had been arrested and was out, but she didn't know he was out on bail. I thought she was interviewing him at the youth center, where all her other interviews had been." My words spill out in a rush, too fast, too much, and I know I'm probably over-explaining, but I can't seem to stop.

Casen shakes his head, processing it all, and Gage chimes in, his voice again laced with that dry wit again. "You know, she actually half-joked about how if you hadn't taken the spyware off her phone, you would've known she was there."

My head snaps up, my eyes locking onto Gage's. He shrugs, like it's nothing, but the reality of that hits me like a punch to the gut. Then we both turn back to Casen, and the guilt that's been simmering beneath the surface crashes over me in full force.

"I'm so fucking sorry, man," I say, my voice cracking under the weight of it all.

Casen shakes his head, his expression calm, almost too calm. "Don't. We all know the risks when we walk into those situations. I had no clue there were so many of them inside. I figured you and Gage would have had that well under control. I'm just glad that kid didn't have better aim."

Gage laughs, the sound unexpected and jarring, but there's something grounding about it, something that pulls me out of my spiraling thoughts. "He was standing close enough to you, his aim had to be really bad, although he did manage to miss the vest."

Casen smirks, the corners of his mouth twitching up. "I think he was actually aiming at my chest. Maybe he didn't want to kill me."

Gage's voice cuts through the tension like a knife, blunt and to the point. "Well, we'll never know because he is definitely dead."

The words hang in the air, a reminder of just how intense everything we went through was. I glance between Casen and Gage, feeling the weight of everything that's happened pressing down on me. But for now, at least, we're all still standing—or, in Casen's case, lying—but alive. And that's something I can hold onto, even as the guilt and the what-ifs swirl around in my mind, refusing to let go.

Gage and I exchange a final, silent nod before we step back, so we can let Casen's family back in to take our place. The heaviness of the moment presses down on us, so we mutter our goodbyes and slip away, the tension still coiled tight in my chest.

My instinct screams at me to run straight to Vallyn, to feel her warmth and hear her voice, but the stink of sweat and blood clings to me—I have to shower and put on clean clothes first.

As soon as Gage drops me off at my condo, I waste no time. The door barely closes behind me before I pull out my phone, my fingers finding Vallyn's number on autopilot. The line rings once before she picks up.

"Hey," she answers, but there's a slight edge to her voice, a hesitation that's far too familiar. It's the same guarded tone she had when she discovered the cameras I'd planted in her house—wary, unsure.

"Hey, pretty girl," I respond, but my voice betrays me, heavy with the emotion still churning inside. I can't hide it, not from her.

"How's Casen?" she asks, concern lacing her words.

"He'll be okay, I think," I reply, my throat tight with the weight of everything left unsaid. "He is out of surgery and we were able to talk to him." The words come out thick, laden with emotions I'm not ready to unpack yet.

"And you?" she presses gently, her voice wrapping around me like a soothing fog.

I let out a breath. "Still covered in sweat and blood," I say with a dark chuckle. "Just got back to my place. I need to shower and change. Your doors locked?"

"Yeah, and the chain," she answers softly, the fragility in her voice slicing through me.

"You doing okay?" I ask, though the answer seems obvious.

She pauses, and I can almost hear the wheels turning in her head before she speaks. "It's a lot, a lot to process, but yeah." A small, tired laugh slips through the phone. "I think I'm just really fucking exhausted."

"You should sleep, pretty girl," I suggest, my voice dropping to a soothing tone, as if I can coax her into rest through sheer will.

"I need to shower, too," she admits. "My uncle is still here, but I probably should sleep if I can. Will I see you tonight?"

"Probably, Little Lotte," I say, using her moniker in a way that's meant to comfort even though there's uncertainty in my voice. "But I'm not positive. I might have to go back to the hospital; I need to check in with Gage first."

"Okay," she responds, her voice soft, almost too quiet, but it's enough to hold onto in this moment.

We talk for a few minutes more. Eventually, though, I know I have to let her go. "Get some rest, pretty girl," I murmur, even as the weight of the day threatens to pull me under. "I'll talk to you soon."

When the call ends, the silence in my condo presses in on me, thick and suffocating. I strip off my clothes, the fabric sticky with sweat and stained with blood—Casen's blood. The sight of it makes my stomach twist.

I step into the shower, the scalding water pounding against my skin, but it does little to chase away the chill that's somehow settled deep in my bones even though it's well into the triple digits outside. I watch as the water swirls red and then clear at my feet, the evidence of the day's violence washing away, spiraling down the drain. The heat is supposed to soothe me, supposed to make me feel human again, but instead, I just feel... numb.

I've been through so much in my thirty years, most of it in the last ten, and I'm pretty sure this is the most I've ever been shaken.

# Chapter Thirty-Five

# The Aftermath

## VALLYN

"You sure you're okay?" my uncle asks, his voice gentle yet laced with the concern he's been trying to keep at bay since we left the crime scene. He lingers by the door, keys in hand, as if he's reluctant to leave me alone.

Nodding, I offer him a small, reassuring smile. "Yeah, I'm sure. What are you going to tell my parents? I haven't said anything to them yet."

He sighs, rubbing a hand over his face, clearly weighing his words carefully. "Nothing right now, Vallyn. You're okay, Blake is okay, it sounds like Casen will be okay... I don't think there's a reason to stress them out, unless you want to."

I shake my head, the thought of involving my parents in this mess sends a wave of anxiety through me. "I don't think we need to, unless something changes."

"Okay," he says, his voice softening. "Lock the door behind me," he adds, stepping forward to give me one last hug. It's strong, comforting, the kind of hug that makes me feel like a little girl again, safe and protected. I nod against his chest, returning the embrace with a quiet determination to hold it together.

Once he's gone, and the door is securely locked behind him, the silence of my apartment presses down on me. The weight of everything that's happened in the past few hours hits me like a bus, and all I can think about is washing it away. I'm so bone-tired, but there's no way I can sleep until I feel clean, until I scrub off the remnants of today.

Making my way to the bathroom, I strip off my clothes with shaky hands. I can't handle the silence so I start music on my bluetooth speaker in the shower. The water is hot, the steam filling the room almost instantly, but it's exactly what I need. I grab the good scrub, the one Blake sent me, and for a moment, I hesitate. Even *thinking* his name feels strange, I'm still trying to familiarize myself with those five letters. But the scent—clean, fresh, familiar—settles me in a way I'm not expecting. I close my eyes and let it envelop me.

This isn't a shower for pampering or indulgence; it's a necessity. For the first time in a long time, I don't waste time shaving or exfoliating. I focus solely on washing away the day, scrubbing my skin until it's red and raw in some places, until I feel like I've stripped off the lingering shadows of fear and adrenaline. When I'm done, I wrap myself in a towel, the softness a stark contrast to the harshness of everything else.

I dress in butter-soft leggings and a long-sleeve, super-soft shirt, craving the cocoon of comfort they provide. I adjust the thermostat, making the air conditioner work overtime so that the cool air justifies the warmth of my clothes and the weight of my blankets. It's not even close to my normal bedtime, but the exhaustion pulling at me is undeniable. The day has taken even more out of me than I realized.

My plan is simple—text Blake and then settle into my bed, whether for a nap or for the night, I don't really care. My body feels like it could sleep for days, and maybe that's exactly what I need.

Me

Hey, I just wanted you to know I'm laying down for a while, but I hope I see you soon

I stare at the screen for a couple of minutes, waiting for a reply that doesn't come. The logical part of me knows he's dealing with his own fallout, maybe in the shower, maybe back at the hospital, taking care of everything that needs to be done. He's probably as exhausted as I am, if not more. The last thing he needs is me being needy, clinging to him when he's barely holding himself together.

So, I let it go. I set my phone aside, pull my blankets up to my chin, and tuck myself in. The comfort of the fabric, the coolness of the air, and the steady hum of the air conditioner lull me into a state of calm I didn't think was possible after everything that happened today.

As my eyes drift shut, I'm surprised by how quickly sleep takes me, pulling me under before I can even process everything that has happened. The last conscious thought I have is of him—Blake—hoping that when I wake up, the world will make a little more sense. But for now, in the safety of my bed, wrapped in softness and comfort, I let myself fade into dreamland, the only place where everything really feels okay.

# BLAKE

"Fucking hell, Keri!" I shout, my heart nearly leaping out of my chest as I find her standing in my bedroom the moment I step out of the shower, barely covered by a towel. The shock of seeing her there, so unexpected, has me gripping the edge of the doorframe. "You're lucky I'm not fucking armed."

Her eyes narrow, but she doesn't flinch. "Casen's parents called Mom and Dad. You weren't answering your fucking phone," she snaps back, her voice as sharp as mine, filled with that no-nonsense assertiveness that runs in the family.

Yeah, she's definitely my sister.

"Fuck," I mutter, shaking my head. "I'm fine. Gage is fine."

But Keri's expression tells me she's not buying it. There's something judgmental in her gaze, something that makes me feel like I'm under a microscope. When she stays silent, just staring at me, I find myself talking, unable to stop the words from tumbling out. "You know the girl... the one you told me to stop stalking?"

Her brow furrows in confusion, like I've just taken a hard left turn in the conversation. "Yeah?"

"She was there, Keri." The confession that comes next is a heavy admission, like it's been sitting in my chest for too long. "It threw me off my game. I feel like it's my fault Casen got shot."

For the first time, Keri's demeanor softens. "Get dressed," she says, her voice gentler now, more like the supportive sister I know. "Then we'll talk."

I nod, grateful for the moment to collect myself. As she steps out of the room, closing the door behind her, I quickly throw on a pair of jeans and a t-shirt, my mind racing the entire time. By the time I join her in the living room, I'm still trying to piece together the mess of thoughts in my head.

"Sit," she orders, her tone firm, but not unkind. I laugh a little, a weak attempt to break the tension, but I do as she says, sinking onto the couch. "Now, tell me what happened."

I take a deep breath, then start from the beginning. "First off, she and I... we're good, that's important to know. But yeah, she was interviewing the guy we were after for her dissertation. She had no idea who he really was, and I had no idea she would be there. It wasn't just that, though—there were eight of them. Even with Gage and all our experience, we were way outnumbered. But when I saw her... I froze. I've never done that before, not in all the times I've walked into hostile situations, but this time, I saw her and I froze. And then I made a couple of wrong moves."

Then I go on to recount the entire thing before adding, "But she's okay, Gage is okay, and Casen... Casen will be okay."

Keri lets my words hang in the air, giving me space to breathe, to let it all out. She's always been like that—knowing when to push and when to pull back.

"What's her name?" she finally asks, her tone gentle.

"Vallyn," I say, the name slipping from my lips like a sigh, like a prayer. I run a hand over my face, trying to wipe away the exhaustion, the lingering fear.

A smirk tugs at the corner of Keri's mouth, like she already knows the answer before she asks, "Are you in love with her?"

The question hangs between us, unanswered for a few beats. Keri has only ever seen me in one serious relationship and that started when I was seventeen. I find myself rubbing my temples and nodding, the truth bubbling up from somewhere deep inside. "Honestly, I think so. It was like love—or obsession—at first sight. And the more I get to know her, the more I like her, the more I want her, the more I want this to last." I look up at Keri, the vulnerability in my voice undeniable. "But I'm worried today might have scared her off, that it might make her have second thoughts. She watched me kill someone, Keri."

"To save someone's life," she counters, her voice steady, reassuring.

"To save *her* life," I emphasize, the gravity of the situation settling back over me like a heavy cloak.

Keri nods, her expression thoughtful. "I think she'll be okay. It's probably a lot for her to process, she's probably decompressing too."

"Yeah, I need to get to her apartment," I say, the urgency building inside me. "Can you let Mom and Dad know I'm okay? I'll call them or stop by tomorrow."

"I can, but don't make me a liar," she warns, her tone lightening just a bit.

I manage a small smile. "I won't."

After a quick hug, Keri heads out, leaving me alone with my thoughts. I check my phone, and sure enough, there are missed calls and texts from my parents, Keri, Gage, and my sweet Vallyn. I fire off a quick apology to her, explaining why I didn't answer, then send texts to Gage and my mom. Casen is sleeping, and they're saying he needs his rest, so I decide not to head back to the hospital.

Instead, I focus on getting to Vallyn. As much as I'd love to clear my head with a ride on my bike, I know I'm not in the right frame of mind to be on two wheels tonight. Even though I still have a few things in that apartment three doors down from her, I pack a small backpack, not sure how long I'll stay, but knowing that once I get to her, I might not want to leave—*ever*.

My mind is spinning, the fear of rejection gnawing at me. What if today *was* too much for her? What if she decides I'm not worth the risk, that my world is too dangerous? The thought terrifies me, but I push it down, forcing myself to focus. I need to see her, to talk to her, to make sure she knows how I feel.

As I zip up the backpack, a plan starts to form in my mind. It might be a stupid plan, but it's what I've got.

# Chapter Thirty-Six

# The Shadow In The Dark

## VALLYN

The haziness clings to me, blurring the lines between dream and reality. I'm not sure if I'm still caught in some half-formed dream or if I've actually woken up. My eyes feel heavy, struggling to open against the darkness that swallows the room, but something doesn't feel right. I instinctively try to rub my eyes, to shake off the grogginess, but my hands won't move. Panic flutters in my chest, quick and sharp, until I squeeze my eyes shut and force them open again.

That's when I see him—Blake. He's sitting on the edge of my bed, just by my knees, his elbows resting on his thighs, his face buried in his hands. The sight of him, so tense, so lost in thought, makes my heart ache with a deep, unfamiliar worry. But then the realization crashes over me that I'm bound, my wrists tied to the headboard. The tension coils in my stomach, but it's not fear—it's confusion and concern.

"Hey," I say softly, my voice barely a whisper in the thick silence. When he turns his head to look at me, I gesture up to my bound wrists and ask, "What's this?"

The room is too dark to see his expression clearly, but I can feel the significance of his gaze, the tension radiating off him like a palpable force. There's something raw and vulnerable in his body language, something that makes my chest tighten with worry.

"Hey, pretty girl," he finally says, his voice low and rough. "I just wanted to make sure you wouldn't run from me."

The words hit me like a blow, the quiet desperation in his tone revealing more than he probably intends. He's afraid—afraid that I'll leave, that I'll slip away from him like a shadow. We've been an *us* for such a short time, and I realize how little I actually know about what's going on in his mind, how much I still have to learn about reading him, understanding him.

Keeping my voice low, gentle, I say, "I'm not going to run. How is Casen?"

He lets out a deep sigh, the sound heavy with guilt and regret. "He's okay. He'll be okay. His parents are at the hospital with him." There's a pause, a hesitation, and I wait, sensing that there's more he wants to say, more he's struggling to find the words for. He scrubs a hand over his face, through his hair, before continuing, "I just feel like it's my fault. That he's there because of me."

I swallow, trying to find the right words, but I'm treading on unfamiliar ground. I don't know enough about what they do, about the risks they face daily, about what was supposed to happen, to offer a perfect response. But I can feel his pain, his self-recrimination, and I can't let him drown in it alone.

"There were a lot more of them than you thought there would be," I say gently, choosing my words carefully. "You guys didn't have the intel and recon you normally do. Fuck, neither you or Gage knew *I* was there."

"Vallyn, I froze," he admits, his voice raw, almost broken. "I completely froze. Then I fucked up and fucked up again. Gage is the only reason you and I walked out of there alive." His gaze drops away from mine, his head shaking in self-loathing as he rubs his eyes like he's trying to erase the memory.

"Untie me," I say quietly, but he doesn't respond, doesn't move. "Blake," I say his name sharply, only the second time I've ever spoken his own name to him, and it snaps his attention back to me. "Untie me." He hesitates, so I add softly, "Please."

With a heavy sigh, he reaches up and unhooks my wrists from the bed. The bindings are still tight around my wrists, but I don't care. As he starts to pull away, I move, not gracefully but with purpose, swinging my leg around and looping my bound wrists over his neck. In a few swift yet uncoordinated movements, I'm straddling him, my body wrapped around his, our faces inches apart.

"Val—" he begins, but I cut him off, pressing my lips to his with a fierce, desperate need.

His sharp inhale tells me I've surprised him, but he doesn't resist. His hands fall to my hips, then lower to my ass, pulling me closer until there's no space left between us. My tongue parts his lips, and he lets me in, letting me taste him—he tastes like mint and tobacco. Our tongues tangle, the kiss deepening with each second, his hand slides up my back to weave into the hair at the base of my neck. He pulls me closer, almost as if he's trying to merge us into one, like he's trying to consume every part of me.

The tension that's been simmering between us since the first time I heard his voice over the phone, the electric charge of our connection, finally snaps, releasing in waves that make my body tingle with a fierce, overwhelming need. The events of the day, the brush with death, the raw emotions, all fuel the fire between us. Everything about this—being close to him, kissing him, feeling him—feels right, more right than anything I've ever known.

Our chests heave as we finally break apart, gasping for air. His thumb brushes tenderly across my jaw as he studies my eyes, searching for something, but I don't know what. "Vallyn," he sighs, my name a breathless sound on his lips, heavy with meaning he's struggling to put into words.

"I'm not going to run," I rasp, my voice rough with emotion. "You saved my life today. Maybe Gage did too, but you definitely did. Even knowing that there were guns leveled at your friends—you saved *me*."

He doesn't respond, but his hand reaches up to gently brush a strand of hair from my face, his touch reverent, like he's touching something fragile and precious.

"Blake," I say softly, his name like a plea on my lips, and his eyes meet mine, locking on with an intensity that makes my heart pound. "I'm not going to run. I'm here. I'm right fucking here."

His eyes search mine one last time, as if he's trying to find the truth in them, and then he pulls me back into him, his lips crashing against mine with a need that mirrors my own. This kiss is different, deeper, laden with all the emotions neither of us can fully express—fear, relief, desire, and something else—something stronger—that's just beginning to take root.

In this moment, we're not just two people caught in the chaos of the day—we're something more, something that feels unbreakable, even in the face of everything that's trying to tear us apart. And I lose myself in him, in the heat of his kiss and the strength of his arms.

My wrists are still bound, the fabric pressing into my skin just enough to remind me of their presence, but I manage to thread my fingers through Blake's hair, the limited motion only intensifying the contact. The gasoline coursing through my veins ignites, turning every nerve ending into a live wire. I don't think I've ever wanted someone so much in my life.

He's undeniably attractive, sexy in a way that's a little dangerous, and built like a fortress. I knew all of that from the very first moment

I laid eyes on him. Our journey to this moment has been anything but smooth—full of speed bumps and his bad choices—but right now, in his arms, it all makes a twisted kind of sense. This is where I belong—where I need to be.

Blake pulls back slightly, just enough to brush his thumb over my bottom lip, his touch soft and deferent. His other hand follows, gently brushing my hair away from my face. The tenderness in the featherlight touch of his fingers is a stark contrast to the strength that defines him, a paradox that both confuses and captivates me. He can be hard, unyielding, but here, with me, he's something softer, something vulnerable.

"Fuck, Vallyn," he rasps, his voice rough with emotion. "You have to be a dream."

A chill runs through me at the way he says my name, like I'm something he's desperately afraid to lose. "Well, if you're dreaming, so am I," I whisper, my voice barely audible over the sound of my own heart pounding in my ears.

I lean in to kiss him again, desperate to close the distance between us, to feel his lips on mine, but he pulls back, just enough to leave me wanting. A pout forms on my lips before I can stop it, the disappointment plain on my face, and the corners of his mouth lift.

"Pretty girl, give me your hands," he says with a soft laugh, his voice warm with affection. He gently guides my arms, pulling my bound hands over his head and down between us.

His hands move to my wrists, and both of our gazes are on his hands as he begins to release the bindings. The room is silent except for our breathing, the moment stretching out as his fingers work at the Velcro. When his eyes lift to mine, he looks at me through his lashes, and the expression on his face nearly melts me from the inside out. There's something in his gaze—adoration, maybe even reverence—that makes my heart stutter in my chest. It's as if he's really seeing me for the first time, and as if he's afraid I might disappear if he blinks.

I can feel the gravity of our brief shared history pressing down on us, the near-misses and close calls, the unspoken fears. I can almost taste his disbelief, the relief that we're here, together, despite everything. He didn't think we'd make it to this point, and the fact that we have probably feels like a miracle to him. I can see the shadow of today's events lingering in his eyes, the fear that I might have been scared off, that today might have been too much.

As soon as my wrists are freed, his hands are on me, one sliding to the small of my back, the other cupping my face with a tenderness that makes my breath catch. He kisses me gently, but there's a restraint there, a carefulness that tells me he's holding something back. When he pulls back to look into my eyes, his expression is serious, almost pained.

"Vallyn, pretty girl, don't hate me, but I'm not going to do more than kiss you tonight," he says, his voice low, rough with a mix of regret and determination.

I can't help but pout again, but he squelches it with another kiss, soft and tender, a promise wrapped in warmth. "I'm just not fully myself," he continues, his thumb brushing over my cheekbone, his eyes searching mine with a sorrow that makes my heart ache. "You deserve for me to be whole, to not have my mind partly off at the hospital, partly thinking about how I should have done things differently today, about how everything that went wrong."

His words hit me like a wave, the truth of them sinking in. He's right, of course. As much as I want him, as much as I crave the closeness, I don't want him distracted or divided. I want *all* of him, and he's telling me that right now, he can't give me that.

I kiss him quickly, softly, letting him feel the acceptance in the gesture before I bury my face in the crook of his neck, inhaling the scent of him, the warmth of his skin against my lips. I press a quick kiss to the pulse point on his neck, feeling the steady beat beneath my lips. "I understand," I murmur against his skin, my voice low and full of the truth I hope he hears. "I'm still right here."

His arms tighten around me, holding me close, and I feel him exhale, a long breath that seems to carry all the tension of the day with it. He's not perfect, not by a long shot, but he's here, with me, and that's enough for now.

# CHAPTER THIRTY-SEVEN
## THE KISS

### BLAKE

Holding Vallyn in my arms, feeling her lips pressed against mine, fuck, it's everything I've *ever* needed. The moment her mouth lands on mine, I am stunned, caught off guard by the intensity of it all.

I knew she wanted this—hell, we both have for a while—but after the chaos of today and the fact that we'd never crossed this line before, I am momentarily paralyzed. Instinct takes over, and so does the desire that has been building between us for so long.

Kissing her feels like coming home, like finding something I've been searching for my entire life. There's a familiarity in it, a sense of rightness that goes beyond anything I've ever felt before. It's like we're connected by something more than just our attraction, something deeper, something that feels almost unnatural in its intensity. Like a force outside of ourselves is drawing us together, pulling us into each other's orbit—we're soul bound.

As I hold her close, the thought crosses my mind—if I hadn't run into Vallyn at that bar, I would still have walked into that restaurant today, leveling a gun at the guy she was interviewing. The whole thing feels too fatalistic, too perfectly aligned to be mere coincidence. It's like we were always meant to find each other, even in the middle of chaos.

It's well after midnight now, and she's still straddling me, her face buried against my neck. I can feel every breath she takes, not just in the rise and fall of her chest, but in the way her warm breath brushes against my skin, sending electric currents through me with every exhale. It's a sensation that grounds me, that makes me never want to let her go.

"Vallyn, pretty girl?" I murmur, my fingers combing gently through her long, wavy hair.

"Hmmm?" she responds, her voice soft, content.

"It's late, and we should sleep," I say, reluctantly pulling back just enough to look at her. "I know you've slept, but I haven't. What are your plans tomorrow?"

She sits up, and the loss of her warmth against my skin leaves me aching. "Um, I was supposed to have lunch with Sasha, but I'll probably reschedule that. Then I have to take Carly to the doctor later in the afternoon."

When I don't respond right away, she continues, her voice tinged with concern. "She has lupus, and she gets infusions every four weeks. She doesn't like to drive herself. It's usually me that takes her, but I can ask her if she can find someone else."

This girl, ready to put everything on hold for me, makes my heart swell with something I'm almost afraid to name. But along with it comes a wave of guilt, crashing over me, reminding me that she shouldn't have to rearrange her life for my sake.

"Vallyn, you don't need to cancel anything for me," I say, holding her gaze, trying to convey the truth in those words.

She sniffs, nodding before replying, "I'm not feeling lunch with Sasha, but I'll still take Carly."

"My only concern is the youth center," I tell her, the thought of her going back there making my stomach twist. "I don't think you should go back there until we know where Elijah is."

She nods in agreement, her expression serious. "Okay. My uncle said the same thing. But, Blake?"

"Yeah, baby?" I ask and her breath stutters at the moniker.

"I don't think that I want full-on spyware back on my phone," she says with a dark chuckle that makes me smile despite everything. "But I think you should be able to see where I am, at least until all this is sorted out." She looks up, her eyes meeting mine with a sincerity that makes my chest tighten. "It would make me feel safer for you to know where I am."

Swallowing hard, the weight of her trust settles over me. "Okay," I agree, nodding. "We can do that tomorrow."

Gage can track her GPS anytime, but it's a lot easier—and less illegal—if it's through a simple phone app. And I'll do anything to keep her safe, to make sure she's okay. Because the thought of something happening to her, of her being in danger again, brings out feelings that are almost stronger than I can bear.

"Ready to sleep?" I murmur, my voice low, eyes tracing the curve of her lips.

She doesn't answer right away, just smirks, a wicked little grin that makes my pulse quicken. With a slow, deliberate movement, she pulls me closer, her lips finding mine again, soft yet insistent. "I guess if you're not going to touch me, then yeah," she purrs, the laugh that follows light and teasing, almost daring me.

I can't help but smile back, my hand grazing her cheek. "Pretty girl, it's not because I don't want to."

"I know," she breathes, her hips rolling into me, the sly grin on her face telling me she's all too aware of how hard this is for me—literally.

"Vallyn," my voice dips, warning her, but it's laced with a heat I can't quite hide. "Don't make me strap you back to the headboard."

Her eyes gleam with mischief, and she tilts her head, a playful pout forming. "You know, it has been a long time, so I'm a little impatient." Her laugh is a melody, sweet and intoxicating, and damn if it doesn't make my blood run hotter. "So, I'm good whenever you decide you are."

The last word barely escapes her lips before I capture them with mine, fierce and hungry. I need her, more than I've needed anything in a long time. My hands find her waist, pulling her against me until there's nothing between us but the thin fabric of our clothes. Her body, warm and pliant, presses into mine, and I feel her center grind against my cock, already straining, already aching.

One swift move and she's on her back beneath me, her laughter ringing out, soft but full of something more primal. I settle between her legs, and the heat of her is almost unbearable.

I watch her face as I take her wrists, guiding them up to the headboard, securing them there with practiced ease. She doesn't fight it; she doesn't resist. Instead, she watches me with a triumphant smile, like she's won some unspoken game. And maybe she has.

When her hands are bound, I lean down, capturing her mouth once more, deep and lingering, savoring the taste of her. I pull back, just a breath away from her lips, close enough that I can still feel the warmth of her breath on my skin. "I said I wouldn't do more than kiss you," I whisper, my voice thick with desire. "I didn't say that had to be limited to your mouth."

Her eyes widen a little, and a sound escapes her—something between a gasp and a whimper—that makes my chest tighten with satisfaction. My smile is slow, deliberate, as I let the tension build between us, knowing that even though I was ready to fall asleep mere minutes ago, the night is far from over.

My lips trail down the curve of her neck, the taste of her skin like a drug I can't quit. Each kiss draws a deeper reaction from her, her breath hitching, her body coming alive beneath me. When her back arches and her pelvis presses urgently against my thigh, I feel her through the thin fabric, and fuck, it's like something out of a dream. Her desire is palpable, seeping into my skin, fueling the fire burning within

I've known all night—felt it when I held her close—that she isn't wearing a bra. It takes every ounce of restraint not to break my promise and let my hands roam over her breasts. But I made a vow of sorts, and tonight, it's even a compromise that my mouth will bring her to the edge. My hand slips beneath her shirt, just grazing the soft skin of her abdomen, but as I lift her shirt I resist the urge to touch her. Instead, I sit back for a moment, my eyes drinking in the sight of her bare chest. Her nipples are hard, begging for attention, but I force myself to savor the moment, to let the anticipation build.

"You good, pretty girl?" My voice is a rough whisper, barely concealing the hunger coursing through me.

Her breath comes in shallow pants, her eyes glazed with need as she murmurs, "Not yet, but I hope you're about to change that."

A soft laugh escapes me, and I lean in, no more teasing, no more waiting. My mouth closes around one of those hardened peaks, and I suck, savoring the feel of her flesh against my tongue. I flick my tongue over her nipple, eliciting a sharp gasp from her, then drag my teeth gently across her sensitive skin as I move to the other. Vallyn writhes beneath me, her body responding to every flick of my tongue, like she's completely under my control—and I love it.

After worshiping her breasts until she's trembling with need, I begin my descent, kissing a slow, deliberate path down her stomach, feeling her muscles clench under my lips. When I reach the waistband of her leggings, I take my time, peeling them down her thighs and off her feet, revealing the rest of her to me. And damn, she's fucking perfect, every inch of her seems designed to drive me wild.

I loop an arm under each of her thighs, lifting them slightly, and begin leaving a trail of kisses up the inside of her thigh, inching closer to her center. I can feel her anticipation building, her breath coming faster, and when I finally reach her, I don't hold back. My tongue parts her silken lips, and her gasp is sweet, her back arches off the bed as she tries to press closer.

Her taste and smell floods my senses, sweet and intoxicating. I slide my tongue down, finding her entrance, and brace her thighs in my arms, holding her steady as I spear her with my tongue. She moans, a sound that reverberates through my chest, and I can't help but think that nothing has ever tasted this good, felt this right.

I spread her with my fingers just enough to expose her swollen clit, then pull it into my mouth, sucking it gently while flicking it with my tongue. She bucks against me, trying to grind her hips into my face, desperate for more. Her whimpers and moans are pure bliss, urging me to keep going, to push her higher.

As I feel her thighs start to tense, her muscles quivering, I know she's close—so fucking close. I keep going, my tongue working her over until she's on the brink, teetering at the edge of release. And then, just as she's about to fall, I stop, dragging my tongue gently up before pulling back just enough to leave her hanging.

She moans softly at the loss, her body twitching in the aftermath, craving what was just within reach. The sound of her frustration mixed with desire sends electricity down my spine, and I can't help but smile.

# Chapter Thirty-Eight

# Edging

## VALLYN

This fucking man—he has me right where he wants me, teetering on the brink of release, and then he just... stops, his lips curling into that maddeningly cocky smile against my skin. He's edging me on purpose, drawing out every second, and I want to be furious, but the promise of that final plunge, of the sweet, merciless release he's holding hostage, keeps my anger at bay.

My body, no longer hanging on that precarious precipice, begins to unwind. The tension that coiled so tightly in my core slowly eases, and just as I think I might catch my breath, he's back at it, his tongue slipping through my folds, slow and deliberate. A shiver runs through me, involuntary, making my toes curl, as I realize I have no control here—not over him, and certainly not over myself. I've never been with a man who has taken my hands out of the equation, and it tips the balance of power firmly in his favor, yet makes him utterly selfless in the act.

I swear I can feel my clit pulsing, each heartbeat a cruel reminder of how empty I feel, how much I need him inside me. How the hell did I go without sex for so long? It's been ages since I even wanted someone, but now... now I want him so badly it's consuming, the most intense, primal desire I've ever felt.

His mouth finds my clit again, latching on with a determination that sends my hips bucking against him, desperate to push him deeper, closer. But with an infuriating expertise, he pulls back just as I'm about to topple over that edge, leaving me gasping, aching, trembling.

I can barely catch my breath before he's plunging his tongue inside me, filling me in a way that's both everything and not nearly enough. The sensation of him moving and exploring teases me to the point of madness, and just when I think I might finally get what I've been craving, he changes tactics again. He flicks my clit, a quick, electrifying motion that makes me arch off the bed, and then he blows gently on my slick skin, cooling the heat he's ignited, only to lick it away once more.

Begging has never been my thing. I've always been in control, but this man, this fucking man, has me unraveling, pleading before I even realize what I'm saying. "I need... I need..." The words tumble out, half-formed and breathless.

His chuckle is dark, laced with a satisfaction that sends a shiver down my spine. "You need what, Vallyn, baby?"

I swallow hard, the vulnerability in my voice foreign and unsettling. "I need your fingers inside me," I whisper, barely able to get the words out. "And I need to come."

"Say, 'please,'" he commands, his voice low, rough, like gravel.

"Please, Blake," I whimper, my pride stripped bare, leaving me raw and exposed.

He's on me in an instant, his mouth crashing into mine with a desperation that matches my own. I taste myself on his tongue, and it's a heady mix of desire and fire that makes me burn even hotter. He breaks the kiss, his eyes locking onto mine with an intensity that sears through me.

"Say it again," he demands, voice tight with something I can't quite place.

"Please," I whisper, but it's not enough. Not for him.

"No, Vallyn, I want to hear you say my name," he insists, his voice rough, edged with emotion that sends a shockwave through me.

"Blake," I murmur, my voice trembling with the severity of my need. "Please, Blake."

His mouth crashes back into mine, and this time, he pushes two fingers inside me. I can't hold back the moan that escapes, muffled against his lips. He pulls back just enough to watch me, his eyes dark and full of intent as his fingers find that sweet spot inside me, curling against it while his thumb circles my clit with a pressure that's both perfect and maddening.

I expect him to stop again, to tease me to the brink and leave me hanging, but he doesn't. This time, he lets me fall, lets me crash over the edge with a force that has me pulling against the binds, my head thrown back as a stifled scream tears from my throat.

"Vallyn, look at me," he orders, his breath hot against my ear. "Eyes on me, pretty girl."

With an effort that feels almost Herculean, I manage to meet his gaze, even as my body shakes and quakes around him, convulsing with the force of my release. When the tremors finally subside, he kisses me again, slow and deep, before dragging his fingers from my soaked center and up my body. He slides them into his mouth, groaning as he tastes me.

"Fuck, you taste good, pretty girl," he says, voice thick with satisfaction. His fingers, still wet, brush against my cheek as he leans in to kiss me gently. "You better now?"

"Much," I reply with a smile, though it's shaky, my body still humming from the aftermath.

He plants a soft kiss on the tip of my nose, his expression warm and almost tender. "Good." Reaching up, he releases my wrists from their bindings and pulls me close, clearly expecting me to curl up against him, to snuggle into the comfort of his arms.

But he's still wearing jeans, and that's just unacceptable. I hitch a leg over his, sliding my hand down to his hardened length, feeling the way his breath hitches as I stroke him through the denim.

"Vallyn," he warns, his tone half-hearted, betraying his own desire.

"Shhh, just let me repay the favor," I murmur, my voice husky as I work at the button of his jeans. I move down his body and his breath catches, a clear indication he knows exactly what I'm about to do.

"Fuck, Vallyn," he groans as I slowly unzip him. My eyes are locked on his, watching every flicker of emotion cross his face as I free him from the confines of his jeans. He sucks in a sharp breath, his head tipping back as his eyes fall closed.

I take him in my hand first, stroking him, feeling the way his muscles tense beneath my touch. Then, I take him into my mouth, savoring the way he responds, the way his body tightens, his hand tangling in my hair as he pushes up with his hips, to move deeper into me.

"Fuuuck," he groans, the sound torn from him as I work him with both my mouth and hand, his grip in my hair tightening as the tension coils tighter and tighter.

I know he didn't plan on this tonight, hell, he probably didn't even plan on kissing me, but now... now he's at my mercy, and it doesn't take long before I feel him start to lose control. He edged himself in the process of edging me and he was close to the brink before I even started. His release is hot and salty on my tongue, and I swallow it down as his hand relaxes in my hair, his breath coming in ragged gasps.

I move back up his body, settling in beside him, my head resting on his chest as he pulls me close, his lips pressing a kiss to the top of my head. "Fuck, pretty girl, that escalated quickly," he rasps, his voice a mix of exhaustion, surprise, and lingering desire.

"And yet, still not everything," I tease, though the breathlessness in my voice betrays just how much I'm affected too.

"But way more than I thought would happen tonight," he counters, his tone light, amused.

I lay there, nestled against him, feeling the rise and fall of his chest beneath my cheek. The quiet hum of contentment settles over me like a warm blanket, but eventually, a soft laugh escapes my lips. "I need to pee," I admit, the mundane reality cutting through the fog of our intimacy.

He squeezes me closer, pressing a kiss to the top of my head. "Okay, pretty girl. I need to change into something more comfortable anyway."

"Oh, you weren't planning on cuddling with me all night in your jeans?" I tease, the playful edge in my voice pulling a chuckle from him.

"No, Vallyn," he replies, his laughter soft, a gentle rumble in his chest. "Although, I'm pretty sure when you decided to climb in my lap and kiss me, anything I had actually planned was out the window."

I tilt my head up, locking eyes with him, and the warmth in his gaze makes my heart skip a beat. "You're welcome," I murmur, leaning in to press a soft kiss to his smiling lips before slipping out of bed and heading to the bathroom.

Back in my bedroom, the quiet air conditioned breeze cools my skin as I gather my clothes from the floor, slipping them back on. I can feel Blake's eyes on me, watching with an intensity that makes my heart race. His gaze is heavy, possessive, as if he's memorizing every detail.

"I need to fill up my water; I'll be right back," I say, grabbing the water bottle from my nightstand, his attention never wavering.

The clatter of ice hitting the metal bottle echoes through the silence, the sound jarring in the stillness of the night. As I walk back into the bedroom, my eyes catch on the pile of weapons on my dresser, the cold steel glinting under the dim light. The sight sends a ripple of thoughts through my mind, and I can't help but start to voice them as I crawl back under the blankets, instinctively finding my place in Blake's arms.

"Hey, I've been thinking about something," I begin, my voice soft, yet tinged with curiosity.

"Yeah?" he prompts, his fingers tracing lazy, random patterns on my arm, each movement sending a gentle shiver through me.

"I want you to teach me how to handle a gun, especially your guns. I mean, if they're going to be around me, I should at least know the basics," I say, a soft laugh escaping at the end, though the request feels more serious than the lightness of my tone.

His hand stills, and he shifts us so he can look into my eyes, the earnestness of my words reflected in his gaze. "That's definitely doable, pretty girl, and you're right—it's probably a good idea."

I nod, but there's more I need to say, something that's been lingering in the back of my mind, growing with every possessive word he's ever spoken. "Remember all those times you told me I'm yours? That I belong to you?"

"Vallyn," he says, his voice gentle but firm, "those weren't just words. You *are* mine."

The certainty in his voice sends a thrill through me, but it also awakens a vulnerability I can't ignore. Swallowing, I muster the courage to respond, my voice barely above a whisper, laced with promise and a touch of fear. "I am yours. But please, don't break me."

His breath hitches, and the endearment he whispers next—"Little Lotte"—is thick with emotion. "I plan on keeping you as mine forever."

The fire that ignites between us is instant, searing, as his mouth finds mine again with a passion that leaves no room for doubt. It's a kiss filled with everything unsaid, every unspoken promise, and as we separate we still are lost in each other, the intensity fades into a gentle warmth, pulling us both into the comfort of sleep, still very wrapped up in each other.

# Chapter Thirty-Nine

# An Even Newer Normal

## BLAKE

My eyes snap open, heart pounding, and I clutch at the sheets, terrified she'll be gone, like *she* is the phantom that will slip away in the night. The darkness is heavy, suffocating, but it's her absence I fear more than the shadows that haunt my mind. I've seen so much death, pulled the trigger so many times that it should've numbed me by now. Yet here I am, in the wake of yesterday's events, the unshakable man who never lost a wink of sleep, terrified like a child afraid of the dark.

*Vallyn... Vallyn changes everything.*

Each time I wake, the panic gnaws at me, irrational and wild. I reach out instinctively, my hand finding her warm, soft body beside me. I pull her closer, as if by doing so, I can fuse us into one, make it impossible for her to disappear. My lips brush her skin, the taste of her soothes the fear inside me, if only for a moment. Her scent, her presence, anchors me in a way nothing ever has. I'm terrified—petrified, really—that I'll fuck this up, that I'll lose the one thing in this fucking world that has ever really felt worth holding on to.

I would still climb mountains, swim through alligator-infested channels for her. I'd kill for her—I did fucking kill for her. I'd die for her. Hell, I'd still burn the whole world to ash if it meant keeping her safe, keeping her mine.

I'm fucking insane, and I know it. There's no logical explanation for this kind of intensity, this obsession that's consumed me in such a short period of time. But logic be damned—she matches my madness with a fire of her own, and that, more than anything, makes this feel real. Real enough to scare the hell out of me, real enough to make me believe that maybe, just maybe, I've found the one thing worth losing everything for.

Morning breaks, and her bedroom is awash in golden light, the kind that seeps through curtains and bathes everything in a soft, forgiving glow. Neither of us bothered with alarms—there's no rush today. She has somewhere to be later, but the day stretches out before us, unhurried and easy. When my eyes finally open, she's sitting up, scrolling through her phone, yet the fingers of her other hand are tangled in my hair, absently stroking.

"Good morning, pretty girl," I murmur, my voice still rough, thick with sleep.

She turns toward me, a slow smile spreading across her lips as she sets her phone aside. Leaning in, she presses her lips to mine in a kiss that feels like a promise. "Good morning," she replies, her voice a warm whisper against my skin.

Instinctively, my arm snakes around her waist, pulling her closer. "I'm glad you weren't just a dream," I confess, the words slipping out before I can catch them.

Her reaction is immediate, tender—a subtle shift as she shifts and snuggles into me, her face nestled in the crook of my neck. There's a vulnerability in the way she melts into me, a softness that tugs at something deep inside. I breathe in the scent of her hair, letting it anchor me to this moment, to her.

"I have to head to the hospital at some point today," I murmur, the thought of leaving her side already feeling like a wrench. "What time do you need to take Carly?"

She pauses, considering. "I'll need to pick her up around one. Her appointment is at two."

I nod, running my fingers lightly along her back. "How about brunch before we do our things?"

"*Get* brunch or *order* brunch?" she asks, her tone playful, teasing.

"Is that your way of saying you don't want to leave the apartment?" I counter with a grin, my own tone matching hers.

"Maybe," she replies, her smile evident even without looking at her.

"Okay, let's order something," I agree easily, happy to indulge her.

There's a strange sense of dissonance as I lay here with her, like today belongs to a different life than yesterday. Yesterday was chaos, a brutal storm of emotions and violence that left us both reeling. But this morning... this morning feels like the calm after, the peaceful quiet that comes after the world has torn itself apart and is slowly piecing itself back together. An afterglow, rather than an aftermath.

Last night, she shocked me when she kissed me. Of all the things I expected from her, affection wasn't one of them. I thought she'd be angry, or scared, or maybe even distant. But instead, she clung to me, kissed me like she needed it, needed me, and in that moment, I realized we'd crossed a line in a way that can't be uncrossed.

I hate to admit it, even to myself, but I'm grateful for what happened yesterday—grateful for the way it pushed us closer, forced us to confront what we are to each other. Not that I'm glad Casen was shot, not that I'd ever wish for any of it to happen again. But there's a part of me that can't ignore the bond it forged between us, the way it brought her—literally—into my arms.

She's been in my arms before, sure, but this is different. *We're* different now. Something shifted, and whatever it is, I don't want to let it go.

After brunch, I send Vallyn off to take Carly to her appointment while I head to the hospital to meet Gage. The weight that has been pressing down on my chest feels a little lighter today. Seeing Casen in better spirits—joking, even—brings a sense of relief I didn't realize I was desperate for. We sit together, laughter bouncing off the sterile walls as we recount all the times our jobs have gone sideways. It's the kind of gallows humor that keeps us sane, binding us together through the chaos.

"Any clue where the fucker is?" Casen asks, his voice laced with curiosity rather than concern.

Gage shakes his head. "No, we think he went south, maybe even crossed the border. Jeremy's old team is keeping an eye out, though."

Casen's gaze shifts to me, his eyes narrowing slightly. "Did you tell your girl she can't go back to that youth center?"

I hesitate, then admit, "Not explicitly, no. But I did talk to her about at least not until we know where he is. I'll talk to her about the possibility of not ever going back, though."

"I'm actually surprised you let her go off alone today at all," Gage cuts in, raising an eyebrow.

I shrug, trying to brush off the unease I already had gnawing at the back of my mind. "We can't live in fear. At her request, I put trackers back on her phone. She just needed to take a friend to a medical appointment. I'm not too worried; they don't know where she lives or her last name."

Gage snorts. "Yeah, but do you know how many Vallyns live in the Phoenix area?"

I run a hand over my face, already regretting where this conversation is headed. "Probably one."

"Actually, three," Gage corrects, smirking. "But still."

"Great," I mutter, a hint of dark humor creeping into my voice. I pull out my phone, needing the connection to her more than I care to admit.

Me

How's it going?

Vallyn

Okay, just sitting in the waiting room, will be another forty-five minutes or so

Me

You want to get late lunch / early dinner after?

**Vallyn**
Yeah, although, can Carly join us?

She is having a rough time at home, I'd like to keep her away for a little while longer

**Me**
That's fine, maybe I'll make Gage tag along too lol

**Vallyn**
Oh geez, but okay lol

**Me**
Be hypervigilant for me, okay?

**Vallyn**
I am, I know that things could get sketchy

**Me**
Okay, pretty girl, I'll talk to you soon

I look up from my phone and pocket it. "You want to grab dinner with Vallyn, her friend Carly, and me?" I ask Gage.

He scoffs, shaking his head before replying, "Sure, but you're *not* setting me up with her."

"Honestly, Vallyn just said Carly needs more time away from home," I explain with a shrug. "I figured she's bringing a friend, so..."

As I finish speaking, Casen's parents walk in. We exchange pleasantries, the atmosphere shifting as we make our exit to give them some time alone with their son. The encounter reminds me I need to check in with my own parents.

Stepping into the hallway, I turn to Gage. "You want to swing by my parents' house with me?"

He chuckles, hands in his pockets. "I've got nothing better to do," he replies, the humor in his voice soothing some of the tension still lingering in the air.

An hour later, Gage and I are sitting in my parents' living room, surrounded by the familiar comfort of their suburban two-story home. The soft hum of everyday life is a stark contrast to the chaos we've been through. As we recount the events that unfolded, I can see the worry in their eyes begin to ease, especially when I tell them Casen is okay, albeit with a few more scars to add to the collection.

"Keri says you have a girl in your life?" my mom asks, her voice laced with curiosity and a touch of excitement. I glance at Gage, who's already grinning like a damn Cheshire cat.

"Uh, yeah," I reply, keeping my voice soft, almost cautious. "It's still in the very beginning stages, but yeah."

Gage lets out a laugh that fills the room. "He's head over heels, don't let him fool you."

I shoot him a glare, silently telling him to knock it off, but my mom interrupts before I can say anything. "Blake, that's amazing. I'm so happy for you."

"Just trying not to put the cart before the horse," I say, adding a touch of humor to ease the intensity of the conversation.

"Well, when you're feeling more sure about it, you should bring her to meet us," my mom suggests, her tone warm and inviting.

The funny thing is, I'm already sure—so fucking sure about her it scares me. But the thought of bringing her deeper into my world, of introducing her to my family, feels like a step I'm not ready to take yet. I want to keep her to myself a little longer, just us in our own little bubble, away from everything else.

"I will, Mom, when it's time," I assure her, keeping my voice steady, even though part of me is screaming to keep this part of my life hidden, protected.

As we sit there, my parents seem genuinely relieved to see both Gage and me doing well—unharmed and in decent spirits despite everything. The normalcy of this moment, in the safety of my childhood home, feels a little surreal after the chaos of the past few days.

After a couple of hours, Gage and I head back to Vallyn's apartment to meet up with her and Carly. The day has been a strange mix of the ordinary and the extraordinary, and as we drive, I can't help but feel the tangible shift in my life.

# CHAPTER FORTY

# THE FRIEND, THE STALKER, & THE SPY

## VALLYN

Carly's eyes are red-rimmed and swollen when she slides into the passenger seat, the remnants of tears still clinging to her lashes like morning dew. Her parents—her dad especially—seem to take a perverse pleasure in breaking her down, each harsh word leaving invisible welts across her tender spirit.

"Keep me away from home as long as possible," she quips, a shaky smile tugging at her lips, her attempt at humor as brittle as glass. The tears haven't quite dried, but she's trying, god, she's trying to hold herself together, even if the pieces don't quite fit anymore. Her hands grip the seatbelt as if anchoring herself to something solid, her body curled slightly as though trying to make herself smaller.

Legally, medically, there's nothing stopping Carly from driving herself. But the reality is different. She's aware of how her reaction times have slowed, how the fatigue settles deep in her bones, making her joints ache like a rusted machine. And though the treatment helps—thank goodness for that—there's no pretending it's easy for her to hold down a job or live on her own. So, she remains under her parents' roof, navigating their suffocating presence and her own frustration.

I remember the slow unraveling that led to her diagnosis, each appointment a new thread pulled until the fabric of her life lay in tatters. We all watched, helpless, as Carly's bright spark dimmed under the weight of it all. But after each infusion, she's a little stronger, if only for a while.

I manage to distract her easily while we drive by telling her about the events of the previous day. I include the parts all about Blake, and how both he and Gage saved my life. She is utterly stunned.

While she's in the infusion suite, I sink into one of the hard plastic chairs in the waiting room, my phone a welcome distraction from the gnawing anxiety in my mind.

When Carly finally emerges, there's a little bit of a lightness to her step. We walk to the car, and I break the news to her, carefully gauging her reaction.

"So, if you want, you get to meet my phantom tonight," I say, the words slipping out with a mix of excitement and apprehension. "And he's bringing Gage with him. They want to go to dinner."

"Gage, the spy?" she asks, a glint of humor lighting up her eyes for the first time today.

"Yeah, Gage, the spy," I confirm with a laugh, the sound surprising me with its sincerity.

"Better than going home to my parents," she declares. "So, do I call your guy 'phantom' or 'Blake?'"

"Blake. Just call him Blake," I answer, laughing along with her, relieved to see her smile, if only for a moment.

When we step back into my apartment, the mood shifts a little. Carly heads straight for the bathroom, a small, grateful smile flickering on her face as she gathers up my makeup and supplies. I hear the water running, the soft rustle of tissues, the clatter of makeup brushes—as she tries to cover the evidence of the tears she shed, the vulnerability she now tries to mask.

It's strange, surreal almost, knowing that Blake and Gage will soon walk through that door as our worlds further collide. Two hours pass in a blur of somewhat nervous energy, the clock ticking down until the inevitable knock at the door.

When they finally arrive, it's like the universe shifts slightly off its axis. Blake, with his calm confidence, steps in first, his presence filling the space in a way that makes me feel simultaneously safe and on edge. And then there's Gage—tall, enigmatic, a little nerdy, but for Carly a shadow brought into the light—outside the night of the only other time she has ever met him. It's not just the strangeness of Blake meeting Carly, a friend who knows the deep recesses of my soul and the sketchy beginnings with my phantom; it's also the unsettling reality of Gage being here, in my apartment, blurring the lines between the worlds we've kept separate.

In the last few days, everything has changed.

Carly, always so vibrant when she is among friends, grows quieter, more reserved. I can see the tension in her shoulders, the way she avoids eye contact, her introversion tightening around her like a protective shell. She's supportive, always has been, but I know there's a part of her that still questions how Blake entered my life, and the shadows that lurk in the corners of that story.

We gather around the kitchen island, the small talk flowing awkwardly at first, each of us trying to find our footing in this new dynamic. We talk about dinner options, debating and discarding ideas until we settle on the Italian place just down the street, the familiar comfort of pasta and wine appealing to everyone.

As we sit at the dinner table and talk, Gage turns his attention to Carly sitting next to him, asking about her Lupus and the treatments that seem to immensely help her life. His questions are gentle, genuine, and I see her soften slightly, her guard lowering just enough to answer him. She speaks more freely, her voice still quiet but less strained, and I'm relieved to see her finding a rhythm, even if it's a slow, cautious one.

Blake, though, he's like a force of nature next to me, his touch constant, grounding. His hand finds my thigh, warm and firm, then his arm slides around my waist, his fingers trailing up my back and through my hair, and I can't help but lean into him. It's as if he's afraid that if he isn't touching me, holding onto me, at all times, I might slip away. And truthfully, I feel it too—that magnetic pull, the need to be close, to secure myself to him in this strange, surreal new reality.

Despite the oddity of it all, the night starts to feel... normal. The four of us, sitting around a dinner table, laughing, talking, even making plans for other days. It's easy to fall into the routine, to let the tension from earlier fade into the background. But every now and then, a thought flickers through my mind—why couldn't Blake have just asked me out from the start? Why did it have to begin the way it did? The thought is fleeting, though, a shadow that passes quickly, because deep down, I know I don't fault him for it anymore. Not really.

And, there's nothing he can do to change it now.

As we're walking out of the restaurant, Carly and I start discussing the logistics of taking her home. I turn to Blake asking if he is going to be at my apartment again, which he blows off as a silly question, because of course he's going to make sure I get home okay. As Carly and I are discussing options, Gage chimes in.

"How about if I take Carly home, and you take Blake back to your place?" Gage asks.

His suggestion would solve the problem, but I'm not sure Carly would be comfortable with that. She surprises me when she almost instantly agrees saying that makes the most sense. And just like that, the logistics are solved.

"Text me when you get home, and if you need me," I say to Carly while I hug her goodbye.

Blake holds the car door open for me and then rounds my car to drive. Once he is settled in the driver's seat I say, "This has been surprisingly normal."

He shoots a smile at me, "I know, and I also know it's a little odd coming off of, well, everything."

As we're pulling into my parking lot I ask, "Where do you live?"

"I have a condo downtown," he answers.

"Like a bachelor pad, condo?" I tease.

"Not so much, no," he answers with a laugh.

As we're walking to my building he grabs my hand, and again this sense of normalcy after everything that led up to the 4th of July and everything that happened yesterday feels out of place and yet completely right.

"Sooo, about that bachelor pad... " I begin while unlocking the door to my apartment.

"What about it, Vallyn?" Blake asks.

"What exactly in your history? I mean, I'm pretty sure you know mine, or most of it," I admit.

"I don't have much of a history, pretty girl," he begins, leaning against the island watching me kick off my shoes.

"Yeah?" I ask, a little in disbelief.

"Yeah, I had a relatively serious high school sweetheart, we barely survived boot camp and didn't survive my first deployment. We were together for almost three years," he answers. "Other than that, it's been very short flings, and not that many of those. There was nothing when I was overseas, and I would be home for short periods of time, but really nothing Vallyn. I told you, you're special. Definitely the only woman I've ever been this intensely obsessed over. The only woman I've wanted to *do* something about in a really long time."

"Were you tested after the last one?" I ask and it takes a second for him to understand what I'm asking.

"I was, a couple of times actually," he answers with a smile.

"And just so you know, I have an implant," I inform him, a little sheepishly. "For birth control."

"I might have known that," he admits, wrinkling his nose, and it makes me laugh a little, even though I know it's creepy.

"You gonna take me to this condo sometime?" I ask flirtatiously, trailing a single finger down his chest.

"Absolutely, Vallyn," he responds quickly and confidently, his hands instinctively coming to rest on my hips. "I, honestly, want to spend as little time apart from you as possible."

Rising on my toes, I gently press my lips to his as I wrap my arms around his neck. I feel him relax against me as his fingers grip into my back. "You staying with me tonight?" I ask quietly.

"If you want me to, pretty girl," he answers, while gently brushing hair out of my face.

"Well," I begin and kiss him again softly. "I, honestly, want to spend as little time apart from you as possible, too."

He studies me for a minute, maybe trying to find the lie in my words, but he won't find it. Then with a firm hand on my neck he pulls me back into a passionate kiss.

# Chapter Forty-One

# Like The Stars Need The Darkness

**BLAKE**

I still can't believe this is happening—that she's real, that her body is here, pressed against mine, and that she *wants* me just as much as I want her. Every time I think back on the things I've done—on the chaos that's followed me like a shadow—I wonder how the hell she's still standing by my side. I was sure one of these insane moments would have driven her away. But here she is, drawn to me like I'm drawn to her, our connection undeniable, electric and magnetic.

Maybe that's all I need to know right now.

My hands instinctively find the smooth skin of her lower back, fingers gliding over the warmth of her body, and without even realizing it, I'm tugging at her clothes, hungry to feel more of her. Her shirt is gone in seconds, tossed somewhere behind us, and the need between us grows feral. I back her into the wall, the cool surface meeting her bare skin as we collide, lips tangled, heat and desperation fueling every kiss. There's a fire burning in the space between us, and I have no desire to put it out.

I pull back just long enough to rid myself of my belt, the weapons I keep with me clattering onto the island behind me. Her hands never leave me. In fact, they're bolder now, fingers hooking into my waistband, and the instant her touch slides lower, my cock hardens even more, if that's even possible. She's got me completely under her spell.

When I turn back to her, my hand tangles in the hair at the nape of her neck, pulling her toward me, and my mouth crashes into hers with raw need. This time, I don't plan on stopping. I can't. I need her in ways I haven't needed anything before. It's like the stars need the darkness—our connection feels just as inevitable, just as consuming. Her soft moans vibrate against my lips, her fingers clutching my shirt as if she can't get enough, and fuck, I'm right there with her.

Reluctantly, I break the kiss, meeting her eyes, dark with desire, and I almost lose myself in their intensity. "Vallyn, pretty girl... are you sure?"

Her breathless reply comes immediately, her body moving into mine, just before her lips find mine again. "I've never been more sure of anything." Her fingers snake around my neck, pulling me closer, and the moment she runs them through my hair, I'm gone.

Her other hand explores my chest, sliding beneath my shirt, and when her fingers touch my skin, it feels like a fuse has been lit inside me. Something snaps. I press her harder into the wall, pinning her there with my body, her soft gasp fueling my desire. Her hips push into me, rolling with a rhythm of need, and I'm done pretending I have control over this.

I tear my shirt off, letting it fall carelessly to the floor, and watch her eyes roam over me—my tattoos, the scars that line my body, the hard lines of my muscles. She drinks me in, but it doesn't last long before our lips crash together again, our hunger too powerful to pause. My fingers trail up her spine, finding the clasp of her bra, and in one swift motion, it's undone. The straps fall from her shoulders, her chest bare to me, and I waste no time before cupping her breast in one hand, my other slipping inside the waistband of her shorts, squeezing her ass. I love the fullness of her curves, she feels like she was made for me.

She's working on my fly, and as she does, my tongue tangles deeper with hers, our bodies burning hot and fast. My jeans hit the floor, but as I reach for her, I growl with frustration, realizing I still have my fucking boots on.

I drop to squat, yanking at the laces while she runs her fingers through my hair, nails dragging across my scalp, sending jolts of pleasure through me. The moment I'm free of my boots, I run my hands up the smooth skin of her thighs, loving the silky feel of her as I stand, kicking off my pants. My mouth finds her nipples on the way up, savoring the way she trembles beneath my touch. Her skin is flushed, begging for more as my lips meet hers again.

She wraps her hand around my cock as soon as she pushes my boxer briefs to the floor, and I groan at the contact. The fingers of her other hand dig into my bicep, clearly guiding me toward the bedroom, and I follow that lead, driven by the primal need to claim her, to make her mine.

When we reach her bed, I scoop her up and lay her on the mattress, hovering above her. My knee slips between her legs, and her hips grind into me, desperate for relief. I smirk against her lips, whispering, "So needy, Little Lotte."

Her only response is to grind harder, her lips claiming mine again. She's insatiable, her need matching mine in every way.

I trail kisses down her jaw, her neck, until I reach her breasts, drawing a nipple into my mouth. She moans beneath me, her hips lifting off the bed, her body writhing. I love how responsive she is—how every touch, every flick of my tongue sends her spiraling.

My mouth travels lower, kissing my way down her stomach, until I reach the apex of her thighs. The moment my tongue opens her, she gasps, her hips bucking toward me, and the taste of her floods my senses—sweet, tangy, and perfectly her—exactly how I remember her. Looping my arms under her thighs, I hold her steady as I feast on her, teasing her entrance, circling her clit with my tongue.

Her moans grow louder, more frantic, and when I push two fingers inside her, I feel her walls clamp down around me. She shudders, her body convulsing, and I know she's on the verge of falling apart. I am more than willing to push her over that edge.

I crawl back up her body, capturing her lips with mine, and knowing she can taste her cum on my tongue drives me wild. One hand grips her hip as I settle between her legs. Her unspoken plea is clear in the way she arches into me, desperate to feel more.

"Last chance to say no, pretty girl," I murmur against her lips, my voice dark and thick with lust.

"Please," she whispers, her hands clutching my arms.

That's all the permission I need.

Pushing into her, my eyes stay locked on hers as her mouth opens in a gasp. I kiss her again, swallowing the sound. As I find a rhythm, I sit back on my knees, pulling her thighs around my hips. Each thrust is deep and deliberate, making sure she feels every stroke.

This still feels surreal, she has felt like she was mine and paradoxically not mine for so long—this is a claiming. I *am* claiming her—leaving my mark on her and in her. Her moans spur me on, and when she braces herself on the headboard, I know I've hit the mark. I fuck her harder, faster, and when she finally convulses around me, her climax rippling through her, I don't stop. I ride it out with her until my own release takes over, spilling inside her, marking her as mine.

I know this is fast, faster than I want it to be in some ways, but we have a lifetime ahead of us for me to make it up to her. Collapsing beside her, I pull her close, her body tucked into mine. My fingers gently stroke her hair, and I press soft kisses to the top of her head.

Her fingers trace lazy patterns on my chest and abs. In this moment, I feel more content than I have in a long, long time.

We lie tangled together, her warmth pressed into me, and the steady rhythm of our breathing is the only sound breaking the silence. I pull her impossibly closer, my arms tightening around her, savoring the feel of her soft skin against mine. I press a kiss to the top of her head, the scent of her hair filling my senses, grounding me. Her fingers are still tracing lazy patterns on my chest, and it's that small movement that tells me she's still awake, lost in the same post-bliss haze as I am.

"You okay, pretty girl?" My voice comes out rougher than I expected, like the fire between us burned through every part of me, leaving only the rawest edges behind.

She shifts slightly against me, her breath warm on my skin. "Very," she murmurs, her voice low, smoky, and full of satisfaction. The single word hums between us like a secret, wrapping us in a shared moment that feels far too fragile and perfect.

I can't help it—I need to see her. I roll toward her, shifting so that we're chest to chest, her heartbeat pulsing against mine. My hand moves to her face, cradling her cheek, my thumb brushing over the soft curve of her jaw. Her eyes find mine in the dim light, and there's something in them that hits me straight in the gut—something raw and unspoken.

"Thank you, Little Lotte," I whisper, my words barely more than a breath, "Thank you for trusting me."

Her hand slides up my chest, fingers grazing my skin, leaving a trail of heat in their wake. When she reaches my neck, she tugs me closer, and her lips find mine, the kiss is soft at first, delicate—like she's savoring the moment. But then it deepens, her hunger coming back to life, and I feel the need radiating from her as her mouth moves against mine with growing urgency.

*She's still needy. Still hungry.*
*And fuck, so am I.*

My body responds faster than I would expect it to, my desire reigniting with a sharp, pulsing heat. I groan into her mouth, and her soft, eager moan fuels the fire spreading through me. I'm already hard, already ready for more, and when her fingers tangle in my hair, pulling me deeper into the kiss, I know there's no holding back.

Round two is coming, and this time, I'll love her better.

# CHAPTER FORTY-TWO

# BATTLE SCARS

## VALLYN

Blake is everything I'd ever imagined he would be and undoubtedly, even in its simplicity, that was the best sex of my life. I don't know if it's because of the intensity of our feelings and interactions, or if it is just the raw sex itself, but I feel like we fit together and read each other the way it is meant to be.

As he sits up with his back against the headboard, I pull the blankets around myself and tuck my knees up to my chest as I face him to talk to him. He weaves his fingers with mine and gently strokes the palm of my hand with his thumb.

Resting my cheek on my knee, I ask, "Can you tell me about your scars?"

He does. He tells me about knife and bullet wounds, about burns and explosions and he gives me a tour of the marks on his body while he does.

When we're done with scars, we get into the meaning of his tattoos, when and why he got them. Some were just for fun and don't have much meaning, while others are coated in meaning—friends he lost on the battlefield, his sister, his parents, among others.

Eventually we move, he needs to smoke. "You know," I begin. "Before you, I always said I'd never date a smoker," I tease, although it's completely true.

He smirks at me as he takes a drag. "It's a bad habit, I know it is, but I don't have many, and, honestly, I don't smoke much." I smile at him and wrap my arms around my waist as I sit in the chair on the patio. It's sweltering outside, well into the triple-digits on this July evening. "Maybe, for you, I'll quit," he offers with a smile.

I shrug. "It doesn't bother me as much as I thought it would. At least not as much as you do it."

Opening my phone which I've barely looked at the last two days, I find messages from my friends. Before I reply, I look back at Blake and ask, "How do you feel about meeting the rest of my friends? I mean, I know you've spent some time around Carly now, but yeah."

"They asking you to do something specific?" he asks.

"Just to see me in person, check on me," I answer with another shrug.

"What would you want to do?" Blake asks with a soft smile. I am definitely aware that he hasn't answered me yet, he's gathering more information.

*Him and his intel—his recon.*

"I don't know," I admit. "Lately it has been all bars, but I'd be okay with brunch, or a lunch."

"I haven't talked to him about it, but I think Carly piqued Gage's interest, you mind if I ask him if he wants to tag along?" he asks.

"I don't think that would be an issue, they've already met him," I answer, feeling the corners of my lips turn up.

"We're still on a self-imposed administrative leave, so we're pretty free. When are you thinking?"

Taking a deep breath in through my nose, I answer, "Tomorrow? Maybe the day after?"

Nodding, he agrees, "That should be fine, just tell me when and where, pretty girl. I'm not planning on going anywhere, so I might as well meet your friends."

"Okay, also next week, most of my week is caught up in my brother's wedding stuff, just so you're prepared for that," I divulge. "And as much as I'd love for you to go with me, I think it might be a little too soon to meet my *entire* family," I add with a laugh. He smiles in response, and I continue, "But I'd love to see you after."

"Oh, I'm sure that can be arranged," he says with a flirtatious smile. "And you're right, your entire family might be a little much right away, but I'll leave that up to you."

Nodding, I look back down at my phone and type out a message in our group chat, the one with just the girls, no Corey.

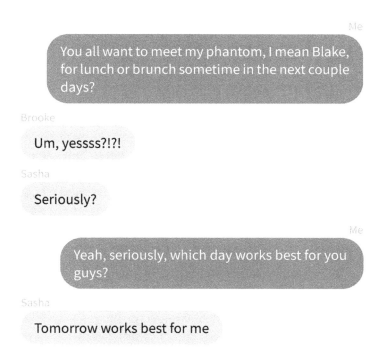

Me

You all want to meet my phantom, I mean Blake, for lunch or brunch sometime in the next couple days?

Brooke

Um, yessss?!?!

Sasha

Seriously?

Me

Yeah, seriously, which day works best for you guys?

Sasha

Tomorrow works best for me

Tori

Me too, I can't believe this is happening can I bring my boy toy?

Me

Yes lol, he's bringing Gage the spy too

Carly

I can do tomorrow too

Brooke

What about Corey?

Me

I don't think that's a good idea for now

Sasha

Me either

Brooke

Okay

As the conversation continues, we plan the where and when and I give Blake the information so he can pass it on to Gage, who is agreeable to going, too. Although, Blake isn't sure if it's because he wants to keep Blake company, or he really does have a little thing for Carly.

I'm not sure how I feel about one of his friends dating one of my friends with our relationship being so fresh, but I also know Carly needs some good in her life.

Blake puts out his cigarette and reaches for me, pulling me to a stand. The air conditioning feels more refreshing than usual as we step back into my apartment. He moves to the kitchen sink to wash his hands, as he always does after he smokes, and I appreciate it.

It's still relatively early in the evening at this point, but it definitely feels like bed time. Blake turns and looks at me as he's drying his hands and I can see in his eyes that we both are feeling a lot of the same things. It feels as if I let him out of my sight he's going to disappear—like there's a precarious fragility to our time together.

As he approaches me, our eyes don't leave each other. The amount of eye contact we seem to be holding on a regular basis should be uncomfortable, but it's exactly what we both seem to need. We spent so much of our time not being able to see each other, we're constantly searching for each other's souls behind the depth of our eyes.

He wraps his arms around me and pulls me close. As I bury my face in his neck, it hits me hard how much he feels like home—how safe and at peace I feel in his arms. How this man that caused so much chaos in my life can be my sanctuary, I don't know that I will ever fully make peace with.

"You think you're ready to sleep, pretty girl?" he asks, his voice soft and deep.

Nodding against his skin, I let out a breathy, "Yeah."

Slowly, he releases me, but his hand runs down my arm and he takes me by the hand, leading me to the bedroom. He pulls me into my bed and immediately pulls me into him, my head naturally finding a place on his chest. Quickly I fade into the tranquility of sleep.

My alarm wakes us in the morning and we're still wrapped in each other's arms, although now I'm the little spoon to his big spoon. I didn't expect us to make it to my alarm, I only set it just in case we slept too late to meet my friends.

"Good morning, pretty girl," Blake rasps, his lips right near my ear. The vibration and breath across my hair and skin instantly sends static and electricity through my body—I instantly feel an ache for him deep in my belly.

"Morning," I manage to breathe out as I turn toward him and my eyes meet his. They're a bright green this morning—absolutely mesmerizing.

His hand reaches up and brushes a few stray hairs off my face. While his eyes track his fingers, mine move to his lips and I'm kissing him before I fully realize what I'm doing.

Fingers tangle in my hair as he pulls me closer and kisses me more deeply. Pulling back just a little, he whispers, "Fuck, Vallyn, you're my fucking everything."

I let out a soft whimper as a chill goes through my body from my lips to my toes and back up, settling in my aching center. His words are enough to do me in all on their own.

His mouth trails kisses from my mouth, down my jaw, then my neck, and with every movement, every contact, my body grows more and more electric. The wanton desire inside me ignites into an inferno.

As his mouth finds my breasts and nipples, I feel like I'm about to be torn apart and the sweet relief I feel when his hand moves to the wetness between my legs is powerful. My back arches into him, willing his fingers to find their way inside me.

He teases the soft skin around my entrance, finding my clit and softly circling it—it's intentionally not enough to make me come, but absolutely enough to get me more worked up and more turned on.

I whimper, grinding against his hand, and he lets out a dark laugh. "So needy," he whispers and then trails his tongue up my neck and back to my mouth. Kissing me softly first, he asks, "Do you want more, pretty girl?

Nodding, I breathe out the word, "Yes," before his mouth collides again with mine.

# Chapter Forty-Three

# Lunch With Friends

## BLAKE

This fucking woman. Everything about her draws me in like a magnet, pulling at me with a force I can't fight—no, I don't *want* to fight. Vallyn is a siren, luring me straight into the depths of her abyss, and now that I'm here, I'm drowning in her. She's everything—my oxygen, the air that fills my lungs. Without her, I'd suffocate. She's my sustenance, the lifeblood coursing through my veins, keeping me alive in a way nothing else ever has.

When my fingers slip inside her, her body arches beneath me, and for a second, I nearly lose it. It's not just lust—it's something deeper, something primal. Sure, I've always enjoyed fucking, but this... this is different. With Vallyn, it's like I'm alive in a way I've never felt before. Needed. Wanted. Her body is my obsession, an addiction I'll never shake, and touching her feels like both the first and last time all at once. I know—I fucking know—that no one will ever compare to this. To her.

Her eyelids flutter closed as my fingers begin their rhythm, but I'm not done watching her yet. I lower my mouth to the curve of her neck, feeling the pulse of her moans hum against my lips. I bite down, just enough to tease, and her soft whimper shoots straight through me, igniting something dark and feral. That sound—it's mine now.

I pull my fingers away suddenly, savoring her gasp of surprise. Her eyes flash with heat, challenging me, but I see the spark of desire beneath it. Pinning her wrists above her head, I let her know exactly who's in charge. Vallyn isn't submissive, not exactly, but she likes this. She likes feeling my strength, my control. And when I claim her mouth again, the taste of her is so intoxicating I could drown in it. Her knees part, her hips rise, and that silent plea is all I need.

I break the kiss, hovering just long enough to catch her eyes, and when I thrust into her, they roll back in her head, lips parting in a breathless gasp. The sight of it, the sheer bliss on her face, almost sends me over the edge right then and there.

*Fuck, she's hot.*

I'm losing myself, but I can't—won't—stop.

Letting her wrists go, I shift back, gripping her thighs with a strength that borders on desperate, on feral. My body moves on instinct, hard and fast, driving into her like I can't get deep enough. Her hand grips the sheets, knuckles white, while the other skims over her skin, brushing her breasts, teasing her hardened nipples. Her quiet moans turn sharp, cutting through the air like the sweetest music, urging me on.

It takes everything in me not to lose control, to not come before she does, but when her body stills and her walls pulse around me, it's over. The tension snaps, and I release with her, riding the wave of her pleasure as it crashes through us both.

We collapse together, breathless and tangled, my arm pulling her close, her fingers tracing idle patterns over my chest. I press a kiss to her hair, and for a moment, there's just silence. Just us.

"Blake?" Her voice is raspy, worn from pleasure.

"Yeah, pretty girl?" I reply, brushing her hair back gently.

She kisses my chest, soft and lingering. "Thank you."

A chuckle rumbles in my chest. "For what, Little Lotte?"

"Again, for stalking me." She laughs, and the sound is pure sweetness. "I still think you could've just talked to me that night. Maybe it would've been better."

I smirk, my lips brushing her forehead. "Maybe. But maybe we needed the drama."

She laughs again, that soft, lilting sound that drives me insane. "I'm just glad we're here now. Doesn't matter how we got there."

"Me too, pretty girl," I murmur, holding her close as the silence wraps around us again. And for now, that's enough.

"Sasha," Vallyn starts, her tone laced with that careful edge, like she's trying to temper a flame before it catches. "This is Blake."

Sasha's eyes cut to me, and I feel the weight of her scrutiny. She doesn't even try to hide it, her gaze raking over me like she's expecting to see warning signs etched into my skin, bright red flags waving from my chest. The air between us tightens with tension as she tentatively extends her right hand. I release Vallyn's arm to meet it, feeling the coolness of Sasha's fingers against mine.

"It's nice to meet you, Sasha," I offer, keeping my voice steady, soft. "I've heard a lot about you."

"Yeah, you too," she replies, but there's a slight hitch in her voice, a hesitation that lingers between us, making the air feel thick. Her eyes flicker with uncertainty, and I can practically see the gears turning in her head, questioning, weighing me against whatever picture she's painted.

The tension snaps as Gage approaches with Carly, his grin cocky, smug even, as their fingers intertwine. I catch the amusement on his face, and despite myself, a smirk pulls at my lips. Sasha shifts when she notices the shift in attention, her body tensing before she lets out a small breath, loosening her shoulders as she turns to greet them.

"Carly," she says, giving a nod that's more formality than warmth. Then her eyes land on Gage. "And Gage, the spy."

Gage's grin widens at the nickname, unbothered, while Carly watches, amusement dancing in her eyes. Soon, Brooke, Tori, and Tori's boyfriend Tyson gather around us, filling the space with chatter, though there's an underlying awkwardness that hums in the air. They've all met Gage before, but it's clear they're still figuring him out, while also still navigating whatever invisible lines exist in this dynamic with Vallyn.

As we all settle into our seats and order food, the atmosphere begins to thaw. I notice how the group's focus is more on Gage and Carly, leaving me under less scrutiny than I expected. Except for Sasha. I catch her staring at me several times—her gaze sharp, like she's still searching for the cracks, the ones where she can see the red flags I've somehow managed to hide from her.

I keep my hand resting on Vallyn's knee, my thumb brushing light circles over the fabric of her jeans. It's subtle, but enough to keep that connection between us, grounding her to me, reminding her that I'm right here. At the same time, I don't want to push it. Her friends are watching, and I don't know how much public display of affection she's comfortable with, especially in front of them. We haven't really talked about it. She was fine with the displays with just Gage and Carly, but I'm not about to start throwing our closeness around in front of people who already have their own preconceived notions about me—at least not yet.

Tyson is the one who finally pulls me into the conversation, breaking through the last of the awkward tension. "So, Blake, you work with Gage?"

I flick a quick glance at Vallyn, gauging her reaction before answering. "Yeah, Gage and I have worked together in one way or another since right after high school."

Gage chimes in with his easy smile, adding, "First in the military, and now doing private investigator work. Though, we've both got our side gigs, too."

Tyson's curious gaze shifts back to me, a flicker of interest lighting up his expression. "We know what Gage does. What about you? What do you do for side gigs?"

"Mercenary work, mostly," I answer, keeping my tone casual. "Still some contracts for the government, but occasionally I take on private jobs."

Tori's eyes narrow slightly, her curiosity piqued. "What kind of private jobs?"

"Security, bodyguard duties... escort gigs sometimes." I don't elaborate, not here. There's no need for too much detail. I steer the conversation away from the loaded silence. "What about you, Tyson? What do you do?"

He chuckles softly, shaking his head. "Nothing as thrilling as that. I'm in corporate sales—medical services, mostly selling to doctors."

Tori's eyes practically glow as she looks at him, her tone filled with admiration. "But he's really good at it."

"You could say that," Tyson shrugs, clearly playing it humble.

Gage leans back in his chair, a grin tugging at the corners of his mouth. "Maybe less exciting, but definitely fewer chances of getting shot at."

As everyone laughs a little, the weight of that statement settles between us, and I bite back the darker thoughts that rise up, forcing a smile instead. With the exception of Carly, Vallyn hasn't told them anything about what happened recently, and I'm not about to spill it here. My lips twitch as I nod in agreement, but I keep the rest of my thoughts to myself.

The rest of lunch flows more easily after that. Conversations drift, laughter lightens the air, and the tension that had once hovered over the table starts to melt away. By the time we all say our goodbyes to Vallyn's friends, the awkwardness feels like a distant memory.

As we walk toward the car, I glance at her, my hand slipping into hers. "Do you want to come with me to the hospital?"

Her steps slow, and she looks up at me, her blue eyes searching. "Are you ready for that? For me to meet Casen?"

"Yeah," I say, with meaning. "You've met Gage, and Casen and I are probably closer. Plus," I pause, the confession slipping out before I can overthink it, "I don't really want you to leave my side right now."

Her hesitation flickers, but only for a moment. "If you're sure you want me to tag along..."

"I'm sure," I murmur, pulling her close, my lips pressing against hers in a slow, soft kiss. When I pull back, I open the car door for her, a quiet smile playing on my lips. "Let's go."

# CHAPTER FORTY-FOUR

# THE HOSPITAL & THE COUCH

## VALLYN

B lake strides ahead of me, his presence commanding even in the sterile chill of the hospital hallway. The sharp scent of antiseptic stings my nose as we approach Casen's room, the quiet beep of monitors the only thing breaking the suffocating silence this afternoon. The door swings open, and there he is—Casen—propped up in the hospital bed, pale but still managing to look like he's in control. Blake doesn't hesitate, closing the distance between them in a few steps, offering that handshake hug guys do, a quick pull before he leans in close, their familiarity hanging in the air like a shared secret.

Blake's eyes flick to mine, pulling me into their orbit, his voice low as he gestures toward me. "Casen, this is Vallyn."

Casen's lips twitch in a smile that doesn't quite reach his eyes, and he shifts, wincing slightly as he pushes himself upright. He extends a hand toward me, the ghost of pain written across his face.

"Well, Blake, I'll give you this much," he says, the hint of a laugh curling through his words. "She is pretty."

Heat floods my cheeks, an involuntary response to the compliment, and I can't help but glance down. Blake's sigh is a subtle thing, almost inaudible, but when he responds, there's a weight in his words. "That, I know."

Casen's gaze sharpens on me then, pulling me back into the moment. "Vallyn." My name feels heavy on his tongue, as if it carries more than just casual introduction. "This isn't your fault," he continues, shifting his attention back to Blake. "And it's not yours either."

The air thickens between them. Blake's jaw flexes, the tension rolling off him in waves, but he just shrugs, his expression unreadable, hiding behind that mask he wears so well. But I can see it, the crack. The shame, the regret. It's there, tucked beneath his cool exterior.

Casen, sensing the heaviness of the moment, breaks the silence. "We all know the risks. There's always the possibility of a distraction, always something that can go wrong."

Blake swallows hard, the muscles in his neck moving as he processes the words, but there's nothing he can say. Nothing either of us can say to absolve what happened.

I clear my throat, the words feeling almost foreign as they leave my lips. "It seems like it could've been worse. I'm just glad you're getting better."

Casen's hazel eyes lock with mine, searching, testing, before he nods. "Yeah, should be out of here in a couple of days." He smiles, but there's something brittle beneath it.

"Really?" Blake asks, there's something vulnerable in his voice, something raw.

Casen looks between the two of us, his smirk faint. "Yeah, I'll probably head to my parents' place. You know how moms are. She'll fuss over me, make me feel like I'm ten again, but it will make her feel needed and special."

Blake's lips quirk up at the corners, a ghost of a smile that barely forms before he offers, "Well, if you're there, I'll come by. Maybe bring you some real food."

"That'd be nice." Casen grimaces, pain threading through the mask of humor he's trying to wear.

Blake squeezes Casen's arm, the gesture filled with an unspoken understanding. "We should let you rest," Blake says softly.

Casen gives a tired nod. "Yeah, it's about time for the meds."

Blake moves around the bed, closing the space between us. I step forward, offering Casen a small smile. "It was nice meeting you, Casen. Blake's told me a lot about you."

Casen chuckles, though it's strained. "Nice to finally meet the girl who's got him all messed up." His eyes flick to Blake, whose eyes roll in exasperation.

I smirk, feeling Blake's presence at my side. "Yeah, well, he lost his mind for a while, but we're good now."

Before I can react, Blake's hand slides into mine, his grip firm but warm. He pulls me close, pressing the softest kiss to my temple, a touch that sends a shiver down my spine. His eyes linger on me for a moment longer before he turns back to his friend.

"Alright, man. Rest up. I'll check in with you tomorrow."

Casen's eyes flutter with exhaustion, but he manages a small smile. "Take care."

As Blake leads me out of the room, the air shifts, a tension slipping away.

Back at the apartment, steam still clings to my skin as I step out of the bathroom, the remnants of the shower like a haze that mirrors the one in my mind. The sound of Blake's low voice floats in from the balcony—he's checking in, speaking softly to whoever's on the other end. The glowing cherry on his cigarette as he inhales draws my attention to him through the window. I dress quickly, the cool air biting at my damp hair, and when I find him outside, the glow of the city beyond throws shadows across his face, making him look both dangerous and irresistible.

Pocketing his phone first, his eyes flick up as I step out to join him. A lazy smile pulls at his lips. "Hey, pretty girl."

That voice. It slips over me, wrapping me in a warmth I can't explain, like his very presence grounds me. "Hey," I respond, and even I can hear the tremor in my voice, the weight of everything pressing down, but also a strange sense of peace.

"You okay?" he asks, his gaze softening, searching my face.

I force a smile, one that feels half-real. "Yeah," I nod, my fingers twisting nervously in the hem of my shirt. "I think I'm still just... processing."

Blake's lips curve into a smile that feels more intimate than any touch. "That's understandable," he murmurs, stepping closer. His eyes linger on me like I'm something he's not sure he deserves. "I still think you're a dream I'm going to wake up from."

I swallow hard, my breath catching as I lace my fingers with his. "Like I said before... if you're dreaming, then I'm dreaming too." My voice is a whisper, shaky, but honest. I tilt my head, meeting his gaze, my heart in my throat. "And I don't want to wake up."

The change in him is instant. My words wake something inside him, and before I can take another breath, his hand snakes into the wet tangle of hair at the base of my skull, yanking me toward him. His mouth meets mine with a force that sends a jolt of electricity down my spine, his kiss tastes of smoke and sin. There's a rawness to it—desperate, possessive—as if he's staking his claim, as if this moment is the only thing tethering him to reality.

The world spins around me, the balcony, the city, everything fading as his lips move against mine. I don't care about the taste of tobacco; it's Blake. He feels like everything I didn't know I needed—rough edges, sharp breaths, and a heartbeat that matches the erratic rhythm of my own. I press into him, needing more, the ache between my thighs growing unbearable, and when he breaks the kiss, I'm gasping, already missing the way he devours me.

He crushes the cigarette under his boot, his eyes never leaving mine. Without a word, he backs me into the door, his movements quick, primal, as if something inside him has snapped. The tension rolls off him in waves, his gaze dark, feral. It's as if he's barely holding himself back, and every inch of my body screams for him not to.

The door slams shut behind us, but I barely register it. His unwashed hands are on me, rough and sure, pushing me backward, and the heat between us is almost unbearable. The fire in his eyes reflects the one burning deep in my core, a hunger so wild, so all-consuming that it leaves me trembling.

I need him. *Now.*

The couch hits the back of my legs, and I fall into it, the cushions swallowing me up in a gasp of air. He's standing in front of me, looming with that predatory intensity that leaves me breathless. Slowly, methodically, his hands move to his belt, loosening it with a metallic clink before he crouches down, untying his boots with quick, efficient motions. It's almost amusing—those boots, the jeans in this Phoenix heat—but the humor fizzles out the moment he straightens up, his eyes locking onto mine. Burning and hungry.

His hands make quick work of his jeans, the zipper a harsh sound in the otherwise quiet room. When they fall to the floor along with his boots, he's standing before me in nothing but a thin layer of fabric and desire so potent it's suffocating. I can't help it—my hand reaches for his when he offers before he pulls me up, his fingers already slipping beneath my shirt. They feel cold against my skin, a stark contrast to the heat simmering between us, and as he pulls my shirt over my head, I shiver.

He doesn't stop—his hands glide around my back, finding the clasp of my bra, and in one smooth motion, it's gone, discarded on the floor with the rest of our clothes. His touch is deliberate, fingertips tracing the curve of my waist before he hooks them into the waistband of my leggings. There's a pause, a breathless moment where his eyes meet mine, dark and unreadable, before he eases the fabric down my legs. It's awkward, stepping out of them, but the second I'm free, his hand is on my ass, squeezing just hard enough to make me gasp, while the other tangles in my hair, dragging me into him for a kiss that feels like it might devour me whole.

His lips are insistent, possessive, as his tongue moves against mine, and I can't help the way my hands reach under his shirt, nails grazing the smooth muscles of his back. He groans into my mouth, breaking away just long enough to rip the shirt off, and then my fingers find the waistband of his boxer briefs. My hands tremble as I push them down, eager, needy, but still wanting to savor every inch of skin revealed to me.

I move, rotating us until the couch is behind him, and he lets me nudge him down into it, his body sinking into the cushions. Before he can react, I climb onto his lap, straddling him, my breasts brushing against his face. He wastes no time, his hands finding my chest, kneading the soft flesh before his mouth follows, lips latching onto my nipple and sucking until I moan, the sound escaping without permission.

I start to grind against him, slow at first, just enough to feel the hard length of him pressing against my clit, but soon it's not enough. My hips move faster, harder, the friction driving me toward a blissful edge. His hands leave my breasts, one threading through my hair while the other grips my hip, feeling my rhythm until my breath becomes ragged and my movements desperate. My head falls back, a silent scream caught in my throat as the climax rips through me, white-hot and all-consuming.

"Fuck, pretty girl," he growls, his voice rough and strained. His mouth is at my neck now, teeth grazing the sensitive skin before he kisses his way up to my lips again, pulling me even closer, as if he's trying to fuse our bodies together. And then, with a shift of his weight, he flips us, pinning me beneath him on the couch. His eyes lock onto mine, and I swear I can see my future in them—every possible version of us, from now until forever. Some people say they see their life flash before their eyes when they die, but I see the future of my life flash before my eyes in the intensity of his gaze. Kids. Gray hairs. Porch swings. All of it flashes through me in an instant, overwhelming and terrifying, but I can't look away.

I want to tell him I love him and I need him. But I can't. It's insane. Too fast, too soon. But then his lips are on mine again, stealing the words before I can really think to speak them. His kiss is deep and hungry, as his hand slips down to lift my thigh. I barely have time to process the shift before he's thrusting into me, and the sensation is enough to steal my breath. I bite down on my lip, trying to stifle the gasp, but he sees it, feels it, and his eyes never leave mine.

This moment—it's more than sex. It's everything. It's trust. It's surrender. It's him, and it's me, and it's the raw, aching connection that makes me feel more alive than I ever have.

His pace quickens, hips driving into mine in a rhythm that feels both savage and intimate. His grip on my thighs tightens, and the pain blends with pleasure in a way that only heightens everything. I can't focus on anything but the feel of him, the heat of his skin against mine, the way our bodies collide in perfect sync.

Suddenly, he pulls back, shifting my hips up with him, and they are now almost a foot above my head—my body almost upside down as he holds me in his lap—he thrusts harder, deeper. It's animalistic now, wild and uncontrolled, and I can feel the bruises forming where his fingers dig into my flesh, but I don't care. I'm lost in the sight of him, the way his muscles ripple with each movement, the way his face contorts with pleasure as he nears the edge.

With a final, deep thrust, he shudders, his release hitting him hard, and I feel him pulse inside me. His eyes find mine again, and for a moment, it's like the whole world stops. Then, as if pulled by an invisible force, he collapses onto me, his lips crashing against mine for a heartbeat before he buries his face in my hair, his weight a comforting heaviness on top of me.

I know we can't stay like this forever, but right now, I don't want to move. His body pressed against mine feels like a promise. So I hold him, my fingers tracing lazy patterns across his back, kissing his neck and shoulder softly, savoring the quiet moment of vulnerability between us.

# CHAPTER FORTY-FIVE

# THE WEEKEND

## BLAKE

The feel of her, soft and warm beneath me, slips away as I roll onto my side. Facing her now, my arm drapes lazily over her waist, fingers tracing aimless patterns across her skin, memorizing the dip of her hip and the curve of her ribcage like they're sacred. Vallyn breathes quietly beside me, the silence between us a language all its own. I don't need words to know she's mine, that this woman is everything.

*How did I ever live without her?*

I can't even imagine a future that doesn't start and end with her in it.

Her eyes meet mine, soft and teasing, and a gentle smile spreads across her lips. "I think I need to pee," she whispers, as if it's a secret, a small disruption to this fragile, perfect moment.

A chuckle escapes me, and I release her, reluctantly. "I guess I'll allow it." Watching her rise, watching the sway of her full hips and the curve of her thick thighs as she moves away, I can't help but marvel at her.

*How do I get to have her?*

I don't think I'll ever get used to watching her.

I pull my boxer briefs back on and she dresses, if you can call it that, slipping into something barely there, and we lazily order pizza, more to sustain ourselves than out of hunger. We collapse back onto the couch, limbs tangled, her warmth pressed into me as we half-watch whatever movies are playing, more interested in each other than the flicker of the screen. Time blurs. Hours slip away. And when the world is quiet and the night has crept in, I lift her—she feels small and weightless in my arms—and carry her to bed.

In the stillness of her room, we make love. Sleepy, slow, like we're moving through a dream—her body against me, her breath mingling with mine, the world fading into nothing but her. There's no rush, no need to be anything more than this, wrapped in each other until sleep takes us both again, our bodies still tangled, as if even in our dreams, we can't bear to be apart.

Casen's call comes early, his voice rough but lighter than I've heard in weeks. He's discharging, but he needs time, wants to settle in at his parents' place before Gage and I disrupt his peace. I respect that. We've all earned the right to breathe for a minute. I promise him a few days, a little distance.

Those days belong to Vallyn. Three long, perfect days of tangled limbs, of bodies intertwined so often I can barely distinguish where I end and she begins. My lips are raw, cracked from kissing her until

I forget to breathe, and my cock... well, I'm not exactly complaining, but there's a certain ache I've never felt before. Yet none of it matters. Nothing would ever stop me from fucking her.

It's not just sex, though the sex is nothing short of mind-blowing. It's the deep conversations that steal my breath just as much as the way her mouth moves against mine. We talk about everything, about life, about kids. Neither of us has a set number in mind, but the idea of a family feels like something tangible now. Something within reach.

But the conversation shifts, turns heavier when she brings up what I do—what I'll do when kids enter the picture. "My Uncle Jeremy never had children," she says, her voice soft, thoughtful. "I always thought it would've been hard for him with what he did."

I exhale, stalling for a moment as I figure out how to answer her. "Vallyn, baby... pretty girl." I stroke her cheek, buying myself just a little more time. "Some of it—it's a calling. The part where I help people, that's not just a job for me. But I've made enough and we could live off PI work if it came to that, especially when it's time to talk seriously about kids. I wouldn't want to be absent. I wouldn't want to miss out on being a father... or a husband."

Her lips twitch in a small smile, but there's something thoughtful in her gaze. "Or a boyfriend."

That coy little smirk she throws my way? I'd burn the world down for her in a heartbeat. Give her anything she wants. Everything.

"Oh, we're putting titles on this now?" I tease, watching her blush just enough to make her even more irresistible.

She shrugs, her smile widening. "You've been saying I'm yours for a while now, haven't you?"

"Little Lotte, you *are* mine," I growl, the words spilling out harder than I mean them to. "Fuck, Vallyn. Yes, you're my girlfriend. My baby girl. My bae. Whatever title you want, you can have it."

The way her face lights up twists something deep in my chest. I want to tell her I love her—to marry me. Hell, I want to drag her to Vegas right now and marry her, but I know that's insane.

Instead, I grin and pull her into my arms. "Come here, girlfriend," I say, wrapping her up tightly.

But then the vibrations start—my phone, my watch—and the timing is too perfect, like he knew she was talking about him. Jeremy's name flashes across the screen, and I show it to Vallyn with a laugh. I answer, "Hey, Jer, what's up?"

"You ready for some payback?" he asks, his tone all business.

My eyes flick to Vallyn's. "You have him?"

"We know where he is. Under surveillance. They won't move on him until next week unless he heads for the border. He has a big team, so we need to gather more information and more resources. Colton's running it, and we could use you and Gage. Think you're up for it?"

"How many?" I ask, instinct kicking in.

"Fifteen, maybe more. That's why we've got recon on him. He's a much bigger fish than we thought. And, Blake, they're planning on moving on him on Saturday, so I won't be there, I'll be at Quintin's wedding."

I nod, already running through the plan in my head. "Probably. I'll call Gage, but yeah. We need to make sure he's locked up."

Jeremy hesitates before his voice softens, "You know Vallyn's still at risk, even if he's behind bars?"

"I do." My eyes meet hers again, her gaze steady, calm, even though she doesn't know the full weight of the conversation that's coming.

"You gonna talk to her?"

"Yeah," I say, my voice low. "And I'll let you know if I need you to back me up."

Jeremy chuckles. "How's she doing?"

I take a moment, absorbing the unspoken care in his question. "She's good. We're good."

"Glad to hear it. She had a rough go with boyfriends in college. I think you two are good for each other."

I let the seriousness of his words—and the things I apparently don't know—settle over me before responding, "She's more than good for me."

"I'm sure she is," he says and then pauses. "Well, let me know what Gage says."

"I will," I answer before we exchange casual goodbyes.

I set the phone down, my thoughts already turning to Vallyn, to what I'll have to tell her, and the storm that's about to come. But looking at her now, I know there's nothing I won't do to keep her safe.

As I hang up the phone, I can feel Vallyn's eyes on me, tension building between us like a coiled spring. "What was that about?" she asks, her voice steady, but I hear the underlying note of unease.

I don't sugarcoat it. There's no point. "They know where Elijah is," I say, watching the way her breath catches, her body reacting to the gravity of the name alone.

I fill in the details—how Elijah isn't just a lone target. He's surrounded, protected, by more than we thought. "They've got him under surveillance for now. Jeremy says there's about fifteen with him. He's a bigger fish than anyone realized. It's gonna take three teams to take him down." I shrug slightly, trying to mask the weight of it. "Although, Gage and I aren't exactly a team."

Vallyn's shoulders slump, the change in her posture instant. The shift in her eyes tells me she knows what's coming. "So, you're going with Jeremy?"

I shake my head. "I need to talk to Gage first. I won't go without him. And no, not with Jeremy. They're moving in on Elijah on Saturday, but Jeremy will be with you—at Quintin's wedding."

Her sigh is heavy, resigned, but she moves toward me anyway. Her arms wrap around my waist, her face pressing against my chest as if she's trying to keep herself in the moment, in me. I hold her close, burying my face in her hair, feeling her breathe. She understands—even when I wish she didn't have to.

"There's something else, pretty girl," I murmur, my voice low. She pulls back just enough to look up at me, those wide eyes waiting for the truth I don't want to give her.

I meet her gaze, steady but soft. "Even if they lock him up, it doesn't mean you're safe. It doesn't mean any of us are safe. We'll still need to stay vigilant, and you—" I pause, hating the way this will hurt her, "—you'll still need to stay away from the youth center."

Her lips press together, her eyes shadowed with worry as she swallows. "Do you think I'll ever be able to go back?"

I exhale slowly, running a hand through my hair. "Honestly? I don't know. Maybe. If you do, I'll want to be there. Probably Gage or Jeremy, too. Someone armed in the van while I'm inside with you, unarmed." I force a small smile. "I know Corey used to go with you, so it shouldn't be an issue."

She nods, but her eyes are distant, and I can see the weight of what she's processing. "No, you being there wouldn't be an issue. I just… " Her voice cracks, and when she speaks again, it's softer, more vulnerable. "I just want to say goodbye to the kids. More than anything."

Her eyes glisten, turning red, and I know the tears are coming. *Fuck*. I pull her in before they can fall, wrapping her up tightly, trying to hold her together with my arms alone. "Pretty girl, we'll get you time to say goodbye. I promise you that."

And then the tears break free, silent at first, then falling harder as she trembles in my arms. I tighten my grip, wanting to shield her from everything, but knowing that no amount of protection can erase the pain that's etched in her heart over this.

# CHAPTER FORTY-SIX
## WEDDING & HUNTING PREPATION

### VALLYN

After running back to his condo while I joined Sonia for her final dress fitting, Blake came back to stay with me until Friday. The little time we have together is interrupted by wedding events. He utilizes the time when I'm gone to coordinate with the other teams, strategizing with Gage, making sure they're ready for Saturday's mission.

At the bachelorette party, I'm trying to focus on Sonia, on the celebration, but she keeps asking about Blake. Every question she asks tugs my thoughts back to him. He's all I can think about, all I want to talk about.

By the end of the night, Sonia's slurring with half-lidded eyes glittering with mischief, and she leans into me, whispering, "He's fucking hot." I follow her eyes to Blake stepping out of his car, pulled up to the curb.

The perfect gentleman, he walks up to greet Sonia and her friends. He's polite and charming when he opens the car door for me with a smile that makes my heart skip. He wasn't going to let me take a rideshare home tonight—that protective instinct of his is in full force.

I only had a couple of drinks, so I'm mostly sober, but the way his hand rests on my thigh as we drive away makes my head spin. There's an intimacy in that simple touch, a promise of safety and something deeper. For a few minutes, the car is quiet, just the hum of the engine and the low beat of music in the background. But the connection between us crackles, thick with unspoken words.

"So, tell me the plan for the next couple of days again," he says, his voice low, thumb grazing my skin. "Just so I've got it straight."

I go over the schedule, detailing the rehearsal tomorrow, the dinner afterward, and how Jeremy and his wife are taking me everywhere. We'll all be staying at the same hotel until after the wedding. I try to keep it casual, but the weight of what's coming—Saturday—hangs between us.

Blake nods, processing, his fingers never leaving my thigh. "Okay. So Jeremy will be with you the whole time?"

"Yeah, he'll be around. Not *in* my room or in every room I'm in, but close enough." I give him a small smile, but it fades when I see the focus in his eyes, the intensity that comes with planning a mission like this.

He squeezes my thigh, grounding me. "I'll head down Friday afternoon with Gage. I know I told you, but he's in Nogales, so it's gonna be a trek. Shouldn't be too bad, though. Hopefully, by the time you're done with the reception, I'll be able to make it to the hotel. And then... I can hold you." His words are soft, but the way he says them makes my chest ache.

"I hope so," I whisper. "I won't have my phone with me during the ceremony. The dress doesn't have pockets, and I can't carry a purse. Jeremy will have his, though. So let Gage know... just in case." My voice trails off, but we both know what I mean. In case something goes wrong.

Blake's grip on my thigh tightens just slightly, reassuring. "Vallyn, I'll be fine. I promise. I'll just be happy to have him behind bars again."

I chew my lip, staring out the window for a moment before asking the question that's been lingering in my mind. "Can I ask you something? Something I should probably already know?"

He glances at me, giving me that silent permission to go ahead.

"Why do bounty hunters handle this instead of law enforcement?"

He nods, taking a deep breath before answering. "We have fewer restrictions. More freedom. We don't have to deal with red tape or getting warrants approved. If we need more guys, we just make a call. If we need more equipment and we want to buy it, we just buy it. There's no jurisdiction for us, no boundaries. We can go to Nogales, no problem. Law enforcement would need to go through red tape, or have another jurisdiction take over, and by then, the target might be gone. We can move faster and sometimes smarter."

I nod, understanding as we pull into the parking lot. But as we get out of the car, something inside me shifts. This might be the last night we have together for a while, and the thought makes me cling to him with a desperation I've never felt before. He holds me just as tightly, as if he feels the same weight pressing down on us both.

The next morning, I wake to the sound of Blake's phone buzzing . When he answers, his voice is already in command mode. He's on speaker, talking to Gage, Colton, and Greg, Jeremy's right-hand man. There's something so grounding in the way they talk, their voices calm despite the tension lacing every word. Colton leads the team, but there's an unmistakable camaraderie, a trust that runs deep between the five men.

They're laying out the plan, a coordinated effort involving a team of twenty men—bounty hunters, private investigators, and tech guys. Eli is holed up in a fortified two-story house with a basement, protected by thirteen armed men. It's a small army, and the stakes seem to be higher than normal for them.

Colton breaks it down with surgical precision. Two teams will surround the house, cutting off all exits. Gage and his guy, Oscar, will disable the security system and scramble any outgoing communications, and a third team will block off the street to prevent any backup from reaching the house and bystanders from getting hurt. The house is rigged with cameras and motion detectors, but Gage and Oscar will handle that—they'll tap into the system, turning the surveillance against the very men it's meant to protect.

Inside the house, they describe a tricky layout. The second floor has windows barricaded with metal shutters, and the basement is believed to be a fortress in itself, but Colton's men are prepared. The plan is to breach from both the front and back simultaneously, using flashbangs to disorient the men inside. They expect heavy resistance, but that's where Blake and Colton's experience comes in. Their job is to neutralize the bodyguards, clearing a path to the basement, where they believe the target is hiding.

They're bringing in drones to heatmap out the interior, marking where each man is stationed. Colton's voice is calm, but the tension is palpable. This isn't a simple grab-and-go. It's a full-scale assault, calculated down to the last detail. Every man on that team has a role, and each role is vital. Timing is everything.

"Blake, you'll take point on the east side. We'll have snipers covering the windows from across the street. Greg, you'll be with me.

We'll breach together, no hesitation. Once we're inside, we move fast. Don't give them a chance to regroup."

As the call ends, Blake looks over at me, his expression unreadable. There's a moment of silence before he reaches for me, pulling me into his arms. I can feel the tension in his body, the weight of what's coming. And it's a reminder of just how dangerous this all is.

But as he holds me, his hand running through my hair, I know that no matter what happens, I'll be waiting for him on the other side.

The afternoon slips away too fast, the weight of our separation pressing down on me like a tightening vice. Soon, there's a knock at the door—Jeremy, punctual as always. Blake walks to his car beside me, carrying my things, his presence grounding me in the chaos of my thoughts.

Their exchange is brief, but charged. I can feel the stress and tension between them, crackling like a live wire. Blake's voice is firm, commanding, as he makes Jeremy promise to take care of me. And Jeremy, my ever-reliable uncle, matches his intensity, making Blake swear to bring Eli back and return unharmed. The gravity of the moment hits me like a punch to the gut, and I swallow hard against the rising anxiety.

Jeremy steps away, giving us space we didn't ask for but desperately need.

Blake's hands are suddenly on my shoulders, pulling me into him, his lips brushing my forehead in a kiss so gentle it feels like a promise. "Vallyn, pretty girl," he whispers, his voice rough with tenderness. "I'll see you tomorrow night. We'll finally be able to sleep a little easier."

I bite my lip, hesitating. My heart races with the uncertainty of what's to come, and I cling to him like he's the only thing tethering me to solid ground. "Can I make a silly request?" I ask, my voice barely above a whisper.

He tilts his head, a soft smile playing on his lips. "You can make any request you want, Little Lotte."

"Sunday... take me to your condo. When this is all done, I just want to be with you... in a place I know is safe," I murmur, thinking of the security he's told me about—how his building, his condo, is a fortress of safety in a world that feels too uncertain right now.

His smile widens, a glint of relief in his eyes as he leans in and presses a quick kiss to my lips. "That can absolutely be done, pretty girl. I'll take you to my condo. I'll *always* make sure you're safe."

I try to smile, but the knot in my chest tightens, and I feel the words clawing at the back of my throat. "You know, I have this crazy feeling of dread." I say, my voice barely steady. "Why am I so terrified something will go wrong?"

He meets my gaze, his expression softening as he runs his fingers through my hair, his touch soothing in a way his words can't be right now. "You know why I know I'll be okay?" he asks, his voice so steady, so sure it makes my heart skip a beat.

"Why?" I breathe.

His thumb traces my jawline, his eyes locking onto mine, unwavering. "Because I've never in my life had something I wanted to come back to and be okay for more than you," he confesses, and the sincerity in his words knocks the air from my lungs.

My arms, already wrapped around his waist, tighten as I pull him closer, burying my face in his chest as his arms envelop me in a bear hug that feels like it's holding me together. The tears come before I can stop them, hot and stinging, falling silently onto his shirt.

Blake's hold on me loosens just enough for him to pull back and see my face, his expression softening further when he notices the tears. He leans in, pressing gentle kisses to each of my cheeks, wiping away the wetness with his lips before kissing me deeply, pouring everything into that moment.

"I'll miss you, Vallyn," he whispers against my lips, his voice thick with emotion. "But I *will* come back for you."

I can't find the words, so I nod, biting back the sob that threatens to escape. He opens the car door to my uncle's car, and I nearly fall into the passenger seat, the sudden rush of emotions has me lightheaded.

The door closes with a soft thud, and I watch through the window as Blake and Jeremy exchange one last nod. It feels final, like a silent understanding passes between them. And then we're pulling away, Blake's figure growing smaller in the mirror.

Jeremy drives in silence, the thickness of everything hanging between us like a fog. I don't say a word either, the tears slipping quietly down my cheeks as I process the overwhelming fear, the dread that lingers in the pit of my stomach. I truly understand the stakes, but now I am really feeling the risk Blake is taking. And the thought of losing him—of not seeing him again after today—leaves me hollow inside.

The rehearsal and the rehearsal dinner feel like a blur. But I hold onto the hope that come Saturday night or Sunday, Blake and I will be together again. Safe.

# Chapter Forty-Seven

# The Apprehension

## BLAKE

"Hey, pretty girl," I answer, my voice soft but steady as Vallyn calls late Friday night.

Her voice, low and sultry, hits me right in the chest as she replies. "Hi. I just got back to the room from the rehearsal dinner. Did you make it to your hotel?" There's a softness, a vulnerability in her tone that I can't ignore.

"I did. Gage and I just finished dinner." Silence lingers on her end, and I know she's holding something back. "You still feeling scared?" I press gently.

"Very much so," she admits. Her breath catches, and I can almost feel the tension from here. "I don't want my fear to affect you, but I can't shake this foreboding feeling. It's deep in my gut, something I've never felt before. Maybe it's just because this is the first time I've had to let you go into a situation like this—why I'm this scared."

I close my eyes, wishing I could pull her into my arms, kiss away her worries. "I think that's probably it, pretty girl," I murmur. "My mom and sister felt the same way the first time they knew what I was getting into. It's normal." I try to sound reassuring, but I know she won't be comforted that easily.

There's a sharp inhale on her end. "I trust you, Blake. I trust Gage and Jeremy's team too. But I'm still scared."

"I know you are, baby. And I'd be lying if I said I didn't have some fear. I always do. But this plan—this one's solid. The heatmap drones, they're a game-changer—they're what we waited for. We've never had that kind of tech on our side before outside of military operations. I swear to you, Vallyn, I'm going to do everything in my power to come back to you. In one piece."

Her soft laugh filters through the line, tinged with nervousness. "Blake... my phantom man." She hesitates, and I can hear the emotion in her voice. "I just need you to hold me so tight the next time I see you, that's all."

"Oh, I will, pretty girl. I'll hold you so tight. Bury my face in your hair, feel you against me. Don't even question that." My voice drops lower, thick with the weight of everything I feel for her but haven't yet said.

We exchange a few more words, small reassurances, promises to each other, before saying our goodbyes. I don't tell her I love her—not yet. But it's there, lingering between us, unspoken.

In the morning I text her.

Me

It's go time pretty girl, I know you won't have your phone, so I'll text Jeremy when it's done

Vallyn

Okay, take care of you

Me

I'll see you soon

A little while later the heatmap drones are deployed, silently marking every man inside. We know exactly where they are—how many on each floor, which room each guard occupies. There's no guesswork, no surprises.

My pulse hums with anticipation as I move into position. The July air is hot against my skin, the sound of our boots silent against the pavement. Everyone knows their role, and there's no room for error. Gage and Oscar handle the security like pros, and within minutes, the cameras go dark. The house is blind, its inhabitants unaware that their own systems are now betraying them.

"Security's down," Gage's voice crackles over the comms. "We're clear."

Colton signals, and like clockwork, the teams move. One more signal has us breaching the front and back simultaneously, flashbangs detonating in sync. The world explodes in a flash of light and sound, and before the guards can even register what's happening, we're inside.

There's no chaos, no panic—just precision. The guards, disoriented and blind from the blast, raise their hands before they even think of leveling their weapons. They know they're overpowered. Not a single shot is fired. One by one, they surrender. I move with Colton through the main floor, securing each room, while Greg clears the upstairs. It's methodical, almost too easy.

"Basement's clear," I hear over the comms from other members of Colton's team, and I exhale, tension easing from my muscles. Less than ten minutes later, Elijah is cuffed, sitting in the back of Colton's SUV, his face a little pale. He knows it's over.

The entire operation runs smoother than we anticipated. No one hurt, no shots fired, and Elijah? He's headed back to Phoenix, his small army dismantled in minutes. Greg and the rest of Jeremy's team stay at the house and wait for uniforms to pick up about half of that small army on warrants.

I pull out my phone, fingers trembling slightly as I prepare to text Jeremy the update. I know they're deep in the ceremony, but there's an urgency to letting them know I'm okay and we're clear. Before I can type a single word, my gaze catches a different text—a message and mirror selfie Vallyn sent earlier.

In her black bridesmaid dress, she's a vision that steals my breath. The fabric dips low in the front—maybe too low—but damn, she looks intoxicating. The dress flows to her calves, hugging her curves in all the right places, the sleeveless design showcasing her soft arms. Her hair, usually a cascade of wild waves, is styled in small, soft curls, pulled back half-up, with tendrils framing her face like a sultry halo.

Her makeup is bold, heavier than I've ever seen her wear. Smoky eyes swirl with sultry depth, and her red lips are a temptation, painted to perfection. It's mesmerizing yet strangely unfamiliar; this version of her feels like a tantalizing secret waiting to be unraveled. I stare at the picture, caught in a whirlwind of admiration and desire, until reality pulls me back.

I close the photo and refocus, determined to send the update to Jeremy as I had planned, even as thoughts of Vallyn linger in my mind like an intoxicating fragrance, wrapping around me, making it hard to think of anything else.

Me

> It's done - was flawless. He's on his way to Phoenix with Colton, Gage and I are on our way back, too.

As I pocket the phone, all I can think about is getting back to Vallyn. I promised her I'd come back, and I will. In one piece, just like I said.

Gage and I crack jokes and let the thumping bass of our favorite playlist vibrate through the van as we slice through the outskirts of Phoenix. The sun is still high in the summer sky, casting a warm glow that makes the suburban sprawl look deceptively peaceful. When we hit a drive-thru, the scent of greasy burgers and fries envelops us. I savor the moment of normalcy. But just as I bite into my burger, my phone buzzes.

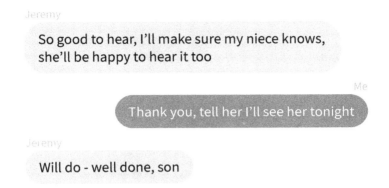

I pocket my phone again, a flicker of warmth threading through my chest. I know Vallyn still has hours of reception to go, so I enjoy my dinner with Gage and then he heads to drop me off at my place, where I plan on showering and getting ready to head to her.

We're nearing my building when another text comes through. Hope flares in my gut—it could be Vallyn—but reality crashes over me like a cold wave when I see the text.

A jolt of ice runs through my veins as I swipe to see a photo. Vallyn is bound in her black bridesmaid dress, her mouth taped shut, sitting in a metal folding chair that looks as cold as the dread creeping into my veins. Her arms are secured behind her, and her eyes scream for help through her smudged makeup. Panic ignites in my chest, and I can feel the blood drain from my face.

Gage, ever perceptive, notices something is wrong. "What the fuck is it?" he breathes, his voice tight with concern.

When his eyes dart to my phone, without hesitation, he jerks the wheel to pull over. The engine purrs quietly as he dials Colton from the dash, his jaw clenched in fury.

"Hey, Gage," Colton answers.

"Tell me you didn't drop him off yet!" Gage barks, his tone demanding.

"We're about to pull up," Colton replies, baffled.

"Take him to the dungeon," Gage orders, the authority in his voice making it clear that this isn't a request but a command.

Colton's agreement is laced with uncertainty, but Gage promises an explanation when we get there. As soon as he hangs up, I dial Jeremy, he rejects the first call and I call back immediately, anxiety twisting in my gut as the phone rings.

"Blake?" His voice is cautious and quiet. I skip the pleasantries, urgency driving me.

"When did you last see Vallyn?" I cut straight to the point.

He hesitates, and I can almost picture him scanning a crowded ballroom, looking for answers that aren't there. "Probably about twenty minutes ago," he replies, finally.

"Well, gather whatever the fuck information you can from the hotel, because Elijah's people have her." My voice drops into a low growl, the words heavy with dread.

"What? Blake, what the fuck are you saying?" Jeremy stammers, disbelief ringing in his tone.

"They sent me a picture of her," I say, my breath hitching. "In her bridesmaid dress—the same dress from the picture she sent me this morning. They've got her bound and gagged in some basement."

"Fuck," he exhales, the gravity of the situation sinking in. "Okay, let me check with hotel security. Where am I meeting you?"

"The dungeon." The word feels ominous on my tongue.

His pause is thick with understanding; he knows the implications—that is where we take people when we need answers. "Okay," he finally agrees, resignation lacing his voice.

I end the call and toss my phone to the floor of the van, the clatter echoing in the tense silence. Gage's grip on the wheel tightens as he accelerates, the city blurring past us in streaks of light and shadow. Colton will likely beat us there.

"You can't kill him," Gage says, stealing a glance at me, my head buried in my hands, the weight of dread pressing down.

"I know," I reply softly, the words a mere whisper against the roar of my heart, each beat echoing the urgency of the moment.

# Chapter Forty-Eight

# The Wedding

## VALLYN

Before I leave my hotel room—my phone to be left with my uncle—I pause to take a mirror selfie. My makeup is bold, edgier than Blake has ever seen, and my hair is styled in a way that feels like a different version of me. The dress clings to every curve, hugging me in all the right places, making me feel powerful, sexy, and confident. I send it to him with a quick playful and flirty message—something to remind him what's waiting for him on the other side of tonight.

Jeremy and Blake both reassured me they'd stay in contact, so I don't hesitate when I hand my phone to my uncle. Anyone who might need me is here, at the wedding, or knows where I am. I take a deep breath, trying to settle the lingering unease in my stomach, and step out of my room.

The suite is buzzing with energy, Sonia and her bridesmaids making last-minute adjustments to dresses, bouquets, hair, and makeup. Sonia looks stunning in her gown, and I know that when Quintin sees her, he's going to lose it. As much as I try to focus on the beauty of the day, there's still a knot in my gut that I can't shake—a sense of dread that I keep pushing down, willing it to disappear.

I walk down the aisle with Quintin's best friend, someone who's known me since I was a kid. His presence steadies me, grounding me in the moment. My uncle, Jeremy, shoots me a wink as I pass, and the tension eases, just a bit. That wink means everything's okay—for now, at least. Blake is okay or there is no news and I cling to that.

The ceremony is beautiful, their vows heartfelt, and the love between Sonia and Quintin makes my chest ache. I can't help but think of Blake. It's been less than twenty-four hours, and yet I miss him so fiercely it's almost laughable.

After the ceremony, I take my place with Quintin, standing in the receiving line between him and my dad. It's all so formal, so traditional, and for the first time, I find myself wondering how I'll do things at my own wedding. When my uncle reaches me, he hugs me a little longer than necessary, his arms wrapped tight around me, and I feel the tension in his grip.

"It's done," he whispers in my ear, his breath warm against my skin. "They're fine, on their way back to Phoenix."

I pull back to meet his eyes, the relief crashing over me like a wave. My chest tightens, and tears sting my eyes, but I manage to smile, to nod. "Thank you," I breathe, and he squeezes my arm, reassuring me with that familiar steady presence, and then hands me back my phone.

The knot in my stomach loosens just enough for me to breathe again, and the suffocating weight on my chest lightens. Dinner is lively, the clinking of champagne glasses signaling toasts and kisses, the room filled with laughter and joy. The cake cutting is sweet, Sonia and Quintin sharing a moment of quiet tenderness, no smashed cake or forced antics. Everything feels light, easy, and for the first time all day, I let myself relax. Tonight, I'll be in Blake's arms again, and that's all I care about.

As they prepare the dance floor, I excuse myself from the head table, slipping away to the restroom. The sound of running water is soothing as I wash my hands, but when I glance up into the mirror, I'm surprised to see one of the caterers emerging from a stall. She smiles at me, a knowing sort of smile that makes me pause.

"You're Quintin's sister, right? Vallyn?"

Her questions catch me off guard, but I smile and nod. "I am."

She doesn't say anything else, just slips out of the bathroom without another word. I finish washing my hands, my mind already drifting back to the reception. But as I step into the hallway, two men are standing just outside the door, dressed in casual clothes—jeans and t-shirts—completely out of place for a wedding.

I hesitate for a second, keeping my eyes down and not really looking at them, but forcing a polite smile as I try to step around them. "Excuse me," I say, but one of them moves in front of me, blocking my path, while the other moves behind me.

The caterer—now standing behind him—nods toward me. "It's her," she says, and my heart stops.

Panic surges through me in an instant. I'm grabbed from behind, an arm locking around my waist while a hand clamps down over my mouth. Hearing my phone hit the floor, I scream, but the sound is muffled against his palm. My legs kick out instinctively, but the other man grabs them, lifting me off the ground. I thrash, my vision blurring with terror and tears, but they drag me backward, pulling me into a storage closet.

Luggage racks, spare chairs, and other items are crammed into the room, but my focus is on the woman stepping toward me—the caterer. She's holding something in her hand, and my heart slams against my ribs when I realize what it is. A syringe.

"No," I try to scream, but my voice is muffled, the sound strangled and desperate. Tears blur my vision as I shake my head, trying to break free, but the man's grip is too tight.

The woman's face is a mask of indifference as she steps closer, the needle glinting under the harsh light of the closet. "Night, night," she says, her voice cold, detached.

I feel the sharp prick of the needle against my neck, the burn flooding my veins. Panic surges through me, but it's already too late. The world spins, my limbs are heavy and useless. My vision narrows to a pinpoint as the drug takes hold, dragging me into unconsciousness.

The last thing I feel is the firmness of the man's arm still wrapped around me, the cold bite of fear clawing at my chest, and then... nothing. Darkness swallows me whole.

When I wake up, everything is wrong. My head pounds, my vision is blurry, but it's the cold bite of metal beneath me that jolts me back to reality. I'm slumped in a chair—hard, cold, unyielding. I try to speak, but my lips don't part. Instantly I realize my mouth is taped shut.

Panic surges through me, and I try to move, only to realize my hands are bound behind me, the cold metal of chains digging into my wrists. The metal links clink together and pinches my skin as I try to shift, the chair scraping against the floor with a sound so sharp, it sends a shiver down my spine. That horrible, shrieking sound of nails on a chalkboard, echoing through the small, cramped space.

Two men turn toward me. One of them—the one closest—makes my stomach drop. I know him. I remember him from the restaurant, the day Casen was shot. The realization crashes into me with the gravity of a nightmare made real.

*Fuck, these are Eli's people.*

I swallow hard, but it feels like a rock lodged in my throat. My pulse quickens, and I instinctively tug at the chains, testing their strength, praying for any give. There's none.

"Look, the princess is awake," the man from the restaurant sneers, his voice cold and mocking. His eyes gleam with amusement, as if this is nothing but a game to him.

A different man, one I haven't seen before, steps into my line of sight. He's holding a phone, and the grin on his face is enough to make my blood run cold. He leans closer, snapping a picture of me. "Smile for Blake," he says, his tone dripping with malice. The men laugh, their cruel laughter filling the room, suffocating me.

I bite down on the scream threatening to tear through me, focusing instead on the room, trying to steady my racing thoughts.

*Think, Vallyn.*

The space is small—fifteen by fifteen feet, maybe less. The walls are old, rough gray brick, and the floor beneath me is cold concrete. My eyes land on a rusted drain in the center of the floor, and dread pools in my stomach. This isn't just some storage room. It's meant for things that they want to be able to clean up.

Five men are here with me. One is the man I recognize from the restaurant, and the other four are strangers. Dangerous strangers. I don't see the woman who identified me and drugged me. She's gone, maybe still at the hotel keeping an eye out for when someone notices I'm missing.

I can feel my pulse in my ears, thundering, as the panic claws at the edges of my mind. But I fight it back, telling myself what I know, repeating it like a mantra.

*My uncle will notice I'm gone. There are security cameras at the hotel—someone will see. Blake will know. He'll know. They sent him that picture, they wanted him to know. And Blake and Gage—they're good at what they do. They'll find me. They have to.*

I keep repeating it in pieces to myself, over and over, trying to drown out the fear. Trying to ignore the sinister reality of where I am and who I'm with. Because if I let it sink in—if I let the terror fully consume me—I don't know if I'll make it out.

I don't know how long I've been here. Time has become slippery, distorted by fear and the constant hum of dread. They've fed me twice, and I've had to go to the bathroom a few times, always under watch, so maybe it's been a day—maybe more. The passing of hours is a cruel joke when every second feels like an eternity.

They take turns standing guard over me. Some of them are quieter, less overtly hostile. But it's always suffocating, knowing I'm never alone. One of them—the youngest, I think—seems different. They call him "Ace." He sat next to me earlier, the flicker of a phone screen catching my attention. He put on a movie, like we were just two people passing the time. I didn't even register what was playing, too numb to care, but it was better than the alternative.

The alternative is "Jigsaw," as they call him. He doesn't talk much, but he watches me—always watches me—with this sickening fascination, picking his teeth and fingernails with a switchblade that gleams under the dim, fluorescent light. Every now and then, he'll glance at me and smile, like he's waiting for something, some cue to do whatever unspeakable thing he's been fantasizing about. That smile makes my skin crawl, makes me want to disappear.

I've tried to keep myself composed, but it's hard. The minutes stretch endlessly, and my mind races with what-ifs.

*What if Blake and Jeremy can't find me? What if they don't make it in time? What if I don't survive this?*

But I have to believe. I have to keep telling myself that Blake is out there, that Jeremy is with him, that they're looking for me. I cling to the thought like a lifeline.

*Blake will find me. They will find me. They have to. I just need to hold on. Just a little longer.*

## Chapter Forty-Nine

# The Interrogation

## BLAKE

Colton is waiting in the garage of the dungeon when we pull up. The van barely comes to a halt before I'm out, heart hammering in my chest. It's really only seconds before I'm ripping the door to Colton's SUV open. Elijah's slouched in the backseat, still cuffed, looking smug like he has any control here.

"Where the fuck did they take her?" I shout, grabbing Elijah by his collar and yanking him out of the car. Forcefully, I slam him against the side of the SUV. My face is inches from his, breathing fury as my fists clench around his shirt.

Gage, Colton, and Oscar stand nearby, silent. They're ready, but I know they're letting me take point. Colton is surely confused, but he doesn't ask questions. The garage door groans shut behind us, sealing us in.

"Where?" I scream again, pushing him harder into the metal, the heat of my rage burning in every word. Elijah's eyes flash, and I see it—the split second decision to fight. He pulls his head back, ready to headbutt me, but I release him before he has a chance to make contact, stepping back, just waiting.

Gage moves in smoothly beside me, his voice calm but laced with a sadistic edge. "You can tell us where your guys would take a hostage now, and we'll play nice. Or... " He pauses, letting the silence stretch, his smile cruel. "Or we can take you downstairs, and it won't be so nice."

Elijah's lips twitch in a half-smile, but it falters. He glances over at Colton, who's watching the scene unfold with a predator's patience. Colton's size alone is enough to unnerve anyone, and Elijah knows it. The tension builds in the air, thick and oppressive.

"If you don't want to cooperate, Colton here has a *thing* for hurting people," Gage adds, his tone conversational. "Your call."

Elijah's gaze shifts between us, his cocky facade crumbling. But then, firmly, he says, "I don't even know what the fuck you're talking about."

"Your boys took Vallyn," Gage states, still calm, still terrifying in its calmness. His words hit me like a freight train even though the knowledge isn't new.

The shock on Elijah's face is immediate and real—he didn't know. His eyes dart from me to Gage, then to Colton. He swallows hard, trying to mask his fear, but I see it as he looks back at Gage.

"I didn't know," he stammers, his voice less steady now. "I *don't* fucking know."

"Let's have a talk," Gage says, grabbing Elijah's arm and steering him toward the door at the back of the garage. We bypass the basement—the actual dungeon—where things would get ugly. It's where we take people to do less-than-legal things to get answers. Instead, Gage leads him to the interrogation room. It's where we handle situations like this when we still want to keep things legal... or at least legal-ish.

Inside, Gage pushes Elijah into a chair and then sits across from him at the table. Rapping his knuckles lightly on the surface before speaking again.

"Here's the thing," Gage begins, his voice still unnervingly calm. "We're probably going to have security footage any minute now. Once we're done talking, we're going to work some magic with the phone number that texted Blake. But this will go much easier for you if you start talking now."

Before Elijah can respond, Jeremy walks in, looking like he just stepped out of the wedding reception. His jacket and tie are gone, but he's still in dress clothes. He glances at me quickly and then hands a flash drive and a cracked phone—Vallyn's phone—to Oscar.

"That's the security footage on the flash drive," he says. "The actual abduction wasn't caught, but I'm almost certain she's on the luggage cart. You'll see."

The blood in my veins turns cold—they took her like cargo. My fists clench, rage bubbling just below the surface, threatening to erupt. All I want to do is put Elijah through the fucking wall, but Gage pulls my attention back to him, voice steady and measured.

"Let's watch the footage," Gage says quietly. I nod, but my eyes stay on Elijah, burning a hole through him. I feel like he's playing dumb, like he knows something.

"I'll stay with him," Colton offers, leaning casually against the wall behind Elijah. His arms are crossed, and even though he doesn't move, the sheer force of his presence fills the room. Elijah doesn't look back at him.

We file out into the tech room where Oscar sets up the footage. Jeremy speaks up as the video starts rolling, "I had them piece it together chronologically from different cameras, it wasn't their first time pulling footage like this. They asked for a warrant, so I might've promised some free services to keep law enforcement out of it."

I nod, my eyes glued to the screen as Vallyn's figure comes into view. She's leaving the reception hall, smiling, unaware of what's about to happen. People are scattered throughout the lobby, chatting, hotel workers moving in and out of frame.

She's right there. Then she disappears down a hallway, out of the camera's sight, about thirty feet behind her, a woman in what is probably the caterer's uniform goes down the same hall.

Jeremy leans in, grim. "That hallway's camera wasn't recording. Looked fine on their screens, but the DVR wasn't picking it up."

Of course that's not coincidental. They planned this.

A few minutes pass, then the female caterer exits that same hallway. Another few minutes pass as Jeremy fast forwards. And then... two men appear, they're dressed casually, pushing a luggage rack with a large duffel bag. My breath hitches, my gut twisting in recognition. *That's her.* Jeremy places a hand on my shoulder, confirming what I already know.

The footage shows them moving the luggage cart through five different camera angles, straight outside to an SUV waiting in the roundabout. The trunk opens, each of them grab an end of the bag and they place it in the SUV, but one of them unzips the duffel, then closes the trunk.

*That's her. That's fucking her.*

Without thinking, I slam my fist into the drywall, the impact shattering the surface and leaving a gaping hole. Silence follows, thick and heavy. Finally Gage breaks the silence.

"You download it?" He asks Oscar, his voice controlled, but I can hear the simmering rage beneath. Oscar nods, and Gage turns to me, locking eyes.

Gage looks at me as he holds up the flash drive and says, "I'm going to take this to the van, see if I can get clear faces and the license plate. Give Oscar the phone number. Show him the texts you got. We'll start there."

I force a nod, but my mind is spiraling. After handing Oscar my phone and him taking the information he needs, I head out to the van with Gage. He's already pulled and enhanced the face shots of the two men from the footage. As soon as I see the first face, recognition hits me like a punch to the gut.

"He was at the restaurant," I mutter, the emotion thick in my throat. "He fled with Elijah."

Gage nods grimly, his eyes scanning the images. "I know." He types quickly, running the license plate through the database, but the second the results pop up, frustration sets in. "Stolen plates. Dead end." He sighs and rubs his jaw. "Hopefully Oscar got further with the phone number, but don't get your hopes up."

I nod again, acknowledging the bitter truth. These guys have been meticulous. Expecting a slip-up now would be naïve. I watch Gage disconnect his tablet, preparing to show the pictures to the other guys and Elijah. He pauses and looks at me, his eyes filled with quiet determination.

"Let me handle this," he says, his voice gentle and firm but also pleading. "I have an angle. If it doesn't work, then you can have him."

My body feels heavy, weighed down by the gravity of the situation. I nod once more, unable to find my voice, and follow Gage back to the tech room. Oscar's waiting for us, his expression serious as he explains, "The phone's a burner. Everything paid in cash. It's bouncing off a foreign VPN, no GPS. They covered their tracks well. Almost impossible to triangulate, but I'll keep working on it."

It's disappointing, but not surprising—of course, they didn't fuck up.

We head to the interrogation room, tension thickening with each step. Elijah's sitting quietly, but there's a shift in the air. Jeremy and Colton are speaking in low voices nearby. I make a mental note to touch base with Jeremy soon—I need to know what Vallyn's parents know, how he's handling this, what our next move is with her family—but that will be later. For now, I let Gage take the lead. I trust him implicitly, and with Casen unavailable, he's the only one I *fully* trust right now.

Gage sits down across from Elijah, setting the tablet on the table, screen dark for now. He scrubs his face with his hands, tension rolling off him before he exhales and calmly speaks. "Here's the deal, Elijah. There's something you need to know before we ask you more questions."

Elijah looks up, cautious but curious. Gage glances at me, then to Colton, Jeremy, and Oscar. Jeremy gives him a nod of approval, and Gage takes that as his cue to continue.

"Vallyn wasn't a snitch," Gage says, voice steady. "She was just as surprised to see us that day as you were. Maybe more. We had an informant watching your mom's house. That's how we knew you left her house and were at the restaurant. Vallyn was there to interview you, just like she interviewed someone from one of your rival gangs earlier. Blake knew she had interviews that day, but he didn't know it was you and he thought they were at the youth center."

Elijah's eyes flick to mine, searching for truth, and when he finds it there, he swallows hard.

"Your boys picked a fight with the wrong people," Gage continues, the tone dropping even lower, more dangerous. "Vallyn isn't just Blake's girl—she's Jeremy's niece." Gage lifts his chin toward Jeremy, who stands rigid, eyes blazing. "The entire bounty hunter population in Arizona knows your guys shot one of ours. And they nearly shot Vallyn, who might as well be one of ours."

Elijah shifts in his chair, visibly a little shaken. He clears his throat. "I didn't know they were going to take her," he mutters, eyes darting to me. "You have to believe me—I didn't fucking know."

The sound of Gage's fist slamming onto the table jolts the room. "This was planned down to the last detail," Gage snaps. "They killed the camera feed, had a getaway car waiting with stolen plates, and stuffed her in a duffle bag like garbage."

I flinch, bile rising in my throat at the image, the thought of Vallyn crammed into that bag.

"And then they texted Blake from an untraceable burner phone," Gage continues. "There's no way they could've known we were going to pick you up today. My guess? This was planned regardless. But now they want to exchange you for her."

Elijah stays silent, his eyes wide but blank, as though he's processing just how fucked his situation is. Gage powers up the tablet and starts with the first man—the one we know. "This guy was with you at the restaurant. We know he's yours and we know who he is. But this guy?" Gage swipes to the next image. "We don't know him. You're going to tell us who he is, or Colton gets to have his fun with you."

Elijah's face goes a little pale. He squints at the picture, recognition dawning slowly. His lips part, and the words that spill out are almost a whisper. "Oh, fuck."

I step forward, my fist slamming down onto the table between him and Gage, the tablet bouncing with the force. They both flinch, and my voice is a growl. "What the fuck are you not saying?"

Elijah leans back in his chair, visibly rattled. He exhales slowly, eyes darting between all of us before they settle back on me. "The one you know—that's Joker. He's relatively harmless." He pauses, clearly hesitant to continue. "But the other guy..."

As the pause grows longer Gage leans in, his calm unnerving. "The other guy?"

Elijah closes his eyes, clearly contemplating his words, then speaks, "They will kill me if they know I cooperated with you, so I'm doing this for Vallyn." He looks at me and then continues, "His name is Jigsaw. He works for my boss' boss—he's cartel. He's the big boss's muscle."

"What else are you not saying?" I demand, teeth gritted. I know there's more, that initial reaction when he recognized him was stronger than what he has told us so far.

Elijah's gaze meets mine, and for the first time, I see real fear. "He has warrants—both here and in Mexico. Drugs, sure, but also murder... and rape."

My blood runs cold as Elijah adds, "He was kicked out of his house for messing around with his nine-year-old sister."

"Geezus fucking christ," Jeremy mutters, turning toward the wall, fists clenched.

"That's not all," Elijah says quietly. He swallows hard and looks at me again, "He is also involved in trafficking for them—*human* trafficking."

The air in the room grows impossibly thick as I process the words. My body hums with rage, more intense than I've ever felt.

"Where would they take her?" Gage asks, his voice tight.

"I don't know," Elijah admits. "But I'm willing to help figure it out." He looks me dead in the eyes and right now he looks every bit of his youth, the teenager he is. "If Jigsaw had my sister, I'd burn the world down to find her. You need to find her."

# CHAPTER FIFTY
# PREPARATION FOR HELL

## VALLYN

It's been too long. My body feels like it's disintegrating, every muscle and joint screaming with the agony of being confined, of being bound in this hellhole for over a week. I convinced Ace to tell me what day it is now and then. It's Sunday. Over a week in this nightmare, and I can barely think straight. My shoulders throb from the constant strain, chained behind my back for what feels like eternity. My head pounds relentlessly, a mix of dehydration, pure exhaustion, and a million other things.

The smell clings to me—sweat, filth, and desperation. They don't even unchain my wrists for the bathroom. Every time it's a degrading ordeal, usually with Ace—because I try to wait until it is him—lifting my skirt, pulling down my soiled underwear because I'm too bound to do anything myself. The humiliation burns, but it's better when it's Ace. At least he tries to make it less awful.

My body is a mess. A mattress appeared a few days ago, but it's filthy and stained, reeking of things I try not to think about. Still, it's better than that cold, metal chair. My fingers flex weakly, trying to stave off the numbness that creeps up my arms from being bound for so long.

I've memorized their names now. Ace, Jigsaw, Joker, Bones, and Lucky. I cling to that knowledge, like it'll somehow help me survive. Ace and Joker are the ones who act human, more or less. But Jigsaw... and Bones... they're something else. There's something dark, twisted in their eyes every time they look at me. Something predatory. And I almost never see Lucky, but they talk about him—he's the highest ranking of them, but there is someone above him.

*Where are you, Blake?*

My thoughts spiral. The fear gnaws at me, hollowing me out from the inside.

*What if they have him too? What if... No. I can't let my mind go there. They'd have no reason to keep me alive if they didn't still want something from him, from Jeremy.*

I've figured out we're not too far from the city. They bring back food quickly—fast food that reeks of grease and normalcy, a stark contrast to the hell I'm living in. They feast while I get toast, peanut butter sandwiches, water, and the occasional soda. It all has to be fed to me, because I can't use my hands. Ace has slipped me ibuprofen a couple of times when the pain was too much to bear. He's probably risking some kind of punishment for it.

He's with me now, sitting quietly, the tape gone from my mouth. The chains are looser today, only loosely tethering me to the chair. There's a strange tension in the air, and it makes the hair on the back of my neck stand up.

That's when Jigsaw and Bones walk in together. It's rare to see them enter the room as a pair. The twisted smiles they share send an icy wave of terror through me. Something's wrong. My heart begins to race, and I feel a sickening dread settle deep in my stomach.

Jigsaw's gaze lands on me first. He grins, pulling out his knife—the same blade he's always playing with—and drags it slowly down his cheek. He holds eye contact with me while he talks to the man next to me. "Hey, Ace, why don't you head out? Watch a movie with Joker or something."

Ace stands abruptly, looking back at me with a flash of concern in his eyes, but then he nods and leaves. He doesn't argue and he doesn't attempt to stay. I watch as Bones casually turns the lock behind him—the backpack on his back catches my attention and my pulse quickens, thundering in my ears. My breathing becomes shallow, every instinct screaming that I'm in danger.

Jigsaw steps closer, tipping my chin up with the point of his blade, forcing me to meet his eyes. His voice is low and dark, each word dripping with menace. "It's been over a week, and nobody's given us Eli, and nobody's come for you. I think it's time we put that pretty pussy of yours to use."

Panic explodes inside me. Pure, cold terror. I kick him in the shin with what little strength I have left and spit at him, my body acting on instinct, even though I know I'm too weak to fight them off.

He laughs. A deep, cruel laugh. "Oh, look, Bones, we got ourselves a fighter."

Bones crouches in front of me, his smile just as sick as Jigsaw's. "First, baby, we're gonna clean you up," he says, his voice almost mocking, as if he's trying to charm me. His hand lands on my calf and slides up my leg, fingers creeping higher.

I kick again, a desperate move, but it's weak. The fear surges in my veins like ice water, and I spit out the only words I can muster. "Blake will fucking kill you."

Jigsaw laughs again, that cruel, mocking laugh that makes my skin crawl. "He has to find us first, sweetheart. So far, that hasn't happened."

I spit again, this time at Jigsaw's face, but I miss, and his reaction is instant. His hand shoots out, wrapping around my throat, squeezing tight. The pressure cuts off my air, and I feel the blood build in my head as the darkness edges in on my vision. "Do it one more time, bitch. I dare you," he growls before releasing me, my chest heaving as I gasp for air.

"Set it up," Jigsaw orders no humor left in his tone, and Bones moves toward the mattress.

I can't see what Bones is doing, but I hear the shuffle of items being removed from a backpack, the clink of metal and the sound of plastic hitting the ground. My heart hammers in my chest, and the fear makes my blood run cold.

Jigsaw leans down to me, his eyes gleaming with twisted excitement. "Toss me the tape," he says with a nod to Bones. It barely registers before Jigsaw slaps the duct tape over my mouth, sealing my lips shut. "Try spitting now, sweetheart."

The tears burn in my eyes as I watch him move behind me, feeling him tug at the chains around my wrists. He releases them, and for a brief moment, there's a sickening wave of relief as I stretch my fingers and arms, my muscles aching from the lack of movement.

But it doesn't last. Jigsaw grabs my arm, yanking me to my feet. I let out a muffled sob as he turns me to face the mattress. I see it now—what Bones has done. Straps, heavy and thick, are looped around the mattress, forming an "X." They're going to strap me down, spread-eagle.

I turn, trying to flee, but Jigsaw grabs me around the waist, lifting me off the ground. He leans close, his breath hot against my ear as he whispers low enough so only I can hear, "You should know, sweetheart, the more you fight, the more I like it."

Tears spill down my face as he throws me onto the mattress, his body pinning me down—straddling my thighs and pinning my wrists. Bones works quickly, securing my wrists and ankles in the straps, pulling them tight until I'm splayed out beneath them. The restraints dig into my skin, and I can't move. I'm trapped. Thoughts of being drawn and quartered go through my mind.

"Fuck, we should have taken the dress off first," Bones mutters, standing over me like I'm some kind of art project.

"We'll do it next time, I'd cut it off of her, but if they do want to exchange, we'll need to put it back on her," Jigsaw says calmly, like they're talking about the weather. "We'll break her in slow," he adds, his voice chillingly casual. "Save her ass for next time, and her mouth until we've fucked some of the fire out of her."

Bones, standing at the foot of the mattress, responds in that same eerie calm, like they're talking about a meal, the first piece of pizza, instead of what they plan to do to me. "Let me have her ass first," he says, no hesitation, no remorse.

"It might be Lucky's," Jigsaw muses, chuckling darkly. "He outranks us, but I'll give it to you if it's up to me."

Their words settle into the pit of my stomach like lead. My whole body feels like it's about to shut down, the cold dread sinking in, wrapping around my bones. I try to scream, but my throat locks up, and all I can taste is bile at the back of my mouth, threatening to choke me. My mouth is taped, sealing me in this nightmare, and my screams are trapped inside.

"Is it time to text him yet?" Bones asks.

"No, man. We gotta get her ready first."

Their conversation washes over me like a wave of pure horror, and I squeeze my eyes shut, willing it all away. Jigsaw kneels between my legs, his voice sickly sweet as he taunts me. "You know, sweetheart," he drawls, fingers tracing along the hem of my dress, "you're lucky this wasn't day one for you. But apparently, you have value. The boss made us wait. But he knows we're impatient. Especially when we have such sweet and pretty pussy waiting for us."

I can't hold back the whimper that escapes me, muffled by the tape. My body trembles beneath them, useless and weak, and I can feel the tears collecting near my ears. He unzips my dress, taking his time, savoring the moment. I can't move. I'm trapped in this horror, helpless, as they strip me of what little dignity I have left.

"Y'know what, Bones? Let's just do one wrist at a time. Lucky'll be pissed if she's not completely naked."

They free one wrist, only to pull it down by my waist and slide the strap of my dress off. They secure my wrist again before moving to the other side. It's methodical, practiced. I'm nothing but a body to them, nothing but prey. Once my dress is down, they repeat the same thing with my ankles, pulling my underwear off too, and soon, I'm lying there, exposed, vulnerable, and powerless under their hungry gazes.

They stand by my feet, admiring their handiwork, like I'm some kind of masterpiece they've created. It makes me want to vomit. Bones grins, leaning over me. "Fuck, bella princessa, you're probably the sexiest girl we've had in here in a long time. We're going to have fun with you."

Jigsaw agrees, his eyes raking over me like I'm nothing more than an object. "Look at that body. Curves and thickness in all the right spots. Milky fucking skin. Fuck, sweetheart."

Another whimper escapes me, and I hate myself for it. I start hoping I'll pass out, that I won't feel or remember what is about to happen.

Bones picks up a pink bottle, and for a second, I can't make sense of what he's holding until I feel the cold cream being smeared onto my legs and armpits, and then lower, between my thighs, over my pubic area and even between my ass cheeks.

"I'm a little jealous you got to touch her first," Jigsaw teases, though his voice is laced with something darker.

"It's the job I was given," Bones replies with a wink. He catches my gaze, and for a second, I see the dark amusement in his eyes. "It's hair remover, sweetheart. We don't like you bitches hairy. Lucky and the boss insist on no hair."

Time seems to stretch and warp as the minutes drag on. Bones wipes the cream away with a dry towel, meticulously removing every last bit of cream from my body. He applies hot wax to my bikini area next, with a sickening smile. "For the leftovers," he says, winking at me again before ripping the first wax strip from my skin. The pain barely registers anymore, swallowed by the overwhelming fear flooding my senses.

They wipe me down with what I think are baby wipes afterward, touching every inch of me, even lifting my body to clean my back and between my fingers and toes. Then Bones slathers lotion all over my skin, the scent of cocoa butter cloying, too sweet, before finishing with too many sprays of strawberry-scented body spray. It makes me feel sick, the artificial sweetness mingling with the cold reality of what's happening.

Bones steps back, surveying me like I'm a piece of art, perfectly prepped for whatever horror comes next. "I think you can text Lucky now," he says, his voice laced with satisfaction as he looks down at me, at my newly exposed, prepared body.

Terror claws at me, my heart hammering in my chest as I try to block out the reality of what's about to happen. My body feels like it's not mine anymore. I'm trapped in this nightmare, and there's nothing I can do to escape.

# CHAPTER FIFTY-ONE

# HELL

## VALLYN

The door swings open with a bang, and my whole body stiffens as the other men walk in. Joker and Ace hesitate, their faces pale a shade as they take in the sight of me bound and exposed. Lucky's voice cuts through the air, cold and menacing. "I brought the babies with me," he says, his eyes gleaming with twisted amusement. "They need to learn how we treat a woman around here. It's about time we make men out of them."

Ace meets my eyes for a brief, flickering second before looking away, his expression conflicted. I know in my gut that he and Joker are young—too young. They can't even be eighteen, just like Eli. Lucky, on the other hand, is older, hardened by whatever life has twisted him into, probably in his thirties. Jigsaw and Bones, they're closer to my age, but those details hardly matter. Sympathy for Ace and Joker's situation flickers in my chest, but it's fleeting, overshadowed by the suffocating terror closing in on me.

"She looks good, boys," Lucky says, his gaze passing over me like I'm nothing but an object on display. "Considering she hasn't had a shower in over a week, you did well." He claps Bones on the shoulder as if they're congratulating each other for a job well done.

Jigsaw's voice cuts in, casual, indifferent. "Bones asked for something," he says, and Lucky raises a brow. "He wants to take her ass first when the time comes."

Lucky chuckles, the sound dark and full of malice. "I was thinking about making one of these two virgins do it," he says, gesturing to Ace and Joker, who both flinch subtly at the suggestion. "But you cleaned her up well, Bones. You might deserve that reward." He steps closer, looming over me, and the twisted grin on his face makes my blood run cold. "I'm just hoping we get to keep her long enough to enjoy her.."

"Oh, me too, Lucky," Jigsaw chimes in, his voice laced with cruel amusement. "Although I do like it when they fight. But I'd love to fuck her mouth for real—those lips, man."

Their words send a violent shudder through me. The room is freezing, my body already trembling from the cold and fear. My nipples are painfully hard from the cold air, and the tips of my fingers, toes, and nose feel numb, like ice. I try to block out their words, to shut down the reality of what they're planning. But it's impossible to escape it, the horror sinking in deeper with every second that passes.

Lucky glances at Bones. "You got the after stuff?"

Bones nods, his expression unreadable. "Yessir."

"Good man," Lucky says, approving. "It's been a while since we had one we wanted to keep for a while. I was hoping you didn't forget that process."

"Nope. We'll break her in a little at a time," Jigsaw adds, his voice practically dripping with anticipation. "But I'm with you, Lucky. I want to keep her, enjoy her."

"Fuck, I'm hard just thinking about it," Lucky says, his tone turning even more sinister. "We'll talk timeline, but she should be able to take all three of us in some way, shape, or form by the end of the week."

Jigsaw laughs, dark and low. "I've been hard since we walked in the room. Let's get this show on the road."

Lucky's tone hardens, as he commands, "Strap her how I want her."

Bones and Jigsaw move toward me, and I can't stop the instinctive surge of panic that takes over. When they unstrap my ankles, I try to kick, to thrash against them, but I'm too weak, my movements pathetic in their control. Lucky watches with a twisted smile, his voice mocking. "Fuck, she's a feisty one. You can move your hips like that while I'm fucking you—try to buck me off. Maybe it'll make me finish faster."

They ignore my attempts to fight, forcing my legs up, bending them at the knee. Bones is first, securing my lower leg to my thigh with thick straps, then attaching that strap to my arm, pulling me tighter into the position they want. Then he moves to the other leg, strapping it down the same way while Jigsaw watches. Within moments, they've positioned me exactly how they want—my pelvis in the air, my pussy and ass completely exposed to all of them.

I close my eyes, desperate for this to end.

I hope my mind can escape while the world blurs at the edges, fading into a hazy backdrop of what's about to unfold. Opening my eyes again, I watch as Lucky moves, a predator settling into position between my legs, his presence commanding and electric. His head dips down, and my breath catches, anticipation thrumming through me like a live wire. His tongue teases, rimming my ass, before he licks a heated path up to my navel, igniting fire along my skin and making more bile climb up my throat.

I squirm beneath him, as my body seems to want to melt into the pleasure, but my brain has the instinct to flee. Both feelings cause me to move.

"Fuck, yeah, woman. You move, that makes this so much fucking better," he groans, voice gravelly and low, like a dark promise. "Outside of outranking all these fuckers, one of the reasons I get you first is I want to taste you. But my goal, sweet Vallyn, is to make you come."

He looks at me until he holds my eyes for a few seconds, then he moves his mouth close to my ear closest to the wall, where the others can't hear as he whispers, "I don't want to hurt you, Vallyn. In a lot of ways I apologize for what has to happen, I want to make this as easy on you as possible, but it *has* to happen."

His words hang heavy in the air, and I shake my head, a desperate denial tinged with an unsettling flicker of hope as he sits back and shifts his focus to my breasts. I instinctively inhale sharply through my nose when he takes my cold-hardened nipple into his mouth, warmth and relief flooding me, as if my body is a traitor to my mind. It's an insidious pleasure, and I hate that I want more. His tongue dances against my skin, igniting a desperate hunger, before he shifts to the other breast, fingers deftly finding the one still glistening from his earlier ministrations.

My body is betraying me and I know it.

When he pulls away, hovering just inches from my face, his breath washes over me. "Vallyn," he whispers, his tone soothing yet filled with a dark promise, "we'll train you to not hate this. That's part of the art of this." The gravity of his words sinks in, focusing on his certainty. "I will make you come tonight. Probably more than once. Your body is just a tool, a tool for you and a tool for us. In less than a week, you'll learn to take three or more of us at once, and whether you believe me or not, eventually you'll like it."

As his words linger in the air, he pushes two fingers deep inside me, and my eyes squeeze shut, instinctively trying to block out both the rising bile and the tide of sensation. "Oh, baby, you're so wet. You *already* like this," he purrs, a dark thrill lacing his voice.

I shake my head, a defiant gesture that feels weak against the way my body is performing to his touch. He only chuckles, curling his fingers up to stroke my G-spot with expert precision. "Oh, you can shake your head no, but your body tells a different story," he responds, that almost charismatic tone teasing at my resolve. "I could have let Jigsaw go first, but he's rough and I want you to enjoy this. I want to pleasure you, too. One of the other reasons I like to go first is that I'm good to go again at the end. And believe me, seeing that cream pie dripping out of you will be so fucking hot."

His mouth finds each of my nipples again, worshiping them with an intensity that ignites the nerves coiling beneath my skin.

I hate my traitorous body so much right now.

Then his mouth descends my body, fingers still relentless against my G-spot, stirring a betrayal within me that I can't ignore. With his other hand, he spreads my lips, running a finger teasingly over my clit causing me to jerk beneath him.

"There she is," he growls, the sound reverberating through me, and then his mouth descends, enveloping my clit with his mouth in a heated, rhythmic suction. He works me with a deliberate cadence, his tongue flicking and teasing, the pressure building to an unbearable crescendo as he continues to explore my depths with his fingers.

The coil within me tightens, and despite the anger and fear simmering beneath the surface, my body continues to sell me out, trying to move against his touch, eager for release. I squeeze my eyes shut, feeling the walls of my core convulse around his fingers, my clit throbbing in time with the mounting pressure. I know he can feel it, too, judging by the way he chuckles against my skin, a knowing sound that sends heat flushing to my cheeks.

"You made that too easy, sweetheart," he murmurs, and just as my resolve crumbles, he pulls his fingers out and spears me with his tongue, igniting a fresh wave of sensation. "Fuck, you taste so sweet."

His fingers trail over my ass, teasing the sensitive skin before pushing one finger inside. "Has anyone ever fucked your ass?" he asks, the question heavy with expectation.

I don't answer, caught in the web of conflicting emotions, unsure of what the right response is—or which answer might earn me better treatment. The tension crackles in the air, and when he smacks my ass cheek hard, the sting jolts me back to reality. "Answer me."

I shake my head no, not knowing how it will shape the moment. At my admission, he pushes his finger in deeper, claiming me with a sense of authority and I shiver.

"We'll go slow, baby. Let me tell you what's going to happen over the next few days," he says, settling back on his knees, his finger still nestled deep inside my ass, moving slightly in and out with a teasing slowness that sends ripples of sensation through my core.

His face is suddenly hovering above mine as he continues speaking low—I'm unsure if the others can hear him. "After we all take our turns tonight, Bones is going to douche you out really well, then give you a thorough enema. Tomorrow, we'll up the ante with a bigger one, and then we'll plug this tight hole while it works its magic."

A chill dances down my spine as he continues, the weight of his words wrapping around me like a dark threat and promise. "When that's done, I'll make you come a few times, ensure this cunt"—he delivers a sharp slap straight to my pussy that makes me inhale quickly, my body reacting with a mixture of shock and involuntary desire—"is full of my cum and happy. I want *you* happy, Vallyn. Then, I'll use my fingers and a dildo to stretch out this ass of yours."

Panic rises within me, and I shake my head, a soft whimper escaping my throat. He notices, his voice steady and filled with a predatory calm. "Vallyn, you'll like it. I promise you will. You're just scared." His gaze pierces mine, as if trying to both reassure me and uncover the secrets buried deep inside me. "I'll use a vibrator on your clit while I stretch you, distract you, keep your cunt happy. Then, I'll let Bones here fuck your ass, but I won't let him finish there. He can leave his cum all over you, but I'll be the first to fill that ass with my cum. These other guys can put their cum wherever they want, except your mouth and ass. Because your ass? That will be all mine for a few days."

Dread courses through me at his words. "Then, in a couple of days, when you're taking us in your ass well, we'll double you up—I'll take your ass for that too. One of them will be in this perfect cunt," he says, his voice a low growl, "while I fuck your ass at the same time. Once you're doing well— being good for us, we'll start training your mouth. And if we need to use an open-mouth gag or a dental dam, we will. I'll be the first one to take that too."

I tilt my head back, a sob catching in my throat, muffled by the unforgiving tape binding my mouth. "Jig, tell her what happened to the last girl that tried to bite you doing that," Lucky prompts, his tone deceptively casual, like he's recounting a harmless story.

Jigsaw chuckles darkly, the sound chilling more. "I choked her until she passed out, then we pulled out all her teeth. After that, her mouth was even easier to fuck."

My heart races, dread pooling in my stomach as I struggle to comprehend the implications of his words. "See, sweetheart, you don't want to fight that," Lucky continues, his voice smooth and coaxing. "Before long, we'll have you taking three cocks at once—one in each hole. I give that less than a week. Eventually, we'll untie you, and you'll cooperate with us. But first, we'll fuck most of the fire out of you. Eventually, the boss will want to have his way with you. He's a sadistic fucker. He'll use clamps, toys, maybe knives. He can fuck you any way he wants, and have any of us join him whenever he pleases. *That's* what we're preparing you for—to survive *him*."

Lucky's words flow like a twisted lesson plan, and I feel the walls closing in, fear and something even darker swirling within me. "But for now, Vallyn, I'm going to fuck this cunt and fill it," he states, a smirk playing on his lips. "Then I'll let all of them fill you, and when they're done, I'll come back around and finish off that cream pie. I think I'll need pictures of the cum dripping from this perfect cunt this first time."

His thumb glides slowly from my taint to my entrance, and then I hear the unmistakable sound of his zipper coming down.

# CHAPTER FIFTY-TWO

# FULFILLED PROMISES

## VALLYN

Everything Lucky promises begins to materialize. He makes me climax four times that first night, each one drawing me deeper into the web he's woven. When his hands can't coax me over the edge, he reaches for a vibrator, turning my body into an instrument. "A climaxed woman is a happy woman," he says, his voice low and sultry, as if imparting a great truth.

Ace and Joker are sent into the scene next, raping me reluctantly, their movements laced with an awkward tension. When all five of them are done, the enema and douching unfold just as Lucky foretold. When it's all over, they strap me back to the cold metal chair, naked and exposed.

Lucky and Bones are the only ones left in the room. "You don't need clothes anymore, sweetheart," Lucky asserts, his gaze possessive. "Your body is ours to do with as we please, so we need access whenever we want it."

And they're true to that, invading me and touching me anytime, and in any way they want.

The following day, Bones arrives with a large enema, his demeanor all business as he inserts it, then uses a plug to ensure I can't release it. The cramps claw at my insides until Bones finally guides me to the bathroom. Afterward, he straps me back to the bed, face down, tucking my legs under me in a way that leaves my ass ready and exposed.

The others file into the room and Lucky follows through on his threats and promises. He makes me come three times, the intensity building with each wave, before he pours lube onto my ass, fingers moving gently but firmly around my rim and in my hole, stretching me as he prepares me for what's to come. The sensation is foreign yet not painful, and I try to think my way through it, each breath hitching as he grips the vibrator.

He fingers my ass while pressing the vibrator against my clit, a dizzying combination that sends me spiraling into another climax. Just as I'm riding the end of that orgasm, he pulls the vibrator away, the stretch in my ass growing more pronounced—probably another finger, I know there are at least two—yet it still doesn't hurt.

Then, he reattaches the vibrator to my clit, and as I peak again, fingers exit and the silicone dildo slides swiftly into my ass, claiming me fully in that moment of unwanted bliss.

"Fuck, you're such a good girl, Vallyn," Lucky praises, his tone dripping with approval that my body reacts to him in ways I don't understand. He begins to slide the dildo in and out of me, never letting it completely leave my body. "You want to know what two of us will feel like, baby?"

I barely have time to register the question before I hear the unmistakable sound of his zipper. He thrusts into my pussy with his cock, the pressure building inside me, there's a synchronization of sensations as the dildo continues its rhythm in my ass. "See, baby? You'll take two of us easily."

He pushes the dildo all the way into my ass, and then, with what feels like an expert motion, he reaches around to press the vibrator back against my clit. He fucks me—rapes me—hard, relentless. "I'm not going to stop fucking you until you come, Vallyn, so let go and release that. Come all over my cock."

A wave of anger surges through me, battling with the overwhelming sensation that's coiling tightly in my belly. I hate that my body is on the verge of giving him exactly what he craves. But I don't fight it; I surrender, thinking that maybe this will make him stop. I whimper softly as my body releases, the pleasure exploding through me just as he fills me completely, our bodies merging in a chaotic dance of demoralizing possession.

He smacks my ass, the sharp sting sending jolts through me, and then he presses on the dildo still buried deep inside. "Bones, that ass is yours, but don't fucking come there," he commands, his voice a low growl that vibrates against my skin.

One by one, they take their turns with me, each of them filling my ass with their cocks, their bodies slamming against mine before they cover my back in hot cum.

My mind drifts away, retreating to memories of my friends, family, and Blake, the warmth of those thoughts clashing with the harsh reality of my situation. I cling to those memories, holding on to them as tightly as I can, desperately trying to dissociate and shield myself from the chaos enveloping me.

Then Lucky returns, his hand gliding over the warm cum smeared across my back. "You should see how pretty you look like this, Vallyn," he muses, a twisted satisfaction lacing his words. "But now, you get to feel what it's like to have your ass filled with cum."

He doesn't hesitate. He fucks hard, filling my ass completely, the sensation overwhelming. Just before he pulls away, he leans in close, whispering into my ear, "No cleanup tonight. I want you to feel my cum inside you."

I'm chained back to the chair, still covered in their cum, naked, exposed and vulnerable.

Over the next few days, Lucky fulfills every dark promise he made. At some point I block out the thoughts of sexually transmitted diseases, even though they plagued me at the beginning. At this point, if they have something, I already have it and it's just part of my fate.

Within a week, I find myself taking three of them at once, a transformation I never thought I'd really undergo. After Lucky fucks my mouth and watches me swallow his cum once, he lets Jigsaw own my mouth. The chilling knowledge that he has pulled out other girls' teeth for biting him keeps me from resisting, each glance from him as his cock slides between my lips a reminder of the consequences of defiance.

Bones has a particular fixation on my ass, so Lucky allows him that "pleasure" most of the time. Usually, Lucky positions himself beneath me, thrusting into my cunt while his hands and mouth explore my breasts.

Occasionally, when Jigsaw finishes, Lucky grips my throat or chin, forcing me to meet his gaze, his eyes holding mine with an intensity that makes me feel utterly owned—I'm his property and he wants me to know it. But Lucky also mouths and whispers reassurances and even apologies to me.

Ace and Joker are required to rape me at least once a day, whether they want to or not, and I begin to count the days by their visits. I know it's eleven days before they feel I'm broken enough to be restrained but no longer strapped to the bed, able to change positions at their will. They force me to straddle them while they rape and sodomize me in any position I could possibly think of.

Then, after Lucky stretches me with his whole hand a few times, they take me two at a time in my pussy. Lucky tells me over and over that he's sorry but he has to prepare me for the four of them when the boss arrives.

It's the twentieth day since they first raped me, my twenty-seventh day in this hell, when Ace tells me the boss has shown up. A knot of anticipation and dread coils in my stomach, knowing that the true darkness may be about to unfold.

# CHAPTER FIFTY-THREE

# WHAT IF I WANT IT TO BE OVER?

## VALLYN

Lucky introduces the older man in the doorway with a half grin. "This is Digger, short for Gravedigger."

Digger's eyes roam over my body, naked and strapped to the metal folding chair, a predatory gleam lighting up his gaze. "Fuck, she *is* a pretty one," he drawls, his voice smooth and dangerous. Then he orders, "You and Bones get her ready."

With that, he walks out of the room, leaving me alone with Lucky and Bones. Lucky grips my chin, forcing me to look into his eyes, and there is an intensity that makes my stomach churn. "Listen, Vallyn," he says, voice low and urgent. "I've been nice to you, even if you don't believe it. Digger *isn't* nice. He will *not* hesitate to hurt you or even kill you if you don't cooperate. Most of what I've done is to prepare you for this. Don't fucking fight him. Understand?"

I nod, the weight of his words pressing heavily on my chest. It's the only response I can give him.

Bones steps forward with a solemn look on his face. He does what he needs to, douching me and administering another large enema. He moves with a surprising gentleness, almost tender in his ministrations. How are these men, who revel in cruelty, so worried about my well-being now?

I look up at Bones while he cleans my body, my voice barely above a whisper. "What if I want him to kill me? What if I just want this to be over?"

He pauses, wiping the baby wipes over my skin, and meets my gaze with unexpected seriousness. "Vallyn, you've done better than any of us thought you would. Whether you believe it or not, we feel a little protective of you. If you want to die, I'm sure Ace will find a way to make that happen painlessly. But what Digger would do to you? It wouldn't be painless. He'd torture you. Just do what he wants, be his perfect whore. Unlike Jigsaw, he doesn't like it when you fight, he wants you to be complacent. He wants to believe you like it."

I nod, swallowing hard as he wipes me down more. As he applies the lotion, he catches my eye again, his expression grave. "Vallyn, seriously—act. Be an actress. He's the best you've ever had; you're happy to please him in any way you can. I don't want to listen to you scream, and I sure as fuck don't want to bury you tonight. I've never said this to any other woman we've had here. You *have* to listen to us."

His words are laced with an urgency that unsettles me.

*What has changed in him?*

He's never cared about hurting me before.

Bones leads me out of my concrete cell and into a real bedroom down the hall, where Digger sits in a chair, waiting. A smile spreads across his face as he takes me in.

"Bones, grab Lucky. Let me see what she'll do for the two of you. Let me see how well you've trained her," Digger says, his tone light but with an edge that sends a shiver down my spine. He circles me like an animal sizing up its prey while Bones walks away, shooting me a warning look.

Digger begins his interrogation as soon as I hear the door close. "They fuck your ass and your cunt at the same time?" I nod, my heart racing. "You swallow their cum for them?" I nod again, the reality of my situation settling heavily in my chest. "Lucky fist you yet?" I swallow hard and nod, feeling exposed under his scrutiny. "Do you speak to them, or have they kept you quiet?"

"I talk to them," I reply, my voice steady despite the fear tightening around me.

"You talk dirty?" he presses. I shake my head, and he raises an eyebrow. "I want you to talk dirty to me. Practice on them. Tell them how much you like their cocks, how much you want them. When you talk to me, I want to believe you."

I nod, the weight of his words sinking in as I hear the door open and assume Lucky and Bones enter behind me. "Boss," Lucky acknowledges, his voice smooth and confident.

"Lucky," Digger replies, then turns to me. "Show me what she'll do for you. Untie her; I want to make sure you have full control of her."

I feel the bindings on my wrists loosen, and Lucky's arm wraps around my waist from behind, holding me securely against him. He buries his face next to my ear, whispering urgently, "Vallyn, everything we do right now is to keep you safe and alive. Listen to instructions."

I nod, resting my hand on his forearm, squeezing it in acknowledgment, a silent promise to comply.

"What do you want, boss?" Lucky asks, his tone shifting into a businesslike edge.

"Just show me what she'll do for you, but definitely fist her—*that* I want to see."

"She'll take three of us, Digger. You want me to grab Jigsaw?" Bones asks, his voice calm and collected.

"No, he's too stupid in these situations," Digger replies, the corners of his mouth twitching into a smile. "If she'll take three and I want to see it, I'll let her take me too. You'd enjoy that, wouldn't you, baby?" he asks, his gaze piercing into mine.

I nod, a mix of fear and dark anticipation swirling within me, and then as he continues glaring at me, I say, "Yes, sir."

Turning me to face him, Lucky tangles his fingers in my hair at the nape of my neck, an intimate yet possessive gesture. He leans in, licking up the curve of my neck before whispering in my ear, "I'm going to kiss you. I need you to kiss me back, and if he kisses you, you kiss him back too."

Pulling back, he searches my eyes, his own filled with a mix of command and empathy. Then he kisses me, his lips pressing against mine with a detachment that feels wrong. As he parts my lips with his tongue, I kiss him back, letting it happen despite the emptiness between us, and I hear Digger laugh, a sound dripping with satisfaction.

Lucky turns me to face Bones, who leans in and kisses me too as he backs toward the bed. "Straddle him and fuck him while I fuck your ass," Lucky commands, his tone brooking no argument. "Bones, control yourself—don't come until we're ready."

We both comply, the tension thickening the air as Digger paces around the bed, his gaze hungry, drinking in every angle of my body. "Let Bones have her ass while you fist her," he instructs after a minute, and Lucky does as he's told, flipping me and shifting his focus with an ease that unnerves me. He holds my weight up while Bones positions himself then pushes me back, so my back is pressed to Bones' chest. He starts with a couple fingers, but quickly is pushing his whole hand inside me.

Digger watches over Lucky's shoulder, a predatory gleam in his eyes. "Prove she can do what I want to do with her," he says, and Lucky's eyes catch mine before he pushes his cock into me with his hand. I remember Digger's earlier words and start to praise how good their cocks feel, how great Lucky's hand is working inside me.

"If you like it, act like you like it," Digger commands, his voice a low growl that sends a thrill of fear through me.

I'm confused, and Lucky sees it. He grabs my hand, placing it on his chest, guiding me with a look that says to follow his lead. I take the hint and reach down to knead Bones' thigh.

"Toss me a vibrator," Lucky says to Digger, and once it's in his hand and humming to life, he presses it to my clit.

For the first time since being thrust into this hell, I allow myself to make the noises I've been holding back—the moans, the whimpers, the not-so-silent screams as Lucky pushes me over the edge.

"Fuck, you broke her well," Digger remarks, a twisted pride in his voice. "Go take her mouth; I'm going to come fast with this one. Bones, I need you to finish fast, though, so I can have all of her."

"Yes, sir," Bones replies, thrusting harder into my ass. I feel him throb, then he pulls out from beneath me, leaving me exposed.

Digger has been gathering items, letting Bones finish. Lucky strokes my hair gently before pressing his cock to my lips. I let him in, fully aware that I don't really have a choice. "Digger is going to play with you. You just need to be a good girl and take it," Lucky says, his voice soothing yet laced with a dark edge.

Suddenly, I feel a pinch on my nipple and realize it's metal. Clamps have been fastened to my nipples now, and then I feel one on my clit as well. Lucky strokes my hair, trying to hold my gaze, giving me a look that tells me to stay focused.

Then I feel a large dildo enter my ass, and pain radiates through me—I'm almost sure he's torn something. A whimper escapes my lips, and Lucky's voice is a low murmur. "Shhh, baby, we know it feels good. We'll make you feel even better. Just focus on sucking my cock."

Fingers delve into my pussy, and I feel the excruciating stretch as he pushes his hand inside, filling me even more. It takes a moment to realize he's jacking himself off inside me, a new and horrific kind of violation.

"You want to tell him how much you like it?" Lucky prompts, and I nod, my voice muffled around his cock. "Mmmhmmm."

He pulls away, giving me the space to follow instructions. "Fuck, that feels good, Digger. Your hand, your cock—all of it."

"You really are a good little whore, aren't you?" Digger replies, a predatory smile on his lips.

"She is," Lucky and Bones chime in unison, their voices blending into a chorus of approval.

Digger finishes quickly, and Lucky, for some reason, comes mostly in his hand, leaving me with very little in my mouth. "Yeah, this one is a keeper," Digger says, pulling free of me before yanking off all the clamps and finally removing the dildo from my ass. "Don't hurt her, or at least don't leave marks on her. Upgrade her accommodations in another week if she's still such good fucking whore. Feed her better; she's too skinny. I hope her boy never finds us, because I want to fucking keep her. She'll be on the rent list, not the buy list—and she needs to come with a high fucking price."

"Yes, sir," Lucky replies, and then he ushers me back to the other room, closing and locking the door behind him without letting Bones in.

He hugs me tightly—I'm horrified and at a loss for how to respond, so I tuck my arms in. "Fuck, Vallyn, you did so well," he breathes, grabbing my face to hold my gaze. "He can be so much worse than that and he doesn't want to sell you. You did so well."

Then he pulls off his t-shirt and puts it over my head, helping me put my arms through the sleeves before chaining me back to the chair. For the first time in three weeks I'm clothed and I'm left confused, the remnants of their cum leaking from me as he walks away, leaving me in a haze.

Two days later, Ace sits with me, his presence a strange comfort amidst everything that has happened. He and Joker no longer rape me; they're no longer required to. And Bones and Lucky haven't touched me since Digger left—only Jigsaw rapes me. While sitting with me, Ace talks about the beach, his voice soothing as he tries to distract me from the weight of my captivity.

Just then, Joker and Jigsaw enter the room with food, the tantalizing scent filling the air. They all exchange words and pleasantries with each other before Jigsaw leans over me, his face close enough that I can smell the sweat and tobacco. "You need to suck me off and swallow before I'll let you have some of this real food," he taunts, a predatory gleam in his eyes.

But before I can respond, I hear the door creak open. I assume it's Lucky or Bones, but I'm wrong.

Ace leaps to his feet, hands raised, backing away like a startled animal. Confusion knots my stomach as I turn to see what's happening. Suddenly, something warm and wet splatters across my face and chest. I look back just in time to witness Jigsaw's body crumpling, blood spurting from his throat. My heart races as I trace the arc of the knife back to my uncle's face, his expression cold and unyielding.

It takes a moment for the reality to sink in—*my uncle is here, and he just slit Jigsaw's throat.* My breath catches in my throat, fear, relief, and disbelief battling for dominance within me. Then, the deafening crack of a gunshot shatters the air, and Joker falls, a gaping hole in his head. I follow the trajectory of the bullet to Elijah.

This must be a dream—a hallucination, I think frantically. *Eli wouldn't work with my uncle. He wouldn't be here to rescue me.*

But then, as my uncle steps aside, my eyes lock onto those hazel-green eyes I've been desperately trying to recall in my dreams. Blake stands before me, and the sight of him breaks something within me. A sob escapes my lips, raw and unrestrained.

Eli has his gun trained on Ace who drops to his knees and puts his hands behind his head.

"Don't—we need one of them to interrogate," my uncle says.

"Oh, I'm not, but he's sure as fuck not moving," Eli says.

Blake falls to his knees in front of me—oblivious to the growing pool of blood. His hand finds my cheek, as my uncle works swiftly to free the chains binding my wrists.

"I'm here, pretty girl," he whispers, his voice thick with emotion, tears rimming his eyes as mine fall down my cheeks. "We'll get you out of here, but we don't have much time."

I nod, the reality of this moment crashing over me like a tidal wave. At this point, I thought this day would never come. As my uncle releases my hands, I fall into Blake's arms, warmth and relief flooding my senses.

"I love you, Vallyn," he says as his arms squeeze me tight, his voice trembling. "I love you so fucking much. I'm so fucking sorry."

I shake my head through my sobs—it's not his fault.

"Let's go," my uncle commands, urgency lacing his words, and for the first time in what feels like an eternity, a glimmer of hope ignites within me. I know I'm finally getting out of this hell.

# To Be Continued